AF579028

Will to Freedom

"Things fall apart; the centre cannot hold;
Surely the Second Coming is at hand.
And what rough beast, its hour come round at last,
Slouches towards Bethlehem to be born?"

— William Butler Yeats, 1865-1939
The Second Coming (excerpt)

"Hegel remarks somewhere that all great world-historic facts and personages appear, so to speak, twice. He forgot to add: the first time as tragedy, the second time as farce."

— Karl Marx

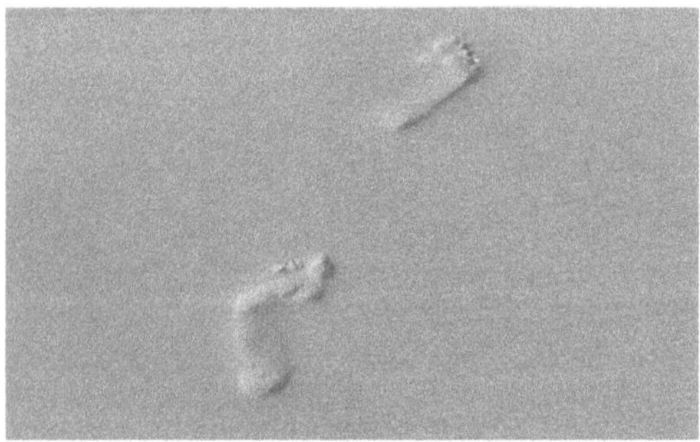

"The second mouse gets the cheese."

— Thompson Smith

"The Second Coming is merely the correction of mistakes and the return of sanity"

— A Course in Miracles

Will to Freedom

Second Messenger

Stephen Ricks

CHB Media
Publisher

Copyright 2023 © Stephen Ricks

All Rights Reserved
including the right of reproduction, copying,
or storage in any form or means, including electronic,
in whole or part, without prior written
permission of the publisher.

ISBN 979-8-9873184-4-7
Library of Congress Control Number: 2023943552

CHB Media, Publisher

(386) 690-9295
chbmedia@gmail.com
www.chbbooks.com

First Edition
Printed in the USA

Revised version of novel previously published as Will to Kingdom, 2015.

"This is a work of fiction. All the characters, organizations and events portrayed in this novel are either products of the author's imagination or are used fictitiously."

DEDICATION

This book is dedicated to the Truth and to the coming brotherhood of inner space explorers who in Peace and Freedom will inaugurate the Kingdom of God on earth.

CONTENTS

APPENDIX CONTENTS

Foreword

Will to Freedom is the story of a spiritual journey that accelerates until it explodes into an adventure. There is nothing I love more than tales of spirit fully realized. My own journey has had many starts, stops, detours, and rewards. Today, I suppose people who like to name names would call me a New Thought Christian. In my spiritual community we follow the teachings of Jesus as a prophet, not as God—at least no more divine in potential than the rest of us. We refer to him as our master teacher. As the divine presence he so fully embodied flourishes within us, we refer to this as the Christ within—much as Buddhists embrace their Buddha heart. It is an inner territory all of us are capable of reaching, the same as Jesus and the Buddha reached it and then encouraged us all to keep walking toward the beauty that is ours.

I began my spiritual journey as a Lutheran, and to this day I thank them for teaching me how to think about the divine, even though my thinking diverged from theirs. As I searched, I began with existential Christian teachers like Paul Tillich, who deepened my perspective, and ended up with thinkers dear to non-Christian spiritual disciples, including Joseph Campbell and Eckhart Tolle. I studied the Buddha and his *Dhammapada,* and also the *Tao Te Ching* to learn how ideas about the divine span different cultures and traditions. For many years I led studies of Julia Cameron's *The Artist's Way*, a path to manifesting divine energy through creative pursuits. Most importantly, I dedicated myself to crafting my own vision of how to understand the divine—God if you will. It was, and is, a grand adventure.

The idea of crafting one's own vision of how the divine displays its power and influence in the world and in our lives is crucial to harnessing that power. When we begin to walk toward that end, we can't be sure how it will take charge of our lives. This is the story Stephen Ricks tells in his novel, *Will to Freedom*. Initially, his protagonist, Richard Holmes, sees "through a glass darkly," as Paul said. But despite seeing only shadows at first, Holmes keeps walking forward in his belief that there's something "more" to be discovered ahead on his journey.

Will to Freedom is a work of fiction and its author, Stephen Ricks, is not to be confused with his character, Richard Holmes. That said, the author—as perhaps is true of all fiction writers—has personal knowledge of many of the things his protagonist experiences, such as receiving insight through visions and being called insane by friends and family who can't accept that this "Indiana farm boy" has experienced revelations they view as beyond the realm for common folk. Holmes' journey becomes an adventure as mystic visitations and ancient mysteries pull him deeper into his destiny.

Another facet of this fictional tale which is based on the author's own experience, is the protagonist pursuing the study of Biblical Greek in order to better understand how the traditional notion of Jesus' identity came to be. In so doing, Richard Holmes encounters a flaw in the translation of a Greek phrase in chapter one, verse six of John's gospel. Holmes, of course, is not a theologian. He is nothing more than a farm boy turned engineer, so he is rightly cautious in calling out "eureka!" But the deeper he looks, the more certain he becomes that the passage was intended to identify Jesus as a prophet come to testify to God's light in the world, rather than to name John as the prophet come to testify to the divinity of Jesus as the one and only "son of God."

Holmes' new understanding, counter-intuitively, does not decrease who Jesus is, but rather manifests his full power. We now see that just as Jesus claimed his full divinity as a flesh and blood human being walking this earth, we too have the same power. It's not an easy journey but it is a simple one if we surrender to it.

Author Stephen Ricks is a student of "A Course in Miracles," and from that course he borrowed a description of Jesus as one who came to show us a bridge over which we can cross into divine presence. But instead of crossing that bridge, we—meaning historical Christianity—opted to worship it. When Richard Holmes, seemingly driven by forces beyond his control, does cross that bridge, miraculous events begin to unfold.

— Gary Broughman,
Publisher, CHB Media

ACKNOWLEDGEMENTS

This story has been a long time in its coming from inspiration to the form in which you have it now. Most recently the Writers at Sica Hall rendered valuable assistance as this story emerged from private thoughts to actual words on paper. My thanks go to each of them. Founder and facilitator, Darlene McRoberts shared her writing experience while showing me real Christian tolerance and patience even as my story challenged her faith. Other members of the widely experienced group, Phyllis , Jim, Lea, Randy, Jim, Sam, Kachina, Sh'mal, Ethel, Peggy, Glenda and others contributed to the story each in their own special way thru sharing their points of view on religion and on writing. Phyllis Lober was most encouraging of the story coming from her Jewish life experience.

Gary Broughman, editor and publisher, promised the story would be better for his involvement. The promise was realized many times over.

My appreciation for the ongoing contribution of Karen, my devoted wife, is beyond saying. She gave me the time and personal space in which to work out the story in my own way.

I feel a need here to say something about the origin of this story. Whatever truth might be found in the various ideas incorporated in the story seems to me to have originated with a willful act of a hidden source. Responsibility for misstatements of course must lie with me. Yet, it must be obvious to those who have known me that I have no real qualification for writing a story such as this. Nothing in my background has suggested that I might someday be involved in expounding on alternative Bible interpretations. We are left then with an unanswered question. Where has this story come from? It has, I believe, come from the same source that has intervened in human affairs and established this county and led us on to where we are today. It is to this source that I give my greatest gratitude.

ABOUT THIS BOOK

Will to Freedom is a fictional account of how a thoroughly secular senior citizen from Daytona Beach, Florida came to be mistaken for the long awaited Jewish Messiah. The story does not fit easily within the established genres but crosses over into several. For some the very nature of the story will suggest the form is fantasy, and at times the action is freely imagined and tempered with a touch of absurdity and farce. Can anything good come out of Daytona Beach?

The essence of *Will to Freedom* is more than just another story of one man's experience—it's a program, a "how to" tutorial showing the way forward for all those who, like Richard with his mid-life crisis, have reached a "what now" point in their lives. Before "going postal" and opening fire on the world, some, a precious few, might willfully choose to listen to Richard as he explains in his own "sermon on the mount" (p. 313-318) his seemingly nonsensical yet straight-forward reason for wholehearted obedience to Jesus' new commandment that we should love our enemies. In choosing the second place these few may find they have entered through the narrow gate and gained the first. Does not scripture say the last (the least able among us) shall be the first to find the way to true freedom?

But this story is too firmly rooted in real life to be dismissed as simple fantasy. From its beginning in Chapter One, the narrative is dramatized memoir. From this honest foundation the story morphs slowly into more clearly imaginary characters and events. Names and circumstances have been changed to protect the innocent. In the event the cover seems at times too thin, I offer my apologies. I have nothing but the deepest respect for every person whose life has touched mine in whatever way.

The heart of the hopefully entertaining story, the thing that makes it matter, is the theology. At times the story may read like a non-fiction scholarly article found in a religious journal. I am not a religious scholar but rather an engineer by training. I believe the research and conclusions regarding the biblical source of the

Christian belief in the incarnation of Jesus are sound, and offer a new direction in which real Biblical scholars searching for an historical Jesus might choose to move. The three Greek words of John 1:6b (*Will to Freedom*, Chapter 8) may well prove to be the three most important words in our world today.

There is also a touch of mystery in this tale, as its protagonist, Richard O. Holmes, perhaps a distant relative of the real master of mysteries, Sherlock Holmes, discovers a new answer to the ancient biblical riddle regarding the identity of the beast who is also a man whose number is 666. We may not like the new answer coming from our modern world of science, but we should find the courage to recognize it is a viable possibility and a sign of the coming new birth of freedom.

The subject matter of the story gives it a certain relevance to today's world in which religious fundamentalism is driving world events. Rather than seeking a solution to violence in further violence, the story endeavors to give life to a more responsible answer in which understanding may come and serve to guide the various competing religious energies into more cooperative and less destructive channels. The story attempts to show a better way out of deeply held religious confusions.

The one overriding theme of *Will to Freedom* is the evolution of spiritual consciousness, both for the protagonist and for the world in which he becomes a catalyst.

— Stephen Ricks, author
Will to Freedom

"Why not give *Christianity* a trial? The question seems a hopeless one after 2000 years of resolute adherence to the old cry of 'Not this man, but Barabbas.' Yet it is beginning to look as if Barabbas was a failure, in spite of his strong right hand, his victories, his empires, his millions of money, and his moralities and churches and political constitutions. 'This man' has not been a failure yet; for nobody has ever been sane enough to try his way."

— George Bernard Shaw
Androcles and the Lion, preface

Chapter One

TURNING POINT

"He dares to be a fool, and that is the first step in the direction of wisdom."

— James Gibbons Huncker

"I coulda been killed," Richard announced. He had been thinking about it on the ride home from Zip's garage and had come to that surprising conclusion.

"What are you talking about?" his wife Celeste answered. They had just returned home after she had gone out of her way to take him to the shop in her car so he could drive his beloved old pickup truck home.

"That guy sent me out on the road without any brakes! *If* I had just paid the bill and driven away like any normal person, I would have left the parking lot and rolled past the stop sign right out into rush hour traffic. And *if* a big truck had been speeding past and *if* he had no room to maneuver or *if* he hadn't been paying attention. And *if* I didn't remember to use the emergency brake in time, *I coulda been killed!*" Richard got madder and madder as he explained his reasoning.

Richard considers himself an average Joe: self-employed, trying to make it in this world as a small homebuilder. He was trained as a civil engineer, but after ten years working in a government civil service job, he turned his back on his profession, believing it offered little hope for achieving his dream of economic self-sufficiency and early retirement.

He worked hard to get where he is in life. He recognizes he isn't normal. He has issues of trust arising from his childhood. He thinks he has to do everything himself. He doesn't know it yet, but he has worked himself up to where he is ready for a mid-life crisis. He is forty-three and has been thinking recently about his mortality and his future, about how he is going to make his mark in the world before he dies. The world doesn't make a lot of sense to Richard. It never has since he left the farm in Indiana where he grew up. He is tired now of playing life's meaningless games.

A few months earlier, for the first time, he read the entire Bible, hoping to find there a way out of his growing sense of living in a meaningless world, his existential angst. Richard is an all or nothing kind of guy and it seemed to him that the crux of Jesus' New Testament teaching was in his command to "love your enemies." But Richard didn't have any enemies. He'd always chosen to be reasonable and so far has always found a way to get around conflict situations. Now, suddenly, an "enemy" has shown up and soon he will be called upon to make a decision that will change his life forever.

He doesn't understand how, but he's invited *me* into his mind to help him make the right decision.

Celeste listened patiently to her husband's tirade against the repair shop. "That's a lot of *ifs*, don't you think? she answered innocently.

"No, I don't think so," Richard responded, taking up the challenge. "It's entirely reasonable. That damn Zip or whoever his name is that owns that place tried to kill me. I'm tired of putting up with stupid people and making excuses for their mistakes. I oughta sue him."

"Whoa, slow down. You're definitely going off the deep end now. You can't sue somebody unless you have damages."

"Damages? I'll show you damages. How about pain and suffering, mental distress, or something. Look how upset I am. Who's gonna pay for that? If I were older I'd be in the hospital having a heart attack right now. It's no damn fault of theirs that I wasn't killed. Who in their right mind, I ask you, would open the hood and check the level of brake fluid in the master cylinder like

I did? Nobody, that's who. Nobody but me, I have to double check every damn thing somebody does just to keep myself out of trouble."

Richard is upset about several things. First, it's the money. It's always about the money with Richard. He thinks the people at Zip's garage are out to rip him off. He thinks they did work he didn't ask for and that they overcharged him for what they did do. They told him it was the government's fault. The law says they can't fix a leak in a brake cylinder, they told him, without putting on new linings and of course they had to turn the rotors to do that.

Bullshit, he thinks. He paid the bill grudgingly. He was entitled, he thinks, to believe that the job was done right.

"I wonder what a lawyer would say about this," Richard continued. "Don't they have a responsibility to do things right? When I opened the hood and found that master cylinder bone dry—and then I realized that I'd already paid their outrageous bill, I was speechless. I was beyond being mad. I didn't know what to think. Then that salesperson said that the mechanic musta *forgot* to add the brake fluid after fixing the brakes. Give me a break. What kind of fool do I look like? *Nobody* works on brakes and forgets to add brake fluid. That's half the damn job, bleeding the air out of the brake lines and getting the pedal solid."

Celeste had enough of Richard's rant and cutting sharply through all the crap asked, "The brakes worked alright coming home didn't they?"

"Yeah, just fine," Richard was forced to admit. "But I'll check it again tomorrow."

"Oh God, What's going to become of us?" he said, as if he foolishly thought the future of all humankind rested on solving his one little problem.

Hold on, that's just Richard. It's a kind of prayer coming from his anguish over living in a meaningless world. It's outward evidence of the little bit of willingness I needed to enter into his mind and help him. Sometimes it's just his first thought of the new day and sometimes, like this morning, he says it aloud while not yet awake.

He doesn't know yet he does it. He isn't religious; he doesn't believe or disbelieve in God. Live and let live has been his philosophy, inherited from his father. He was however, impressed with how the God of the Old Testament loved and took care of His people, telling them over and over, "My loving kindness is forever." That was when he began to wish against his better judgment that God was more than just an idea.

This morning Richard is working at home, calling sub-contractors and paying bills. Soon he remembers the problem with his truck and goes outside to check.

"Damn," he said aloud, seeing the master cylinder is only half full. *It's the same problem I had before Zip's 'fixed' it. Now what do I do?* he asked himself.

That's my opening—that little bit of stillness that comes with uncertainty. He thinks first about suing the guy—whoever it is—that owns Zip's garage. Then his thoughts turn darker and I wait for a break in the string of meaningless thoughts of violence. And right after he fantasizes about slashing that clerk's tires and firebombing Zip's garage, I suggest, Stop payment on the check. He likes the thought and believes it is his own. I knew he would like it. Richard really doesn't want to sue anybody, he's never done it before, and he's afraid of what it might cost. Besides, he doesn't have the stomach to sue anyone. It goes against his nature to try and force his will on anyone. Richard is a lover and not a fighter. That's it, he decides, I'll stop payment on the check. It seems to him an acceptable way to get even.

The strategy worked and two days later Richard got a call from Andrew who said he is the owner of Zip's garage.

"Are you Richard Holmes?" Andrew asked. Then he listened as Richard angrily vented his frustration about the problem that is still a problem.

Andrew was calm and his voice soothing. "Give us another chance," he proposed, "and I will personally see that the job gets done right and I promise you there will be no additional charge."

Andrew's words are exactly what Richard wants to hear. He experiences them as being sweet as honey. Richard is beguiled by the sweetness, but not entirely convinced this is the right thing to do. In the mind space created by his uncertainty I push this thought at him, forgiveness. It stops him for an instant as he wonders where it came from. Then he remembers it's from the Bible. The thought is enough to get him past his uncertainty, coming down on the side of trust. He commits to trusting Andrew. Oh why not, he reasons with himself, the guy is promising to fix it right and no additional charge. I'll never get a better deal than that.

"All right," he told Andrew; "I'll bring the truck back."

Richard is peaceful with his decision; his stomach isn't churning as it does when he thinks seriously of suing someone. And I am pleased with it too. It isn't the big life changing decision that is barreling down on him but he has made a commitment to trust and forgiveness. It's an important step for Richard and I know he's the kind of guy that doesn't abandon his commitments easily. That's a fact I can use to help him make the right decision when the time comes.

One day after the truck was returned to Zip's garage, Richard again got a call from Andrew.

"Richard, we have your truck ready. It was a leaking master cylinder. You can pick it up anytime and it will only be seventy-five dollars more."

The words hit Richard like a sledge hammer. The thing he feared most had come upon him; his trust has been betrayed. He has made the wrong choice in giving Zip's a second chance. *Only seventy-five dollars more! What the hell is this!* flashed into his mind.

But all that came out through the budding rage was a rather weak, "You said no additional charge."

"Well, I have to charge you for the part," Andrew responded, his words no longer sweet but sharp and biting.

Immediately, Richard's mind is closed to me and he is possessed with a compulsion to hold Andrew to his promise. "You promised me," he begins calmly but firmly, "no additional charge."

Andrew said something in his defense, but Richard had heard enough.

"You *lied* to me!" he accused Andrew.

"I didn't lie, you have to pay—"

"You lied! There was nothing said about my paying for anything; NO ADDITIONAL CHARGE. Those were your words. That was your promise to me."

Andrew was tired of being condemned for his standard business practice and said finally, "All right, have it your way, I lied to you. The bottom line is this. If you want your truck you'll have to pay the bill."

Richard's anger was appeased by this confession of guilt from Andrew and saying nothing more he hung up.

Richard's reason returns quickly once he is alone with his thoughts and his mind again opens to my suggestions and guidance. I can see what he is thinking. His first instinct is to see everything that happens as his own fault. By trusting Andrew he left himself vulnerable to being betrayed. He was distracted by Andrew's sweet talk and overlooked the important fact that he was in control when he had his truck and had stopped payment on the check. Andrew successfully wrested that control from him with a few sweet words—a lie—and now, having possession of the truck, he is in control.

This was it. Richard began wrestling with his big, potentially life-changing decision. What will he do now? What can he do? His behavior was constrained on one hand by his Midwestern values of being reasonable and responsibly accepting the consequences for his actions, and on the other hand by his nonviolent constitution which is easily upset when he considers using force. Checkmate. He saw no way to get around Andrew's power over him. He saw no way except letting Andrew run over him and in his mind that had become totally unacceptable. Wrestling with the problem, his thoughts eventually turned to consideration of other ways of accepting defeat. He considered letting Andrew have his old truck rather than the alternative that seemed like death—giving in to Andrew, letting Andrew control his behavior.

I'll be damned if I'll do that, he thinks. I see an opening here and saddle him with this thought, And you'll be blessed if you forgive him a second time. He doesn't like this thought and is tempted to reject it as his own. His mind narrows and the light dims but before he can rebel and try to buck the thought off, I pull the saddle strap tight, saying seven times seventy. He knows what it means. Then in the stillness of his uncertainty about his new thoughts ***I*** *climb up into the saddle, reminding him of his own judgment of the crux of Jesus' teaching: "Love your enemies."*

Then ***I*** *hold on tight, expecting a storm of protest, but to even my surprise, he seriously considers this approach to his problem. Instead of rebelling, his mind takes another tack and looks for reasons why this could be the most reasonable way for him to go. With my help, he avoids thinking of all the problems that might come in the future with a decision to love your enemies, and instead he stays present and focuses on only the enemy before him. He likes the fact that in further forgiveness he can keep his commitment to forgiveness. He wasn't wrong in his initial decision to trust and forgive. Following Jesus' command, he thinks, is a way of getting around Andrew's demands while keeping his self-respect. He sees that this is another direction in which he can move, a direction previously unseen. In siding with Jesus he will be rising up and going over Andrew. And in addition to solving his immediate problem, he thinks, this new direction offers a possibility of blessing, of possible release from his anguish of living in a meaningless world. He is curious to see what lies down this road.*

Behind Richard's conscious awareness of being curious to find what lies ahead going this way was his forgotten longing for adventure. Richard's desire for adventure was aroused in his teenage years through reading the exploits of Huck Finn and Tom Sawyer floating free down the Mississippi River on a homemade raft, and sharing vicariously in the exploits of cowboy scouts Kit Carson and Buffalo Bill going alone into the unknown wilderness to find a way for others to follow. Later he developed an enthusiasm for reading science fiction that kept alive his dreams of exploration and new discovery while extending its boundaries to include other forms of life and whole new worlds.

Richard had forgotten his naïve excitement at the dawn of the space age when he heard a newsreel announcer's voice at the local movie theatre thundering above him from the big screen, saying, "The next frontier is only twenty miles from home." Richard was sixteen with his first car and he knew he could easily explore anywhere within twenty miles of home. That wasn't news and the thought left him a little bewildered. *Where is this new frontier?* he wondered while awaiting the answer. Then suddenly his hopes were dashed as the booming voice announced the true yet impossible answer**,** "Straight Up!"

It was obvious as the space age took hold that Richard didn't have the right stuff to be an astronaut. In fact, at every point in his life Richard had chosen duty over answering the call to "boldly go where no man has gone before." Yet the spirit for adventure was still alive within him.

"Can you take me back to Zip's tomorrow?" Richard asked Celeste, finding himself strangely excited at taking this first step into the unknown to put his face-saving plan into action.

"You gonna give him the extra money?" Celeste asked.

"Yeah," Richard answered, giving no hint of his private thoughts for deciding to do so. "It seems like the only reasonable thing to do."

Celeste agreed to the trip, saying, "OK, but this had better be the end of it."

*Richard is quiet on the twelve mile drive to Zip's, and impressed with his acceptance when I saddled him with seven times seventy and love your enemies. I push another radical thought into his mind***.** *Go the second mile, I advise; knowing that if he could make such a radical break with the past, he might actually have a shot at being The One. He quickly translates the abstract thought into practical action and gets the idea of not only paying Andrew the amount he is unjustly demanding but of paying him more that he asks. He thinks that he needs to show himself that money isn't everything. Having seen Andrew sell his soul for a lousy seventy-five bucks, Richard is ready to prove to himself that money is not his God. True to his nature as an "all or nothing" kind of guy, he is "all in" on his commitment for forgiveness.*

He liked the idea of paying double the amount of the bill. Then he rationalized that would be more than required to make his point and unfair to his children, who he hoped to be able to send to college. In the end, he paid the bill by writing a check for about ten percent more than the new amount. And he was happy to do it; he noticed that this way seems right to him and his gut agreed.

As he handed over the check, the clerk dropped the final bomb. "There will be a three day waiting period for the check to clear before the truck can be released." Remarkably, this did not disturb Richard's peace. True he did not see it coming, but he knew that he should have. It seemed an entirely reasonable and predictable thing for Andrew to do, seeing that he had already stopped payment on one check.

> *Richard is in fact rather pleased to have one more thing to forgive. I am impressed, Richard is a natural.*

But on hearing this latest insult Celeste went off like a gun. BANG! She attacked the clerk directly and anyone else within hearing distance in her loud school teacher voice, "What do you mean we can't have the truck? He's paid the goddamned bill. I wanna talk to the manager. Look I've made two trips down here and I'm not going to make a third. I'm not leaving this time without the damn truck." She continued in this way attacking both the clerk and the manager and blaming them personally for all the trouble in the first place. The owner, Andrew, was either not there or was laying low in his upstairs office. The manager calmly informed Celeste she will have to quiet down or he will be forced to call the police. She did not calm down and continued to make a scene, disrupting the normal operation of Zip's garage. A real uniformed gun-toting policeman materialized in the lobby in no time. Celeste's anger was not tempered by even this and she continued repeating everything in profane detail until the policeman threatened to take her to jail if she did not get control of herself. It's the first and only time in their twenty years of marriage that Richard had seen his wife react to anything with such intensity. He was amused in his calm acceptance of the delay, but wisely did not let it show.

On the trip home, Richard preached to Celeste on his idea of what Jesus' teaching is really all about. She did not attack him and had surprisingly little to say about religion. She did not understand why he was not upset about having to make yet another trip to Zip's.

Arriving home about noon on a hot summer day, Celeste proceeded upstairs to their bedroom, saying she has a headache. It was hot outdoors and the big old house they had owned and lived in for eleven years was not yet air-conditioned. All the windows and doors were open to catch the breeze coming off Daytona's ocean beach two city blocks away. Richard set his body down in the wooden swivel chair behind the big old mahogany desk in the office. His intention was to meditate on what had just taken place.

He was beginning to realize that what he had done was beyond normal and the dark idea that he had made himself a complete fool was trying to work its way into his consciousness. He resisted the increasingly insistent temptation to look at the dark side of his decision and closed his eyes while asking an urgent question*, What now? How does following Jesus' command to love your enemies work?*

He lifted his eyes behind closed eyelids, this sincere question heavy on his mind, and entered into a more profound stillness than he had ever known before. Richard had asked a question and was now waiting in infinite patience for the answer. His blind, all or nothing, obedience to Jesus' command had brought him to this point in his life. Having cut all earthly ties, he had an unqualified need to know. He cannot continue beyond this point without the answer. He had reached the limit of the world's teaching and was ready to go beyond it.

> *In the next instant, Richard finds himself in a wonderful new world where everything was Love. He is separated from his body, which he knew remained seated in the old wooden desk chair. He is somewhere else, some place new and entirely unknown; yet he is alive and well, surrounded by—permeated through and through—by a living Love. Being separated from his body does not frighten him; rather he is excited to know the freedom he felt. The Love all around and within him gives rise to a constant Peace and Joy, deeper and more satisfying than anything he ever imagined possible.*
>
> *"Oh, oh, big mistake," he realizes immediately, thinking*

regretfully of the life he has led without faith in the existence of a greater reality.

"Why didn't someone tell me about this, he asks in his wonderment at this new world?" This is the answer, he knew, to his search for meaning. This New World, this amazing Reality he has stumbled into exists beyond time and space. In a single holy instant he is released from all limitation; he is free in union with Love. This is the answer to everything.

As Richard revels in the limitless and unchanging peace and joy, his sense of self shifts involuntarily from the limited world of separation and bodies—from which he had been released—to a new and greater knowing of who he is. In this perfect world where all is Love, he knows himself as Love. Love has created him like itself, as part of its self, and he realizes that this timeless moment is unmistakably the point of Jesus' apparently nonsensical command to "love your enemies." The command could only be understood in the doing of it. He has entered through the narrow gate.

I serve as guide and show Richard around our true home, knowing our visit will not last long. First I direct his attention to the innermost heart of all things and show him the source of all the Love. He watches in awe as LOVE generates endless thoughts of Love like itself. And he understands that he is one of those holy thoughts of the Creator, identical to the original thought and to all the others. Then in response to his desire to know of the world from which he believes he has just escaped, I take him to the outermost wall of unknowing. And there he sees how the created thoughts of Love could not extend themselves beyond the wall. And through the bars he sees his other world, beyond the reach of Love, where everyone lives in unknowingness, oblivious to the presence of Love, which alone is real.

He realizes his wife Celeste, his children and all the others are in that world. And he wants them to experience this greater reality with him. The choice he has to make comes into clear focus and I know our visit is ending. He wants to stay in his Home, the New World he has just discovered but now duty is calling and he knows he has to first return and tell the others of his discovery of this wonderful New World of Love. He must encourage them to follow in the ancient way he has discovered.

His dream of being an explorer, of his having the right stuff and courage to enter the unknown, is fulfilled, and being realized, it now merges with his duty to return and tell the others of the important wonder he has found.

I watch over his return to the familiar world and help him adjust again to the limitations imposed as he again gives life to the still warm body he had so briefly escaped.

His mind was alive with new ideas, and he immediately attempted to capture something of the experience in words. As his consciousness returned, he began to write on the desk pad before him with the words "the Oneness of God" running through his mind. The words were laid out carefully as though it were to be the title of a book relating his experience. Then he found he had no patience to write anything more; his heart was on fire and he had to tell someone about the *New World*. There was only Celeste.

"I love everybody," Richard innocently told Celeste when first he saw her after returning to this world. While waiting for her to come downstairs he had tried to contain his enthusiasm and considered it might be best if he didn't say anything about his vision of *Love* for a while, until he understood it better.

They were in the kitchen and he could not contain the good news any longer. He had to share the joy and it came out suddenly. "I was meditating and something happened," he explained. "*Love* is *Real*. I love everyone completely."

"What?" she said, mistrustful of what she was hearing and all the while trying to relate it to the scene she had made at Zip's garage and the sermon she had endured on the trip home.

"I just sat down at the desk to meditate and suddenly this world was gone. There's another world, a world of love and peace where we belong. I love everybody."

"What? I don't understand you. What's going on?" Celeste struggled to find an explanation that would enable her to make sense of what she was seeing and hearing. *What's happened to Richard, where is he coming from?* she asked herself. *He's different. His eyes are opened wide. Why is he telling me this? What's wrong with him?*

Richard knew that something important had happened to him, a progression of some sort, like a graduation. He fully expected Celeste would soon see that and share his joy. But Celeste wasn't feeling joyful.

"I love everyone," Richard told her again. And then to help her understand better he said, "I love the neighbor lady, Dr. Goldsmith's wife, the same as you."

Celeste, on hearing her husband say he loved another woman, a woman she doesn't even know, the same as he loves her, exploded in a fit of rejection. "No," she said loudly, giving strong voice to her disapproval, "I'm your wife. You love me; you don't love another woman the same as me. You had a crazy dream, that's all."

"What I saw wasn't a dream. This world is the dream; it isn't real and we don't live here," Richard said in a calm matter-of-fact manner. Hearing himself say this, he began to recognize the fundamental shift that had taken place in his sense of self. He had tasted life beyond the body and accepted it as his own.

Surprised and frustrated by the insane certainty of Richard's response and feeling herself powerless to reach him, Celeste impulsively grabbed a nearby pan and hurled it at Richard. He saw it coming but made no move to save himself. "Bang," the pan ricocheted off the kitchen cabinets, missing its mark by a wide margin and falling noisily but harmlessly to the kitchen floor.

"Wait! Stop! What are you mad about?" Richard asked as Celeste grabbed a skillet and took more careful aim. He didn't understand Celeste's anger and was surprised by her throwing the pan at him. She'd never done that before and so he thought it was just a misunderstanding. Not being angry himself, he made no attempt to return fire as he narrowly avoided being hit by the flying skillet. More pans and pots, dishes—whatever was handy—followed the skillet, some hitting their mark.

Many changes lay ahead for Richard but he would always recall this as the day his old life ended and his new life began. He remembered how he had raised his arms in front of his face to defend himself against the barrage attack, and sinking slowly to the floor had curled up in a tight defensive posture, a fetal position, until Celeste quit throwing things and left the kitchen, all upset and crying.

Chapter Two

THE TURQUOISE WAKE

"Why are you blowing like that?" Passenger Celeste Holmes sounded impatient as she deplaned, walking side by side with her recently retired husband Richard through the covered corridor linking their Delta Flight 228 with Hartsfield International terminal, Concourse C. Their predawn flight from Daytona Beach had arrived safely in Atlanta on time, 7:45 a.m. Monday morning.

Richard, surprised at the harsh early morning intrusion into his fantasy world, answered reflexively. "Huh? What blowing? I didn't realize I was doing anything." And then on second thought, he added defensively, "What the heck—do I have to watch even how I breathe with you? Why? Does it bother you?"

"You've never done it before," answered the woman who knew him possibly better than he knew himself.

"Maybe I should see a doctor," Richard came back sarcastically, then added, "I guess it's the cold. I left my jacket in the carry-on bag and they took it—won't see that again now till Reagan International in Washington D.C." It was the perfect cover story, he thought, to explain his unusual behavior.

Truth was, in all his seventy years Richard had never before sat so close to such a physically beautiful woman. It was having an invigorating effect on him—not exactly sexual but certainly something lively was going on. He wasn't a bad looking man, but he certainly wasn't a candidate for a magazine cover. Attractive women usually never gave him a second glance. This was new and a little frightening. He wondered what had changed.

As standby passengers, Celeste and Richard had been the last to board the full flight, not knowing until the last minute if they would be allowed on. As usual on full flights, their seats were not together. And this time, with no room left in the overheads, the crew had unexpectedly required them to check their carry-on bags at the door of the plane in warm Daytona Beach. Now they were in Atlanta in March and it was cold—fifty degrees in the walkway. It was reason enough to be breathing differently, he thought. Yet Celeste seemed unreasonably disturbed by his vigorous staccato breathing. Was she upset at having seen him talking with the beautiful woman and helping her retrieve her also beautiful bag from the overhead compartment?

Celeste had led the way onto the plane with Richard following closely behind. Her assigned seat was farther to the rear of the plane. She pointed out his row as they came to it and then continued on back. Without the carry-ons to worry about, Richard paid little attention to where she was sitting and stopped in the aisle where she had pointed. His seat was 32B, as usual the middle seat between two already settled in passengers.

The woman in the window seat was unconcerned with his arrival, seeming not to notice. Richard caught only a glimpse of her face as she looked up briefly. She was young, though definitely a woman and not a girl. Her face was exotic, with perfectly smooth complexion. She was maybe of Middle Eastern heritage. She had long brown hair and full lips. She looked a lot like the recently announced *Sports Illustrated* swimsuit issue cover model. She was beautiful.

The older man in the aisle seat, who was about Richard's age, got up when Richard made it known the middle seat was his. Richard eased his six-foot-four, two hundred pound body, together with his travel bag, into the middle seat sandwiched between the beautiful woman on his left and the polite man in the aisle seat, whose attention was directed toward his wife seated opposite him across the open aisle.

The beautiful woman's legs—Richard found it impossible not to notice—were sheathed in shiny nylon stockings with a good portion of her thighs exposed above the knee. His view was stopped only by the bright turquoise hem of her skirt or dress—he couldn't tell which it was. Muscular but feminine, he thought, then tried to distract himself by wondering what Celeste might be encountering in her assigned row. The experience made him smile internally, recalling how as an adolescent he often felt himself on the outside looking in, as if standing before the temple door guarding the entrance to the Holy of Holies in ancient Jerusalem. Only the very few were entitled to enter, and he wasn't one of them.

The reality of the predawn flight became clear when the external power umbilical was disconnected and the cabin was suddenly thrust into darkness. When the onboard power took over, the cabin light was more subdued, with only a scattering of overhead lights here and there like stars in the sky.

Richard reflected on his situation. Hardly an hour ago he was in bed with Celeste, his wife for forty-seven years, sleeping in his arms. Then after a flurry of activity, here he was, seated in the dark improbably close to an unknown, exotic-looking young and beautiful woman with thighs partially exposed and only a movable armrest separating their bodies. He took a deep breath.

Once in the air, the beautiful woman was intent on getting some sleep and rested her head and upper body against the window wall. She was wearing a long white, open sweater or coat, which she used as a blanket over the bright turquoise something. Richard didn't push his luck by trying to make small talk.

The passenger directly in front of him suddenly chose to recline his seat into Richard's lap, leaving not enough room for his knees. He quickly moved his knees to either side to avoid them being trapped by the falling seatback. In doing this his left leg momentarily brushed the young woman's right leg. He then crossed his feet at the floor as he had long ago learned to do, making it possible to lower his leg bones below the reclining seat back. Doing this brought them nearly within his own seat space. Still, his left leg intruded slightly into the borderland between himself and the beautiful woman.

While the jet engines droned on steadily outside the window, she seemed to drift in and out of sleep inside. Her right leg brushed briefly now and again against his left leg. The two of them were coming together unseen, felt only below the thin movable armrest enforcing the separation of their two bodies.

The effect on Richard was electric, with energy flowing into his psyche at each contact. He sat erect and motionless between the two passengers, seemingly himself asleep while actually meditating and now once again he was floating free in a sea of *Love*. The beautiful woman too, he imagined, appreciated the human contact. Her leg seemed to naturally want to fall against his, and he imagined it was relaxing for her to let it do so. More and more it came to rest against his and for measurably longer periods of time. Finally it decided to stay put and soon he felt the warmth of her body blending with his own. Richard considered that maybe she was awake and teasing him. It was impossible to tell. It didn't matter.

The plane landed smoothly and the woman and Richard came alive. Their spontaneous clandestine rendezvous beneath the armrest was over. When the plane rolled to a stop at the gate, and eager passengers jumped up into the aisle, Richard turned to his left and asked, "Are you in a hurry? Because if you are, I can let you out into the aisle, but I don't think anyone is going anywhere for a while."

"No," she said, "I'm fine." And it was music to Richard's ears in the midst of the chaos swirling around them. She understood there was nothing to be gained by standing in the aisle. So they sat together in mutually agreeable silence a few minutes more until the way began to clear. And when it was their time to exit, he stepped into the aisle and back a little creating a space for her to go before him. Seeing she was concerned about the overhead, he offered his help.

"Which one is it?" he asked before spotting the bright turquoise suitcase. "Got to be this one," he said, and she rewarded him with a genuine, movie star quality smile. As she came fully out into the aisle, sliding into the protected space he had created for her, she raised her arms and stretched a little, facing him with her back against the crush of frantic travelers. And arching her back, her chest, until now hidden beneath the simple, bright turquoise dress, pushed out as close to him as possible without touching.

Her body language, Richard considered, was screaming something impossible, something that he had believed himself too old and too married to hear. He lowered the matching rollaway he had been holding over his head to the floor between them and pulled up the handle as he always did for Celeste. And then she was gone down the aisle with him standing entranced, watching her go. He blindly offered a man across the aisle opportunity to go next but the man surprisingly deferred. Richard found himself pulled along up the aisle in the wake of the beautiful young woman who had spent the early morning with her warm and wonderful leg pressed against his and who had just now flashed her memorable turquoise-clad breasts at him. Hadn't she? He knew so little about women.

Another time and he might have stepped aside and waited for Celeste to come up the aisle, but this time he followed the other woman up the aisle and out the door onto the covered walkway to the terminal.

Outside the airplane and on the cold breezy runway, she turned to shift her load slightly—he supposed in preparation for the long walk into the terminal. Her long white sweater was somehow brushed aside in this action and her bright turquoise behind momentarily came into view.

He was not disappointed. But it was too much and the trance was broken in the cold air. Richard stopped following in her turquoise wake and stepped aside, waiting for Celeste. It was then, while he was standing still and watching her go, that he saw her turn and take a quick look back in his direction. Their eyes met in a totally magic moment and then the catch in his breathing—the blowing, as Celeste called it—began.

* * *

No fool like an old fool, he reflected later. He decided the genuinely beautiful and warm woman had been a tease. Yet he took even that as a compliment. Richard looked younger than he was and suffered none of the debilitating effects of old age, but he had never known himself to be attractive to women, and the young woman must have known he was old enough to be her father.

Still, she had been comfortable enough to play with him and the encounter had been enjoyable—he hoped for both of them. It was in a way a kind of celebration, a coming back to life event fully twenty-five years in its coming.

He was relaxed now and ready to enjoy the rest of his life—excited even and looking forward to seeing what the next few years might bring. But it hadn't always been like this. For the past twenty-five years he had been obsessively driven, single-mindedly pursuing this day when his work as a home builder would be done. But was a new kind of work waiting for him? Was the surprising interaction with the woman in turquoise somehow meant to introduce a new chapter? What did she signify? Richard's thoughts went back to the time long ago when it had all begun—the episode at Zip's garage which had opened his eyes to the possibility there was more to be seen and done.

Chapter Three

JENNY

"Remember how electrical currents and 'unseen waves' were laughed at? Knowledge about man is still in its infancy."

— Albert Einstein

"Jenny, what's going on? Didn't you hear the phone ringing?"

"Was that *my* phone?"

"Well, hello—yeah!"

"Oh."

Bina softened her incredulous tone. "It's okay I got it for you—nothing to worry about. I've been covering for you all morning. Haven't you even noticed?" It was obvious to her that something was distracting her co-worker.

"No. But if you say so, thanks."

"You're welcome. You know you've been out of it all morning."

"What? How?" Jenny said.

"I've never seen you upset like this before."

"What upset? I'm happy. That's all."

"Happy? Jenny, you're nearly comatose. It's like you're not even here. Anyone else and I would say it was drugs."

"I guess I am a little preoccupied . . . thinking about it."

"Thinking about what? Did something happen over the weekend I should know about? Jenny, did Bill finally ask you to marry him?"

"The weekend? No. No, not Bill. I've been thinking a lot about

Bill. He's so immature. I'm not sure I even like him anymore."

"Well, what then? C'mon, Jenny, we're best friends. Let me in."

"Well, if you must know, it was the most exciting experience I ever imagined. I'm just still all aglow."

"Sex? Is this about sex?"

"No, not at all, but the excitement was like that, only different. It left me all aglow. Haven't you ever felt all aglow like that?"

"Yeah, right. I know all about being 'all aglow.' Maybe once or twice in my life, I know. But you said, not on the weekend. When?"

"This morning, on the airplane."

"Jenny! You had sex, or something like sex, on the plane? No! You didn't! How? I can't believe it. Did Bill come back with you?"

Jenny woke a little from her dreamlike state in response to this excited accusation of improper behavior coming from her best friend.

"What? Bina! What are you thinking? No, of course not. I didn't say I had sex on the plane. Do you think I would do that? All those people . . . watching."

"I'm trying to fill in the blanks. You said it was on the plane this morning, the best . . . something . . . whatever, you ever imagined."

"I said, the excitement was *like* sex only different."

"Oh, well, excuse me valley girl, that explains everything. Jenny, what in the world can you do on an airplane that is like sex but is not sex and not drugs?"

"I don't know. Something happened, that's all. I'm happy. It's like I'm all wrapped up in a *Love* bubble, warm and fuzzy. Don't ask me any more questions, alright. You're supposed to be my friend, don't spoil this for me. I don't have the words to explain what I felt. I'm happy. Just let me be—can't you?"

"Okay, sure, I can do that. But then after work you've got to tell me everything. I want some of your happiness for myself."

Jenny didn't respond, seeming not to hear while all wrapped up in her "love bubble." Her best friend and boss, Bina, continued to cover for Jenny's absent-mindedness the rest of the day.

Bina had a PhD in linguistic science from Jerusalem University in Israel, where she had grown up. She was a research librarian, one of many working for the Library of Congress—the LOC—and Jenny was her personal assistant.

Bina couldn't stop thinking about the "love bubble" excuse Jenny gave. What kind of language was that? And did she really say that she wasn't sure she even liked Bill anymore, that he was too immature? Where did that come from? They were engaged to be married, for Christ's sake, and Jenny made frequent trips to Florida and Daytona Beach on the weekends, away from her job in Washington, D.C., because she wanted to be with Bill, a used car dealer Bina considered a little "dodgy."

She had been telling Jenny for years that Bill wasn't the one for her. What had happened that she was suddenly able to see it? Was Jenny coming awake somewhere inside her "warm and fuzzy" happiness bubble?

Jenny was a beautiful woman and could attract any man she wanted with nothing more than her smile. But she could be a little simple minded at times. Maybe that's all this "happiness" business was. Yet, it seemed to be a real mystery and Bina loved to get to the bottom of things.

* * *

Leaving their underground work station in the Adams building LOC at the end of the day and exiting onto Independence Avenue, Bina steered Jenny away from the Metro and toward the *Hawk and Dove* bar and grill on Pennsylvania Ave. It would be happy hour and the drinks were free for single women, and on a Monday night there wouldn't be a lot of guys to bother them.

They took a table at the back and ordered drinks—a gin and tonic for Jenny and a Budweiser for Bina—and one order of sweet potato fries, the house specialty. With drinks in hand, Bina resumed her interrogation.

"OK Jenny, now tell me what you did on that airplane that's better than sex? My imagination is running wild."

"Nothing. I got on the plane; Bill took me to the airport, and I was normal. Then when we arrived in Atlanta to change planes, I was just so happy."

"That's it? I waited all day to hear this? Jenny there's got to be something. Did you have a drink—coffee or orange juice? Was there some guy watching you who might have put something in your drink?"

"No, I didn't have a drink, not even coffee. It was dark on the plane and I was sleepy. I was in the window seat and I leaned against the wall and tried my best to get some sleep."

"All right, now you're telling me something. What do you mean you *tried* to sleep? Was somebody bothering you so you couldn't sleep?"

"No, it wasn't like that. He wasn't bothering me; we barely talked at all."

"Oh, so there was some guy. And he was sitting next to you?"

"Yes, he came late and he was tall and so he squeezed into the empty middle seat next to me. But it wasn't like that. He wasn't a guy. His leg brushed mine."

"Not a guy? What was he then—a girl? Jenny, this is like pulling teeth. What are you trying to hide? Did you do something you're ashamed of?"

"No. Yes, maybe, sort of. I mean, well he was an older man and I flirted with him. I guess it was flirting; I was friendly. His leg brushed mine when the seatback came down. But he was real polite and he reminded me of Forrest Gump. It was cramped and we were close together. I brushed my leg back against his."

"Okay, let me see if I've got this right. There was an older Forrest Gump sitting next to you and you flirted with him and you're ashamed you did it because . . . why? Don't tell me—you thought maybe he supposed you were making fun of him. Is that what you want me to believe?"

"Not exactly. After the plane landed, I was feeling really happy and playful. I just assumed—somehow it was obvious to me that he had something to do with it. I'm not sure if I was just flirting. I wanted him to follow me."

"You mean you were trying to get this innocent Forrest Gump man to follow you home?"

"Maybe, but it wasn't sexual. I don't know what it was. My body responded kind of like it was sexual, but it wasn't! I just wanted to keep him on my radar."

"And why would you want to do that."

"Because I was just so happy."

"Well, now we're back where we started.

"Let's go back to when you were playing footsies with this guy, excuse me, not a guy, this older Forrest Gump. How did he react to that? Did he look at you?"

"Nope. He was sitting straight up in the too small seat and he didn't move—it looked to me like he was sleeping standing up, and that's what reminded me of Forrest Gump."

"Jenny, I'm guessing here—stop me if I'm wrong—but I think you were feeling happy before you tried to pick up your father."

"Honestly, Bina, you can be irritating. Haven't you ever been attracted to an older man? He wasn't my father."

"Okay, sorry. I deserved that, my bad. So it sounds like you're telling me that it made you happy just to be close to this guy."

"Yeah, except that after a while it was more than just being close."

"What? Wait! I need another drink before you go there. Waiter . . . yes, she needs another, too. Thank you. And bring us another order of those sweet potato fry things, will you?"

After a few minutes, the conversation resumed. "Okay, now Jenny, what exactly do you mean, 'more than close?' Did this guy come on to you?"

"No, it was me."

"You? Jenny! What did you do? No, wait. Do you remember that poor guy you smiled at that day and he backed up and fell off the Metro platform onto the tracks?"

"He wasn't hurt."

"I know. Thank God. But the point is—I wonder if you have any idea of what you do to men."

"I think I do—sometimes."

"Okay. Now, what did you do to this Forrest Gump?"

"Well, since he had brushed his leg against mine first, I brushed him back. And then . . ."

"And you were wearing that turquoise jumper and those shiny nylons and it came halfway up your thighs, didn't it?"

"Yes. So?"

"So? Jenny!

"What?"

"Well, you know. Or maybe you don't know. But you should know. Men of a certain age . . . well, you could have blown the poor guy's fuse. And then …"

"Anyway, then after the first time I brushed his leg it felt so comfortable and natural that I did it again. And then again. Finally my leg just rested against his and we both were sleeping. When the plane landed and we woke up our legs were pressed tight together and I couldn't tell if he was doing it or if I was."

"So close together that no light could come between?"

"Yes, I guess so."

"That's from Genesis, the Bible, it's how close the rabbis say a man cleaves to his wife and they become one flesh."

"Bina, you've got a dirty mind, you know that? It wasn't like that. I didn't marry the guy."

"Oh, so you admit he was a guy?"

"No! He was a real Forrest Gump. He was polite. He got my bag down for me from the overhead."

"Jenny, have you ever had to get your own bag down when there was even one guy or man-child left on the plane?"

"Well no, but—"

"And what did you do for him."

"I gave him a big silly smile. It was real funny, and that's when I realized how happy I was and I didn't want to leave him."

"And what did that do to him? I bet he melted in a puddle like Frosty the Snowman."

"Bina, where do you get this stuff?"

"I don't know. I just thought your warm smile would be too much for him to keep his cool."

"No, and he didn't melt. He smiled right back, real innocent like. And so then when I stepped out into the aisle, into the little space he made for me, I stretched a bit and arched my back so the outline of my body under my sweater was, you know, visible—I wanted him to feel what I was feeling, and follow me. My body was nearly touching his and I might have moved in closer except . . ."

"Except what? Don't stop now, you're on a roll."

"Except there was a woman glaring at me two or three rows back. I was being free and shameless, and I guess she thought I had gone too far. Anyway her look sobered me up a little bit and I turned and took my bag by the handle he had ready for me and then I walked up the aisle toward the door. I was sure he would follow. I mean I've never met a man who wouldn't have."

"Well, what was he?"

"What?"

"Was he a man or a mouse? Did he follow you?"

"Yes, but he didn't follow real close. I guess he was—"

"He was probably having a heart attack and needed a moment to recover. You might have killed him if your breasts had actually brushed against him like your leg did."

"Very funny. And then—"

"There's *more*?"

"Yes, just one more thing. Outside the plane, I stopped on the ramp into the terminal and waited for him to come out. Then when he did, he stopped just outside the door like he was waiting for someone. I didn't know what to do, so when I saw him looking at me, I kind added some extra wiggle as I walked. I was kind of desperate, using whatever tools I have, you know?"

"We don't all have the same tools."

"Remember, you asked for this."

"I remember, go on."

"Well, when I looked back he was still standing there and he saw me looking back. Our eyes met and I was embarrassed. I realized the game I was playing was the wrong game for this moment. I turned around and went on into the terminal. I never saw him again. But, the happiness stayed."

"Whew! Try and imagine what the old guy musta been going through."

"Oh, one more thing. That lady, the one that glared at me in the plane, was coming up to him like she was the one he was waiting for."

"I might have guessed it if I was just a little smarter," Bina said. "A few minutes ago I would have said none of this made any sense—I don't mean the part about how you affected him, I mean the way he affected you—but it's starting to . . . come on and drink up, we've got to go."

"Go? Where are we going?"

"Well, I'm putting a lot of stock in your intuition about this guy and the extraordinary effect he had on you, but if he is who I think he is, we're going to find your Forrest Gump before someone else does."

"Who?"

"I think Homeland Security is looking for him, but they don't know it yet. The effect you had on him would be easy enough to dismiss, but the effect he had on you makes no sense unless—"

"Homeland Security? Why would they want to find him?"

"Well, if you can believe it, I think someone there may want to kill him."

Chapter Four

HOMECOMING

If strangers could now sense something extraordinary in this older Forrest Gump, it was a long time coming. For Richard's family it was always difficult and had been from the beginning. Shortly after his big, out-of-this-world experience, he traveled with Celeste and the kids back to his boyhood home on the farm in Indiana. He recalled that road trip as magical, but he also remembered his disappointment at being thought crazy when he shared his surprising experience with his extended family.

"Where are we?" Richard suddenly asked Celeste with concern and some urgency even though he was the one driving. He had been at the wheel of their plush, custom Chevy van pulling the humble Coleman pop-up tent trailer every mile of the way from their home in Daytona Beach to wherever they were now, somewhere north of Atlanta.

It was Monday about noon, the third day of their trip to visit relatives in their home state of Indiana. The trip had been planned for months, and although their relationship was now strained and uncertain since Richard's big experience on Wednesday—and Celeste's skillet throwing overreaction to the sudden loss of her husband's special love—they had decided there was no real reason to change their plans. Their two children, Annette, 11, and Timmy, 7, were along for the ride and were now lost somewhere in the back of the big gray van carrying them toward Indiana for a visit with their seldom seen grandparents.

The first night away from home they stopped at High Falls State Park south of Macon, Georgia. The main campground was full and the ranger said they were lucky to find a spot to set-up in the new annex on lower ground near a river. They decided to stay over on Sunday and spent a pleasant family day in the park. They rented a rowboat and rowed themselves back and forth across the still water of the lake above the dam. And they swam in the flowing water of the river at the protected beach area below the dam. Then, they watched as a small boy carefully crawled out on the slippery rocks under a waterfall at the end of the dam. Richard followed the boy's progress and was thrilled when, finally in position, the boy was immersed in the falling water. Richard enthusiastically imagined that something special in the way of baptism was taking place. Annette and Timmy were soon following their father out onto the slippery rocks where they too received the water baptism. Celeste did not participate in this "baptism," nor was she impressed.

Back on the road the next day, Celeste was startled to hear Richard ask her to pinpoint their location. "What do you mean, where are we? Don't you know?" she answered. And when Richard didn't immediately answer she added, "Are we lost?"

Each time she spoke, Richard leaned his ear in her direction to better hear through the thick fog of his overexcited mind. There was another voice far more interesting than hers that he was intent on hearing. Finally he roused himself from the celestial music coming from somewhere deep in his personal dream world and answered, "No, we're not lost. But we must have turned off I-75 somewhere. I don't know exactly where we are, somewhere North of Atlanta on I-85. Take a look at the map and see if you can figure out where we are and how we can best get back to our usual way home on I-75."

While she searched the map, Richard was busy recalling the game of kickball he had played with Timmy at the state park the day before. Immediately after the game, he had momentarily lost consciousness. Now this wrong turn was apparently a second time he had done something unaware. This time he had taken a wrong turn and didn't yet know where their new direction was taking them.

The kickball game Sunday evening before dinner had begun by kicking a lightweight rubber ball back and forth with Timmy on an unused baseball diamond. Timmy was athletic and being only seven, full of energy. The lightweight ball was about the size of a basketball, and even when kicked really hard it would drift slowly through the air like a balloon and not go very far. The object of the spontaneous game became to keep the ball in the air using nothing but feet.

Richard kept up with his son for quite a long time. When the ball finally hit the ground he was exhausted and ready to take a break. He sat down on the end of a picnic table and then apparently lost consciousness. For how long was impossible to tell, but when he came to there was a stick in his left hand and a geometric drawing scratched in the dust of the Georgia red clay at his feet. It was obvious to Richard that he had made the drawing with the stick in his hand but he had no memory of doing so. He had no idea what the figure meant. It was something new and exciting and he, unlike Celeste, was sure it was important.

He finally had something tangible to show as evidence of his inward experience. He was impatient to know what the drawing was. He wanted to preserve it and carry the red dust itself home in a box, but that was impossible. Not having a camera, he preserved the drawing by carefully making a copy of it on the back of a business card he kept in his wallet.

After dinner that evening, park rangers came by warning of a severe storm. They suggested that campers might want to leave the low lying annex campsites, where Richard and his family were, and move to the main campground on higher ground. Richard did not heed the warning and the storm never reached the campground. It had apparently done severe wind damage a few miles away to a wide circle all around the park and campground while they remained at its calm center with their sleep undisturbed.

And then Monday morning before they returned to the road, a young park ranger, a woman with big blue eyes, had been surprisingly willing to search out some information for him on the meaning of the strange figure he had drawn in the red clay. It looked like it might be an Indian symbol of some sort. Their efforts had not borne fruit but all these happenings and more contributed to a feeling, in Richard's mind, that he was not alone and this was going to be an enchanted trip.

And now this unexpected wrong turn. Where would it lead? It wasn't really a wrong turn, Richard knew, it was an invitation to adventure. He realized that his attention, his thoughts, had not been on the road that he and Celeste had traveled many times; but never before had he made a wrong turn like this. What was the reason for it? What was waiting for them up ahead? Where were they being led?

Celeste's voice intruded in his reverie, from somewhere outside his personal paradise. "Here we are. It looks like we're about half way to Greenville, South Carolina," she said. He lent her an ear. "About fifty miles out of Atlanta," she added.

"Fifty miles!" Richard reacted. "You mean I was out of it for nearly an hour? That's too far to have to go back. Let me see the map. Maybe we can find a new route from here."

The big gray van continued its northward journey, its driver imagining a mysterious loving presence guiding it along the way, its big V-8 engine running smoothly, effortlessly pulling the small pop-up trailer. The van's tires rolled out a satisfying hypnotic rhythm, echoing the concrete pavement of the interstate highway beneath them, leading directly toward the Great Smoky Mountains less than a hundred miles away but not yet visible on the horizon.

Richard sought to reassure Celeste about this unexpected new route and about his state of mind. "We used to go this way before the interstates were built. I remember we came through the mountains once at night in a rainstorm. Do you remember driving that narrow two-lane road snaking through the valleys, going up and down the mountains, like a roller coaster? That was a long night." Of course they both knew it wasn't like that anymore.

A thought came into his mind in that mysterious way that thoughts often do, and Richard remembered having read somewhere about the interstate highways being inspired by an ancient prophecy from the Bible: "… knock down the mountains, fill up the valleys and make straight the way of the Lord." Richard thought it a strange connection—modern highways and ancient texts. His thoughts took a flight of fancy, imagining a heavenly traffic controller following the progress of their van, appearing as a tiny golden blip on his heavenly viewing screen as it moved along this modern highway, straight through the knocked down mountains and filled-up valleys exactly as it had been foretold.

Celeste interrupted his daydream. “I do remember that trip. That might have been the last time we went this way.”

“Yeah, I think that was it.”

“Are you OK?”

“I feel great. Sorry, I just wasn’t paying attention back there. I’m all right now.”

“You seem a bit dreamy; want me to drive?”

“Dreamy . . . what is that?

“Oh, I don’t know, preoccupied, I guess.”

Traffic was light, the miles rolled by and the family inside the van grew quiet watching the pleasant countryside outside passing by: small farms with modest houses and barns at the end of long lanes off gravel roads. Sometimes clouds of dust could be seen rising behind a car or pickup truck traveling country roads that cut through the fields, some planted with corn, green and growing fast now under the summer sun. They spotted a few wheat fields beginning to ripen to a golden color, but they mostly enjoyed gently rolling pastures, some with cows or horses, and here and there a few sheep and goats.

Unnoticed, the van drifted into the left lane and imperceptibly slowed to just below the allowable limit. Running on cruise control it was not bothered by traffic using the right lane to enter or exit the highway, and what little through-traffic there was politely passed on the right with no one seeming to mind the inconvenience

Richard relaxed at the wheel and perhaps feeling the mood of his own carefree days growing up on the Indiana farm—the end point of their trip—was again seduced into opening his mind to the loving presence. Soon he was in *Love* again in a most literal way, his mind willingly joined with the loving power that came forth upon invitation and joyously held his attention. The world receded somewhere outside, seen only dimly as through a fog. This time there was something, the slightest loving hint of something, residing so tenderly within the limitless love as to be completely overlooked, missed entirely if one were not already inside that something, already a part of what it was. It was not demanding, not asking, yet Richard felt drawn to it as if it somehow was for him.

"Richard. Richard," a voice intruded from somewhere outside through the fog.

"What is it?" he answered without diverting his attention from the something holding him captive within the *Love* surrounding him.

"What's going on? Why are you crying? "

"I'm not crying."

"Yes, you are. You're weeping, tears are streaming down your face."

"Love," he confessed.

"Love? Honestly, Richard if this is about that woman again, I swear I'm going to leave you." Celeste's tone made it clear she meant it. She turned away from him, feeling again the threat of some undefined love beyond the love between them, a mysterious love having power to make her husband shed tears of joy like she had seldom seen.

"No, not like that," Richard answered, taking the opportunity to communicate through the fog separating them. He turned to his wife for help, as he often did, this time with the internal *something* waiting for his attention.

"Country," he said. The word seemed to come from somewhere outside him.

"What? You love the country?" Celeste knew her husband missed living in the country. Was he experiencing some kind of psychological release from the anxieties and pressures of living in the city too long? Was it the countryside passing by outside—so like his Indiana home—that he was remembering with love?

She decided to try and reach him, "You're remembering growing up on the farm aren't you. You loved the farm. That's it, isn't it."

"Not that kind of country," he said, and laughed a little on his side of the fog.

"Well, what then?" Celeste asked.

"USA" came out immediately, directly, surprising both of them, making Richard ask himself, *What am I—an answering machine?*

"Oh, I get it you love the U.S.A., this country, America."

On hearing this, Richard felt the attractive something dissolve peacefully back into the oneness. "Yes," he answered, "that's it. Thank you." So that was what it was. That inexpressible something so gently calling to him had been a message, a communication from the *Living Love* itself. In some special way, he knew, God loved the U.S.A. This was God's country.

"Wait, there's something else," he realized. And then, their heads lifted up and with eyes wide open they looked out the front windshield and saw it together. There filling the horizon in the near distance, magnificent rolling foothills in front, and beyond the hills, range upon range of higher yet tree covered mountains stretching from left to right as far as they could see. Clouds above played with light and shadow, and moving across the mountains created a spectacular panorama. The mountains seemed alive, more than beautiful, simply regal and majestic. It was of course, the Smokies, and they were surprisingly yet unmistakably, in Richard's eyes at least—purple!

"Hey, look at the purple mountains," exclaimed their daughter Annette.

And then seven-year-old Timmy said, "Yeah, I see it too, purple, cool."

The two children had pulled themselves away from their electronic toys in the back of the van and were competing for their parent's attention by trying to squeeze themselves into the narrow space between the two captain chairs up front. Everyone had suddenly come to life, seeing the same thing at nearly the same moment. This, Richard realized, like the still unknown figure, the sign he had scratched in the red dirt yesterday, was not just his imagination.

With this confirmation of his seeing purple mountains, Richard jolted awake out of his unitary mind space. The fog dividing his inner and outer worlds dissolved, and he came back into his separated self. Very simply, he was Richard again.

"Hey, here's a riddle for you. Do you see what I see? It's a song." Richard gave his Purple Mountain Kids what they wanted, his attention, by challenging them to see if they would also confirm what he had just suddenly realized. “See if you can guess what song it is,” he said. “Here’s the clues, first—love of our country, America, and second, purple mountains.”

Annette spoke first. “I know it. It’s the National Anthem,” and she began to sing, “America, America—”

“No,” Timmy interrupted, “that’s not the anthem. *It’s* all about fireworks, ‘the bombs bursting in air—to show our flag is still there.’”

“Oh yeah,” Annette said and then asked, “Well, what is my song? It’s the one you’re thinking of, isn’t it Dad?”

“Yes, it is Annette; you win. But Timmy’s right too. Your song isn’t the National Anthem, it’s called, *America the Beautiful.* A lot of people think it should be the National Anthem and right now I agree with them.

“Timmy, buddy, I know you really like fireworks. We can buy some in Tennessee and then we’ll let Uncle Fred in Indiana help us shoot them off on the farm on the Fourth of July.”

“Yeah, fireworks,” sang Timmy as he retreated to the back of the van and to his video game.

“Now, let’s see if we can remember some more words to that song.” In Richard’s mind, the words to the song had to be part of the message. “Maybe we can get Mom to help us. I remember, ‘amber waves of grain’—those wheat fields we saw a while ago, beginning to ripen, that will do for amber waves of grain. And there’s the ‘purple mountains majesty’ right in front of us.”

“Well, I should know all the words because we used to sing it at the school I went to,” Annette volunteered, and then continued, “‘America, America’. Oh yeah, this is it, ‘God shed his grace on thee, and crowned thy good with brotherhood from sea to shining sea.’”

On hearing those words, Richard tuned out and began fumbling around among their collection of maps with his right hand while keeping the left on the wheel. His eyes darted back and forth from the highway to the maps; he was looking for something and having trouble finding it.

Celeste offered her help. “What is it? I’ll get it. You keep your eyes on the road. There’s more traffic now, and you might want to get back over in the right lane."

"Oh . . . Okay," Richard said slowly, seeing the situation and taking full control of the van. "I was looking for those pictures of the van that came from the guy who customized it. It should be with the owner's manual and stuff behind the maps—there somewhere. I want to see if the logo on the spare tire cover is what I think it is. How long we been driving in the left lane?"

"I'm not sure. I think I fell asleep for a while. Maybe half an hour."

"Oh, and nobody honked?" *That's surprising*, he thought, wondering if it would be irrational for him to see it as another sign that they were not alone on this trip.

"Not that I heard. Where were you? Can't you just wait until we stop and then take a look at it?" Celeste asked, suspicious of something not quite right in the urgency of his request.

Richard ignored her first question and answered the second one, finishing with an assertion of his rights. "I could, and I will do that too, but I'm impatient. Why shouldn't I see it now?" He was gaining confidence with each supposed sign, growing reckless now of Celeste's concern for his sanity.

"Here it is," Celeste said finally. She looked at the picture and saw for herself the small coincidence in it, but knew Richard would see it as another important sign. She practically threw it at him.

Picking up the sales flyer, Richard scanned the company's letterhead, *Imperial Custom Vans, Tallahassee Florida*, written at the top above the two pictures of their exact van. It had been the company owner's personal van. The first picture was a front and side view, and below that was a rear view clearly showing the company logo painted on the round metal cover on the spare tire bolted on the rear door which was only a few feet behind him. And it was, as he was even now convinced it should be—a crown. It was a proper symbol for the presence Richard believed was with them, guiding their way home.

* * *

"Richard, hurry up," Celeste said. "It's time for the movie to start."

"What movie is that?'

"The museum orientation movie we've been waiting fifteen minutes for."

"I'm coming. Just want to finish reading this exhibit."

"Honestly, Richard you are the slowest. What is it you're looking at? You haven't moved past that one exhibit since we came in the front door."

Celeste came over to where Richard was being held captive. It wasn't much, just an unprofessional full scale diorama of a local hillbilly, a stuffed dummy dressed in a plaid shirt and Oshkosh denim overalls, posed in a rocking chair on a wooden platform in front of a wall mural of a log cabin with mountains in the background. She took in the title of the exhibit: JOHN HENDRIX — THE PROPHET OF OAK RIDGE.

"Prophet?" she said aloud. "What's that religious crap doing in here? This isn't a church. It's a United States tax-supported Museum of Science and Energy for God's sake." She turned to Richard and in an accusatory tone said, "You knew this was here, didn't you?"

"No I didn't. Honestly I'm as surprised as you," Richard responded truthfully. "It was your idea that we stop here, remember? You said it would be a good opportunity for the kids to learn a little American history. Well, I guess this is just part of that history."

"Look at this," Richard pleaded. "This is incredible. A local hillbilly, John Hendrix, heard a voice, 'as loud as thunder,' he said. The voice told him to go out into the woods and sleep on the ground for forty days and forty nights and then he would be told the future. Well, he did what the voice told him to do and then he saw visions of what was going to happen here forty years before it really did happen."

"Incredible is right," Celeste protested. "Stuff like that just isn't credible at all. You don't believe that crap do you? Well, do you? Yes, you do, I can see it in your eyes. Oh God, Richard, it's just a bunch of rumors and made up stories by a bunch of half-wit hillbillies. It's crap."

"Well, maybe I wouldn't have looked twice at it before, but now, I know what a *vision* is. I can understand also why you feel the way you do about it, but really, this is history. It's well documented. The guy told everyone who would listen about the visions. He even marked the trees where the buildings would be built. And he named names of people who would be living and who would see it happen, and names of others including himself who would be dead. You said yourself why would something that's just crap be in this official government museum? The obvious answer is, this isn't crap. It really happened. It's real.

"Look, here's the important thing for us today. John is quoted as having said there would be a bunch of factories built here 'that would,'—this is the direct quote, 'help toward winning the greatest war that ever will be.' Did you hear that? 'The greatest war that will ever be.' The work done in the factories here resulted in the atomic bomb that ended World War Two. So, it seems to me that John is saying there won't be any greater war than that. There won't be a World War Three. I think that since he was right about what he saw in his visions we should give him a break and consider believing this good news part about no more war. One less thing for us to worry about, right?"

"Honestly Richard, you are incredible. Sometimes, I'd just like to drop a bomb on you. Come on, let's go see the movie. Timmy and Annette are already in there."

Richard nodded his okay to that and turning toward the theatre said, "Maybe there will be something in it about John Hendrix—the official government approved Prophet of Oak Ridge."

The movie was a standard sort of short historical documentary. It was full of old newsreel clips and photos of life in Bear Valley, Tennessee, before the Defense Department of the United States federal government decided to build a secret facility there. In the early 1940s they moved the local people off their land on short notice and built a huge facility and developed procedures to refine uranium such that it could be used to make the first atomic bomb. There were pictures of the land being cleared for construction of the giant buildings used in the refining processes but there was no mention of a prophet named John Hendrix marking the trees forty years earlier to indicate where the buildings would be constructed.

There were photos of the people who were recruited to work there, and others showing how the modern city of Oak Ridge rose from its beginnings as a community of temporary housing for the workers. Emphasis was given throughout to the importance and enormity of the undertaking and to the extreme measures taken to preserve the secrecy of the whole operation.

Altogether, Richard thought the history of the area was well documented, but he was disappointed about the lack of recognition given to the Prophet of Oak Ridge.

The grand finale was impressive documentary footage of the nuclear explosion that took place at Nagasaki, Japan, on August 9th, 1945. The final scene showed the unconditional surrender ceremony of Japan on the battleship Missouri, marking the formal end of WWII.

Timmy's enthusiasm for the Oak Ridge museum was immediately evident when the film ended. He and Annette quickly located their parents near the back of the theatre.

"Wow, Dad, did you see the fireworks with that giant smoke cloud? We were on the front row and when they dropped it from the airplane—boomzilla! It musta been the giantest explosion ever. I wanna see some more stuff. This place is neat."

"It isn't fireworks Timmy, it's a bomb. And there's no such word as giantest." Richard sought to restrict his son's enthusiasm for war and destruction just a bit. "A lot of people were killed in that explosion."

But Timmy seemed not to hear. "Well, we have some cherry bombs and some smoke bombs. Wow, I hope they go off like that! Hey, we need an airplane to drop them out of. Does Uncle Fred have an airplane?"

Annette's reaction was more subdued, showing sympathy for the plight of the people in the Oak Ridge area who were asked to leave their homes on short notice. "Mom, did all that really happen? How could a whole city be kept secret?"

They left the theatre together and then Celeste and Annette followed the signs toward the exhibits dealing with the human aspects of the history while Richard and Timmy went the other way, down the road of scientific discovery toward the mock-ups of the "Little Boy" and "Fat Man" atomic bombs.

When they met up an hour later they had all had enough history and were ready to leave. Richard asked a museum employee for information about nearby campgrounds and he was given a brochure for *The Happy Cricket.*

"It's not the biggest but it has a restaurant and a swimming pool and is still quiet enough so you can enjoy the outdoors." The helpful man told him. Richard was skeptical of any commercial campground big enough to have a restaurant, but then his eye noticed a single mention of the "Prophet of Oak Ridge" on the backside of the information sheet.

"*The Happy Cricket* is located in the woods near the spot where John Hendrix—the Prophet of Oak Ridge—is believed to have spent forty days and nights seeking his vision of the future." It was simply stated, and it was enough.

* * *

"Where are we going?" Celeste asked. "Isn't the Interstate the other way?"

"Yes, but I've got a better idea. If we go straight home now it'll be too late when we get in. I think it would be better if we stay here tonight at a campground and then arrive in Indiana tomorrow afternoon."

Celeste was caught off guard. "What campground?"

"It's called *The Happy Cricket.* It's in the woods just a few miles out of town." Richard handed Celeste the brochure for the *Happy Cricket* hoping she wouldn't read it close enough to notice the mention of "the Prophet" in the fine print on the backside. Evidently, he thought, Prophet John Hendrix wasn't a big drawing point.

"How did you decide on this one? We usually decide together."

"Well, yes. But, I thought you'd be pleased, not to have to worry about it. Relax, we're on vacation. The guide at the museum recommended it and gave me this advertisement. It looked good to me. He said it has a popular, fun restaurant and a swimming pool."

"A fun restaurant? What is that?" Celeste asked, curious about this change in plans.

"It's got a water wheel and you cook your own sausage and pancakes at the table."

"A swimming pool sounds fun to me, Mom," offered Annette.

"Me too. Let's go," Timmy said, adding his approval of the new plan.

"Okay," Celeste said, and it was decided.

"By the way," she told Richard, "there was nothing about that mountain man, so called prophet, in the other exhibits we saw. I knew it was nothing."

"There wasn't any mention of it in the movie or anywhere else that we saw either," Richard answered, neglecting to mention that they were heading directly toward the place in the woods where John Hendrix had received his inspiration a long time ago. Richard was feeling a kinship with the plight of this mountain man mystic and wanted to know everything he could about him.

* * *

"Look at this," Celeste said. "Here's a book about that hillbilly Prophet."

"Oh?" Richard said, trying to look merely surprised through his excitement at what Celeste had found in the campground store.

The store clerk overheard their conversation and said, "Yes, ma'am. We've got all them books anybody ever wrote about John Hendrix. And I reckon you know about 'Inspiration Point'. Just follow the signs. It's about half a mile down the trail there right outside the store."

"No, I didn't know," Celeste responded, surprised. "Richard we didn't know about all this, did we?"

"Well, maybe I did—just a little bit," he answered. "There was a mention of it in the brochure. Didn't you see it? But I didn't expect to find all this."

"Oh, yeah," the clerk said. "We're kind of a big center for information about the Prophet."

"I can see that," Celeste said. She began questioning the clerk. "Tell me, it's all just a bunch of old stories, right? There's nothing credible about it is there?"

"Oh no, ma'am. It's all very real," he said. "There's lots of folks around here that's got relatives that knew John and heard him talk about his visions. My own Pa was one who heard him. It's all there in them books."

"Hmmm," Celeste murmured as she laid a carton of milk and box of Cheerios on the checkout counter.

Richard added a small book, *Back of Oak Ridge*, to the stuff they were buying and the talkative clerk said, “That there’s a real good’n you picked out for yourself Mister.”

“Ma’am, if it’s any interest to you, we find that it’s mostly the men that are interested in the Prophet. I don’t know why that is. It’s just the way, I s’pose. O’course there ain’t many of any kind much interested anymore.”

“Tell me,” Richard said, “why is that?”

“Well, I reckon the world has just moved on past that sort of thing.”

Celeste took that opportunity to move on herself, saying, “I’m going to check on the kids at the pool.”

“Okay, I’ll find you later,” Richard said, happy to have an opportunity to talk with this older gentleman alone.

“We saw the exhibit at the museum. You know anything about that? By the way, my name is Richard.”

“Pleased to meet you Richard; mine’s Curtis. I know all they is to know about that museum exhibit. Me and some others was responsible for getting it put there. They didn’t want nothing to do with it at first.”

“Is that so?”

“Yep, that’s so. Them’s my old Oshkosh overalls that ol’ John Hendrix dummy is a’wearin. An I knowed right off when you walked in that door yonder that you was interested in the Prophet.”

“How’d you know that?”

“Oh, it’s a kind of look a man has when he’s seen a vision or two.”

Richard took a walk that afternoon with Curtis out to Inspiration Point. The path was cleared and easy to follow. It meandered a bit though the forest but it was all on nearly level ground, altogether an easy walk. Inspiration Point itself was just a small natural clearing in the dense woods. There was no broad vista or waterfall or other interesting natural feature one would normally expect to see at a place called Inspiration Point.

Curtis stopped on a leaf-covered spot of bare ground. “Right here’s the spot, near as we can tell, where my great aunt found John one winter morning with his hair froze to the ground. Course they’s no reason to say this spot is somehow more holy than the rest; John wandered all through this area preaching and hollerin' for anyone who would listen to him. You know they all said he was crazy.

"Your great aunt?"

"Yep, my grandfather's sister was married to the man that built the mill back yonder that's now a restaurant. And they had a house where the store is today. They owned all this land around here."

"So, are you now the owner of *The Happy Cricket*?"

"Well, it's a family affair, but I'm the oldest an' the one in charge."

* * *

That night after having dinner in the Mill restaurant, the family bedded down in the comfortable beds in the tent trailer. Annette and Timmy were soon asleep, having played hard at the pool. When Richard was certain Celeste was asleep he gently eased himself out of bed and into his clothes. He found the flashlight and was surprised when Celeste roused herself and said, "Where are you going?"

"I gotta pee" he said. She was satisfied with that and went back to sleep. But Richard didn't have to pee; instead he was being irresistibly drawn again down the path to Inspiration Point. It seemed a foolish thing to do, walking in the dense woods in the dark, but he had the flashlight and there was some moonlight coming through the trees.

The path was cleared and well defined, though not well worn. And of course he had just visited the place with Curtis earlier in the day. It seemed to him now that his mind had known that he would be returning in the dark and had made note of certain trees and boulders to be used as landmarks and turning points to guide him. Yet every step was an adventure, a step into the unknown. All his senses were alive, helping him find the way.

Finally, he was at the special place in the small clearing in the woods that Curtis had shown him. He told himself that he would just lie down in the leaves for a while, maybe fifteen minutes or so to get a small taste of what the prophet must have felt. He found the ground harder than he expected and there was only a thin layer of leaves and his clothing to cushion it. But still he brushed even the leaves away under his head so that it was in direct contact with the ground. He wanted no transgression of the formula that had worked for John Hendrix when he responded to the voice telling him to "go into the woods and sleep with your head on the ground …"

* * *

With dawn breaking among the trees, Richard woke and found himself, not in the forest, but again in that other world, that perfect place where all is Love and Peace. There were others with him this time there in the Oneness, and they were all singing with great enthusiasm. They were obviously singing in celebration of some unknown great event. There were four of them singing, as was made clear by the words of the song. Richard took it to be himself and three others—three of his best and closest friends, friends who he knew were, in this perfect place, as much a part of him as he was himself. Yet he didn't know who they were. When he dared ask, the answer overwhelmed him. He tried not to think of it, because the revelation in his vision exceeded his wildest imagination. His three friends were Jesus, Moses, and Elijah.

And they were all singing: "*Glorious, Glorious, One keg of beer for the four of us*."

It was wild and energetic, each chorus more joyous, more festive, and louder than the last.

"*Glorious, Glorious, One keg of beer for the four of us*."

They sang on as though in ultimate defiance of some law forbidding singing.

"*Glorious, Glorious, One keg of beer for the four of us*."

Richard lost himself in the celebration, he was singing his heart out and then suddenly . . . it was over.

The perfect place and the joy he felt in singing with his friends were simply gone. Instead a grotesque and repulsive creature was in his face, demanding all his attention. The gargoyle-like beast contorted its ugly face in one fierce and menacing expression after another, opening and closing its gaping mouth to reveal sharp pointed teeth ready to rip and tear its victims. Richard felt the creature's red eyes burning into his consciousness, demanding obedience and threatening annihilation for transgression of its law. It was a fearful sight and in response, in compliance with the beast's demand, Richard opened his eyes and the hideous creature was gone.

He found himself again awake, this time in the forest, among the trees at the dawning of a new day. He was disoriented and confused about who he was, having only a vague recollection of his life in this imperfect world of separation. And he was possessed—on fire it seemed, with a need to fulfill a serious responsibility. He was charged with waking this world to the truth that it wasn't real but only an illusion, with *Reality* entirely something else beyond what was apparently real. It was a mission impossible that to him wasn't impossible because of the *Reality of the Living Oneness*, and of his three friends who had celebrated the passing of the baton of truth on to him. They were expecting him to bring it home again and to bring the whole of the world along with it. He had to find a way to do just that. The celebration had been in his honor, a fitting send-off for this final leg of their shared mission to save the world from the dream of itself. The wild celebration had all been designed to attract the attention of the guardian, the repulsive beast he had seen. Its fearsome nature had caused him to expel himself from the perfect world, back into the dream of separation and fear, charged with knowing the truth that brought with it the need to do what was impossible.

Driven by the fire lit within him, Richard set out to tell the world the good news that its end was near. He ran through the trees shouting, alone in the forest with only the trees and the hills to hear, searching for someone, anyone and everyone having ears to hear. He took no thought for the path out of the woods, not really remembering it was there or realizing that it was the only way that would lead him back to where he belonged in this world. He was quickly, hopelessly, lost. Every tree and rock looked exactly like every other. He was soon exhausted and vainly going in circles, when suddenly Curtis was there with him.

Richard stepped up close, like to a brother and said, "Curtis, this world isn't real. They sent me back to tell you. It's a sham world Curtis, a dream. There's another world, more real than this one, where we belong, where we are happy all the time. We can go home whenever we're ready, Curtis. I've been sent back here to tell everyone the good news."

"Hold on there Mr. Richard, and calm down now just a bit and you'll be fine. You was just afixin' to get yourself lost in these woods fur sure. I knowed you might be comin' back to the clearing tonight, so's I was keeping an eye out for you. It's a good thing too, that you was a'hollerin' out loud so. I like to of thought it was ol' John Hendrix, hisself that was out there. Might never have come across you myself 'cept for that hollerin'. A fella can wander around out here for days once he gets hisself all worked up and lost."

"Let's take us a short walk back to the store now and you can rest a bit there in my office. I'll get you a cup of coffee and whatever you want. The missus'll be looking fer you soon as she awakes."

As they walked back to the camp, Curtis asked, "I take that better place you be talking about to be heaven—spend some time there tonight did ya?"

At the mention of heaven Richard took up his mission impossible again. "Heaven, yes, that's where I was. And I didn't want to leave, but they sent me back, Curtis. They were singing a glorious song and there's only four of us and just one keg of beer, one truth. It's *real* right now, Curtis, *Heaven* is ready for us. We don't have to wait. The gate is open. There's a creature, a big ugly thing, standing guard, but if we aren't afraid we can slip right past it."

"Why heck, Mr. Richard, folks around here been knowing heaven is real for a long time, forever I reckon. That ain't nothing new."

Undaunted by this, Richard asked, "How many of them have been there and come back to tell you about what it's like and how to get there right now?"

"Well, I don't rightly recall any of 'em doin' zactly that. The preachers I know mostly been telling folks heaven is a place ya go to when ya die if you've lived a good life. There's no other way to get in there that anyone ever told me of. If you can tell folks how to get into heaven without dying, I expect they'll be lots of 'em clamoring to hear about that. Why you might even want to build you a little church here in the woods and preach 'bout that yourself on Sundays."

Once in the office, Richard accepted the cup of coffee Curtis offered him and then, still deeply confused about his identity, he wanted to learn whether he could exert any power and authority in this world. “Would you get me a pack of cigarettes?” he asked Curtis.

“Why shore, Mr. Richard, I could do that. But I never knowed you to smoke.”

“I don’t” Richard said, “I was just wanting to know if you’d do it for me.” He paused a moment to think and then asked, “Curtis, would you bring some water and wash my feet?”

Curtis stiffened slightly and stood a bit taller on hearing the unusual request. “Well now, I reckon that’s somethin’ you best be doin’ fer yourself, Mr. Richard.”

“I’m sorry, Curtis. I don’t want anything from you. It was just a feeling I had. I needed to know. There was no other way that I could think of to find out.”

Richard became quiet, as if he were taking in some new information, and was surprised by a desire to call home. He asked Curtis if he could use his phone.

“Shore, go right ahead. It’s there on the desk,” Curtis offered. “But you might want to wait a bit to get your legs under you again, so to speak, before talkin’ too much to people. Maybe you ought to talk to the missus first thing? I’ll go and call on her for ya. Whyn’t you set here a spell and wait for your mind to clear a bit?”

* * *

Curtis found Celeste on her way back to the campsite from the bathhouse. The sun had just climbed above the horizon, and he approached her with his eyes down, not nearly so talkative as he had been in the store.

“Ma’am, my name’s Curtis,” he said. “You and your husband was in the store yesterday.”

“Yes, I remember you, Curtis,” Celeste answered. He was very polite and seemed harmless. She knew Richard had spent some time with him yesterday.

“Your husband’s fine, ma’am. He’s back in the office at the store right now. I found him wandering in the woods out beyond Inspiration Point. I knowed right away when I first seen him that he might be wantin’ to sleep in the woods. And then I reckon he lost his way coming back.”

"What? Richard slept in the woods? No, he didn't he's ..." She began to protest then stopped, realizing she didn't really know where he was right now. She asked, "Why in the world would he do that? Is he all right?" Celeste felt a surge of emotions for her husband, which were impossible to sort out in the moment.

"He'll be just fine ma'am. But right now he's confused a mite, and thinkin' he's somebody else. I've seen that before—most ever preacher feels that way at one time or another. He'll soon be over it, but it might be a comfort to him to talk with you."

"Of course," she said. She wanted to go to him and help him anyway she could.

When they walked into the office, Richard seemed fine but did not look up to acknowledge them. He was talking intently on the phone.

"Mom, I need to know if there is something you haven't told me about my birth. Was I adopted or something? Are you my real mother?" After a pause, he continued. "Well is Dad my real father? You know we don't look anything alike. There's something I don't understand going on about my birth that you haven't told me."

"Richard!" Celeste exploded, "is that your mom? You can't talk to her like that. Let me have the phone." Richard handed it to her, his unusual and insensitive conversation with his mother apparently over.

"Mrs. Holmes? This is Celeste. I'm sorry about Richard calling you so early. He's confused. They said he was lost in the woods overnight. He's okay physically, I think, but he's been having unusual thoughts for a few days."

Richard stepped outside the small room with Curtis as Celeste continued to talk with his parents in Indiana.

"Yes, we're still coming. We're in Tennessee at a campground right now. And we should be seeing you this afternoon. But, I'm warning you he's becoming too much for me to handle. I'm going to need some help. The man here says Richard thinks he's some famous preacher or something, but that he'll get over it. I don't know."

Celeste listened intently for a minute before speaking. "Well, I don't mean to sound like I'm blaming you, I'm not, but this all started when he finally got around to reading that Bible you sent him a few years ago. Now, he's confused and I think maybe he needs some help. We can talk about it when we get there. I've got to go now. Sorry, bye. See you soon. . . . Yes, the kids are fine."

Richard came back into the office and for the first time noticed a picture hanging on the wall. He stopped suddenly and asked, "What's that?"

"Oh, that there's a calendar we had made up for advertisin' *The Happy Cricket*," said Curtis.

"No, I mean the picture, what is that beast?"

"Oh, that there is a wild boar. It's a big ol' ugly wild pig what lives in the woods around here. The whole calendar is about animals found in the woods here. There's a picture of some deer and there's a bear—"

"Is it dangerous?" Richard asked, sheepishly considering for the first time that his imagination might have misled him because the picture was suspiciously like the hideous beast, the guardian he had seen earlier. "I mean would it attack a man sleeping on the ground?"

"Nah, I never heard of anythin' like that. They don't see too good and they will attack when they are surprised or feel threatened. But they mostly roam around through the woods looking for nuts. They use them fierce looking tusks to root the nuts up outa the ground." Curtis decided it wouldn't serve any good purpose for him to say he'd seen a particularly big and ugly wild boar in the woods this morning just before he found Richard.

"Richard, are you all right now?" Celeste asked.

"Well, I'm feeling a whole lot more like Richard and not somebody else if that's what you mean."

"Oh, good, because we should be getting on the road if we're going to be in Indiana today."

"I think I'd like to take Curtis' advice and rest up here a minute. Why don't you take the kids and go to breakfast at the restaurant? I'll join you in a little while."

"Okay," Celeste said, "we'll pack up and be ready to go when you are." She stepped close to Richard and they embraced and kissed before she went out.

Curtis said, "Well, I need to be opening up the store—folks'll be needin' things." He took a King James Bible from his desk and handed it to Richard, saying, "Whyn't you read a bit from this here Bible as you are gathering your thoughts. I'm sure you'll find something in there that'll speak to your trouble." And then he left Richard alone in the office.

* * *

Richard was feeling properly humbled as he sat down in a cushioned chair to quietly review in his mind the events of that morning. Could he sort out what might be real from what was maybe only his overactive imagination? He smiled, thinking of the absurdity of some fierce looking but mostly blind wild pig searching in the woods for nuts and, finding him asleep, getting up close in his face before finally moving on, never realizing he had found the biggest nut in the forest and maybe even the whole wide world.

After a while he picked up the Bible and thumbed through it randomly searching for some words to console himself. Eventually he turned to the Book of Revelation and read to himself verse six of chapter fourteen:

"And I saw another angel fly in the midst of heaven, having the everlasting gospel to preach unto them that dwell on the earth, and to every nation, and kindred, and tongue, and people."

Then, having turned the page, and with verse seven clearly in view, he was surprised beyond anything he had ever heard of at seeing the words emboldened and standing up off the page in the third dimension and vibrating at a high frequency as though they were alive. He felt his head lifted up and the words spewed out automatically into the room with only himself to hear:

"Saying with a loud voice, ***Fear God, and give glory to him; for the hour of his judgment is come: and worship him that made heaven, and earth, and the sea, and the fountains of waters***."

It was his voice, he knew that, and yet it wasn't him using it. The voice was different. It was attractive, having overtones and a quality he had never suspected it could have.

With this fantastic happenstance, came a great emotional release and Richard felt he had in some way come full circle. He felt that he was in total control of himself for the first time since three days ago, when, after loving an incompetent mechanic in response to Jesus' command to "love your enemies," he had lifted his eyes in peace and non-judgment.

“Wow,” he exclaimed aloud though there was no one there to hear, “I’m an angel!”

Energized and no longer confused by the night’s mysteriously wonderful event, he got up from the chair, returned Curtis’ Bible to the desk and then, buoyed up in the renewed knowledge that he was not alone, he went out looking for Celeste and the kids with his feet only lightly touching the ground.

He caught up with them in the restaurant and they were happy to see him.

“Mom says you were lost in the woods!” said Timmy.

“Right she was about that, good buddy. I was lost and now I am found.”

“We popped the tent down by ourselves, Dad,” Annette told him proudly.

“You did! Great. Who worked the crank?” Richard asked, already knowing the answer.

“I did,” she exclaimed. “It was easy; I did it just like you showed me. And I stowed the crank back in its place in the door so it’ll be there next time.”

“Good girl. How’s the pancakes? I’m hungry after being lost in the woods.”

“Oh, just like home,” Celeste said, pouring more batter on the grill in the middle of the table. “You’re in a surprising mood from a while ago,” she continued. “We left a change of clothes for you and your shaving kit so you can take a quick shower.”

“Thanks,” he said, then offered, “I’m an angel.”

“This is fun,” Timmy said, using a spatula to fool with the pancake cooking in front of him.

Richard smiled down at his son. “Didn’t I tell you it’s a fun restaurant?”

Celeste looked at him, wondering what was behind the remark about being an angel. And she wondered why she had never noticed before how his face seemed to glow as he talked.

“What’s an angel, Dad?” It was Timmy, who hadn’t seemed to be paying attention.

“Well, I don’t know yet exactly; we’ll have to look it up.”

"Can you fly?"

"No," Richard laughed. "Not that kind of angel, I think."

"Are we gonna see Grandma today? Mom says so."

"Yes, we are. But we've got to get on the road to do it."

After eating his fill of pancakes and sausage, Richard left the table to shower, leaving Celeste with time to pay the bill and browse the gift shop.

"And, dear," he said as he left the table, "see if you can find one of those calendars with the wild boar picture on it for me."

"Will do, O Holy One," Celeste answered. It was the first time she playfully called him by that name.

Half an hour later they were on the road again.

* * *

The final day of the journey home was filled with music and synchronistic happenings that solidified Richard's belief that they were not alone.

Timmy was soon bored with the passing scenery on Interstate 75 as they traveled north from Oak Ridge, Tennessee.

"Hey, you all want to hear my new *Thriller*—Michael Jackson tape?" he asked.

"Sure, why not?" Richard answered. No one vetoed the request and so Timmy put the *Thriller* tape in the front dash tape player.

At once, the new and exciting music filled the van with its infectious melodies and words, all to Timmy's obvious delight. *Thriller, Billie Jean, The Girl is Mine, Beat It* and several other songs played over and over for the next hundred miles or so. Eventually everyone joined in as Timmy led them in a sing along. Somewhere south of Lexington, Kentucky, everyone but Timmy agreed it was time to give it up.

The light-hearted, festive mood changed dramatically when their van was caught up in a traffic jam just outside of Lexington. Richard refused to accept that this was just a random event intruding itself harshly into what otherwise had been, for him, a magical trip. He switched on the CB radio thinking he would listen in on the trucker's conversations to learn something about the cause and severity of the traffic tie-up.

"Jesus Christ," an anonymous trucker's voice boomed out

unexpectedly loud into the van, "I can see all the way around the bend, this F'N snafu must be at least five miles long—I reckon it'll take at least an hour, maybe two, before we'll be movin' again."

"God Damn!" came a slightly less annoying reply as Richard found the volume control. "Here I am standing still with a load of lettuce—got to be in the Big Apple by dawn. Shit."

Richard pushed the talk button for the first time ever and said, "Breaker, breaker. Can't you guys talk plainly without using profanity and bringing God into it?"

This brought a chorus of responses in reaction, seeming to come down on him all at once.

"Well, well, what we got here? A goody two shoes?"

"Must be some kind of preacher."

"Maybe an angel come down to save us. Ha, ha, ha!"

"Hey, Buddy! In case you ain't noticed, this ain't Sunday and you ain't in church. What you drivin'? I'd like to run you over."

Richard figured he had made his point and switched off the CB radio.

All was quiet in the van as it sat unmoving in the hot July sun with everyone fully expecting to be stuck there for some long time. Richard reached down and picked up the King James Bible he kept beneath his seat. He read at random and then began to realize that the words he was reading seemed to fit the situation he was in. The words weren't darker than the rest and they didn't stand up off the page or vibrate as if they were alive as before in Curtis' office. And it was only his normal voice he heard as he looked up through the skylight above him and read aloud:

> "Be pleased, O Lord to deliver me: O Lord make haste to help me. Let them be ashamed and confounded together that seek after my soul to destroy it; let them be driven backward and put to shame that wish me evil. Let them be desolate for a reward of their shame that say unto me, Aha, aha."

Soon, cars directly in front of them began to move out of the left lane, they were jockeying around for position and honking as though they were under some compulsion to get out of the left lane, which was the lane for through traffic that the van was in. They moved quickly forward before encountering another brief stoppage as more cars seemed to be scrambling to get out of their way. Then the road was clear ahead and the van quickly came up to speed and continued on its northward journey.

"It worked!" Timmy exclaimed, clearly impressed.

Celeste was just as clearly not impressed, though she was happy to be moving again, and Annette could only smile a little. The two of them said nothing about what to Richard was an obvious and unmistakable cause and effect reaction between his prayer and the breakup of the traffic jam.

A few miles further up the road Celeste put in a tape with Elvis Presley singing gospel songs. It was one of Richard's favorite tapes and he was surprised to hear a new deeper meaning in old familiar songs like *You'll Never Walk Alone, Who Am I?* and *I Believe.*

A tall, young, black man suddenly appeared standing on the side of the roadway with his long arm extended and thumb up. He obviously needed a ride. Richard slowed and brought the van to a stop on the shoulder, a ways down the road beyond where the man stood.

"What are you doing?" Celeste asked. "You're not thinking of . . ."

"Man needs a ride. We've got room," Richard answered. He opened his door and slid out to meet the young man whose pure dark color and general appearance reminded him of a young Nat King Cole. He was running along the road's shoulder to catch up to where the van had come to a stop. He looked clean and was carrying a duffel bag.

"How far ya goin'?" Richard asked.

"Williamstown," the man said. "It's the next town—just up the road a ways."

"What's your name?"

"Darnel," he answered.

"OK, hop in," Richard said, seeing no reason not to give the young man a ride.

He opened the big side door and found Annette and Timmy already in the third row bench seat, leaving the center area open for

Darnel. He introduced Timmy and Annette and then shut the big door.

As the van again got underway, Richard found himself unexpectedly concerned for his children's safety. Darnel wasn't much of a talker, offering only that his family was in Williamstown and he was going home on military leave from the army.

Richard felt uneasy about the situation and checked the rearview mirror frequently to see what, if anything, was going on in the back. It was unlike him to pick up hitchhikers—he had never before done it with the family on board. But there was something about this man, maybe the way he extended his long arm, that caught Richard's attention and made him think that he should stop. He had acted on an impulse, but now he was having second thoughts and could only imagine that Celeste and Annette, maybe Timmy too, were in shock because no one had said a thing.

While looking uneasily in the rear view mirror, Richard suddenly realized that Elvis was still singing and now his attention was being called to the words Elvis had just sung. What was it? It sounded like a message. There it came again: "*Don't fear the dark.*" Wow, it was enough to set his mind at ease. Have no fear, he thought. God *is* with us.

They dropped Darnel off and Elvis continued singing gospel songs as the miles flew by. Then as the van approached the Ohio River Bridge crossing into Cincinnati an upbeat song about Jonah and the whale began to play. The bridge was a huge, silver colored steel-frame structure carrying interstate traffic on two levels. And as Elvis sang about Jonah being swallowed up in the belly of the whale, the van was swallowed up into the lower deck of that huge bridge with its shining steel girders dripping water from a sudden summer shower. Richard thought they looked very much like the bones of that big fish might look from the inside.

"Hey look, everybody, we're in the whale," he said. It didn't take a lot of imagination to see the similarities. Timmy and Annette saw it right away.

"Oh, yeah. I see it," Annette said.

"Neat," Timmy added.

Then with Elvis singing his heart out about the whale delivering

Jonah safely onto the beach of his homeland, the van shot out of the lower deck of that bridge into the sunlight of Ohio and on the Indiana side of the big river. Richard thought it would have taken a choreographer some time to work out all the elements so that the timing of the song with their passage through the bridge in heavy traffic would be so perfect. In his mind it was further proof of something more than simple coincidence at work.

They turned off I-75 onto I-74 going northwest toward Indianapolis. Soon they crossed the state line into Indiana and there were corn fields everywhere. "Knee high by the fourth of July" was the old saying but with modern nitrogen fertilizers the corn grew faster and this July second it was already up to the top of the fences.

They left the Interstate highway going north on an Indiana state road and then in no time at all it seemed, they were turning into Grandma's driveway. It was four o'clock in the afternoon of a Tuesday.

* * *

The reunion was an awkward affair. Richard held nothing back and told everyone about his experiences with God, beginning with his reading the Bible his mother had sent him. It was plain to see that Richard's mother wasn't comfortable being in her son's presence and listening to his stories. She was still hurting from his accusation that she wasn't really his mother. Richard's father listened patiently and tried to understand but said very little. Celeste privately talked with Mrs. Holmes and tried to reassure her that Richard was better now and that she was sure he just needed some time to return to his normal self.

Richard and Celeste spent the night in the camper. The kids stayed in the house.

The next day, Uncle Fred showed up and immediately approached Richard saying he had some friends downtown who wanted to talk with him. It sounded to Richard as if Fred's friends might be part of the "brotherhood" that he was sure would be showing up sooner or later. He was enthusiastic and ready to go talk with them, hoping to find someone who could appreciate what he had been trying to share with people who had no interest in hearing about such things.

It would have served no useful purpose at this point for me to intervene and tell Richard the brotherhood he was looking for would not come into being until after his fated meeting up with Jenny and Bina more than two decades yet in his future.

Uncle Fred, who really wasn't his uncle but his brother-in-law, escorted Richard downtown to a small office building. He stopped at a door clearly labeled *Community Mental Health Clinic*. "What's this?" Richard said in total surprise. "You think I'm crazy?"

"Don't worry about that," Fred responded. "There's people here that want to talk to you, just like I told you."

Richard looked inside and saw Celeste and his sister Nancy—Fred's wife—sitting side by side as if waiting in a doctor's office. Celeste jumped up on seeing him come through the door and hurried to him.

Her brown eyes met his blue and seeing the disappointment there she said, "Richard, I'm sorry. I didn't know anything about all this. I told them you were okay. They wouldn't listen to me. It was that phone call from the campground; they thought I was asking for this kind of help."

Seeing the sincerity and helplessness in her voice and manner, Richard looked at his wife and said, "It's okay, Celeste, really it is. I believe you. It's just that this is such a surprise; I didn't know I was making them so afraid of me. I guess I'd better be careful and watch what I say."

"They don't know you anymore. You're not yourself, you're different. They don't understand. How could they?"

"I thought it was best to let it out, to share everything. I wanted them to know."

"Well, this might be a good time to begin watching what you say."

"You think they want to have me committed? Can they do that?"

"I don't know," Celeste answered truthfully.

They sat together in silence for a while then Richard said, "I didn't know this town had a mental health clinic. Who's paying for this?"

Fred answered, "Your dad."

"That's a laugh," Richard said as he thought of his frugal father spending his hard-earned money to have his own son's head examined.

"Mr. Holmes, Mr. Richard Holmes!" The nurse was calling for him; Doctor Peterson was ready to see him.

* * *

"So, Mr. Holmes," Doctor Peterson began, "I'm told that you are hearing voices of people who aren't there. Tell me about that."

"It's not like that. I heard a voice but it was my voice."

"Your voice? But it wasn't you?"

"That's right."

"It was someone who wasn't there?"

"No."

"No?"

"It was someone who is really there but you can't see them."

"An invisible someone?"

"I guess that's right. It was a spirit person."

"I see. And is this spirit person still with you."

"Yes."

"And how do you know this to be true, Mr. Holmes?"

"I get messages, answers."

"Are you feeling all right, Mr. Holmes? Any physical complaints, pain?"

"My brain is sore."

"Tell me about that."

"Well, it's all around my head on the inside. It feels like when a muscle is overworked, it's sore."

"What do you think is going on?"

"I think every connection in my brain is being rewired."

"Why would that be happening?"

"Well, I read the Bible and God became very real to me. And now everything I ever knew before is being revised to make room for that fact. It changes everything."

"You believe your brain is rewiring itself to make room for God?"

"Have you read the Bible, Doctor Peterson?"

"No, but I've read many other books on the brain and the mind."

"You need to read the Bible on top of all those other books."

"Mr. Holmes, do you have suicidal thoughts?"

"No sir."

"Any thoughts of hurting others, your wife, anyone?"

"No."

"I'm writing you a prescription, Mr. Holmes, for some pills that will slow your mind down—stop it from racing. Take this medication, one tablet a day for three days, and you'll be all right."

"That's it?"

"That's it. You're free to go."

Richard went back out into the waiting room and Celeste went inside to talk with Dr. Peterson.

* * *

The following day was the fourth and all of Richard's considerable extended family gathered at Nancy and Uncle Fred's place in the afternoon to visit and wait for sundown when Fred put on his fireworks show. Timmy was having the time of his young life playing with his cousins and following his hero Uncle Fred around asking every few minutes if it was time for the fireworks.

Richard was quieter, more restrained in his conversations than before. He understood now what the word unbelievable really meant. Even his own mother thought he was crazy. Imagine, his own mother, who knew better than anyone that he had never in his life made up stories or told lies to get attention, even she had dismissed him without a second thought. It could only be that what he was trying to say was literally unbelievable. At least it was to her. He realized now that not everyone was ready to hear what he had to say. He would have to learn to be careful about whom he was speaking with and to watch what he said lest his testimony be simply ignored and his fate end up like that of John Hendrix. He would have to find a way to be taken seriously.

* * *

On the day after the fireworks celebration Richard's father brought a Methodist minister to the house. He had never before in Richard's memory done anything like this, having decided long ago that religion would play no part in his life. It was clear that he had invited the man so that he could talk with Richard. After lunch

Richard and Rev. Rasmussen sat outside in the shade on the back porch and had a conversation.

"Richard," the minister began, "your father is worried about you and thought that I might be able to help you understand your experience. Do you want to talk about it?"

"Well, I'm not sure I want to get into that again. Everyone thinks I'm crazy."

"An unexpected encounter with the Divine can sometimes cause a person to momentarily lose his grip on reality. God is very powerful and if one's mind isn't prepared, a direct experience can be very traumatic. It's something I've seen before. I call it temporary *Divinity* to distinguish it from temporary *insanity*. The two experiences can appear the same from the outside, but they come from opposite ends of the spectrum."

"Is that so? You sound as if you might have had your own experience."

"Every preacher has a calling. The experiences are quiet varied."

"You should tell that to Dr. Peterson; he's never even read the Bible."

"Your father told me that's what caused your experience—you read the Bible?"

"Yeah, I'm forty-three and I finally got around to reading it last year. That's where I got the idea to love my enemy. And then when I did it, the world, this world we see, the whole of time and space just disappeared and I was in a better world where there's nothing but *Love*.

"This world of time and space isn't real, preacher. It's a sham world. The other world of *Love* where I found myself makes this world seem like a dream and it just disappeared like a dream goes away when we wake up. I don't remember any preacher ever telling me that this world isn't real. And I'm beginning to wonder why. Do you truly believe God is real, Mr. Rasmussen? What do you tell people about God?"

"I tell them that God is Love."

"Do you tell them that *He* lives in a world where *All* is *Love*? And do you tell them that world, not this nightmare, is their *Home*?

And do you tell them that they don't have to take your word for it, that they can follow Jesus and go see it for themselves. My father is right; there is no God in this world. But what he doesn't know is that this world is all a big illusion to keep us from *Reality* where all is *Love* and where we belong. I think that's important to know. Don't you? Why aren't you preachers telling people about this? Don't you know what the truth is? Don't you believe what Jesus said about loving our enemies? Don't you know only *Heaven* is real?"

"We preach the truth as it is given us to know it. The Bible tells us God created this world."

"And I'm telling you, it's all an illusion. You think a God of *Love and Life* created this world of fear and death?" A world of *Love* is what he created and we are part of it—it's our home. We don't belong here. I read the Bible my mother sent me and I loved my enemy, an automobile mechanic, like Jesus said to do. My God, haven't any of you preachers done even that? And then this world that we think is so important, and so very real, just disappeared—like the dream that it is. I was home—the constant *Love*, peace and joy I found there is beyond anything imaginable in this world. I was home—I was welcomed there and I knew I belonged there. But as soon as I realized that no one had told me anything about this other world of peace and *Love*, I realized that this was important for everyone to know. I knew I had to come back to tell everyone—my family, everyone; I thought it was important. I saw it as my duty. It seemed to be the right thing to do. I guess I just naturally thought everyone would believe me and never imagined that they wouldn't want to hear it. I thought they would be happy to learn that this world of war and death is only a dream. But no one wants to hear it. They're afraid of me. They think I'm crazy. Even my mother.

"Do you know what I'm talking about, Mr. Rasmussen?"

"Sounds to me like you have had a religious calling Richard, and a very strong one. Many denominations within Christianity have begun with one person having an experience of God."

"I'm not aware of any of them teaching that this world isn't real."

"Your experience was for you, Richard. You need to take some time out now to study and understand what has happened to you and to put it into context with the religious experiences of other people and the religions that have grown up based on their experiences of God. For instance, I know that some forms of Eastern Religion teach that this world is only an illusion. Are you aware of that Richard?"

"No, I'm not in the God business, Mr. Rasmussen. I grew up here on this farm from the age of ten, and I loved it here; then I left the farm at eighteen. We didn't go to church much growing up, my mother did a little. After high school I went to Purdue where I studied science and engineering, and so until last year, when I was forty-three and finally got around to reading the Bible, nothing I had ever heard of prepared me for the joyful surprise—the shock and awe really, of learning that this world of time and space isn't real, and instead another world of pure *Love* is the only thing that is real and is in fact where I truly belong, where we all belong."

"Well, then, I suspect that studying about religious experiences and about some other religions and particularly those that believe as you do would be very interesting to you. I recommend that you start by taking a look at William James' book, *Varieties of Religious Experiences*. It a classic and—"

"You don't understand, preacher. God can't wait for me to spend years studying religions. People need to know right now that they are living an illusion. God wants people to know *Him* and I can't think of anything that would change human behavior quicker, end all the suffering, than learning that the world and everything in it that people fight and kill each other for is nothing but a dream."

"How's it going, trying to tell people that?"

"You know damn well how it's going. I'm sure they told you." Richard was surprised at the anger welling up in him which he had directed at this preacher. "That's exactly why you're here. So far, everyone thinks I'm crazy. Jesus Christ! They took me to have my goddamned head examined.

"What do you think, preacher? Is God real? Is there another world of *Pure Love*? Or is it this world of death and destruction, of suffering and pain, that is His creation made in his image? What is it you tell people about God? Maybe if you and all the other preachers knew what the hell you were talking about I wouldn't be in this situation. Don't you people know that God is only *Love*?

"I'm beginning to understand what 'unbelievable' really means. I'm wondering now how I myself would react if it were you telling me this story that this world is a sham and if I were the one hearing that for the first time. I like to think I would at least hear you out and then give it some serious thought. But I might just ignore you and maybe even put you away if I had the opportunity and power to do it and you wouldn't shut up about it."

"Look, Richard, I don't blame you for being angry. Right now you are being tempted to yield to judgment and perhaps even separate yourself from your family in bitterness over what you see as their rejection of you. I hope that doesn't happen because you need the strength and the grounding that your family can give you. Maybe what you need is to try another approach."

"What other approach?"

"Well, like I was saying before, maybe you want to take sufficient time out and study the religious experiences of other people and look at how they responded."

"That's very interesting, Mr. Rasmussen. But can God wait on a man? I mean, I make my living by building houses for people, and when someone contracts with me to build them a house they generally want to move in right away. And often the bigger the house or the more important the people are, the quicker they expect the job to be done. They want to see me start working on their house right away, and they expect me to finish in good time.

"This situation seems to me like that. I feel a need. I've been 'called,' as you put it, by the most important person to build a house, so to speak—really to tell a truth big enough so that we all can live in it together, in peace. That person is God, and I figure He wants it done right away. And surely there is no one who deserves faster service than God. I haven't been asked or called to go off and spend years studying religion before going to work."

"Yes, God can wait on a man," Rev. Rasmussen said. "God has infinite patience. He will wait and be with you all the while you do His work. And besides, there's precedence for taking a time out before beginning your work."

"What do you mean?"

"Well, do you remember reading about how Jesus, after his

baptism went off in the desert for 'forty days and forty nights' before he came back and began to teach?"

"Yeah, but that was the time he was tempted by the devil. He wasn't off studying religion."

"No, but it was a time-out between his baptism and his ministry. I think that's where you are now, Richard. You need to take a time out, like Jesus, sufficient time out, whatever it takes, for you to discover what it is you really have to say and just how to say it to best advantage so that it can be taken seriously. You might find that you eventually want to write a small book to better share your ideas, your understanding of what this world is and what meaning it has."

"I like the idea of writing a book," Richard said. "I think I have the title already: *The Oneness of God*. I wrote it down on my desk calendar right after the Vision. There was even a kind of outline of the contents. I had forgotten about that in all the excitement."

"You could see all that excitement as you being tempted to step away from the original message."

"If that's the case, I guess I didn't pass the test."

"Don't be too hard on yourself. They haven't locked you up and thrown away the key yet, have they?"

"No, all they really did was think I was crazy."

"There's biblical precedent for that too. Jesus' family thought he was 'beside himself,' which means they thought he was crazy. And that happened after his time-out."

"I guess I missed that part. Where does it say that?"

"I believe you'll find that in Mark 3:21.

"Blast off!"

"Excuse me?"

"Oh, that's like saying 'gesundheit' when someone sneezes. It's something I learned to do living in Florida. Whenever there's a rocket launch they do a countdown, like you just did. 'Mark 3-2-1,' blast off! Get it?"

"Got it. I guess you won't have any trouble remembering where in the Bible people said Jesus was crazy, too."

"Right. There's something else I wanted to ask about. . . . Oh, you keep saying I need 'sufficient time,' while the Bible says Jesus' time of temptation was 'forty days and forty nights.' "

"Well, the Bible uses the expression 'forty days and nights' several times. In Genesis, it rains for forty days and nights," Rasmussen said. "Bible scholars today think the expression wasn't meant to be taken literally, but rather meant something like 'sufficient time.' "

"I don't know about that," Richard said. "My experience came from taking Jesus' command to love your enemy literally. Maybe people who see it as something else are missing the point."

"I certainly agree that there are parts of scripture that are meant to be literal and others parts that can be more loosely interpreted. Wisdom lies in accurately judging which is which, 'learning to rightly divide the word of God' is how the Bible puts it. It isn't all one way or the other."

Richard had no further questions, and as Rev. Rasmussen got up to leave he added, "It looks to me like we've successfully routed the tempter for the moment; it's time for me to be moving on. Let me know how the book comes out, if you decide that's what you want to do. Send me a copy."

"Sure, Mr. Rasmussen—look for it in the mail in about forty days, give or take a week or two."

Richard's father rejoined the two and walked Dr. Rasmussen back to his car, thanking him for coming out.

"Your boy is going to be all right, Mr. Holmes. I think his experience is genuine. It's been very traumatic for him, but he is showing signs of coming out of it okay. He's more relaxed and his sense of humor is back. What eventually comes of his experience is up to him. I wouldn't be surprised if his life takes a whole new direction."

* * *

On Saturday, the day following his conversation with the preacher, Richard woke up very early and, going into the house, he found his mother alone and working in the kitchen.

"Good morning, Mom," he said.

"Good morning, Richard," she responded. "I see you are feeling better."

Richard supposed that she had heard Dr. Peterson's evaluation of his mental health. She seemed willing now to relate to him as before.

"Yes," he answered, "the preacher helped me see some things differently. I'm sorry, Mom, for that phone call. I guess I was beside myself for a while. I was excited and not thinking clearly."

"Oh well," she said, "I was thinking about that yesterday when you were talking with the minister and it seemed to me that maybe I should share some of the responsibility for that."

"What do you mean, Mom? It was all my idea, my mistake."

"Yes, but we never shared the whole story about the time you were born and I was thinking that maybe if we had . . . I know it would have been more memorable for you."

"What rest of the story, Mom? I know I was born in a hospital in Indianapolis and that you were a nurse working there."

"That's all true but there's more we never told you. I was too ashamed to tell the rest of it. Your dad and I just agreed not to talk about it. It was nobody's business but our own."

"And now you're thinking that I have a right to know about what you were ashamed to tell?"

"Yes," she said, pausing before continuing. "Well, you know about December 7th of course, what happened that day, the attack on Pearl Harbor in Hawaii. President Roosevelt called it 'a day that will live in infamy'. It wouldn't have been a good day to be born, but you were almost born that day."

"What? Tell me what happened?"

"There was a terrible snow storm the night before and all the power was out. We lived in a little house on five acres of land just west of here. It was twenty miles from the hospital. About two o'clock that Sunday morning I decided it was time that you were going to be born and we had to get to the hospital. I was a nurse and I was trained in childbirth; I knew all the signs. You were on the way; I was sure of it."

"It was hard for your father to drive in the storm—the wind was blowing from the west and directly at us all the way. We knew the way very well because I made the trip every day but it was hard to even see the road in front of us. It was worse when we got in the city. We knew the streets, of course, and all the shortcuts, but the storm—the wind was blowing snow in all directions and piling it up in drifts—was a real blizzard and everything looked different.

Some streets we didn't dare turn into because the drifts looked too deep. The streetlights were all out and the traffic signals were out too. Anyway, we got lost, 'turned around in our minds,' your father says. We didn't know which way the hospital was. I think that's why he agreed not to talk about it; he was ashamed to admit he lost his way at such an important time. But it was understandable, in the storm and the darkness. We were desperate to find the right way and then your father got out of the car to brush snow off a street sign so he could read the name. And while he was looking up at the sign, away off in the distance he saw the light. It was like a miracle to us. We both saw it and we soon figured out what it was. It was the lighthouse!"

"Lighthouse? What lighthouse?"

"On top of the Methodist hospital in Indianapolis there's a small lighthouse. Not many people know about it now, but it's still there. It's the only hospital I've ever heard of with a lighthouse on top. I think it was meant as a Christian symbol—you know, Jesus as a light in the darkness and the hospital as a sign of his healing power. Anyway, we navigated our way to the hospital by going toward the light until we were close enough to see the building all lit up in the darkness with its emergency generators.

"We went in the emergency entrance and they took me up to the maternity ward where I knew everyone, all the nurses, and then after all that it was a false labor. You weren't ready to be born. I was so embarrassed. It was a mistake that an inexperienced person would make. They kept me there almost all day to be sure and Dad had to wait in the waiting room. He said he didn't get the news of the Pearl Harbor attack until later when I was released and then we just returned home. The storm was over and the snowplows had been working so there was no trouble. After that, all the talk was of the war and, well, we just never told anyone about that night."

"Wow, that's some story."

"Yes. And you haven't heard it all yet. They said the light in the lighthouse didn't work. It wasn't on that night. I suppose we should have told them that we saw it a mile or more away, but we didn't want to call attention to ourselves and maybe be ridiculed, so we kept quiet. I've always wondered about that and about how I was so sure you were on the way, and then it didn't happen, you never showed up. It was almost like you knew it wasn't a good day to be born."

Richard was quiet on hearing all this and his mother continued to talk, reminiscing about when he was just a baby. "We were so proud of you. You were what we lived for. We didn't have much extra money in those days. . . ." She paused, went to an upper cabinet and took down a flour container. She reached inside and pulled out a small, heavily tarnished metal cup, which she handed to her son. Although it was old, he could clearly read his name, Richard, engraved in fancy type. "But, we bought this silver-plated cup," she continued, "for a keepsake, instead of having your baby shoes bronzed like other people did. And see, I still have this old cup to remind me of those happy days."

Something living stirred within Richard upon seeing the old cup. He said, "I remember seeing that cup when I was very little." In his mind there was a visual memory of a time when he was only five or six and the cup was used every day. He saw himself as a child looking at the cup and not understanding the letters written on it. But the world was a mystery at that age and so this didn't trouble him. He was just learning to read and may not have even understood that the letters on the cup were supposed to be his name. But now he could see in memory that the name he saw at that young age had not been Richard but was instead *Emmanuel.*

Emmanuel? What kind of a name is that, he wondered, thinking it sounded and looked somehow Spanish. Then, he remembered Emmanuel was the name he had read from the Bible and that had caused him to tell Celeste, "This doesn't make any sense."

It was while they were at the campground in Georgia, where he had played kickball with Timmy and then, exhausted, had scratched that yet-to-be-understood figure in the red clay. It was after the kids had gone to sleep and he had stayed up around the campfire with Celeste that he happened to read, in Matthew's gospel, the story linking Jesus' birth with the Old Testament prophecy about a virgin birth. He was troubled at the time by a logical inconsistency in the story. The Old Testament prophecy said the son was to be named Emmanuel and that didn't square with the fact that they named

Mary's boy Jesus. Why didn't they name him Emmanuel? And how could they claim that Jesus' birth fulfilled this prophecy unless they did? There was a footnote in his Pilgrim's edition King James Bible that said many people had noticed the inconsistency and it offered an explanation that tried to explain it away. But the explanation was labored and he hadn't bought it—that's when he had spoken out to Celeste, "This doesn't make sense." Making sense was important to Richard; he would discover that it was his way.

Seeing the name Emmanuel on his cup as a child meant nothing to him, but now he recognized that it was a memory that, if true, meant that God had been working with him his entire life. The implications of this name were too great for him to accept it uncritically and he refused to consider it, instead reminding himself that his mind may be racing again and misleading him. Probably, it was just his imagination, fired by his wish for his life to have some special meaning, altering his memory of the name he saw written on his cup. After all, he had the real cup in his hand and the name on it was Richard and not Emmanuel. But was there some connection between the name and the mysterious figure drawn in the Georgia red clay? Maybe he hadn't just happened to read the story linking Jesus with the Old Testament name, Emmanuel. Wasn't it just possible that he was being guided, being led step by step toward acceptance of another name, another identity, one having a special function in God's plan? He took a deep breath and tried to quiet his mind by listening only to his mother's voice as she finished her story. And then his dad joined them in the kitchen and he let the thought be forgotten for the moment. It could wait for another time.

* * *

Celeste and the kids, Timmy and Annette, returned in the afternoon from their overnight visit with her parents. Timmy ran in the house ahead of the others. "Grandma sent you some cookies, Dad. They're really good. If you don't want them, Mom says I can have them. Do you want them? Huh? Do you? And Grandpa let me push his lawn mower. It was fun. They don't have much grass like this grandpa has, or a barn.

Richard finally found a gap in the one-sided conversation. "Hey, you bet I like Grandma's cookies too," then playfully advised his small son, "Don't you eat them all. Save some of them to share with the rest of us.

"How are Grandma and Grandpa?" he asked.

"Okay, I guess," Annette answered as she came into the kitchen. "They got a new car. It's purple. It's kinda neat but it only has two doors. Grandma drives really fast and honks her horn a lot. It's funny. Boy, I'm tired," she went on, changing the subject. "I slept on the living room couch and it wasn't too comfortable. Mom stayed up late talking with Opal in the kitchen. I could hear them. Why does she hate black people so much? She told Mom a story about how a black lady had cut her off and taken her parking spot in front of a doughnut shop. She was really mad."

"Oh, Holy One," Celeste greeted him as she joined them in the kitchen. She was obviously in a good mood. "Where is everybody?"

"Mom and Dad went grocery shopping. I think we're eating them out of house and home. And I wanted to be alone for a while so I could write down what I remember about everything that has happened on this trip," Richard explained.

"I had a talk with my mother this morning. I apologized for the phone call and questioning whether she was even my mother. She told me an interesting story about the time I was born."

"Good. I'm happy to hear all that," Celeste said. "My parents asked about you; they wanted to know why you didn't come too. I told them what you said about the house being too small for all of us and that you weren't feeling well and needed a rest after the long trip."

"Well, that's true enough," Richard said and then, seeing that Timmy and Annette had left the room he added, "Did you tell your mother about how you threw all the pans she gave us at me."

"No, of course not," Celeste said and then added defensively, "Why would you ask such a thing? That was a stupid thing you did and you deserved what you got. Maybe you are crazy."

"The preacher said they called Jesus crazy too."

"What are you talking about? What preacher?"

"Rev. Rasmussen. He's the minister at a big church in town. My dad invited him to the house yesterday when you were gone."

"Your father invited a minister to come talk with you? I can't imagine that happening. I don't understand why, but your father has never wanted anything to do with religion."

"You're right about that. I don't know what he thinks about religion either, but he's the only one honestly trying to understand what I'm talking about and not just giving up on me as crazy."

"I haven't given up on you."

"I know. But you're not giving me much encouragement either. You just want me to take some pills and have everything be like it was before."

"What did the minister say about Jesus being crazy?"

"He said there's a story in Mark's gospel about Jesus' family calling him crazy. I checked it out. Jesus was drawing a big crowd with his preaching and when his family heard about it they tried to tell everyone not to listen to him because he was crazy. And then the hypocrites came to check him out and they told him he had a devil and that he needed to take some pills to get rid of it."

"All right, that's enough talk about pills. Seriously, it actually uses that word, crazy?"

"Well, no. It says Jesus was 'beside himself.' But the preacher said it means the same thing. He said every preacher has an experience of being called and I gathered that some of them can be pretty far out. He seemed to be comfortable with the idea and even knew the chapter and verse, Mark 3:21. It made me wonder if there was a time in his life when people thought he was out of his mind."

Oh great, Celeste thought, *Just what I need, the crazy leading the crazy*. But, she said, "Maybe the preacher was trying to make you feel better about what happened. It seems to have worked."

"Yeah. And I found out there is more to the story of Jesus being called crazy. After they called him crazy he was again preaching to a large crowd and they told him that his brothers and—get this—his mother were outside and wanted to see him. And then he seemed confused, like me, about who his mother was. He asked the crowd who was his mother and brothers? And then he told them that everyone who does the will of God is his brother and his sister and his mother! Reading *that* made me feel better about that phone call. And it made it easier to apologize for it too. I told my mom I was 'beside myself.' "

"That doesn't seem like the same thing at all to me," Celeste said.

"Well, it sure seems like quite a coincidence to me. How many stories have you ever read about someone being confused about who their mother was? And this morning I woke up with a poem in my head. I've never before in my life written a poem. Listen to this. I call it *Crazy Two*. That's t-w-o. '*If you want to, call me crazy. Please be my guest and do. For I'm only following Jesus, And they called him crazy too*.' That's t-o-o."

"Nice. What else did the crazy preacher say?"

"He said I need to take a time out—as long as it takes, he said—to reflect on what has happened. That's why I'm trying to write down all the stuff that's happened so I can look at it later. And he said I need to study about religions and about experiences like mine that other people have had. He said Jesus took a time out before he began to tell people about the good news. He said I might want to write a book about my experience someday. That reminded me that I had written something on the desk pad right away while the *Vision of Love* I had was fading. I'm anxious to get back and see what I wrote. The preacher also said God can wait on me."

"That all sounds like good advice to me. I was afraid you were going to go off and be one of those street preachers who paint Bible stuff on their cars and pickup trucks and yell at people, calling them sinners and saying the end of the world is near."

"For a while, I could see myself doing that. I know where they're coming from. But I think there's too much of my father's irreligious attitude in me for that. I can't see me calling my father a sinner just because he doesn't go to church. My message isn't going to be the same as theirs. Besides, the preacher says I've learned a valuable lesson that the direct approach doesn't work. I think I'm past that sort of wild-eyed stage now. It seems to me the book idea is a better way, you can talk to people and reason with them and they can read it and take it or leave it."

Celeste thought that she would probably leave it, whatever it was. But she said nothing.

* * *

The next day, Sunday, was the last day of their visit and in the afternoon they all gathered in the living room to look at old family albums and pictures. As memories of past years were triggered by the photographs, Richard realized how trouble-free his life and that of his family had been. He had always been healthy and had never even so much as broken a bone. His had been a charmed life it seemed. They were not rich but had never been poor either. His father was successful enough in his business to have provided a comfortable life for them all. And he had generously provided a college education for each of his children, so Richard had never struggled financially. If his had been a religious family, he thought, he might have supposed that his charmed life was due to angels watching over him in answer to prayer.

Among the happy memories were a few that didn't add up and had been a source of recurrent wonder all his life. There was the memory of the rotten egg that bounced off frozen ground when it should have gone "splat" like all the others. He had thrown it some long ago sunny winter afternoon of his childhood—with a dozen or so others—from their barn's big haymow window into the garden forty feet below. It could not have bounced, it was impossible, yet it did bounce on the first hit and then went splat on the rebound. He saw it hit the ground and then rise up in the air again and he never forgot it, wondering.

Another event he never understood was when he slipped and fell unexpectedly to the ground while climbing over closely packed farm machinery stored in the dark interior of the barn. He had taken a leap over a sharp-pointed rotary hoe with the intention of landing in a hay wagon, but he missed an important hand hold and found himself falling backward, helplessly, toward the ground with his head and back unprotected and sure, he thought, to land hard on the sharp metal below. He expected to be seriously injured but miraculously, it seemed, he had landed in a soft patch of hay between the pointed wheels of the rotary hoe and the hay wagon. He remembered thinking while falling how badly he was going to be hurt and when he wasn't hurt at all he never quite accepted it as the legitimate outcome dictated by the laws of physics. Even today he sometimes wondered about how he had been so lucky. It seemed now that events like these had prepared him to believe in miracles.

Celeste moved next to Richard on the couch where he was leafing through the album. Just when she sat down he turned a page and there was a group photo of their wedding reception. The reception had been a very informal affair, held at Celeste's parent's house in the city the weekend after the wedding and the last weekend before they packed all their belongings into a small trailer and moved to their new life and jobs in Florida. It was a beautiful fall day with the trees burning with color and the air filled with the subtle fragrance of dry fallen leaves. The event was held outdoors in the driveway area between the house and the garage—an old unpainted wooden building that had been cleaned up and used as a bar and serving area. Richard thought the old garage was about as close as you could get to actually being a barn in the city and he was very comfortable in the humble setting.

The photo captured images of most of their two extended families, twenty or thirty people of all ages, gathered around the two of them seated at a small table in the front center of the picture with the open garage/barn in the background. The overflowing familial love captured in that moment was plainly evident. And now as Richard looked at the picture he saw the *Love* in it and was suddenly overwhelmed with a realization of the truth that this picture was a miniature of a developing situation placing him at the center of something unimaginably bigger, more powerful, and hugely loving.

His heart stopped and for a long moment he could not draw a breath. The impact was what he had imagined it would be like to be struck by lightning. It felt as if a switch had suddenly closed somewhere on a high voltage electrical potential and now a new high energy current was flowing through his life. He saw, in his imagination, ever widening concentric circles extending from his central position in space, and he imagined that a long-standing psychic energy wave had suddenly found an outlet through his loving thought and had grounded itself, collapsing and concentrating all its ancient energy on him. It was an implosion, with him at ground zero. New energy flowed lavishly into his heart and mind.

He realized in that single, heart-stopping moment that much had been given him and now much was being asked in return. He could not refuse. It was in that moment of willing acceptance of his duty that he felt as though he were Atlas and the weight of the world had suddenly been dropped on his shoulders. He was Prometheus, running hard to escape, having just stolen fire from the Gods, or Colonel Tibbets flying his Enola Gay toward Japan destined to drop the bomb that would alter the course of the world. Images of opportunity and responsibility blended in his mind: he was the first caveman to see the potential for the wheel in a rock rolling downhill, and Albert Einstein on his first hint of knowing the equivalence of mass and energy, a Las Vegas gambler watching as the wheels spin and the winning symbols line up without end. He was like a safe cracker turning the dial in darkness and listening as the tumblers guarding the Secret of the Universe fall into place and then watching in rapt wonder as the door opens on a vast golden treasure. And finally he saw himself as Ulysses, sighting his homeland and hearth at long last, after having fought the good fight and journeyed far and wide searching for something half forgotten. He was Hamlet, deciding *To Be*, and Adam waking to find God his father loving him all the while he had slept.

It was, perhaps, the final phase of the change he believed was taking place in his brain, with new connections replacing the old. He imagined the change had reached a critical mass and then gone nuclear to its end point with billions and billions of new connections created in a moment. His consciousness expanded. He was sealed, a new creation. There was no turning back. He was what he was. He was ready now to think unthinkable thoughts, willing to ask new questions and able to see reasonable, responsible, possibilities where others saw nothing.

His heart began beating again with renewed strength, enough to carry him through the moment as the new *Life* within him whispered, “You are my beloved son. This day have I begotten you.”

The shining moment passed, unnoticed by everyone in the room save Celeste, who alone felt Richard draw the first deep breath of his new life. He did not cry out prematurely as before, seeking to share this new revelation. He had learned to contain the *Power* inherent in the moment. He had learned these thoughts, though truer than true, were unspeakable and were not for the present time and place. Celeste too had learned—not to ask.

And so the moment passed unheralded. The important birth—Richard's second—was accomplished in silence. The delivery had been difficult and traumatic, for him and particularly for Celeste, but it was over and now he was free, breathing the pure air of a new life.

"Science cannot solve the ultimate mystery of nature. And that is because, in the last analysis, we ourselves are a part of the mystery that we are trying to solve." — Max Planck

Chapter Five

HOMELAND SECURITY

Bina and Jenny left the *Hawk and Dove* and headed toward the familiar Capitol South Metro Station on D Street.

"Do you know what your seat number was on the plane?" Bina asked as they walked in the brisk springtime wind and cold.

"I have the ticket here in my purse. It has the flight number and everything. What are you going to do?"

"I'm calling Julie in Atlanta to see if she can help us put a name to Forrest Gump. It shouldn't be too hard. You remember Julie, she works for Delta."

"Yes, I do remember her—from the party," Jenny said. "She was nice . . . here's the ticket, and this is my seat number, 32a. So he was sitting in 32b."

Bina took the ticket as she removed her cell phone from her purse, touched the screen several times and put it to her ear. "Hello, Julie? This is Bina from Washington D.C. You remember we met last year at a party in Arlington?"

. . .

"That's right. I'm still at the Library of Congress. And you remember my friend Jenny?"

. . .

"Oh sure, she's good. Yes, still gorgeous. Life isn't fair. She's right here with me. Listen, Julie, we have a problem and I think you may be able to help us."

. . .

"Well, Jenny was on a Delta flight this morning, flight number 228, 6 a.m. from Daytona Beach to Atlanta. She was sitting in a window seat, 32a, and she had a fascinating conversation with a man who sat next to her and now she wants to know who he was."

. . .

"No. No, it's not like that. He was an older man. We're thinking that maybe he was a preacher or a guru or something."

. . .

"Yeah, I know, privacy rules are terrible."

. . .

"I don't want you to get in any trouble, but I thought it might still be on a computer screen somewhere."

. . .

"Well, listen, we know the man and his wife were the last ones on the plane. So I was thinking they may be 'Delta family' people. Would that make a difference?"

. . .

"It would? Oh good."

. . .

"Thanks."

. . .

"Call me when you get something, anything. And if ever I can help you here at the library, call me. Bye."

They boarded the Metro and took a seat, with Jenny by the window. They were both quiet while Jenny stared out absently at the passing buildings. After a moment she turned to her friend and spoke softly. "Bina?"

"Yes."

"I've been thinking. Are we doing anything illegal or dangerous? You said Homeland Security is looking for this man."

"Relax, nobody is looking for him—yet. I'm probably wrong. But what I said was, I think they should be looking for him but that they don't know it yet. They are looking for a much younger person. Our hero is a senior citizen."

"How do you know that?"

"Well, you said he was older. And you only have to be fifty now to join AARP."

"No, not that. *I* told *you* he was a senior. But that's really all I told you—all I know. What makes you think Homeland Security is looking for some 'guru,' young or old?"

"Jenny, did I say they were?"

"Not in so many words. But, you think I'm right, don't you—that he had something to do with my feeling so good today? And that's unusual, isn't it, that someone could stir up those feelings in me without really doing anything? All I know for sure is I've never met anyone like that before."

"Yes, I think the two of you made a perfect couple. I think he was probably meditating while sitting in that tight middle seat next to you in the early morning darkness. That would account for the erect posture that reminded you of Forrest Gump."

"But how would that affect me?"

"I don't know how, but I have read that many followers of Eastern holy men claim that just being near their guru can elevate their feelings—make them feel happier. How that could be true nobody knows for sure. But it's a possibility at least."

"This man was more Forrest Gump than any guru I ever saw," Jenny said.

"Right. I thought of that. It may be the first time he has meditated with someone like you so close to him."

"What do you mean, someone like me?"

"I just mean that you are a beautiful person on the inside too, very accepting of everyone and nonjudgmental. You're not always trying to analyze everything like I do. Your mind is open to new things."

"You're saying it probably wouldn't have happened to you?"

"Yeah, I most likely would have missed out on the whole feeling good thing."

"Maybe that's why you don't know about the 'afterglow' I get after good sex. This was like we just bypassed the sex and went right into the good feeling. But it was like afterglow on steroids.

"I can't really describe it and I want to," Jenny went on, turning her gaze back toward the window. "It was more than just being happy. It was like when you fell down and your mother kissed you and told you everything would be all right. And you felt all better inside. It was like that too."

"Hummm, sounds really peaceful and comfortable; wish I coulda been there."

Jenny turned back to her friend and put her hand on Bina's forearm. Her voice, which had been almost dreamy, was now full of earnest concern. "Bina, I know you're a smart person and all that, but why did you say you think someone wants to kill him? There's no law against making people feel good is there? What do you know that I don't?"

"Let's wait till we get home and I'll tell you everything I know."

Half an hour later Bina and Jenny were settled in the two-bedroom townhouse they leased in the less expensive Alexandria area south of the Potomac River. While sharing a dinner of salad and a pizza, Bina told Jenny what she knew about a secret project in the Homeland Security office.

"I got a call last month from Lucy—she works in the executive office of Homeland Security. We had lunch with her once. Remember, kind of a tall woman? She said her boss had told her to call the Library of Congress and get him—quote—'everything they have on the Second Coming and'—now get this—'some information on gurus.'"

"On what?"

"Exactly. That was my response too—and maybe hers—but I didn't say anything. She called me, instead of going through the normal procedure because she had no idea of what books to get and she knew me and thought I would do the research for her and get her the right stuff so she would look good for her boss."

"She's that tall brunette with the real Southern accent," Jenny said.

"Yes, that's her. I think she was Miss Alabama or something a few years ago. Anyway, her boss loved the stuff I sent and rewarded her by taking her out for a big dinner when his wife was out of town."

"Bina, this salad is really good. What did you put in it?"

"Jenny, that salad is two days old; you've had it before."

"I can't help it. It's never tasted like this before. It's really good. Maybe it fermented or something. Don't you taste the difference?"

"No, I don't taste any difference. I think your taste buds must be happy too."

"I'll bet you're right. I'm happy all over, inside and out. But forget my taste buds; go on with your story about Lucy."

"She called me a few days later to thank me. It was late in the day and she said she was alone in the office. So, I asked her what it was all about. I was curious why someone at Homeland Security was looking into the Second Coming.

"I've never told you, Jenny, but I did my PhD thesis on the Jewish Messiah. That was when I was in Israel at Jerusalem University. In fact, I included my published thesis, *Ten Character Traits of the Jewish Messiah*, on the recommended reading list I gave Lucy's boss."

"I never knew that about you."

"Oh, yeah. I'm full of surprises. My grandfather belongs to the oldest Jewish sect in existence and has never left Israel. They are still waiting for the promised Holy One. I grew up listening to his stories."

"Is he the one you call every week?"

"Yes, we're still close. I'm still his little princess, his only grandchild. He wanted me to stay in Israel and doesn't understand why I left. He was responsible for me being named Bina."

"This pizza is good too. Where did we get it?"

"You want to hear the rest of this story or not?"

"I'm sorry. So what did Lucy tell you?"

"First she said she didn't know what I was talking about. I suppose they are trained to answer like that. Then I jokingly suggested that maybe someone expected Jesus to come back soon and we could let him take care of all our problems.

"Well, I might have thought the phone was disconnected it was so quiet. I guess she was deciding what to say next.

"Finally she broke the silence and said, 'Bina you are so close, I just have to tell you. I have to tell someone.' She asked if she could trust me not to tell and I told her she could. And then she said something I never would have imagined. '*They think he's already her*e' she said. '*And now they are trying to find him.*'

"Now I was speechless for a moment. I couldn't believe that

she was telling me those hardheaded realists in charge of Homeland Security had bought into the Jesus myth. My mind was searching for another way to understand her words. 'He's already here?' I mumbled, not wanting to ask a stupid question."

"'They believe he is,' she answered.

"Who?" I had to ask, even though it felt like I was about to be caught up in that old Abbott and Costello 'Who's on First' routine.

"'Jesus, of course,' she answered. Then to my relief she added, 'At least I believe it's Jesus. I can't ask anyone. I'm not supposed to know anything. They don't say *Jesus*, they say *a great soul*. But I know its Jesus, who else could it be?' "

"Bina!" Jenny exclaimed, "Have you lost your mind? Do you think the man on the plane with me today was Jesus?"

"No, I don't think that," Bina answered. "I'm Jewish, remember. I don't believe in Jesus. But I do think that the idea of a great soul has some possibility. Lucy says all the secret intelligence agencies—FBI, CIA—are cooperating in a big effort to find him. She said it's code named *Cinderella Search*."

Just then, Bina's purse began playing the Israeli National Anthem. She picked up her cell phone and answered, saying simply, "Bina." The call was from Julie with Delta Airlines in Atlanta. Turned out she was able to get the mystery man's name without breaking any rules. He was Richard O. Holmes, and his wife was Celeste Holmes.

"That's H O L M E S," Julie carefully spelled out. "They live in Daytona Beach and their daughter Annette began with Delta in the mid-90s."

Julie admitted to being curious about the guy and said she had Googled him to see if he were somebody special.

"Oh," said Bina, "what came up?"

"Nothing," Julie answered. "There is information on several people named Richard Holmes but no Richard O. Holmes of Daytona Beach."

"Oh well, we'll catch up with him on Facebook—"

"Nothing there either."

"You checked already?"

"Yes, I'm curious to know how this guy is flying high, yet off the radar. You and Jenny be careful. Let me know what you find out, okay?"

"Okay," Bina promised. "But don't hold your breath and keep it to yourself will you? We don't want to scare him off till we find out what he's all about."

Bina made a note of the names—Holmes, Richard O. and Celeste—and thanked Julie warmly for her help, again telling her to call if ever she needed something from the Library of Congress.

"Julie says he's a nobody. The internet has nothing on a Richard 'O' Holmes," Bina told Jenny.

"That's unusual, isn't it?" Jenny asked.

"Yes, but it's not bad. In fact, I think I like it. I should have expected it. I wrote in my book that the Messiah's experience would separate him; he would be one of a kind."

"You mean something like the Lone Ranger? Hi-Yo Silver, away."

"Yes, I suppose so. Now, where was I?"

"Cinderella," Jenny offered.

"Oh, yes, the *Cinderella Search*. Well, later the same day that I talked with Lucy, I thought of a way I could check out that part of her story. I went to see Leah in the evening after work. She lives in a townhouse like ours just down the street and she works in the J. Edgar Hoover building on Pennsylvania Avenue."

"The FBI."

"Yes. I asked Leah if there was something big going on. She denied it until I said 'Cinderella,' then she began asking me what I knew. I told her a little of what I suspected and it was apparent that I knew more than she did. I asked her to call me if she learned any more about Cinderella. She said she would."

"Well, that's interesting."

"Yes, and Lucy told me something else interesting. There is a defense contractor working secretly at Oak Ridge, Tennessee, on something related to the search."

"What?"

"I don't think she knows. She said it was going to cost a lot. Then I asked her how they know 'he' is here now."

"Good question," Jenny said. "I was wondering about that too. How did all this craziness get started?"

"What Lucy told me sounded far-fetched, but for some reason the intelligence agencies latched on to it. She said a spiritual writer noticed there was a sharp jump in human consciousness in the late 1980s around the time of a widely publicized 'harmonic convergence.' Then years later a brain researcher showed if only one mind first experienced the jump that higher level of consciousness would spread at the speed of light to all other minds. Working together, the spiritual writer and the secular brain guy came up with the idea that a 'great soul' had been born into the world in the 1980s. And then lots of people bought into the theory for various reasons."

"Harmonic convergence?" Jenny said.

"It was a worldwide meditation event in 1987 that coincided with an unusual alignment of the planets and was foretold in ancient texts. Apparently it left a lasting imprint, which is where the birth of the 'great soul' comes in."

"So now he—or she?—would be maybe thirty something, right?"

"Jenny, that's right. How did you do that so quickly? You hate math."

"It was 6th grade arithmetic."

"Yes, but you … anyway, that's why I told you they weren't looking for our senior citizen."

"Dr. Oh!"

"What?"

"Our senior citizen, Richard 'O' Holmes—Dr. Oh, because he made me feel, Oh so good."

"Jenny you are amazing."

"Thank you. Now go on. You were about to explain why you said Homeland Security should be looking for Richard."

"Oh, that. It was what you said about your fiancé Bill that caused me to put two and two together."

"What did I say?

Remember? You said Bill seemed immature and maybe you didn't even like him anymore."

"Yes, so?"

"Well, I've been trying for years to help you see that used car salesman 'Big Dollar Bill' isn't right for you, and you never seemed to hear me. So, what happened today to change your mind?"

"I don't know. What do you think happened?"

"I think that, besides being happy, your consciousness has been raised."

"You mean like what that writer said happened to all of us in the 80s?"

"Yes, that's what I mean. And I've never heard of a mere guru doing that."

"Okay, maybe that's a little bit the same thing as what I felt, and so maybe Richard does know something about it. It sounds crazy, but if I go by what I experienced it makes sense to me too."

Jenny felt a gentle warmth moving through her body. She had a strong desire to let it carry her away, as had happened on the plane. But just as she was feeling engulfed in peace, a logical thought entered her mind and startled her. "Just one more thing, Bina, that I don't understand. If some great soul was supposedly born some twenty or thirty years ago, how does that fit with my Dr. Feelgood? He must have been born sixty or maybe seventy years ago."

"I thought of that, too. The answer is in the book I wrote about characteristics of the coming Messiah. I explained how the Messiah will be someone who is a bit of a misfit, someone who has a hard time finding his place in the world. He probably won't be an accomplished person. That's why I shouldn't have been surprised when Julie googled him and nothing came up. A number of things may contribute to his condition. He may be left-handed, for instance. Scripture says he won't have a shape that we will desire. He won't be handsome and maybe his clothes don't fit well."

"Dr. Oh didn't fit well in the airplane seat. He was squeezed in there; it couldn't have been very comfortable. That's what caused his leg to brush mine in the first place. And he was left-handed too, like you said. But what's the point of his being a misfit?"

"Jenny, again you amaze me. You didn't always think like this. Anyway, the point of his being a misfit is that it will be easier for someone who isn't totally in love with the world to eventually turn away from the world and turn whole heartedly toward God, perhaps in a last chance attempt to find his place in the world—maybe I should say *out* of this world. I actually wrote that 'in midlife he would have a traumatic life changing experience of the reality of God.'"

"Okay, well, mid-life for Richard, I suppose would have been when he was forty something. That would put his life changing event, if he had one, in the range of the harmonic convergence."

"Right, that's what I realized when I said Homeland Security should be looking for an older person. Richard's experience of God would be a kind of restart, a second birth, for his life."

"Restart? You mean like when you push the restart button on a computer? Like when everything gets in a big mess and all you can do is push restart and hope for the best?"

"Jenny, I could not have found a better metaphor myself. And then after the restart button is pushed, everything is total confusion for a while as lights and a crazy jumble of words and numbers flash on and off the computer screen while you watch and wonder if it will ever work right again. Finally, if you are lucky, it settles down and begins to rearrange things again in a logical and useful way."

"You're saying that Richard's life may have been a total confusion since his experience and he may only now be coming out of the fog?"

"Yes, I wrote in my book that 'the coming Messiah, after his experience of God, would be on fire with the need to communicate what he then knew to be true.' He may first try to tell people directly what he knows but his enthusiasm and the believability of what he is saying may make it seem he is out of his mind. If he keeps pushing he will sooner or later be told he is crazy and that will cause him to have to draw back and rethink things. He will have to start over and find a way of communication that resonates with the people he is trying to reach without freaking them out about the reality of God."

"What's that mean, resonate?"

"It means he will have to learn to translate the love of God into the common language of the people so they can understand and so some of them, maybe at first others disillusioned with the world in some way, will want to go and see for themselves what God is all about really. Today the common language is reason. Science and logic determine what we are willing to believe is true. In our increasingly logical society something has to make good sense or we will refuse to hear it. That's why, in my opinion, organized religion is dying."

"Excuse me, Bina, but I thought religion was all about having faith and just accepting certain things as true."

"That has been the way of religion for a long time. But the age of faith is coming to an end. The coming age is about wisdom and understanding. That's what the messiah concept is all about, the end of one age and the beginning of a better one."

"Oh, you mean it isn't going to be the end of the world?"

"No, of course not. It may seem like the end of the world for some people; but that end of the world stuff is just a misunderstanding to scare people into going to church."

"Boy, I'm glad to hear you say that. My cousin says World War Three is coming and that will be the end of the world. He goes to church a lot."

"Well, I prefer to think the Messiah is coming and through the understanding and wisdom he will bring we will learn how to turn ourselves around and quit killing one another. I speculate in my book that the coming Messiah may be someone schooled in science and logic, maybe a scientist or engineer. He will be trying to tell us about God in the language of reason, using logic and understanding. And in his attempt to communicate, I think, he very likely will write a book.

"Now you know why I left Israel and took this job at the Library of Congress, the biggest library in the world. I have a dream of someday finding that book."

"And you think Richard could be that one?"

"Yes, I think he could be. It's not like the Messiah will be some exotic thing, an angel flying in from heaven or something. I think he will just be an ordinary sort of man."

"It's been maybe forty years. How long does it take to write a book? It must be a big one. What do you suppose he has been doing all this time?"

"We have to remember he will be trying to do the impossible and that will probably take a long time. First he will have to regain his sanity. People who believe in science aren't known for believing in God also. So that will be hard, and he won't be getting much support from either scientific or religious people. And then he may have to ask himself and decide over and over if he wants to do this or not. He most probably will have a wife and family and how will he deal with that? He may be trying to live two different lives at once. And there's another thing. When he comes he won't be alone. In some mysterious way God will be with him. He will have to learn that there is a Plan, but he won't necessarily know every detail of it. He will find he isn't in charge of when or how things happen in his life. He will have to learn how to listen for signs and he may even be hearing a voice no one else hears. And beyond all that the world will have to be ready. That's a lot to ask of any ordinary man. It seems to me forty years may be about right."

"There was nothing ordinary about the man I met."

"Well, you know what I mean; he will be an ordinary man with an extraordinary experience."

"And a power to make people happy."

"That too, it would seem."

"Bina, you know what?"

"No. What?"

"I'm glad we had this talk. But why would Homeland Security want to kill someone for writing a book about God?"

"Lucy said her agency classifies the supposed 'great soul' as an unknown intelligence and therefore a threat. Their rules say unknown intelligences have to be dealt with under the protocol for extraterrestrials and UFOs. She is afraid 'Jesus' will be killed again, this time by Homeland Security following a policy of shooting first and asking questions later."

"That's stupid. What if he wrapped up the whole world in a love bubble—poof, no more wars!"

"Lucy thinks that's what they are afraid of—peace, the end of our way of life."

Chapter Six

ENCOUNTER WITH CHRISTIANITY

"For God is not the author of confusion, but of peace as in all churches of the saints." — I Corinthians 14: 33

"The Christian ideal has not been tried and found wanting; it has been found difficult and left untried."
— G K Chesterton 1874-1936

Richard and Celeste returned to their home in Daytona Beach from visiting family in Indiana. Richard was more certain than ever that his vision was real and he knew absolutely that it had changed him. The Richard who had thought himself little more than an animal and who had found no real purpose for his life was no more. He knew himself now as belonging in the unchanging world of pure Love he had discovered. He had chosen to leave that world in order to tell others of its existence. The visit had convinced him that it wasn't going to be as simple as he had at first thought. He had accepted an important new purpose for his life. But he had yet to learn it was a purpose at odds with his and Celeste's life together.

He chose with some care those who he told of the big experience which had changed his view of the world and of himself. However those first attempts to communicate, like the direct sharing he had done with family members in Indiana, were unsuccessful.

It was time for a new beginning, a restart. Richard was sure the information he had gained in the Vision was important and he felt it was his duty, his reason for being, to find a way to effectively communicate what he knew to be the truth. He would need to find a new approach.

Rev. Rasmussen had shown him the beginnings of another way. He would take a time out, sufficient time, to study and learn about religions and then set down his ideas in an orderly, reasonable fashion in a book which people could read, and then accept or reject as they saw fit. He had no idea that "sufficient time" would turn out to be more than twenty years before his book was finished and he and Celeste would find their way to Washington D.C.

The rejections had taught him to hold his peace with people who were not interested in understanding the world in a new way. Since the source of his inspiration was the Bible and the words of Jesus, it was inevitable that he would soon find his way to others who studied the Bible and who held Jesus in high esteem—Christians.

* * *

The trip back from Indiana to Florida and Daytona Beach was uneventful and the Holmes family tried to resume their lives as before. But it was soon apparent this was not going to be possible. Richard and Celeste were at odds over their belief in God. They had been equally yoked before, in that neither of them had any use for religion. Now they were pulling in opposite directions. It was soon apparent to Richard that he would have to pursue his goal quietly to maintain peace between them.

To Celeste it seemed that Richard had given up his insane idea that he had been chosen to bring a special message to the world. She expected that, perhaps after a brief period of healing, her husband would again be as before. But Richard did not give up his belief in having found a special purpose for his life. He merely went underground with it. He banked the fire once burning openly for all to see, and it remained, still hot and smoldering, but out of sight within him. His mission was apparently not going to be easy. It was going to take time and study but Richard was in it for the long haul. He was struggling now, learning how to balance living two lives. His old life was lived on the surface of things, apparently normal as before, while his new life survived in his private thoughts.

Richard was anxious to return home and revisit the holy

place where the unexpected Vision of Love had first surprised and overwhelmed him. He wanted to sit in the old wooden swivel desk chair again, this time in his own mind and body, and to see what it was his hand had written on the desk pad there. The Indiana preacher had suggested that Richard might eventually want to write a book about his experience, which had caused him to remember that something had been written there. "The Oneness of God," was all he could remember, but he knew there was more to it and hoped it was an inspired outline for the book he now felt destined to write.

What he found written on the desk pad was not an outline for the contents of a book but was only an uninspiring few words that seemed to be a title page. It read as follows: from the top in capital letters, was first written ONEISM, with the ISM crossed out and NESS, written above it. God, it seemed, was prone to having second thoughts. And his own memory was also proven imperfect in seeing only the one word title, ONENESS, in place of the four words, THE ONENESS OF GOD, he had remembered.

Below the one word title ONENESS was a thirteen word subtitle written on six lines in all capital letters centered on the page. It read: first line, "A." Second line, "GUIDE TO FAITH." Third line, "FOR." Fourth line, "UNCOMMITTED GENTILES." Fifth line, "WHO." Sixth line, "KNOW THERE IS A GOD." The last line, like the ONENESS title, had been edited. It was first intended to include the word "surely" between THERE and IS so that it would read, "KNOW THERE SURELY IS A GOD." But the spacing didn't work and the attempt was given up with the word "surely" crossed out, which was a good thing because it was misspelled, "SHURLY." It looked then as if God was not only prone to having second thoughts but also had trouble with spelling.

Yet another interpretation was competing for recognition in his mind. It said that if we were going to recognize "shurly" as being misspelled, we should also take another step and recognize there was another possible spelling, Shirley. Then, if by chance, the "there" in line six had been wrongly written in place of an intended "that," lines five and six together would read, "who know that Shirley is a God." Of course, Richard rejected this interpretation on the basis of its apparent absurdity, an odd comment on the extent to which his mind brought every possibility to his attention, no matter how unusual or ridiculous.

At the very bottom was a single line, which read, "Inspired by GOD." Then neatly spaced across the page was the date, July, 1985 A.D. Richard recognized the July date as another mistake because the Vision had actually taken place June 26 according to the record of events he had written. He quickly crossed out the "Inspired by GOD" line and wrote over it, Richard O. Holmes. Altogether the visual effect of the title page was pleasing and the words "uncommitted gentiles" were helpful in that they showed that the book would not be for everyone.

The writing was definitely not the Divine point of beginning he was hoping for. It seemed clear that he was on his own in this impossible mission having apparently been abandoned by God at the outset. Seeing this, the fire within him died a little.

> *Richard is difficult to reach right now. His mind was open to me when he was uncertain; now he is tempted to believe that I am no longer with him. It was easy at first to put ideas in his head that he quickly embraced as his own—ideas which led him to let go of his familiar world and allowed him to see its illusory nature. Now disbelief coming from those he had expected to accept him has produced doubt about how to reach them. His experience showed him that beyond this unreal world only seeming to exist in time was the truth of an eternal world of Pure Love. He still knows that and he started out confidently, straightforwardly pursuing his objective of showing others the way he had found. But now he needs reassurance he hasn't lost his mind and time. When he's ready he'll busy himself searching this illusory world of human flesh and blood for his own special way to share what he has learned. It isn't surprising that Richard is caught for now between two worlds—and not open to any new initiatives from me. For a time Celeste proved more attuned to hearing my voice than Richard.*

A few days after their return home, Celeste told Richard that they were invited to a distant neighbor's house for dinner. The neighbor was a well-known doctor who was also a fundamentalist

Baptist. The doctor's wife had somehow learned of Richard's experience and now they wanted to know more about it. Richard, having once been disappointed by trusting others who professed to have an interest in his experience, was cautious. The first time, his trust given freely had landed him in the Mental Health Clinic and the memory of that indignity was still fresh in his mind.

The doctor and his wife lived in a big new house on the Halifax River. Dinner was served at a long dining room table in a huge family room with an impossibly high cathedral ceiling. Every wall of the room held a multitude of stuffed and mounted heads of once alive and wild animals. The centerpiece of the room was a fifteen-foot tall stuffed grizzly bear posed in a menacing posture reared up on his two hind legs. His appearance was presumably exactly as it had been in the last moments of his life when the hunter/doctor had gunned him down at close range, just in time to save his own life.

The dinner consisted solely of fresh blue crabs taken from the river and served with melted butter on brown paper sacks. After the feast, and with the dead grizzly bear looking down on them, the important doctor who lived in the big house on the river listened impatiently as Richard cautiously told his story with a minimum of details. He was cut off even before he was finished as the Baptist roared his unreserved approval, saying, "My Boy, you've been born again!"

There was no doubt about it. And the only thing to be done now, he advised, was to get Richard baptized and then enrolled in a Sunday school class at his own First Baptist Church. The baptism couldn't wait and the ceremony took place that evening after dinner. Richard and the doctor stripped down to their undershorts and walked out into the river at the big house.

The lady of the house counseled Celeste and Richard repeatedly on the necessity of "keeping the family together." It seemed to be her specialty. Keeping the family together was all that she could see. Evidently she too was familiar with the born again experience and the havoc it could wreak on a normal family's life.

Richard thought it was better to be "born again" than labeled crazy. At least, he thought, you could evidently be born again while living a normal life and not have to hide one life inside another as he was finding necessary in order to keep his marriage together.

So it was that on the first Sunday morning following their arrival back home, Richard and Celeste found themselves at First Baptist in a Sunday school class for born again adult believers. Richard was subdued, content it seemed to be among those who presumably understood him from the inside out, having had their own born again experience. Celeste was there against her better judgment, doing what she thought necessary to keep the family together.

The first Sunday, the Baptist doctor personally led them though a serpentine maze of hidden hallways and stairs deep in the bowels of the large old church building. When they arrived at the classroom he had chosen for them, he introduced them to the teacher, a friend, who like him was an older gentleman and a lifetime Baptist.

Celeste soon understood that the so-called Bible study teacher was there primarily to teach proper Baptist doctrine and guard against heresies. Richard didn't know it yet but the fire burning within him was a substantial source of Baptist heresy. Indeed, in time, he would come to know himself as the proverbial loose cannon on the deck of the ship of Christianity.

The teacher was particularly outspoken about his belief in the rapture, which he was fond of saying would be sudden and might happen at any moment. This teaching was new to Richard and it fascinated him because it seemed to fit in some respects with what he had experienced. He listened intently as this otherwise sane, reputable, politically important man professed what to Celeste seemed an absolutely insane belief in the sudden disappearance of a large number of people—vanished in an instant off the face of the earth.

Richard also thought the literal disappearance of human bodies was highly improbable, yet he did not reject the teaching entirely but instead tried to understand it in a more reasonable way. He remembered Celeste saying that after his experience she missed the man she had married. Well, where was he? It seemed to Richard not unfair to say that he had been "raptured" in that first, sudden experience of otherworldly love. That man was gone.

Celeste, however, was in no mood to be understanding of a

teacher she felt was old enough to recognize an absurdity and should not be irresponsibly teaching nonsense to others. She was continually biting her tongue to avoid airing her views and making a scene. After all, it was still a free country and what people chose to believe in the privacy of their own church was their business. She was a guest and could leave at any time. So she tried to overlook the teacher and his insane teachings while watching Richard for signs of his own insanity reappearing. She was thankful each Sunday for that holy instant when the class was over.

With one notable exception, they faithfully continued their Sunday morning meetings with the born-again class for nearly a year. One Sunday they didn't go to church but took the kids to Disney World and had a great day. Well, you might have thought someone had discovered a prostitute hidden in the preacher's parlor for all the fuss their transgression caused. It was all the gossip when they returned that next Sunday. The teacher made a point of announcing their sin in class so no one would miss it.

For a while, Richard and Celeste were on the same page again. It was a wake-up call for Richard that these born-agains did not share his radical sense of freedom. In hindsight he would come to know the event was strike one against him.

Strike two came a few weeks later when Richard stayed after class to ask the teacher a question regarding the lesson, which was a reading from the book of Revelation. The lesson was a warning about the danger of taking the mark of the beast. Richard's question was about the identity of the beast, old 666. He began his questioning by asking the teacher if he was certain the number of the beast was 666 and not 616 because there was a footnote in his Pilgrim Bible that some ancient manuscripts showed the number might be 616.

The teacher never answered his question but took immediate offence at Richard daring to question his wisdom. He said bluntly, "Richard, this is the second time I've had trouble with you. Now, if it happens again, I'll have to ask you to leave my class."

Strike three came soon after as Richard continued to wake from the illusion he was among others like himself. The class was reading from the Gospel by Luke, a message to the disciples where Jesus is heard to say "Love your enemies, . . . " The request is repeated, and then there followed a statement where Jesus quite plainly stressed the necessity of doing what he says, "And why call ye me, Lord, Lord, and do not the things I say?"

The temptation was too great for Richard to resist. He thought this teaching was clear and inescapable. So he purposefully asked the obvious question in his mind, "Why don't we love our enemies like Jesus asks us to?"

There was an immediate sympathy for his question among the newer members of the class. But before the heresy could really get going, and even before the teacher found his voice to respond, another member of the class, a man well-grounded in Baptist Christian teaching, answered, saying, "That's called 'going on to perfection.' We aren't asked to do that at this time."

Richard was stunned by this response. It indicated that these people were not, as he had thought, simply failing to understand the importance of giving up their own judgment and going all the way in doing as Jesus taught. The response showed that someone responsible for formulating Baptist doctrine had in fact seriously considered Jesus' command and found a way to avoid doing it. The darkness had been institutionalized.

Rejection of doing as Jesus taught, at least for this present time, had apparently become official Baptist doctrine. Richard had never heard of the teaching of "going on to perfection" and knew nothing of the reason for saying there was an acceptable time to pursue it. In order to be a good Baptist, one needed only to confess that Jesus was Lord and profess to love him. At this time, it was not necessary to do as he commanded.

The darkness in this approach was too great for Richard to see through and without knowing the source of this unknown teaching he was unprepared to confront it directly. The teacher finally found his voice and ended the discussion by requesting Richard see him after class.

It was strike three and Richard was out. The teacher had apparently exhausted, at two, the number of times he was willing to forgive. Richard saw it fell far short of the seven times seventy times Jesus had said were necessary to enter the kingdom of God.

Celeste was overjoyed that Richard no longer felt himself one with the Baptist born-agains. Perhaps now, she thought, he would be normal again and pay more attention to her and the family.

Their friend, the doctor who had baptized Richard in the river, was disappointed in their decision. He told them about the Baptist teaching of the "priesthood of the believer," which apparently meant that they were free to believe what seemed right to them as long as it was based on the Bible. He said that he personally disagreed with much of what the Baptist preacher taught on Sunday mornings. He tried to get them interested in another class and another teacher.

Richard had learned much about Christianity and Baptist Christians in particular in his year spent with them. But now he was ready to move on in search of a church home more suited to him. He was looking for people who had been radically transformed, instilled with a reverence for life, born-again, raptured, whatever, through doing the radical teaching of Jesus.

* * *

In the second year after his big experience, Richard began visiting another Baptist church. Celeste chose not to go with her husband, saying that she'd had enough Sunday school to last the rest of her life.

The Seventh Heaven Baptist church was different from the First Baptist in many ways. It was a small church that had been in existence at the same location for more than a hundred years. And even though it sat just a stone's throw beyond the front door of the Catholic Basilica of St. Paul, the largest church building in town, it was not well known.

The church members were few in number but faithful in attendance. They were mostly older and many were descendants of the church founders. They had been born into their faith and had been loyally supporting their church all their lives. Richard's attendance, each time he came, was an event and was welcomed as a positive sign that the old church wasn't dead yet. His Sunday school class was taught by a middle-aged husband and wife team who were helpful and harmless. Sometimes Richard was the only student, with never more than three or four attending.

Richard was attracted to the church because of its distinctive belief in the importance of keeping the seventh day Sabbath. Their worship service and Sunday school was held on Saturday rather than Sunday. It wasn't that the day of the week was important to Richard because he knew next to nothing about the controversy. But he thought that a church that would go contrary to the established practice in what seemed a small matter, just to be true to the Bible, might also try to follow Jesus' teachings more closely.

The people in the church were nonjudgmental about Richard's experience and accepted it as an ongoing work of the spirit with which they should not interfere. There was no talk about the importance of being born again at Seventh Heaven as there had been at First Baptist. Richard made friends with an older gentleman, a retired minister, who helped him learn the proper use of a Bible concordance so he could do his own Bible research. This small friendly church was good for Richard; it calmed him down a bit by being a safe place where he could freely share his feelings.

At home it was getting impossible to speak openly about God within hearing distance of Celeste. She became upset every time the subject came up, and Richard was careful not to unnecessarily offend her. His experience had changed him in many ways and some of them were very troubling to Celeste. For one thing, his ambition was gone. He was no longer interested in working hard and getting ahead. He had been there and done that. They had enough money and investments, he told her, that he didn't feel the need to work so hard as before. This disturbed Celeste and she began to talk about going back to work herself, resuming her career as a school teacher. Richard assured her that this was not necessary. They had enough, he said, to live comfortably and take care of the kids. Although she realized they were better off than many others, Celeste didn't understand how it was possible for anyone to say they had enough money. Nobody ever had enough money. Richard's life clearly had a different focus. She didn't understand it and that made her anxious about their future.

Richard and Celeste were sometimes unexpectedly at odds over small things. Each spring Celeste had to do battle with Richard to get him to mow the lawn for the first time. The spring flowers were flourishing. The bright yellow dandelions, deep blue Jacob's tears, thistle blossoms and other flowers covered the lawn, and Richard insisted it would be an unnecessary massacre of the innocents to mow them down in full bloom. He resisted mightily, making Celeste's life miserable for a week or two each year.

When a friend of Richard's, a builder like himself who also was a preacher with a small church, came by for a visit and saw their situation he told them they were unequally yoked together. Truer words were never spoken. However, he offered no solution to the problem. They had been equally yoked when they were married. But now the change in Richard brought on by the sudden intervention of his faith in Jesus' words had come between them. They were stuck with each other, held together by the seriousness in which they had taken their marriage vows.

Richard's life was slowly being taken over by his concern with God and religion. This worried Celeste greatly but there was little she could do. Richard told her to think of his endless reading of books as his all-consuming hobby. He said her situation was no worse than those wives who were "golf widows," or whose husbands were workaholics. Celeste was not pleased with this comparison. She missed the man she had married and wanted him back.

Her concern was relieved somewhat when fate intervened. A small notice in the local newspaper said the junior college was offering classes for adult students. Among those listed was one on world religions. Celeste brought the class to Richard's attention, thinking it would be far better for him to spend his time in a classroom than to be absorbed in private reading and attending church meetings where who knows what sort of superstitious nonsense was taught.

Richard enrolled in the World Religions course and found it was being taught that semester not by the usual college professor, but by a local rabbi. The rabbi, he discovered, taught such courses as part of his liberal Jewish congregation's community outreach program. Meeting each week with the rabbi was Richard's first prolonged exposure to someone of the Jewish faith. The rabbi seemed to be a very reasonable person. The way he made sense of difficult religious concepts was much like the simple straightforward way Richard had learned to think working with his father growing up on the farm in Indiana. The rabbi seemed more like a member of his family than any Christian he had yet known.

Christians he had known seemed to have their own way of thinking. It was a way that Richard didn't always understand or appreciate. He was only ten the first time this fact came to his attention. The family had just moved to the farm from the suburbs of Indianapolis. His father said he could have a BB gun, but he would have to earn the money to buy it himself.

He signed up with a mail order company to sell packets of their All-American flower and vegetable seeds in order to earn prizes, one of which was the coveted BB gun. Sales were going slow when he happened to knock on the Sunday school lady's door. She was called the Sunday school lady because she taught Sunday school at the local Methodist Church and each week she would go around and pick up a bunch of kids and take them to the church. Well, Richard was happy when she bought a large order of seeds, nearly enough so he could get that BB gun. But after the sale was made and he was about to leave, she said, "Now you have to go to Sunday school with me for the next three Sundays." That conclusion didn't follow logically at all in ten-year-old Richard's mind. That hadn't been part of their agreement. He was confused but believed the woman and went with her to Sunday school as she said he "had to." But he always believed that the Sunday school lady, who was an adult and a Christian, had tricked him and treated him unfairly.

Richard came away from the World Religions course believing that Christianity was out of step with both Judaism and Islam with respect to its understanding of the nature of God. Both of these other major religions held decisively to the idea that God was One. Judaism declared, "Hear, O Israel, the Lord your God is One." And Islam was even more pointed in its declaration, insisting that "There is no God but Allah," and "God has no Son."

Only Christianity had the confusing, hard to understand teaching of the Trinity, which said that God was indeed One, while yet being comprised of three distinct persons. It did not compute logically for Richard. He thought it was a bit like wanting to have your cake and eat it too. It was a mystery that apparently required the Christian way of thinking to accept. His father and the rabbi were among those he knew who did not accept it.

A second point of disagreement among the three religions, in which Christianity was again the odd man out, was in how they viewed the person of Jesus. Richard was surprised to learn that Islam accepted Jesus as a prophet though a lesser one than their Muhammad. Judaism did not have much to say about Jesus except to refuse to accept him as their long awaited Messiah who they expected to come in the flesh. It was unthinkable in Judaism that a man could be also God.

In sharp difference to these two human responses to the question of who Jesus was, Richard learned that Christianity taught that Jesus had a dual nature; he was uniquely one hundred percent God and one hundred percent man. Again, this belief, like that of the Trinity, was amazing, difficult to explain, and hard to understand.

Reflecting on these two fantastic and confusing beliefs, Richard saw that the first—belief in a three-in-one God—rested logically on the second belief in a dual nature of the man Jesus. For if it was accepted that this one man was also God, then it was at least logical that the strict oneness of God would have to be broken and reworked somehow to allow him to be a part of that oneness.

It was apparent then to Richard that the Christian belief in a dual nature of Jesus was the fundamental point of disagreement. This belief, which he learned was not explicitly stated in the Bible, was the source of confusion and the main thing standing in the way of an important theological sameness that might hold a promise for peace among the three major world religions.

Richard, of course, realized that these two essential but non-biblical teachings that made Christianity what it was had played no part in his experience.

> *Richard is absolutely going down the right path. He is a product of his time and his is the age of reason. He has been brought, first through his personal Bible study with Christians and then through his classroom study of Christianity in comparison with other religions, into close personal and intellectual contact with what seems to him to be the basic problem leading to the lack of peace in the world. Christianity simply doesn't make good logical sense. He isn't the first to notice this, of course, but his experience of the power available for the transformation of human nature, through following*

Jesus' teaching has furnished him with the right stuff to stay with the problem until it is resolved. He clearly sees the most logical way for him to accomplish his goal is to root out the source of the logical problem holding Christianity back from being all it could be. He will be on his own now for a while. I can run interference for him and open doors when he needs them to open, but it will be a while before he will reach an impasse in his work that will cause him to open his mind to me again in complete willingness to hear my voice.

Making sense of things is Richard's way of dealing with problems. He understands the process of trouble shooting and his life on the farm and his training as a civil engineer has endowed him with the personal characteristics, determination and perseverance, to succeed in solving this problem as he has with others. Of course, the logical problem of Christianity was different from any he has encountered before. It was a human problem for one thing and the subject matter was unfamiliar, but Richard had confidence that when he was able to get to the heart of the matter he would find it was just a question of some misunderstanding standing in the place of truth.

Richard had naturally accepted Jesus as being only one thing, a man, and a prophet who spoke the words of God — powerful words that when accepted as true surprised Richard with a life-saving experience of the Reality of Love.

I know Richard will always remember these things about Jesus, and I know he will continue to search until he has found the mistakes responsible for the present theological nonsense he has encountered. He knows that until this is accomplished he can't convince people to take the leap of faith necessary to jump the chasm that separates this world from the true world of his Vision. He has already shown me he can love his enemies and go the second mile, and I know he will perfect these abilities as he works his way through the maze in which time and circumstance have hidden Jesus' truth. Richard is the One, all right. He's a lover and a thinker; the Father has done the right thing in choosing to set him free in the world. He will not return to his newfound home alone.

Looking for a way to make his personal peace with the Christian teachings, Richard considered that perhaps the unreasonable belief of Jesus being one hundred percent man and one hundred percent God might ultimately prove to be true but that maybe it was just too great a formula to be understood all at once. Maybe it was like the scientific theory of the nature of light which he knew treats light as either a distinct particle or a continuous wave but never both at once.

He knew it was certainly beyond his own straightforward way of understanding to say that Jesus was two different things at the same time. And maybe it was beyond human understanding, in which case it would be necessary to choose, at any given time, how to relate to Jesus. He could be accepted as a man, a prophet who spoke the words of God demanding obedience to love. Or he could be seen as God and made an object of worship. But to try and do both at the same time looked to Richard to be clearly impractical, perhaps a form of madness and certainly a source of great religious confusion.

One thing at least seemed certain, the accepted formula of Jesus having been one hundred percent man and one hundred percent God seemed way overbalanced in the one hundred percent God direction. There seemed no lack of people willing to worship a Jesus who was fully God, while precious few were found willing to hear his advice on loving their enemies. Realizing his experience had come from following a human Jesus, Richard began to dream that maybe it was in his power to work toward developing the one hundred percent man side of the Jesus equation.

* * *

Beyond the two Christian theological confusions, the teachings of the three in one God and the two in one Jesus, Richard was troubled by another confusion that was more personal in nature and that had begun with his other-worldly experience.

Unlike the two theological confusions which he knew were shared by many others, he seemed alone in his new understanding of what he was. His sense of self had shifted during the experience in sympathy with the reality he found there, and it had not shifted back. Richard was sure that it never would. He believed that it was a permanent change. He had not yet come to realize how great this confusion about his personal identity was. The nature and extent of it was brought into clear focus over a years' time, beginning with a chance event that occurred on a beautiful spring day in the third year following the experience.

Richard was his own boss and could choose how he spent his time. More and more he chose to spend less time on the job watching over sub-contractors and more time in libraries pursuing his interest in religion. As far as Celeste knew he was still working long days building houses for sale. It was on one of these recesses away from a construction site that Richard happened to pass through the front door of the City of New Smyrna Beach public library where he unexpectedly ran literally into a creative display of poetry.

To entice readers, the library staff had transformed the entrance hall of the library into a sort of art gallery for poetry. They had created attractive freestanding displays on which they posted information on poets from all nations and times, together with examples of their work. It was one of these exhibits that unexpectedly greeted Richard that fateful spring day.

There on a wall directly in front of him as he walked through the front door—and exactly at his eye level—was a verse of poetry he found impossible to ignore. It was titled To A Skylark and was accompanied by a picture of a small bird that reminded Richard of the Meadowlark he knew from his days on the farm in Indiana. The exhibit said an English poet, Percy Bysshe Shelley, who lived from 1792 to 1822, had written the poem in 1820—two years before he died by drowning.

"Teach me, half the gladness thy brain must know," Shelley wrote, commanding the small bird to share with him what compelled it to sing so beautifully and freely. Then the poet continued, "Such harmonious madness from my lips would flow."

Richard was immediately struck by the words, "harmonious madness." He read the words again excitedly and very nearly out loud, in a sudden recognition of the aptness of the phrase for describing what was inside him, straining to be released.

Richard was struggling still, as he had been struggling three years now since his first attempt to find the right words to describe the experience. That first attempt had ended in Celeste's disastrous misunderstanding when he blurted out that he loved everybody the same, that he loved the neighbor lady the same as her. He was struggling to find words to express the inexpressible. It was apparent to him that he had to find a way to give effective voice to the reality he knew to be true and which he believed was the answer to everything. That God was real, was for him, the answer to all problems great and small—personal, national, even international.

"Harmonious madness," he loved the sound of it. The two words seemed to perfectly combine his growing suspicion that, even if he were able to find words to advance a perfectly reasonable harmonious exposition of what he knew to be true, it would still appear to be madness. There was a kind of healing, a relief in realizing this. No matter how well he could present his evidence, it would always be the responsibility of the reader to hear it and give it credibility, or not. Communication was a two-way street and at best, he could take it only part way. He could not compel the hearer to believe, as he had unwittingly been trying to do. He could only put it out there and let the response be whatever the hearer was ready and willing to do.

Communication of his truth would require him to freely express his madness. Until now he had been trying self defensively to hide his insanity in more normal, acceptable forms of speech. Those who heard his harmonic madness must be free to embrace it with sympathetic understanding or dismiss it with perplexity and perhaps even ridicule.

In the days, weeks, and months that followed, words came to him and aligned themselves with other words in a rhythmic, rhyming fashion that was enjoyable and fed on itself, calling forth other words which all together served to express ideas which had previously escaped expression. The theme soon became plain. Richard's private confusion was harmonious madness about Creation.

He called his first poem A Trip to The Library. It was a straightforward exposition of what had happened that day.

A TRIP TO THE LIBRARY

There on a wall in front of me,
was this verse of poetry:
Look at this, I said in time,
these words, they do rhyme.

"Teach me half the gladness,
thy brain must know.
Such harmonious madness,
from my lips would flow.

The world should listen then,
as I am listening now."

Harmonious madness! I said with glee.
That's what's inside of me!

I feel as though I have been taught.
And now it is as though I ought
To let it flow,
That which I at once did know.

Such harmonious madness as you will see,
Has been bottled up inside of me.
That the world will listen, I'm not sure,
Using madness as a lure?

Richard read other poems by other poets but nothing inspired him like the words "harmonious madness" had done. Something about the rhythm and rhyming felt just right for him. His readings showed him that madness was common in the lives of many poets. And he found a definition of poetry that fit his interest. Perhaps not surprisingly it too was by the English poet Shelley.

"Poetry is the record of the best and happiest moments of the happiest and best minds."

— Percy Bysshe Shelley, 1792-1822, English poet

The second poem was longer, a record of his experience, which was definitely the best and happiest moment of his mind. It was by far his best attempt to describe the Love that had so captivated him. He called it The Vision.

THE VISION

"Love is Real," I'm here to say.
What I have seen won't go away.
I stood before Love Divine.
So immensely strong, near lost my mind.
What a being! Love so pure!
Free the captives? That's for sure!
Love enough to go around,
As I could see, it knew no bounds.
No expert I, on Love at all,
Yet unlike any I recall.
Like a strong magnetic force,
But works on such as we of course.
The Joy I felt was utter bliss.
"Myself," I said, "More of this."
Could not be more in intensity,
The more I sought was eternity.
It was a Vision in my mind's eye.
Yet, it was Real, this world the lie.
Not a dream, wasn't night,
Sitting still, no wish to fight,
Caught me quite by surprise,
Looking up were my eyes.
My brain controlled for just a while,
Not for a billion, would I touch that dial,
I was enraptured, gone was strife,
Loved all others as my life.
A window opened, just for me,
A window through which I could see – Reality!
It's been so long, and still I know,
Love is Real, and that is so.

The Vision went on for two pages and Richard was pleased with it, though it never seemed to find a final form and was constantly being reworked. In time there came a Vision – Part Two in which the identity confusion that was only hinted at before came into sharper focus. It began:

How did I warrant this, unbridled grace
To stand before His holy face?
I was there, right time, right place;
Yet there is more to win this race.

It became clear that the "race" in the stanza's last line was the human race. For Richard the human race, the striving to get ahead, was over. And in this poem the start of a radical reinterpretation of the biblical creation story on Richard's own authority was clearly seen.

That God is Love has been said before,
But have they come from Love's door?
Know that He is, and be set free
From all who practice hypocrisy.
Know what you are, it's not what you think.
Like God created, does not stink.
Dare to be just what you are,
Knowing this will take you far.
God is Love and Wisdom, two.
Love is He and Wisdom She.
She turns you right who have gone wrong.
Then the Love above, He comes on strong.

There were many other poems written in that third year. There were short ones like; Humanist, Here and Now, Prophets, Dream Come True, Changed, Please Answer Me, A Live One. And there were longer ones including; Christians, Nothingness, Nobody, Being Human and The Body Barrier. The longest one was a six-page instructive writing called The Way.

Richard's identity confusion was nakedly displayed in *The Body Barrier*.

In love with the body, I know that you are.
You love it more dearly than your house or your car.
You love it so much, you think it is you.
By love you are blinded. Oh, how to get through?
Think of your body, not you, but an 'it.'
You God created, like him you are.
The body evoluted from bits of a star.

I draw no pleasure from flesh or from bone.
All that I want is to get my self home.

I do not live here and neither do you.
Let us see clearly, with this world be through.

And in *On Being Human* he openly attacked the idea of being human.

Buddha has told us, I think it's no lie:
"All composite bodies are destined to die."

Human is composed of matters two,
Body and Spirit—just which are you?

To be human is to suffer much. You pass through time,
Live and die, suffer, suffer, along the way.

You wish to live, always be young,
Yet these are not what a human becomes.

We have been deceived, you and I,
Led to believe we live and die,

While all the while it is not so.
Being human, it's the wrong way to go.

Richard was ready when again a small notice in the newspaper seemed to show the way forward. It was a call for entries in a local poetry contest. The winners were to be awarded a weeklong study with a recognized poet. The entry rules called for the submission of twenty-nine pages of original work. Richard thought this was excessive but found that if he included everything he had written he had twenty-nine pages. He pulled it all together and sent off the required six copies of everything.

He was reluctant to share the one-page poem Christians because he believed it might easily be misinterpreted as a mean-spirited attack on those blind guides who continued to teach that God created human beings. Yet it was needed to meet the twenty-nine page requirement and so it appeared to him fated that it be included.

CHRISTIANS

Such a worthless bunch,
As I surely know, even if by hunch.
A self-righteous group – better than we.
Even though God has said, "I hate hypocrisy."
"We are God's people."
That's what they say,
"And all of you will be blown away."

He entered the competition, but his call to greatness as a poet never came. Later, Celeste showed him another newspaper notice saying, "O Holy One, isn't this something you're interested in?"

It was an announcement of a public reading of the winning entries for the poetry contest. Richard went to hear what sort of poetry had been favored over his.

The readings began and after hearing just a few lines, which spoke lovingly without rhyme of the magnificence to be found in the color of autumn leaves and the beauty of an evening sunset, Richard saw the truth. Earth-bound poetry had won the day.

Of course! How had he been so blind? Not all poets were given to madness. And these poets were quite apparently aggressively addicted to being human. It was simple, really. Human beings believed themselves earth-bound creatures and so they dearly loved earth-bound poetry. Their kind would not be won over easily by a few rhyming words telling them that what they loved and what they wanted to be was not the truth. Reaching them would require something more substantial.

His recognition as a nobody-genius, savior of the human race from itself, would have to wait for another day and another way.

Celeste was sensitive to his mood when he returned home. "What's the matter?" she asked.

"Oh nothing," he said. Then he added, "I guess the impossible is going to take a bit longer than even I thought."

Celeste sighed.

In the days that followed, Richard accepted the rejection of his poems as evidence that it was not his destiny to be a poet. He was disappointed of course, but took encouragement in the fact that he had boldly submitted his ideas to public view and no one had come in response to take him away, saying he was crazy. This strengthened his determination to persevere in his quest to find an effective way to share his truth. He could only trust that another form of expression would present itself when the time was right and he was ready.

He was concerned, however, that his poems were ahead of their time and would be misunderstood. Of special concern was his poem regarding Christians. He knew its harsh words were born of his frustration in not finding any Christians who would follow Jesus into "love your enemies" territory. He had not really meant to condemn the whole Christian religion. His mission, as he now understood it, was to reform Christianity by inspiring it to follow Jesus more closely.

Chapter Seven

A NEW BEGINNING

Once again it was Celeste who, sensitive to my leading, showed Richard the way to a new beginning when the door unceremoniously closed on his small dream of being a famous poet.

Richard was intent on visiting every sort of church in the area in order to learn something of their distinctive beliefs. He was having a hard time understanding that otherwise sane everyday people actually held fantastic and unreasonable beliefs such as the rapture and the incarnation. He felt that perhaps he was missing something that everyone but him knew.

One Sunday morning Celeste was suddenly stricken with a feeling of dread about a small store-front church Richard had chosen to visit that day. Following her intuition, she showed up at the small church during the service and, making only a minor disturbance, managed to persuade her husband to return home with her. She then suggested that he look for another college course in religion somewhere.

Following her suggestion, Richard learned that the friendly Rabbi who had been his teacher for the *World Religions* class also taught classes on the Bible at a local private college. It seemed a good place to begin again.

Once Celeste had pointed Richard toward the academic study of religion there was no holding him back. He had learned to be at home in the classroom and in libraries through the years he had spent in college and graduate school.

He took course after course at the local historically black college, gathering information about various aspects of Christianity. He found the multi-volume classical commentaries on the Bible in the library and was amazed at the time and effort that must have gone into producing them. There were courses on the life of Jesus and the life of Paul, the apostles, the gospels and even a course on the highly symbolic book of Revelation.

Richard wasn't simply gathering knowledge for its own sake, there was a method to his madness. During his and Celeste's year with the First Baptist Church, he had learned firsthand the particular points of theology that were leading Christians to believe the proper response to Jesus was to worship him in place of actually following his teaching.

Now he was keeping an eye and ear out for anything which might be the source of the misunderstanding.

He supplemented his college course work with outside reading and soon learned of the ongoing quest for the historical Jesus. The quest was famously written about by Albert Schweitzer and although its motivation was different, it was undeniably closely allied with his own quest for a one hundred percent human Jesus. Schweitzer had concluded there was not enough information from the Bible and other sources to allow the historical Jesus ever being found. Schweitzer was a recognized genius yet his conclusion had not stopped others from continuing the quest. Richard read that Schweitzer had chosen not to search in one of the four gospels for his historical Jesus and thought it was a surprising decision. He filed the fact away in his memory.

There were other books that contributed to Richard's growing store of facts regarding the probable life and times of an historical human Jesus. One of these was by a Jewish author and offered a particularly Jewish understanding of the early years of Christianity. Another author writing on the history of events following Jesus' death was certain there had been a protracted struggle between two competing groups holding incompatible views of who he had been. The conflict had lasted for maybe four hundred years, he believed, before some great event had caused the distinctive Christian beliefs to win out.

Richard continued to read Christian literature, books and other articles wherever they were found, even illustrated missionary tracts found in restrooms and other unexpected places sometimes gave a new slant on something already known. In time he came to notice how the fourth gospel was often referenced in defense of Jesus being one hundred percent God. Often it was the only gospel source mentioned. Other scriptural support for the troublesome belief came from the writings of the late arriving apostle Paul.

Once noticed, the importance of John's gospel to the essential Christian belief became clearly visible. John's gospel was known as the "most beloved" gospel. Virtually every commentary devoted a few sentences or a full paragraph to render homage to the exalted understanding of Jesus found there. Seeing this, Richard recalled Schweitzer's choosing not to include John's gospel in his quest for the historical Jesus and wondered about the wisdom in that decision.

And it wasn't only in the gospel generally where Christian devotion was focused, it was in the prologue particularly. The important prologue to John's gospel was where the WORD of God, ever present with God in the beginning, was equated with Jesus. In John's prologue Jesus' existence was pushed back beyond time to eternity. There was nothing else like this in all of Christian scripture. Richard saw this unsupported, soaring declaration was why Christians loved John's gospel.

Richard's extra-curricular reading and research took on a sharper focus following his discovery of the importance of the fourth gospel and especially its prologue in Christian beliefs. Outside the classroom he was surprised to learn the prologue, in the opinion of several scholars, had been an early Christian hymn added onto an earlier version of John's gospel. This widely recognized fact was troubling to Richard, who thought it dishonest. It reminded him of the deceptive practice of the cowbird in Indiana that laid its oversize eggs in other birds' nests for them to hatch and raise believing they were their own kind.

The experts, however, were not concerned. They assumed the earlier writing was also Christian. To them the cowbird had simply laid its egg in another cowbird's nest and they saw no harm in that.

Chapter Eight

MAKING A DIFFERENCE — IN GREEK

"He winked. His eyes twinkled. 'All right, forget what I've said. But for God's sake, learn to look beneath the surface,' he said. 'come out of the fog, young man. And remember, you don't have to be a complete fool in order to succeed. Play the game, but don't believe in it—that much you owe yourself. Even if it lands you in a strait jacket or a padded cell. Play the game, but play it your own way—part of the time at least. Play the game, but raise the ante, my boy. Learn how it operates, learn how you operate – I wish I had time to tell you only a fragment. We're an ass-backward people though. You might even beat the game. It's really a very crude affair. Really Pre-Renaissance – and that game has been analyzed, put down in books. But down here they've forgotten to take care of the books and that's your opportunity. You're hidden right out in the open – that is you would be if you only realized it. They wouldn't see you because they don't expect you to know anything, since they believe they've taken care of that. . . ."

— Ralph Ellison, *Invisible Man*, 1947

A door opened for Richard to take his understanding of New Testament scripture to another level when Dr. Sane, head of the religion department at the small local college, came out of semi-retirement to again offer his two-year study of Biblical Greek. I reminded Richard of how the Rabbi who had taught his World Religions class had said that anyone wanting to make a difference in how scripture was interpreted had to work in the original language. For the Old Testament that language was Hebrew but for the New Testament and the Gospel of John the required language was Greek.

My reminder was hardly needed, Richard signed up for the new challenge at the earliest opportunity. He was excited and fully expected that this knowledge would be an important next step in his search to find a way of overcoming the Christian confusion deterring others from following Jesus' powerful "love your enemies" commandment that had set him free.

After three semesters of Greek study Richard found the source of the Christian muddle. It was a mis-translation of a verse at the beginning of John's gospel. It appeared that when the Christian hymn had been attached, the opening line of the early gospel, verse six, was reinterpreted as being idiomatic, when in fact it was not. It was a great satisfaction for Richard to have found the truth he sought. Yet it was near impossible to share it because the Greek language was, well, Greek to nearly everyone. The devil was alive and well it seemed, living in John 1:6b, the second part of the sixth verse of chapter one of the fourth gospel.

The explanation required an open mind, together with knowledge of the rules of Greek grammar. Richard would always remember how his Greek professor, who was also a committed Christian, had triumphantly exclaimed, "It's idiomatic," as he struggled in class to translate literally the three Greek words of the second part of the verse. Later, Richard saw how his intelligent, educated professor had only repeated an error made by others. The professor was unable to hear Richard's reasonable untangling of the confusion surrounding the important verse. It took some time before he realized the professor's commitment to Christian doctrine had closed his mind to the possibility of the new understanding.

Untangling the confusion had required an understanding of the ways mistakes have been known to enter into scripture. The particular type of error causing confusion in the interpretation of verse six was something called "dittography." Whenever a repetition of letters was noticed by a copyist there was a possibility of an unwarranted repetition—the error of dittography—having crept into the text. Of course it was always possible that the repetition of letters was purposeful and not an error. An unnecessary "correction" of the last two Greek letters of verse six to avoid a repetition, a supposed error of dittography, with the first two letters of verse seven was found to be the problem. It was an ancient typo.

The two Greek letters in question were omicron and upsilon – 'o' and 'u'. The "ou" constituted a possessive case ending on the proper name John. Richard saw these two letters were vital for conveying the idea the original author of the gospel had wanted to express. This original idea was lost in translation when someone at some time chose to "correct" what appeared to be an error of repeating letters – ouou. The omicron and upsilon were replaced by two other letters, eta and sigma, which when transliterated read – ace. The "ace" ending was a subject or direct object case ending. Its use introduced problems in the Greek grammar. With the original two letters restored, verse six obeyed the laws of Greek grammar and made sense. It then read: *There was a man sent from God whose name was given by John.* With the eta and sigma letters in place the verse was grammatically inconsistent. The experts declared it "idiomatic" and interpreted it to say: *There was a man sent from God whose name was John.* The thought of the original author was lost. And in the darkness of that lost translation Christianity had grown and flourished.

Richard reflected on how easy it was now for him to speak about the repetition of letters while remembering the difficulty he had in finding what was now obvious.

He had believed fully in the importance of his discovery of an error being made in translation but he continued to search for an understanding of how the shift in the identity of John's "man sent from God" might have taken place. He was suspicious of the simplicity of what he had found. He asked himself how it could be possible that his alternate translation of John 1:6 had not been discovered previously. He was ambiguous about sharing what he knew, fearing it was possible that he had simply rediscovered what had previously been known and widely rejected for some as yet unknown reason. He was not a theologian and was afraid that without a fuller understanding of how the error was made, his discovery would be rejected and he would again feel the disappointment in being thought insane. He was cautious about what to do.

> *I knew Richard would not commit himself to stepping forward into the world alone. He would wait until he knew the time was right and that would require his receiving a clear message that it was time to act. In fact there was yet more for Richard to discover. Instead of a message to go now, I was able to emphasize a line from another song from his past. "Gonna wait 'til the midnight hour!" He turned it over and over in his mind, seeking to remember the song it came from. Finally it dawned on him that it might be a message to wait. It made good sense. His was a small light. It would go unnoticed in the light of day. When the time was right, both he and the world would be ready and doors would open effortlessly. His doubts would evaporate and nothing would stand in his way. Richard got the message—his time had clearly not yet come. I reminded him of the book he dreamed of one day writing with the expectation it would open his way into the world. He responded thinking that perhaps what he had learned was only a chapter, maybe there was yet more to come. He resolved to wait, continuing to study until a clear message was received. His was the age of reason, he thought. The age of making claims of revealed knowledge and giving encouragement to act on faith alone was over. He needed more facts.*

In time, Richard's reading brought him to several sources that helped him understand how it was possible that his reinterpretation of John 1:6 could have escaped being seen. He learned that the earliest Greek manuscripts which might have contained his "of John" reading were gone, never to be found. He dreamed of their showing up someday but believed it would take an act of God, which for him was not out of the question.

A book came into his life that seemed to have been written just for him. It was a layman's guide to the New Testament text. The book had many photocopied pages of old handwritten New Testament text, which immediately caught his attention. He had long known from his reading that the oldest text was written in a continuous stream of capital Greek letters, called uncials, with no punctuation; but to actually see this with all its human variety and imperfections was a new thing. He was surprised and pleased to see that several of the example sheets were reproductions of the first page of the Gospel of John that included verse six.

Richard remembered now how it had taken patience to search the long lines of continuous Greek uncial letters for those three most important words, written in continuous upper-case Greek letters: ONOMAAYTWIWANNHS. He was surprised how unfamiliar the uncial, capital, Greek letters were. He was forced to go back to page one of his Greek textbook in order to review them. All his work with Dr. Sane had used the smaller letters, the miniscules.

When the words were at last found he had been surprised to find his subject three-word phrase seemed on first sight to be mysteriously placed between two OYs. The mystery was soon solved as he relearned that what appeared to be a capital letter Y was really the Greek upper-case, uncial, letter “u.” The seeming enigmatic Yiddish word “OY” following the word John was in reality the first two letters of the following Greek word.

Reading the layman’s guide had informed him about the process of copying the texts and the various ways in which errors could be made—both unintentionally and, it seemed to him, in misguided efforts to align the text with prevailing orthodoxy.

Eventually, he had come across a review of a one-man translation of the New Testament into English that had set a goal of making a literal translation while maintaining the word order of the original Greek—similar to what he had tried to do in Dr. Sane’s class before being told to accept the phrase as idiom. The book review contained a statement of the author’s guiding principle which excited him. The author’s “constant aim” for his translations, he said, “has been to suppress any tendency to think that I know precisely and unmistakably, here toward the end of the twentieth century, what my originals “meant to say” – linguistically or theologically . . .”

The review contained an example, which perhaps by chance, was Richard’s John 1:6 passage. His heart leapt when he saw a rendering closer to his own than he had seen anywhere before:

"**Came a man sent from God, John by name**." Only one small change was needed to make it correspond to his exactly and that change involved, of all things, word order.

Only another literalist, Richard supposed, someone like himself, with an Interlinear New Testament close at hand, would have noticed that the translator did not, himself, adhere strictly to his ideal of preserving the original word order of the Greek in translating John 1:6. Was he unable, in this instance, to bring himself to do it?

Richard saw that correcting the translation to reflect exact word order yields a statement which for many committed Christians is unthinkable: **"Came a man sent from God, name by John."** There it was, a translation that was as close as Richard was going to get in support of his position. He believed his study had revealed a clear and reasonable possibility: his radical alternative reading might be the thought the original author had intended to write.

But this intelligent educated Christian, earnestly seeking to understand the text in a new way, had not been able to see it and had actually violated his own self-imposed rule of maintaining original word order *to avoid seeing it*. Richard knew it was said you could bring a horse to water but you couldn't force him to drink. Was it also true that you could bring a Christian face to face with the truth but you couldn't force him to see it? Were human beings somehow constructed so as to be unable to see a truth they thought would destroy them? After all if this man has accepted Jesus as his personal savior, his life depended on Jesus being God. For him to entertain the thought that Jesus was simply a man, even a man sent from God, was impossible.

The three small words of John 1:6b were, in his estimation, the three most important words in the world, not because of what they were thought to say, but because of what they could reasonably be understood to mean and the importance of that heretical meaning to a possible reformation of Christianity which could bring it into peaceful conformity with Judaism and Islam. Yet the new reading was based only on a few words of the established text and the rules of Greek grammar.

Though he greatly preferred his understanding, he had to admit the existing reading was also possible. After all it was the reading found in every Bible ever printed; it was the accepted reading and Christianity and the world were what they were because of it.

Richard saw his word study had gone as far as it could. It had revealed significant internal evidence supporting his understanding. But it had raised some questions too. Questions that had caused him to wonder if the proposed change in meaning of John 1:6 had taken place innocently over time or if something more overt and historical had forced it to take place suddenly and purposefully. He had a suspicion that something dishonest had taken place to cause the shift in name from Jesus to John. He was beginning to smell a rat.

I saw his thoughts as he contemplated the resistance he would have encountered if he had gone off into the world acting only on faith and asking Christians to just believe on his word as revealed truth that their understanding of scripture was wrong. It would have been an impossible task. He saw now even if he were armed with limitless unquestionable facts, the deceiver had protected the Christian mind against the entrance of any new truth.

Instead of this being a discouragement to him, I was pleased when he logically turned and asked himself, who then, if not for Christians, was the truth he was uncovering intended to reach?

This uncertainty allowed me to remind him of what he had written on his desk pad immediately upon seeming to return to his still warm body from his experience of the world of Love. He remembered there was a title: ***The Oneness of God*** *and then there was something more. It was something awkwardly worded about the book being* ***a guide for uncommitted gentiles who knew there surely was a God****. On this remembering he experienced an emotional release and his mind went in two directions at once. First he wanted to know who were these uncommitted gentiles whose God was named Shirley—his sense of humor was working again—and simultaneously he was filled with thanksgiving for my help while realizing he had forgotten the truth he had learned again and again on that magical trip from Daytona Beach to his home in Indiana.* ***He was not alone****. How could he so easily forget that fact?*

He was like a child it seemed fearing abandonment by those who had given him birth. No, more like a baby who when the mother is out of sight believes she never existed.

At this point in his seeking to solve the mystery of how the error in translation of John 1:6b might reasonably have taken place, he had relaxed in the renewed realization he was not alone.

"I need a break," he had told Celeste, and she was surprised though glad to hear it. She had been conspiring for just such an event. She hadn't approached Richard yet, but her cousin Bob and his wife Sally had asked if she and Richard were interested in going on a trip with them to England. Of course Celeste was immediately on board with the idea and now it seemed Richard was also ready to get away for a few days.

They arrived in England at Heathrow Airport and while deciding what to do first, Richard found an information exhibit that made him feel at home. Sir Malcolm Campbell's home, the exhibit explained, was only a few miles away in the English countryside. Sir Malcolm was a Daytona Beach hometown hero. Richard knew he still held the world's record speed of 276.82 miles per hour set in 1935 on the sand of Daytona Beach. His Bluebird V racecar powered by a Rolls Royce aircraft engine had roared across the very sand where Richard frequently went on early morning walks The car was on exhibit at the Daytona Speedway. This discovery was the first of several surprising findings as the four of them toured the country from London to Edinburgh in Scotland. Bob was on a quest to visit a family cemetery somewhere in the north near the seaside town of Whitby. They rented a car and with Bob driving on the wrong side of the road they were off. First stop London, where they took the traditional double-decker sightseeing bus and visited all the standard tourist places including Westminster Cathedral very near the Big Ben landmark. They stayed overnight and saw a farcical play about a totally blank canvas being hailed by experts as a great masterpiece until the fraud was exposed by someone simply speaking the truth.

Stonehenge, a must see on everyone's agenda, was the first stop of the second day in England and then on to see an excavated Roman bath in the historic town of Bath. They worked their way across the middle country staying a night in Shakespeare's home town on the river Avon, where they watched a production of *A Midsummer Night's Dream*, a story about the chaos resulting from the actions of unseen forces causing an important misunderstanding.

The prestigious Oxford College was found to take its name from its location on a stream of water where Oxen had historically crossed. It was the place where the familiar story *Alice in Wonderland* was written. A small Garage long ago owned by someone named Morris was said to be the beginning of the famous MG automobile—the letters standing simply for Morris' Garage.

A visit to the city of York gave immediate realization that the founders of our own New York City must have first known this place. The name hadn't sprung from nothing. In many ways Richard saw that for an American, a trip to England was like going home for the first time. America's roots were in England, the connection was stronger than he had ever imagined.

North of York, they found the small seaside town of Whitby on the northeast coast of England near the Moors. They were charmed by Whitby, a fishing port and tourist resort which reminded them of Daytona Beach, their own small hometown in the USA. The Moors was a landscape unlike any Richard had ever seen. The extensive area was covered by a type of deep dense vegetation that protected the land from the ravages of the North Sea. He saw what appeared to be a farm implement, an abandoned disc/plow standing ten feet high which he imagined had been used in an unsuccessful attempt to plow under the native vegetation in hope of turning the land to some productive use.

Bob found the family cemetery he had come looking for and tried to imagine the life his ancestors may have lived. Richard knew his own father had made a similar trip to another town in the south of England in search of his own family's roots. In talking with Bob, Richard learned that under the English system the first son traditionally inherited the family home and a second son was thus forced to leave and find his own place in the world. America was historically known to be a place first colonized by many discontented second sons from England.

Edinburg, with its fortress castle and monstrous cannon high on a rocky hill overlooking the city, was fascinating and endlessly historic. They toured the castle and saw the Stone of Destiny. Visiting a second castle at the end of surprisingly named Prince's Street, they relived the history of the legendary Bloody Mary, Queen of Scots.

Bob and Sally left for home from Edinburgh. For Richard and Celeste the final destination on the nearly weeklong tour was Manchester, a big modern city on the western edge of England. Faced with a one-day delay in departure, Richard and Celeste found themselves on a self-guided tour. They came across the Rylands Library during visiting hours, and doors opened in response to a simple declaration that, yes, Richard was a visiting Bible scholar from America. They were then allowed a viewing of the oldest piece of New Testament manuscript in existence. The small fragment of a second century copy of John's gospel was kept under lock and key and handled only by a trained attendant with gloved hands. The fragment was from the 18th chapter of John's gospel and the text in full was a confirmation of Jesus' role as witness to the truth. The unexpected finding was a special moment and a fitting end to their trip.

Returning home, Richard had resumed his study in a more relaxed mood. The brief interlude allowed him to see what had eluded detection before.

Richard looked again for the first time in seven days at the continuous stream of capital Greek letters—"ONOMAAYTWIWANNHSOYTOS"—which constituted the words of John 1:6b. This time his eyes unexpectedly continued on past the three important Greek words and on to the next word, the first word of the following sentence. He had intentionally read the last syllable of John, the last word of the important phrase as though he were seeing it with his supposed "ou" ending, in place of the "ace" ending that was actually written. The supposed "ou" ending made the translation read "of John and not simply "John." There was a natural pause in the rhythm of the syllables as he mentally verbalized the important OU and then surprisingly continued on to a previously unseen second OU, the first syllable of the next word. The previously unseen second OU had escaped notice because being written in uncial Greek letters it appeared as OY.

I knew the surprise he found was coming and I shared his

joy in hearing the repeated OU for the first time. "OU OU?" He said it out loud and as though it were a question. "Are you kidding me?" he said reflexively, and I knew his mind was spinning already realizing it wasn't a question but an answer. He paused suddenly and said, "Thank You." It came sincerely, naturally, from his mind filled with gratitude. And we both knew it was for me. It was an answer to the question he had been asking: How could the improbable change from "ou" to "ace" have taken place?

Richard remembered how he had reveled in finding the now obvious second 'ou' that had been waiting for him to discover. "OU – OU," he said again, aloud. The effect was striking and inescapable each time he said it. "Ou ou" or "Oh Oh," he thought, is the recognized sign of serious trouble, even disaster just ahead. Richard saw it's what we say when the phone rings and our call waiting tells us it's the IRS. We say it when the rent is due and the wife says she spent the money on shoes –"Ou Ou!" Or when the gas gauge says *E* and the nearest station is fifty miles away, "Oh Oh." And in fact, in any situation where the enemy in whatever form has breached our defenses and is banging on the door—Oh Oh! Big trouble!

He had continued to listen to the sound of the syllables of the two competing forms of the Greek name "John"—"ee – oh – whan – ace (ou)" until he imagined every syllable of the word had a special second meaning. The first two syllables "ee" and "oh" were by themselves expressions of fright and surprise. What were the odds of that? He had asked himself, And then the term "ace" is widely known to indicate a triumph or victory over an opponent. Finally, he had imagined even the syllable at the heart of the word had a special double meaning. In his exalted state of mind he heard the word "whan" in the heart of the Greek word for John. He thought it not impossible the "whan" referenced the concept of a magic wand as though simply by waving this word some great change had taken place. To him it seemed the world was literally spellbound, being held captive, in a constant state of religiously motivated wars, by an evil incantation: EEE OH WHAN ACE. He dreamed of one day being able to magically set it free by again waving the magic whan while reciting a different incantation: EEE OH WHAN OU.

Taken altogether, the two competing versions of the Greek word John appeared to be carrying the weight of a hidden history and somehow the enigmatic Jewish expression OY, in fact a double Oy, was involved. The concentration of high energy particles indicated a serious disagreement regarding the correct spelling of "John" may have been at the center of a clash of cultures at the time of the birth of Christianity. Richard believed he was hearing ancient echoes calling to him across nearly two thousand years. And like the poet Shelly had advised in his memorable poem *To a Skylark*, the world should listen soon as he was listening now.

The effect of the mistranslation was to elevate the roles of both John the Baptist and Jesus. John was promoted from being only an announcer, a voice crying in the wilderness, a role he was born to play, to also being the gospel's "man sent from God," a witness to the light of God, a role which he denied was his.

Jesus was forced out of his role as "man sent from God," witness to the light, the role which the original author had given him and a role which he is heard to affirm at least thirty-five times. With John firmly seated in Jesus' place, Jesus was then understood as the "Word" made flesh. The Word was a foreign idea to the original writing. Like the cowbird's egg, it was an idea introduced into the original gospel by the Christian hymn added to it.

Richard believed he had discovered the way in which an early gospel of unknown origin had been taken over by an emerging Christianity. The extent to which the early John gospel conflicted with Christianity was immediately evident as verse eight now powerfully and unmistakably declared that the man sent from God, Jesus, was *not himself* the Light, but was sent to *bear witness to* the Light. Verse eight, a previously powerless statement when believed to refer to John the Baptist was now a direct denial of the essential Christian claim for Jesus. The new interpretation released Jesus from being the Word incarnate and allowed him to be a prophet, a fully human Jesus, *a witness to* the Light, and not absurdly *the Light* itself. Here was a human Jesus accessible to all humanity in a reasonable way.

The strange familiarity of the transliterated case endings, the "ou-ou" and the "ace," suggested that something of great cultural significance had taken place. Someone, it seemed, had played an illegal "ace" and had thereby triumphed over their opponent. There were no known manuscripts having the "ou ou" reading. Proponents of the original gospel may have bitterly fought its takeover by a hated enemy. And in the end may have succeeded only in leaving these few surviving echoes of a great clash of religious ideas. It was not beyond belief that something more, perhaps a fragment or a copy of an ancient manuscript, may yet be found hidden away in some dark place waiting for a new world having ears to hear.

This was the place where the idea that Jesus was coequal with God took root and grew. From this simple beginning, the disastrous misunderstanding of who Jesus was had eventually grown into a major world religion in conflict with Judaism and Islam.

In Richard's mind, somewhere below consciousness and not yet formulated into words, lay the beginning of a question he was feeling, that perhaps the explanation he had found was too simple and straightforward. Not all theologians were committed Christians; why hadn't one of them seen this possibility? He wanted to know the unknowable—who had changed the "ou" to "ace" and why had they done it? I knew that eventually he would discover and appreciate the beauty of the larger Plan beginning to come together. But for the present I had let him discover all he needed to know.

I allowed myself to relive the moment, a long time past, when a young manuscript copyist had stopped his work and solicited counsel with his superior. The copyist had come across the then existent double "ou" and had recognized it was the sort of thing he had been advised might indicate an error had crept into the manuscript he was copying from. His superior, a monk named Liebowitz, had been uncertain and they had prayed together seeking guidance on how to proceed. I answered their prayer and guided Liebowitz to change the first "ou" to "ace" and they washed their hands and proceeded accordingly. It was satisfying for me now to see my plan coming together. Yes, the time was right; it was the flowering of the age of reason and understanding.

It was the seventh year and Richard felt a great

responsibility to share his discovery of the ancient typo. There was yet more discoveries to be made before his book would be written and it would be his hour. But his mind was made up and he was determined to make some effort to share what he knew with someone. I opened a door for him in a safe place where he could scratch his itching conscience and learn that without my help his effort would be unproductive.

Chapter Nine

THE NON-CHRISTIAN CHRISTIANS

"I trust that there is not a young man now living in the United States who will not die a Unitarian."

— Thomas Jefferson, 1822, letter to Benjamin Waterhouse

Richard liked talking with Marjorie. She was friendly, and about his age. She was easy to look at too, a trim dishwater blonde with green eyes and a ready smile for everyone. She had taken care of herself; the years hardly seemed to matter to her.

"Whatcha been doing?" she asked him.

"Oh nothing new. The usual—you know."

"What's going on with your experience? Still trying to write something?"

"Yes. I have been making some progress on that. And, to be honest I've reached a point where I need some feedback. I think I need to share it with someone. Maybe with you Unitarian Universalists, I'm not sure."

"Can I help? What's it like?"

"It's like what the early Unitarians were into. Have you read some of that history?"

"I've been a UU all my life and my father was a Unitarian before they joined with the Universalists in the early 50s. Is that far enough back for you?"

Richard suspected she was accustomed to having plenty of money in her life. She had grown up in Massachusetts, where both

Unitarianism and Universalism had their roots in this country. She was a real UU but she was new to the local group. Her family was grown, and now newly divorced she was on her own for the first time in her life. She apparently loved it. Just returned from a trip to Machu Picchu, she was on a quest to bring greater spirituality into her life.

She and Richard had both chosen to go with the small group that had agitated for change and split off from the long established UU congregation last year. Marjorie was a full member of the struggling fledgling group while Richard was a perennial visitor. They were talking now after a Sunday service in the rented space the new congregation had chosen for its temporary home.

"Nah," Richard said, "you've got to go further back—a few years even before your father was born." Richard was understating the case. "There was a man named Michael Servetus; remember him?"

"Maybe," Marjorie bluffed. "Refresh my memory."

"He wrote a book that some people didn't like and got himself killed—burned at the stake."

"Whoa, when was this?"

"October 27, 1553. It should be a national holiday in all UU churches."

"*Long* time ago," Marjorie said in her funny, friendly way. "What was the charge?"

"He committed the heresy of teaching anti-trinitarianism. His book, *On the Errors of the Trinity*, was the original Unitarian manifesto. To make a long story short, he was tried, found guilty and when he wouldn't give it up, he was tied to a stake and burned to death by John Calvin and the protestant Council in Geneva, Switzerland."

"Geneva? I've been there. I don't think they do that kind of thing anymore. You sure this is the guy you want to follow?"

"Have you been everywhere?" Richard asked rhetorically. "Servetus was like Harry Truman. He just told the truth and they thought it was heresy. Besides, the price of speaking heresy has gone way down. "

"That's the way it is with you, isn't it? Like it was with him, you have to speak your truth."

Richard didn't know how to answer that and so continued his history lesson. "After Servetus was killed, Unitarianism was born teaching toleration for other beliefs and it seems to me it has never got beyond doing only that."

"And so now you think it's time they got back to speaking heresy again—to see if the lesson has been learned?"

"You understand real good. Yes, I do think Unitarians ought to speak their distinctive truth if they want to grow. That's what this group is all about isn't it—growth? New members? If you want to grow you've got to be connected with your roots, for nourishment and support."

"You learn that back on the farm in Indiana?" Marjorie kidded him.

"Yeah, I guess so. But it's obvious isn't it?"

"For you it is. Wanna have some coffee?"

"Sure. Hey, how was Machu Picchu? My wife and I might want to go there someday."

The following Sunday Richard arrived at the storefront church early and reading the bulletin board his eye was drawn to a new notice: "*UU Men's Group. Want to talk about it?*" There was a place for those interested to sign up and a date set for a first organization meeting. Then at the bottom Richard was astounded to read: "*See Richard Holmes for information.*"

It was a bold move, a step Richard would never have taken himself. It could only be Marjorie's doing. She knew him well enough not to ask his permission but just to do it. Richard was surprised but quickly got used to the idea and gave Marjorie a thumbs-up when he caught her eye during the service. She answered with her signature smile. Later she explained that the women had decided that the new church should have a men's group, and it was her idea to "kill two birds with one stone." So now he knew how it felt being a dead bird.

Two men signed up that first day and two more before the first meeting took place one evening a couple of weeks later. Richard explained to each of them before the meeting that he really didn't know anything about organizing a men's group but that he wanted to use the first meeting to show them something he thought they would be interested in. Richard really only wanted to make some UUs aware of what he had found. He was sure they would be interested in hearing how he thought the doctrine of the trinity was founded in an ancient typo. He was hoping to strike a spark in someone more capable that himself who would take his idea and run with it.

In the days leading up to his attempt at sharing his revelation, Richard prepared his argument carefully in a way he thought would appeal to Unitarians. He took as his beginning point the often quoted principle for interpreting scripture from William Ellery Channing, in his 1819 landmark sermon "Unitarian Christianity":

> "Our leading principle in interpreting Scripture is this, that the Bible is a book written for men, in the language of men, and that its meaning is to be sought in the same manner as that of other books.... With these views of the Bible, we feel it our bounden duty to exercise our reason upon it perpetually, to compare, to infer, to look beyond the letter to the spirit, to seek in the nature of the subject, and the aim of the writer, his true meaning; and, in general, to make use of what is known, for explaining what is difficult, and for discovering new truths."

From this guiding principle Richard intended to first make a statement reminding them of the importance of John's gospel to the Christian teaching of the Trinity and the divinity of Jesus. Then he would show them how the concept of a "man sent from God" was the pervasive subject matter of that gospel.

To illustrate this fact he first carefully read through the gospel and made a list of each statement he found relating Jesus in some way to the idea of being sent by God. Using this list he prepared a visual presentation of the surprising total of forty-three references he found throughout the gospel from chapter three to twenty. This was accomplished by using a photocopy machine to reduce the size of each of the pages of the gospel such that all of them could be fitted on a single double wide sheet of paper. On this he used a yellow highlighter to mark the position where each of the statements occurred. The point of this was to illustrate that John's gospel was throughout a story about the coming into the world, the short life and tragic death of Jesus, a man sent from God.

Then Richard intended to look back to Chapter one of the

gospel and point to John 1:6 as a possible topic sentence of the story: "There was a man sent from God whose name was John." He would state that there was actually no corroborating evidence that John had been sent by God. And in direct contradiction of the idea that John was the author's intended "man sent from God," was John the Baptist's no nonsense answer to the Pharisees sent from Jerusalem in which he denied being "the anointed, the Christ, or that prophet." He intended to first point out that John's direct denial of the role assigned to him was an obvious flaw in the Christian gospel.

Richard assumed that he would be talking to a more or less friendly audience. Maybe they would have little interest in theology but certainly, he thought, none of them would be committed to Jesus as "incarnate God."

But that assumption turned out to be wrong. One of the men, Phillip, was a new member who Richard did not know. He had apparently been attracted to the UUs by their liberal policy as a welcoming congregation. Unknown to Richard, Phillip was a retired Presbyterian minister. He and Robert, a UU from the Universalist tradition were best friends. In matters of theology Robert deferred his better judgment to Phillip.

Richard began his argument, as he had intended, with a strong statement regarding the importance of John's gospel to the whole of Christianity. He said, "The prologue to John's gospel is the "sine qua non" of Christianity."

Then before he could even give the literal meaning of the obscure Latin phrase, Phillip exploded at him saying: "That's not true!" and "You don't know what you're talking about." Not knowing yet that the distinguished looking man with the full head of wavy white hair was a retired Christian minister, Richard had no clue as to why his words had evoked such an emotional, even hostile response.

It was obvious that Phillip's friend Robert and the other two younger men had no idea what "sine qua non" meant and therefore no understanding of the disagreement. They were soon clamoring for an explanation from someone while Phillip continued to berate Richard for his ignorance of the scriptural foundation of Christianity.

Finally Phillip paused to take a breath, and Richard was able to bring the others up to speed by telling them that "sine-qua non" is a Latin phrase meaning literally "without which not." He then said that he had only meant to say that without the famous prologue to John's gospel Christianity would not be the thing that it is. This restatement of his opening remark again set Phillip off.

"Only in your opinion is that true," he began. In retrospect and after learning in conversation with Marjorie that Phillip was a Presbyterian minister who had 'retired' after his wayward sexual preference had been discovered, Richard thought that perhaps he had simply been angry and on guard against an attack by Unitarians on his Trinitarian beliefs. He seemed irrational in his unwillingness to admit the unique importance of John's prologue to the essential Christian beliefs. But for whatever reason he again launched into an obviously informed and scholarly monologue on why Christianity did not rise or fall on only a few words at the beginning of the fourth gospel. Richard thought he protested too much.

This time Richard was able to defend himself against the attack a little. He countered with, "No it is not just my opinion. Nearly everything I have read about the Bible and Christianity has something to say about the singular importance of John's prologue." Richard knew the famous prologue was much loved by Christians and not without reason. "Only here," he reminded Phillip, "is Jesus said to have preexisted with God and as God. The prologue is the most reputable source of the Christian teaching of Jesus as God incarnate." It had seemed to Richard that this first step in his argument was widely accepted, and he had not expected to have to defend this fact as being more than simply his own opinion.

Phillip did not allow the discussion to get past this sticking point, insisting that there were other equally important sources for the teaching of the divine nature of Jesus and the trinity. He repeatedly tried to lead Richard into a discussion of one or another of these other sources.

Richard moved past the controversy by granting that perhaps

he had overstated the importance of the prologue. Moving on he introduced the concept of a "man sent from God" and presented his visual aid to show the pervasiveness of the concept in John's gospel. Phillip misunderstood its purpose and held it up to ridicule for being too small to read. The others agreed with Phillip's assessment and the visual aid to understanding became instead an obstacle to be overcome.

Richard recognized in Phillip's disruptive behavior attempts to take over and guide the discussion. In spite of this, Richard stayed doggedly with the steps of his planned argument. When Phillip finally understood that Richard was calling into question the identity of John's "man sent from God" he objected simply saying the attempt was nonsensical because, "The verse says his name was John the Baptist. How much plainer could it be?"

Again Phillip felt the need to educate the small group and treated them to a review of the gospel story's involvement of John the Baptist. He retold the story from its beginning when the temple priest's tongue was loosed and he declared that his miraculous new son would be named John. He continued on through John's finest hour baptizing and giving witness to Jesus as the light and finally retold the circumstances of his death by beheading. He could not be dissuaded in doing this from start to finish, apparently thinking Richard was ignorant of the story and convinced that once so informed he would surely accept the gospel truth that John the Baptist's name was John.

Richard listened politely from start to finish and then appeared to ignore the "new" information by continuing in his search for John's name. Phillip was flummoxed at this apparent audacious ignorance and demanded to know by what authority he was engaged in this needless inquiry. "Do you imagine that you know more than the scholars and experts?" he asked.

Richard knew he was on solid ground when Phillip again attempted to redirect his efforts, saying: "Richard there are many things in the Bible that are unclear and could use some new thinking. But this verse you've selected is not one of them. No one is looking to be enlightened on the matter you've chosen to question. Everyone

I know likes it just the way it is."

Of course that was exactly the problem and the opportunity as Richard saw it. Yet it was impossible for him to point to a solution where others did not see a problem.

The discussion never got off the ground as the hour set aside for it ended in confusion. Reflecting on what had taken place, Richard felt he was justified in his belief that Christians, even these Unitarian, non-Christian Christians were not interested in finding a theological basis for a human Jesus. These people had no ears to hear what he was intent on saying. His was a solution for a problem that did not exist in their minds. Yet the discussion was useful for Richard because it had raised some issues that he would need to consider and find a way to answer.

His attempt to arouse their interest in a possible flaw in the gospel and to enlighten them had been weak and ineffectual. Yet Wisdom, he knew, says it is impossible for a man to be persuaded of a truth that he believes will kill him.[1]

Still, Richard found it difficult to shake the feeling that he had succeeded in disturbing the ancient peace and somehow Michael Servetus' spirit had been roused from its deep sleep and was now allied with him in his effort to make the truth known.

Chapter Notes

1 "It is difficult to get a man to understand something when his salary (or his life) depends on his not understanding it."

— Upton Sinclair

Chapter Ten

EVERYDAY JEWS

"To go against the dominant thinking of your friends, of most of the people you see every day, is perhaps the most difficult act of heroism you can have."

— Theodore H. White, American political writer 1915-1986

"My feeling as a Christian points me to my Lord and Savior as a fighter. It points me to the man who once in loneliness, surrounded only by a few followers, recognized these Jews for what they were and summoned men to fight against them and who, God's truth! was greatest not as a sufferer but as a fighter."

— Adolph Hitler, *My New Order*

Celeste quickly picked up on her husband's mood when he returned home after the unusual evening meeting with the Unitarians.

What's the matter?" she demanded. "What happened to you?"

Not wanting to get into it with his wife, Richard said, "Aw, I think they're all a bunch of homos." It was a small-minded statement not supported by the facts but one feeding into the popular suspicion surrounding men's groups in general. Richard enjoyed talking in stereotypes and using improper words with Celeste. She could never tell when he was serious or just kidding.

"Well, what did you expect?" Celeste asked, thinking she was one step ahead of him.

It looked like she wasn't going to take the bait this time.

"I expected that, maybe, one of them might be interested in

talking about what's wrong with the world today."

As he said it, Richard remembered the very first quotation he had saved. It was something about small minds wanting to discuss small things and only great minds being interested in talking about ideas.[2] Evidently great minds were hard to find.

The collection of quotations had grown now to several thousand covering a wide variety of subjects. They served to help him find proper words for thoughts he had but which he had trouble communicating.

"You know you can't talk like that around other people."

"Like what? Oh, you mean 'homos'? I reckon anyone born in a barn like me who learned about sex by watching farm animals do it can say whatever he wants."

Celeste frowned and Richard knew it was time to quit teasing her. "I know," he said. 'I just wanted to see how stupid you thought I was."

"So you're not going to join the men's group?"

"What for? I doubt my sex life would interest anybody."

"Well, maybe they will surprise you. Give it a try."

Richard thought that might be a good idea, especially since he had left a package of handouts with details of his big idea—including the crucial Greek part he never got into—with each of the four Unitarian men and realized that there was still a slim chance that some one of them might actually look at it and have a question or want to talk about it.

"How was your day, dear?" he asked, feeling better for having reverted briefly to his childhood and spoken a few words in his uncensored barnyard English.

"It was okay, until I read in the newspaper where they're going to cancel Annette's graduation ceremony."

"What the heck? They can't do that."

"I think they already have. Here, you can read it for yourself."

It was their daughter Annette's senior year in high school. She had been only eleven and her brother just seven when he had had his experience, and they had taken that wild trip to Indiana together in the big gray van. He wondered how much she remembered, maybe the swimming pool at the Happy Cricket campground, probably not much more.

And now all at once, seven years later, she was looking forward to wearing the cap and gown and walking across the stage to get her diploma. It would be a disappointment for her if that was cancelled. And they had company coming for the big event; his mother who had thought he was crazy and his father who had recruited a Christian minister to help him, and his brother and sisters from Indiana, they were all planning to be there. Maybe Celeste had read the story wrong. It was too late now to cancel such a big event without any notice.

"*Graduation Ceremony Cancelled*" was the headline of the small article on the first page of the local section. The story began, "*A traditional graduation ceremony held each year has been suddenly canceled due to objections raised by families of two graduating students.*" It seemed real enough.

"It was on the TV news too," Celeste said as he continued reading the newspaper article.

"They said two Jewish families—"

"Jewish? What have they got to object about?"

"They got a lawyer and he threatened to sue the school board for requiring their kids to attend a ceremony where prayers were offered in the name of Jesus." He demanded the prayers be dropped or be made to God only."

"Oh I bet you loved that."

"It's all a bunch of crap. They interviewed a preacher, one of those fundamental Baptists, who vowed he would never be ashamed of the name of Jesus. So the school board voted to drop the ceremony from the official program."

"Wait a minute. Something's not right here. They don't have prayers at the cap and gown thing."

"No! It's not that graduation ceremony."

Well what then? I thought you were saying that—"

"It's the baccalaureate program," Celeste said.

"What's that?"

"I don't know. Look it up. It's religious, is all I know. We had one when we graduated."

Richard raised his hand, palm out, to ask for more time. "Let me finish reading the newspaper story." He was surprised at how two Jewish families had come suddenly into his life. Until now he hadn't given any thought to how Jewish people coexisted with their religious beliefs in the dominant Christian population.

The news article told him only that the Baccalaureate ceremony was traditionally held on the Sunday before the diploma ceremony and that it was a Christian ceremony in celebration of graduation and that prayer would be offered, undoubtedly in the name of Jesus, for thanksgiving and for the success of the students in their new life.

The encyclopedia said much the same thing: "*The Baccalaureate ceremony is a service of worship in celebration of and thanksgiving for lives dedicated to learning and wisdom.*" Additionally, he learned that the event is often of an inter-faith religious nature.

It was understandable how Jewish families who did not believe in Jesus would object to their children having no choice but to be included in a Christian ceremony. The obvious solution was to make the ceremony inter-faith. But evidently that wasn't possible, so the school board withdrew their sponsorship of the ceremony. It seemed somehow a shame to lose a traditional graduation event but it was a sign of the changing times.

Coincidentally, or perhaps it was just his new awareness of Jewish people, the following evening Richard heard the TV news anchorman use the word "Christ" as a synonym for Jesus.

"Did you hear that?" he asked Celeste.

"What?"

"The way that news guy just said 'Christ' meaning 'Jesus' as though it were a matter of fact."

"So?"

"So, I wonder what those Jewish families who stopped the Baccalaureate ceremony think of that? They don't believe that Jesus was Christ. How do the news people get away with offending them like that?"

"I don't think the TV people even think about it."

"You're probably right. I never thought about it till yesterday.

CHAPTER NOTES

2 "Great minds discuss ideas, average minds discuss events, small minds discuss people." —Admiral Hyman G. Rickover 1900-1986. Father of America's nuclear navy

Chapter Eleven

TOWARD ANOTHER JESUS

"In every generation there has to be some fool who will speak the Truth as he sees it."
— Boris Pasternak, 1890-1960, Russian author and poet

Richard's personal quest to be useful in helping others find their own deep transformative experience of God's Love was temporarily at a standstill due to his failure to make contact with the Unitarian men. It would be more difficult than he had imagined motivating these people to reconnect with their unique anti-Trinitarian founding beliefs. Yet it still appeared to him that they were the group best prepared to hear his truth and perhaps recognize it as their own.

Celeste's advice that maybe the men's group would surprise him proved right. After that first disastrous meeting, the four men all went out of their way to be friendly to him. Robert appealed to his better judgment saying, "You can't quit the group without at least giving it a try. After all, it's your group. You started it." This appeal to his reasonable nature was persuasive, and realizing that getting to know Phillip and the others better would be helpful in his attempt at reaching them, Richard continued to meet regularly with the new group.

The unexpected way in which the failure had happened was a concern. The open landing space had first been sighted in reading about Unitarian Universalists beginnings. Of all religious people he had visited with, the UUs had appeared to be potentially the most receptive to his idea of a fully human Jesus. Then with Marjorie's help he had quickly entered into a landing pattern. But on final approach Phillip had appeared suddenly and without warning he stood in the open space and blocked the attempt at making contact. Maybe it was just that the timing was not right. Or maybe the open place existed only long ago and had since been filled in with other beliefs. For whatever reason, the approach at landing had been too high and too fast. A second attempt would require another go around.

Reading and meditation continued to be important pursuits. There was something new coming into his world. People were writing books and speaking openly about Near-Death Experiences. These personal testimonies of people leaving their bodies under extreme circumstances and having encounters with a heavenly realm of light and love had much in common with his experience. Maybe this was a new door opening for him to take the place of the failure with the Unitarians where the door had seemed to suddenly close. Richard was very interested in learning all he could about Near-Death Experiences while continuing to work with the Unitarians.

He was so intense in his desire to find a way to express his salvation that many times he would fall asleep lost in thought with a book in his lap. This intense focus on books and learning was troubling to Celeste.

"We don't do anything anymore; you're always reading some old book—or writing," she complained. "You're not the man I married."

And his relationship with his son suffered. When the young boy, Timmy, asked him to coach his Boys Club basketball team, he chose the books. The disappointment was palpable. But, he told himself, "The need of the many exceeds the need of the one." His life was not his own.

Once he awoke suddenly to hear a voice, his own voice saying, "You've got to go slow." It was strange hearing his own voice—through his ears only without any inner voice thought connection. It wasn't clear exactly what his voice had said because of the unexpected suddenness of the happening. It was as though another person had intervened and used his voice to deliver a message. He was sure it wasn't him who spoke. It was like the disembodied voice he had experienced at the *Happy Cricket* campground after he had been found wandering lost in the woods years ago. That time the words he had both said and heard—though it was, paradoxically, not him that said them—were written in the Bible held open in his hands.

This time there was uncertainty of exactly what he had heard. Was it, "you've got to go slow?" or "you've got to grow slow?" Either way, the clear message was that he needed to slow down and take it easy; everything it seemed would come to him in time. It was a reassuring message. Evidently he was on schedule toward whatever destiny was his.

Timmy's basketball team found they had a new assistant coach who showed up for most practice sessions and Timmy was glad when both his parents attended all the games. Slowly the fog lifted and it became obvious that the problem with the failed approach to the Unitarians was in large part that the landing craft was too small. The John 1:6b switch from John to Jesus was by itself inadequate to handle the power he was attempting to tap into, and the attempt had quickly tripped the Unitarian Universalist circuit breaker of believability, making contact impossible. The men had been unable to take him seriously. This failure mode was way better than the result of earlier attempts to tell his truth. Not being taken seriously was several notches above being thought crazy. There was hope.

It was unmistakable that growth was taking place but it was imperceptibly slow. A bigger vehicle, something with more size, greater width and length was needed. It was true that the next approach would have to be lower and slower but if he were bringing more with him he would be easier to see and harder to ignore. Once they saw some value in reconnecting with the historical roots of their denomination, surely then they would turn on the landing lights and not stand out on the runway. Being welcomed would greatly help the chances of making contact, of at last being understood.

> *At first it wasn't clear what could be done to add weight to his argument, but as his mind continued to relax I helped him to realize there was a strong possibility that the substance of the revelation could not exist in isolation.*

If his understanding was correct—that John the Baptist had mistakenly or otherwise been placed in the role of 'messenger from God' which role he believed properly belonged to Jesus — there most probably were other instances where the roles of Jesus and John reflected that confusion. Finding one or more of these would add a new dimension to his argument which would broaden the appeal of the discovery and enhance its believability.

Richard anticipated that by raising his sights and looking beyond his narrow focus on verse six in John's gospel, by taking a broader view of the respective roles of Jesus and John, he might discover something that would lend support to his conception of a fully human Jesus, a special messenger, a man sent by God, whose authority and leadership could only be accepted or rejected without having the deceptive and devastating, power robbing alternative of being worshipped as "God incarnate."

Chapter Twelve

BEHOLD THE MAN

"To be great is to be misunderstood."

— Ralph Waldo Emerson

Moses Spoke Of Me

Rereading John's gospel, Richard found two disconnected references linking Jesus back to the Old Testament and to the early Israelites and to Moses. Phillip first claims to have found Jesus and says he is the one Moses spoke of. Later Jesus himself claims that Moses spoke of his coming. The two references support his understanding that Jesus is the gospel's main focus.

A third link to Moses was found hidden in John the Baptist's comprehensive answer to the Pharisees in which he denies being "that prophet." Research into the meaning of "that prophet" revealed it is a reference to a declaration found in the eighteenth chapter of the fifth book of the Torah. Moses informs the early Israelites that YHWH has promised, in accordance with their wishes, he would never again speak to them directly as he had at Mt. Sinai. YHWH had personally delivered the Ten Commandments from atop a quaking mountain amid smoke, fire and thundering which frightened the people so severely they "thought they would die."

Richard saw a similarity in this revelation to the emerging Israelite nation, perhaps upwards of a million people, to what near-death researchers were calling a "fear-death experience." Like the better known "near-death experience," a "fear-death experience" was very impactful and invariably left the experiencer knowing God was real.

Rather than ever again speaking directly to his people, YHWH promised to send a special prophet to speak his words in his name. The people were told to never forget the time their god had spoken directly to them and to continue the remembrance through teaching their children. They were told to wait for this prophet and to be sure to do what he says for they would be held accountable. The Pharisees asked John the Baptist if he were "that prophet." This was evidence the prophet had not yet come and was still being expected at that time.

Richard took special interest in the statement that YHWH would put words in the prophet's mouth and the prophet would speak all that he was commanded to speak. He found a statement attributed to Jesus in John's gospel that fit with this like two pieces of a puzzle. Jesus declared the special words he spoke were not his own but were words he was commanded to speak. This further strengthened the understanding that the Jesus portrayed in John's gospel was a special prophet like Moses. The author of John's gospel clearly portrayed Jesus as the man God had promised he would send. Jesus can be heard claiming the authority of this prophet.

Richard accepted literally Jesus' claim that the words he spoke were not his own. He knew what that was like. He recalled his experience in Curtis' office at the *Happy Cricket* when at a time of high excitement exactly that had happened to him. And again a second time, more recently, when he had awakened suddenly in time to hear his voice say, "You've got to grow slow." These were words spoken by himself, yet he knew they were not his own words.

* * *

This Is He

Richard was beginning to get with the program and was not concerned with sharing his latest revelation. He was learning to wait and listen for my voice.

The discovery of Jesus the man, a special prophet, spilled over into two of the other gospels when Richard's attention was caught by a logically confused interpretation of a story involving Jesus and John the Baptist. The famous story, found in Matthew 11:10 and also in Luke 7:27, began with John the Baptist sending two of his disciples to ask Jesus, "Art thou he that should come? Or do we look for another?"

Richard saw the interpretation was logically confused when he temporarily set aside the irrelevant material coming between the question and its answer. When the question, "Art thou he who should come?" was brought together with its answer, "This is he," the accepted interpretation was as if John had asked Jesus, "Are you the one who should come?" and Jesus had answered, "No, you are." This nonsense interpretation was used in support of the Christian misunderstanding that John the Baptist had been Elijah who must come before the Messiah.

Richard found the key to understanding the question and answer differently was in recognizing the phrase "this is he" was a common response used in telephone conversation. When a caller asks to speak with the unknown person who has answered his call, it is common for the person called to identify himself saying, "This is he." With this understanding in place, Jesus' answer to John's question was, "Yes, I am he who should come." Jesus' answer was then a claim to be a prophet, either Elijah or "that prophet" spoken of by Moses. This Jesus, Richard was pleased to see, was consistent with the man-sent-from-God, the Jesus he had found in John's gospel.

Corrected in this way the story appears as if it were part of the early John tradition. This view is strengthened by the intervening statements praising John the Baptist. John is said to be the greatest of all those born of women. Yet he is destined to be less than the least of those who will be in the Kingdom of God. These statements echo Jesus' teaching of a second birth found only in John's gospel. Evidently John, unlike Jesus, was not born of the spirit but only of the blood of woman.

There is also validation of John's self-proclaimed role of being an announcer. John the Baptist is honored above all other prophets who had only been able to speak about what was to come. John's role was superior to theirs in that he was privileged to identify Jesus as the anointed one, saying in effect, not simply that the God sent messenger was coming, but being privileged to actually announce his arrival.

Richard realizes there is the beginning of an elusive harmony of the four gospels in this new interpretation. The key to a peaceful understanding lies in giving up the Christian insistence on placing John the Baptist in Jesus' place. These two newly realized expressions of a fully human Jesus—a man who came claiming to be a prophet, a unique messenger sent from God—one illustration found in the Old Testament Torah and a second demonstration from the New Testament gospels, fulfilled Richard's hope of finding broader support for his John 1:6b interpretation of Jesus as a man-sent-from-God. It seemed misplaced pieces of a great puzzle were falling logically into place.

Chapter Thirteen

THE MESSIANIC SECRET AND THE JESUS PROPHECY

"The worst lie is the truth misunderstood."

— William James

Another year was ending and newspapers, magazines and television programs were full of stories by experts and others making their predictions for the coming new year. Richard was taking in all the various entertaining and sometimes serious predictions when a thought came reminding him that this modern tradition had something in common with the Biblical prophets.

He recognized this was no idle thought but was actually the first step in a process that he was beginning to understand. It seemed to him that he was being led. The surprising thoughts he sometimes had, coming seemingly out of the blue, were not his alone. The leading was subtle, gentle in the extreme. He was free to ignore the thoughts, refuse to look at them, label them crazy, or otherwise deny them for long periods of time—months, even years. But always they would return and in the end he would consider them and follow them to their logical conclusion. Sometimes his thinking would go off track and he would get stuck in some dead-end or other. But always the guidance would come to rescue him and lead him on.

Being led by the *Spirit of Truth* was not a bad deal but it could be exasperating, especially, Richard knew, for his wife Celeste. By now he knew what to expect from the process. This new and unexpected thought indicated to him that some new revelation was at hand. But poor Celeste had no idea what was going on nor did she want to know. From the very first she was sure her husband had gone off the deep end and lost his mind, which in a way was true. For her, every day since then had been a struggle to regain their normal life. At times Richard would seem to be getting better, returning to some semblance of the man he used to be, but then he would go off again on some tangent that she didn't want to even know about. And she would have to wait, often impatiently, for him to return.

The revelations were beginning to pile up. Individually they seemed powerless and of little consequence, but Richard was beginning to see the new ideas as elements of a new system of thought. Together, they would provide a framework for a new understanding. In the same way that a single piece of 2x4 lumber would look nothing like a house to a caveman, two 2x4s stood vertically to suggest walls and two more laid across their tops resembling a gable roof might begin to reveal the potential in the new building material. Similarly, he believed, his ideas taken together would begin to suggest a new way of thinking, a new system of thought.

The first two revelations were simply reinterpretations of the creation story from Genesis. They dealt with a new and yet biblical understanding of what God had created. Next there were several revelations regarding a new understanding of who Jesus was. The first of these, like a firstborn child, had been the most difficult and had required a two-year study of biblical Greek to formulate the breakthrough idea. The second one, like a second child, had come easier. Now, this coming revelation might deal with something new. He was anxious to pursue it.

"All right, dinner's ready," Celeste called a third time. Richard was so taken with his new idea that Celeste's voice failed to penetrate and her call to dinner had simply not reached his conscious mind on the first two tries.

"Just a minute," he answered hoping to gain a few minutes to scan the article he had just found in Unger's Bible Dictionary dealing with the function of prophets.

Half an hour later, having read the article, Richard saw that if his Jesus was in fact Moses' special prophet, he should have had something important to say about future events. Unger's article said:

"It was an important part of the message of the biblical prophets to disclose the future. However, this was not mere foretelling to appeal to idle curiosity. The genius of prophecy was a prediction of the future arising from the conditions of the present and was inseparably connected with the profoundly religious and spiritual message the prophet was called to proclaim to his own generation."

Building on this train of thought led him to see that the greatest future event bearing on the life of Jesus was the coming of Christianity with its intense unfailing opposition by Judaism. Was it possible that his Jesus had foreseen the coming of Christianity? What did he know and when did he know it? What if Jesus knew his role would be misunderstood; what if he had seen in a vision that he would be mistaken for YHWH in whose name he had come? Would he have tried to tell his people what was coming? Had he warned them about a coming heresy?

Dinner that evening was cold, black-bottomed grilled cheese and lunch meat sandwiches with potato soup. They ate in silence, but still they were at the table together. Richard had learned not to share his thoughts with Celeste. She wasn't interested. But she stayed with him through the years, honoring her marriage vow of "for better or worse." He loved her for that.

At some level, he thought, she seemed to understand that his work was important, but he couldn't be sure. He clearly didn't understand her motivations for doing anything. She was always pushing him to reclaim some aspect of the life they might have had together if things had been normal. This week she had stripped the wallpaper from their bathroom walls and was trying to get him involved in choosing a new color. He couldn't care less. Compared to the possibility of discovering if Jesus had foretold the rise of Christianity, choosing a color for bathroom walls was nothing. Whatever she chose would be fine; he trusted her judgment. It wasn't what she wanted to hear. She wanted him to pay more attention to her.

Through the years she had managed to get him to go with her on several trips. They could still have fun, she knew, if she could get him away from the books. They had been to England a second time and Ireland once. They had toured the Bavarian castles in Germany and had even spent ten days in China. Halfway around the world, they realized it was the furthest they could ever get from home. One step in any direction would bring them closer to Daytona Beach.

Celeste was still hoping for a chance to see the pyramids and Richard wanted to combine a trip to Egypt with a visit to Israel. Celeste wasn't interested in visiting the Holy Land. Maybe she was afraid it would trigger another religious attack. Theirs wasn't a bad marriage.

Richard searched the gospels for anything Jesus may have said that sounded like a prediction of future events. He knew he was looking for something that was open to being misinterpreted—something that seemed questionable or not well understood. It might seem to be out of place, labored in its interpretation or otherwise somehow not quite right. It would have a bearing on how Jesus' life would be understood and on the birth of Christianity.

The first thing he found was a discussion between Jesus and his disciples regarding who the people thought he was. It was known as Peter's great confession of faith. A version of the story is in each of the four gospels. Jesus begins by asking his disciples in private who people are saying he is. Various answers are given; *John the Baptist, Elijah, Jeremiah, or some prophet of old.* Then Jesus asks the disciples who they say he is. Peter answers, saying Jesus is the Christ, the Son of the living god.

In Matthew's gospel Peter's answer is highly praised by Jesus, who says Peter is blessed because it was his Father in heaven, and not flesh and blood, which has revealed this to him. Only in Matthew does Jesus say Peter's confession makes him the rock upon which he will build his church and promises to give Peter the keys to the kingdom of heaven—power to bind and loose things on earth and in heaven.

Following Peter's confession that Jesus is the Son of the Living God, Jesus issues a strict order to all the disciples that they should not tell anyone what Peter has said. This commandment not to tell anyone he is Christ is called, by Christian interpreters, "The Messianic Secret." Richard finds that there is a great deal of uncertainty among the experts as to exactly why Peter's understanding of who Jesus is should be a secret.

The order not to tell anyone that Jesus is the Son of God is found in the three gospels but not in John, where Jesus replies to Peter's confession by saying, "Have I not chosen you twelve and one of you is a devil." In Matthew's gospel, only three verses after his praise of Peter, Jesus is heard strongly rebuking Peter for refusing to believe his teaching that he will soon be put to death. Jesus says that Peter is "an offense" to him and calls him Satan, saying: "Get thee behind me, Satan." Jesus criticizes Peter for being more concerned with the flesh and blood things of the world than the things of God.

Richard thought this stern rebuke was peculiar following so closely the unparalleled praise of Peter for his great confession of faith. He pondered all of this, seeing that Peter was either a spiritual genius who saw what the other disciples were unable to see, *or* he was dumb as a rock. Richard thought it was the latter. The idea that Jesus said Peter's confession should be a secret was, for Richard, a Christian spin on the obvious fact that what Peter had said was simply not true. Jesus had rebuked Peter, characterizing him as a devil and Satan because he was wrong-headed. The over the top praise Jesus heaped on Peter in Matthew's account was obviously a Christian addition inserted into the gospel at a later date to make it appear Jesus had appointed Peter to be the head of a new church.

Richard and Celeste had visited Rome and St. Peter's cathedral. They had seen the crypts of ancient Popes lining dark corridors and knew of the claim that the crypt of Peter himself, the first Pope, lay somewhere in the dark depths far below. The expansive palatial sanctuary above was filled with priceless sculptures and paintings, symbols of the worldly wealth of the church which had grown up from Peter's great confession of faith. The church appeared true to Jesus' view of Peter as a Satan "savoring not the things that be of God, but the things that be of man."

Beneath what seemed an obvious Christian insertion of Peter's great confession of faith, Richard saw there was indications Jesus had known a false idea of who he was had taken root even among his small group of twelve disciples.

It was a real possibility. It fit with Richard's conception of another Jesus, a Jesus who was a man, a prophet with a message and not absurdly God in the flesh. But it was not the direct warning against a coming heresy Richard had hoped to find.

* * *

THE JESUS PROPHESY: BE YE NOT DECEIVED

"See all these buildings here, the Capitol building, Library of Congress, the Supreme Court, the Washington Monument and Lincoln Memorial? There shall be nothing left—not one stone shall remain stacked upon another."

"When shall this be, Master? Tell us. And what will be the sign of the end and of your coming the second time?"

Richard was dreaming, having fallen asleep trying to imagine what it must have been like for Jesus and his disciples in the temple area of first century Jerusalem when Jesus began to tell them of things to come after his death.

"Be careful that you aren't fooled. Many people are going to come to you after I'm dead saying Jesus this and Jesus that and asking you to have faith, and trying to convince you that I was the Messiah. And they will say that any day now I will come back and if you don't believe them you will be left behind when Judgment day comes.

"So now I've told you and you know what's going to happen ahead of time. Don't believe these people. And whatever you do, for God's sake, keep the faith and don't become one of them, a Christian.

"When I'm gone and all this starts to happen, remember what I said and you will know I was a true prophet. Your life and that of your family depends on you remembering to do what I said and you need to keep yourself and your family away from these people."

"Ding-dong; Ding- dong; Ding-dong; Dong-ding.

"Remember I said that they will be coming to your houses, ringing your doorbells and they will be insistent . . ."

"Ding-dong; Ding- dong; Ding-dong; Dong-ding.

The eight-note Westminster chime in the foyer of the big old house sounded off a second time and broke into Richard's daydream, rousing him back to the twentieth century.

He got up from the comfortable brown leather sofa Celeste had found at an estate sale, nearly tripped over the small white dog that inexplicably saw no reason to get out of the way, and slowly ambled shoeless toward the front door.

Opening the door he saw the rear ends of a man and a woman already down the stairs and about to disappear out of sight around the front corner of the house.

"Hey!" he said. The people stopped their retreat and turned around. Seeing them he knew at once who they were, though he'd never seen these two before in his life.

"Oh, it's you—again. You people sure are persistent."

They were always the same—well dressed and carrying brief cases with Bibles and pamphlets—ready on a moment's notice to launch into it with some unknowing person who chanced to open a door to them.

"Don't say anything," Richard told them. "Listen to me. I've heard it all before. I've got two questions for you. First, in whose name are you ringing my doorbell?"

The two visitors glanced at one another, and then answered in unison. "We come in the name of Jesus," said a small white man with a bandaged hand, and a large black woman wearing a sensible print dress and a burgundy colored wig. They stood side by side at the top of the stairs on the small porch just outside Richard and Celeste's front door.

"That's what I thought. Now here's my second question. Why do you keep after me—coming back and back again?"

Again the two Jehovah's Witnesses turned to one another and silently synchronized their thoughts. Looking back at Richard they again chimed in unison, "The end is near."

"That's enough. I've heard enough. Listen to me; you people don't need to be coming around here anymore. I want you to take that message back to wherever it is you all come from. And make sure that all of you get the message. I've entertained you here at my front door for years. Now, I know my wife has not been friendly to you at times, but we have heard what you have to say and now it's time to stop. I don't want to be rude. But I have it on good authority that you people are deceived. You ought to learn to read your Bibles for yourselves and quit believing whatever your leaders tell you is the truth. Sorry. Now, goodbye."

With that, Richard shut the door even as the man offered a pamphlet titled "Who Was Jesus?" with his good right hand.

"Was that …?" Celeste asked, coming out of the kitchen and into the foyer to see what was going on. She was wearing an apron and carrying a paring knife in her right hand.

"Jehovah's Witnesses? Yes," Richard answered. He was now wide awake.

"Did you just tell them—"

"To go away and not come back."

"Well, Hallelujah! Glory to God . . . but . . . why?"

"I just read the most incredible thing."

"I've been telling you for years to stop talking to them," Celeste said. "What did you read?"

"Something Jesus said."

"All right, I'll bite. What did he say that would make you do that?"

"He said not to go with them."

"Who? Jehovah's Witnesses?"

"Christians. All of 'em. Catholics, Baptists, Methodists, Jehovah's Witnesses, the whole bunch. Anyone who says Jesus was the Messiah and the end is near."

"Where did you find that?" Celeste was curious to know.

"It's in The New Testament gospels, Matthew, Mark and Luke."

"Well, it must be hidden because Christians evidently haven't found it."

"It's hidden all right, right out in the open. Christians can't see it because they have let themselves be deceived. They aren't following Jesus; they're following Paul.

"Jesus delivered the truth, once for all, and he warned his people that many would come saying he was the Messiah and that the end was near. He told those who knew him not to be deceived."

"Whatever," Celeste said. She turned and went back to her warm kitchen.

It was another piece of the puzzle Richard was still working on. With this surprising piece, the picture was coming into clearer focus. The "many" who Jesus had said would come were here. They were Christians. And Jesus' people had apparently heard his warning against going with them. Jews rejected the idea that Jesus was their Messiah from the beginning when the self-appointed, late coming, apostle Paul, first began preaching in their synagogues that he had been. And Richard knew Jews continue to this day, nearly two thousand years later, to reject Jesus as Messiah. Who knew they were following their Jesus in doing this?

Who knew the historically important enmity between Christians and Jews was based in something Jesus said? It was a surprising thing to consider.

Before falling asleep, Richard had found the direct prophetic words he was looking for. Again it was in a private conversation between Jesus and his disciples. The conversation, found in the three gospels, is known as the Olivet Discourse and is sometimes called "The Little Apocalypse" because it includes some of the end-of-the-age prophecies found in the book of Revelation.

In discussion with the disciples Peter, James, John and Andrew, Jesus tells them the temple will be knocked down in the future. The disciples want to know what will be the sign when this will happen. Jesus answers warning them against being deceived by many people who will come in his name saying he was their Messiah and many will believe it.

Richard saw it was a sign recorded in Matthew's gospel still alive across twenty centuries of time; available to anyone with eyes and ears to comprehend it and a mind willing to receive it.

He found Luke's gospel included the warning against being deceived and included a second important detail bearing on the identity of the many who would come; they will say the time is short and the end is near.

Richard knew Christians had been expecting Jesus to return practically from the day he was crucified. Jesus' failure to show had been a continuing scandal requiring adjustments in theology through the years to find ways to explain it. These two beliefs, Jesus was the Messiah and he was coming back soon, practically defined Christianity. Jesus had seen the future and then he had, prophetically speaking, nailed it by warning his followers against becoming

Christians before Christianity came into the world. In the game of religion, it was Touchdown Jesus.

Richard had fallen asleep after reading the warning against being deceived and while wondering if his Jesus had foreseen something that would serve to establish him as a true prophet. His dream had let him see a new way of understanding the words which were thought to be a warning against false prophets who would come claiming to be the Messiah. There was a clear warning against false prophets but it was separate from the first warning against deception.

The test of a true prophet was whether what he says comes true. In Richard's new understanding Jesus had foreseen the coming of Christianity and had thus shown himself to be a true prophet and therefore he was a prophet whose words should be trusted and obeyed.

The greatest thing that happened after Jesus left this earth was the coming of the Christian Church. Think of it, what if Jesus knew his role would be misunderstood; what if he had seen in a vision that he would be mistaken for YHWH in whose name he had come? Wouldn't he have tried to warn his people against what he knew was coming? Wouldn't he have told them not to be deceived by the deceptive lie, the Messianic Secret, he knew would be told about who he was? What kind of a prophet would he have been if he had failed to see this?

Chapter Fourteen

CHRIST-INANITY (*TIME OUT FOR THE BIRD*)

"We must not assume the existence of any entity until we are compelled to do so."

— William of Occam, 1284-1347, English philosopher

Known as Occam's Razor, this famous principle guided philosophical thought for centuries.

"KISS," Acronym for "Keep it Simple Stupid."

— Anonymous

A modern incarnation of Occam's Razor.

Helen, the woman sitting on Richard's right at a table in the third row, secretly watched his progress as he worked slowly with his left hand creating a pencil drawing of a rustic outdoor landscape. There was a river flowing through it from the center left down to the bottom right. The river was bounded on its right bank by reeds and swamp grass. On the upper left bank were a few scattered boulders at water's edge, bounding a small meadow in front of a low range of distant hills. It wasn't what they were supposed to be drawing, and although it was none of her business, Helen wanted to know what it was

He was supposed to be drawing a leaf. The former nun teaching the class had described the fine points of how to draw realistic close-ups of leaves and twigs. "See how the veins in the leaf structure radiate outward? Now turn the leaf over and see how the structure underneath reveals itself above in line and shadow." Richard had listened, but followed his own inspiration.

He had enrolled in the free class for bored retirees to see if he perhaps had an unrecognized artistic talent. He was still searching for a way to express his Truth. He fantasized that maybe he might be destined to take his place with those famous artists whose lives had been spent painting imaginative yet realistic looking scenes illustrating the life of Jesus.

However, he found pursuing the fundamentals of light and shadow rapidly exhausted his willingness to concentrate. After laboriously drawing a few life-sized leaves, one of them attached to a small branch, his attention had wandered, and the river landscape had almost magically begun to take form. Richard recognized that the leaf drawings he made were more realistic than anything he had ever before drawn. It was a testament to the nun's teaching ability. But the river landscape was a reflection of what was in his mind. He knew what was yet to be drawn, but Helen didn't and she continued to watch, saying nothing as the picture developed.

Helen's attention was lured away from Richard's developing sketch for a few minutes while she worked, following the instructor's direction to illustrate the fern-like foliage of a cypress tree. It was clear the ex-nun was in love with the world and its beauty expressed in the foliage of trees. The cypress greenery, she said, offered a special challenge for an artist because of its unusual construction. When Helen again thought to look carefully to her left at Richard's drawing, she found there were now two small men, drawn looking away from the viewer, standing waist deep in the middle of the small river. Above the men, above the low hills, and clearly the focal point of the drawing was a larger than life-sized white bird with wings outstretched, seeming to be suspended in the air. A free-form starburst was drawn around and behind the bird to call even more attention to it.

At the very top of the picture among the clouds, Richard had drawn another free-form starburst.

He was finishing up the last of four words in the highlighted space, which read: *THIS IS MY SON.*

Taking it all in, Helen exclaimed, "Oh, the baptism."

Richard looked up, seemingly unaware that the mature woman

with the no-nonsense manner had been watching him. "Not so loud," he playfully advised, "The nun will find us out and we'll be excommunicated."

"It's all right," the woman said. "The class is over."

Richard looked up and saw Helen spoke the truth. "Oh, well then, we are saved by the bell."

"It should read, '*YOU ARE MY BELOVED SON,*'" the plump, nosy woman said with authority.

"Oh, you think so?" Richard answered. Then, realizing he didn't know the woman's name, he paused to introduce himself. "I'm Richard, and you are?"

"Helen," she said.

"Well, Helen would you like to join me for coffee? The lunch room is just next door. We can talk about what it should be."

"I guess so. Why not? I've got some time before I need to be getting back. But I'm certain the Bible says *You,* and not *This*."

They were soon settled in at a table near the center of the room in the busy junior college's student cafeteria. Helen had a steaming cup of black coffee and Richard a glass of cranberry juice and a sweet roll. Richard cut the roll in two and offered half to Helen.

"No, I shouldn't," she said, then remarked, "I can't remember ever having come under threat of excommunication before, Richard. Is that your greatest fear?"

"That was just a joke, Helen. The instructor is a nun so I thought, what's the worst she could do to us for disrupting her class?

"She *was* a nun. I wonder why she left her order," Helen replied.

"Once a nun, always a nun. Anyway she sure knows her subject. It looks to me like she has fallen in love with leaves and twigs. Maybe her love of the world conflicted with her love of God. The eternal triangle, you know: Man, in this case Woman, World, and God.

"To answer your question," Richard continued, "I've never been communicated so I have no fear of being ex-communicated. It's my natural condition. I was born outside the church."

"The Catholic church?"

"All of them—Catholic, Baptist, Mormon, Jehovah's Witness, Evangelical. Have I hit home yet?"

"Pardon me?"

"You obviously know the Bible. I'm guessing you study with a church."

"Baptist. My father was a Southern Baptist minister and my husband is a minister. I should have told you, my name is Helen Gospel."

"Your husband is Dr. Johnny Gospel of Second Baptist?"

"Yes. And I've heard the baptism of Jesus preached many times. I remember, '*You* are my beloved Son.' "

"And you are entirely right; the Bible does say, "*You* are my Son."

"If you knew that, why did you write, *This*?"

"Because the Bible also says, '*This* is my Son.' And that apparent conflict can be traced directly to the fact that the Bible is more than one book."

"The Bible is the greatest book ever written."

Richard paused before saying, "To be great is to be misunderstood."

"Be that as it may, the Bible is still the best-selling book ever."

"It seems to me that it is a library of books. Your Protestant Bibles have sixty-six books," Richard said. "And the Catholic Bible has a few more."

"Baptists have always believed that all the books of the Bible have one author."

"It's an anthology then? A bunch of stories by the same author."

"No, it's one story by one author, God."

"Be *that* as it may, the books of Mark and Luke agree in saying, *You*. "

"Then Matthew and John have *This*?"

"Yes. Actually it's only Matthew that has God saying, "*This* is my Beloved Son." John's baptism story, as I'm sure you know, is different. It does say "*This*" but it is John and not God who gives the testimony.

"You obviously prefer *This*—why is it important to you?"

"I'm looking for an interpretation, a theology that makes sense. So that—"

Helen is suddenly impatient and interrupts Richard. "And it

doesn't make sense to you that God would speak to His Son saying, '*You are my beloved Son in whom I am well pleased*'?"

"Oh, I'm perfectly happy to let God speak to His Son in any way He chooses. I have no problem with that."

"Well, then exactly what is your problem with accepting, 'You are my beloved Son'?"

Richard, recognizing Helen's frustration with his refusal to agree with her, tries to steer the conversation in another less threatening direction. "Maybe," he says, "We should talk about the nun some more. My drawing seems to have upset you. I wasn't trying to convert anyone; I was just looking at a possibility—trying to express a thought in a picture."

"No, it's all right. I'm trying to understand where you're coming from."

"Now there's an expression I haven't heard in a long time. I seem to remember something in the Bible, someone saying when Christ comes, no one will know where he is coming from. Are you familiar with that? Whatever that story is, it could be where that expression came from."

"Do you imagine yourself the Messiah because I wondered where you are coming from?"

"No, it isn't that at all. It's just that I'm fascinated by how many expressions there are in our everyday language that have their roots in the Bible.

"Such as?"

"Oh, things like *kiss of death* and *nailed him. Turning the tables* is very common. It's in the newspaper two or three times every week. And, I'm sure you are aware of many more.

"Maybe you should write a book."

"It's been done. But there's always more to find."

Helen looks at her wristwatch and then taking a drink of her still hot coffee, steers the conversation back to its original intent. "You said you saw a possibility in saying, '*This* is my Son.' What did you mean?"

"*This* offers the possibility of a more reasonable understanding that I think might appeal to more people than just Christians."

"You mean unchurched people like yourself?"

"Yes, and anyone who finds the gospel to be unreasonable."

Helen seems surprised at this and is compelled to ask: "Let me ask you Mr. . . . what is your name?"

"Holmes, Richard Holmes."

"Are you a Christian, Mr. Holmes?"

"I like to think I am. I believe in God and also in Jesus. Does that make me a Christian?"

"I suppose that depends on the nature of the Jesus you believe in."

"My Jesus is a man, one much like any other man, except he was a special prophet."

"Well, then I would say you are not a Christian, certainly not a Baptist.

"I can live with that. I have trouble with the belief that Jesus was both one hundred percent man and one hundred percent God. My mind won't stretch that far. My reason won't let me go there. Maybe I'm sort of a semi-Christian."

Helen again returns the conversation to the baptism by asking, "What possibility do you see in '*This*'?"

"*This* allows us to understand the baptism in a logical way. Tell me, what does *this* stand for? "

"What do you mean?"

"*This* is a pronoun. What does it refer to?"

"Why—Jesus, of course."

"There's the problem, right there. That understanding is Christianity or Christ-inanity as it seems to me would be a better name for it.

"Christ-inanity!" Helen repeats sharply drawing the attention of several students at a nearby table. "That's a terrible thing to say. Inanity means insane or . . ."

"No, it's not that serious. Inane is merely stupid, silly, foolish, frivolous, ridiculous—take your pick," Richard offers.

"You think Christianity is ridiculous?"

"In what it believes about Jesus, I do." This baptism scene is a case in point."

"Explain."

"Okay, choose again. Look at the drawing. What else could *this* refer to?

"I don't see any other choice, unless you mean John?"

"No, not John, but you are getting warmer. There's another person in the picture."

"Another person? Who? Where?"

"Okay. Look. Try to imagine that you are Jesus. Put yourself in his place, standing in the middle of the Jordan River beside John. Maybe you've been there already, visiting in Israel I mean, with your husband and church group."

Helen nods her head yes, as Richard continues, "According to the account of the baptism in Matthew, *you* see the heavens opened and looking up, *you* see the Spirit coming down. And then *you* hear a Voice from Heaven, The Voice speaks to *you*, saying, '*This* is my beloved son.'"

Helen's mind opens a little and light, understanding, floods in. She exclaims, "Oh, the Spirit. You think *this* refers to the Spirit coming down?"

"Isn't it obvious? Third *person* of the Trinity." It looks to me like Jesus heard the Voice just before or immediately after the Spirit joined with him and he was overwhelmed by a new *Spirit of Love*. I'll bet there was no question in his mind as to what *This* referred to.

Helen and Richard are quiet together in the noisy cafeteria. Helen drinks coffee while considering what she has heard, while Richard privately recalls his experience, reliving the exhilaration and joy of finding himself free in an unbounded sea of *Love*.

Then she says, "I have to admit, it seems technically a possibility. But you have taken literalism to a new level. That's extreme to the point of absurdity."

"I hadn't thought of it in that way. Maybe literalism is an extreme sport. Maybe to make it work you have to go all the way with it."

"How do you think of it."

"Well, it seems to me that my understanding is a refinement of the old belief—rather like how Einstein expanded on the Newtonian laws of motion. The old laws are still valid but now we are aware of their limitations."

"Einstein was a genius. Do you think you're a genius?"

"Genius is oftentimes just common sense. Do you think it's

absurd to see the Holy Spirit as God's beloved Son? The Spirit has been accepted as a person from the early Church Councils. Whose son do you think he is?"

In the ensuing silence, Richard asks Helen another question. "Baptists believe that God created this world don't they?"

"Yes. There is some division over whether the creation was done in seven literal days. But, yes, of course, Baptists believe God created the world."

"Have you ever been to a zoo in the springtime?"

"I think so."

"Do you remember seeing all the new baby animals? The mother elephant with her baby elephant, maybe some tigers with their newborn tiger cubs and then, of course, the new giraffe in with the hippopotamus."

Helen comes to life at this saying, feeling certain, she strenuously objects. "Hippos don't give birth to giraffes."

"They don't? Why not?"

"That's just the way it is. Like begets like."

"No exceptions?"

"None."

"God's law?"

"Yes."

Why do you suppose God would make "like begets like" a law of His creation?

"I have no idea."

"Maybe so we wouldn't be deceived when He sent His Son into the world? John has it that God is a Spirit. So His Son would logically be …?"

"A spirit, like Himself."

"Now you're being reasonable. See how the parts fit together logically and make sense? Feels good, doesn't it? Like a breath of fresh air. And since there can be only one "Only Begotten Son," I choose the Spirit. There's no need to make Jesus '*God of very God*'. The *Spirit* already is all that. Occam's Razor is satisfied. We have not unnecessarily complicated things."

"What is that, Occam's Razor?"

"Occam's Razor is a rule of philosophical thought that came

into use in the 1300s. It says we should not imagine a second solution to a problem when one will do. Most people are more familiar with its modern incarnation, KISS, which being interpreted is "Keep it simple, stupid.

"The basic Christian beliefs, the dual nature of Jesus and the Triune nature of God, were decided on in the fourth century, about a thousand years before we learned how to think reasonably. Those beliefs were sacred and therefore untouchable, so Occam's Razor was never applied. The result is that we've been stuck forever with a religion that can be accepted only by faith because it's a logical mess. It's time for a gospel makeover."

"You have an unusual way of looking at the baptism."

"And you, I can see, are being remarkably patient and tolerant of my view."

"That doesn't mean that I am persuaded by your argument. My husband would probably say your argument is the most confused, backward, upside down and just plain wrong theological understanding he has ever before heard from any man."

"Sounds to me like you are trying to say that what I see, my visage, is more so marred than any other man."

"See, there you go again. Who do you think you are?"

Richard acknowledges Helen's question with no more than a smile while asking another of his own, "You recognized a Hippo-inanity right away," he said, "why is a Christ-inanity so hard for you to recognize?"

Helen responds surprisingly, remembering what she knows of early Church history. "Mr. Holmes," she begins confidently, "I believe you have fallen prey to an ancient heresy called Gnosticism. Like the Gnostics, you are obviously trying to reason your way to God when the only way is to come by faith."

"Helen, you are very close to the truth. I do feel a kinship with the Gnostics. They were wrongly condemned. Gnosticism is a heresy only because a Roman Emperor decided it wasn't in his best interests and made laws against it. He tried to get rid of all the Gnostic writings, but the truth can't be buried forever.

"It seems to me that Jesus himself was the first Gnostic. Gnostics were condemned for claiming to have secret knowledge of God. Jesus obviously had knowledge of God that others did not have. It might be called secret knowledge except for the fact that he was desperately trying to give it away to anyone having ears to hear."

Helen again tests Richard sanity asking, "Do you imagine yourself like Jesus?"

"Don't you?" Richard replies. "Aren't all good Baptists challenged to be like Jesus? Don't all born-again believers have a special, even secret, relationship with God? Are not we all striving to be like Jesus by letting the mind that was in him be in us?

"I've drawn a picture of that great event in Jesus' life, the time when according to the gospels he let the Spirit of God, God's beloved Son, enter into his mind. It's called the baptism here but it was also the moment he was born again from above. Here also in that moment is the resurrection. Jesus was changed in that one shining moment, He was raised from the dead and born again into new life. It's all one great experience. Occam's razor says we don't need all these different confusing—"

"Wait. You're saying Jesus was born-again? And the resurrection and the baptism are the same thing?

"Yes. It's simple. It's all one thing. There is only an experience. All the theology is unnecessary and its getting in the way of seeing the one important thing.

"We don't know Jesus' experience happened in the river with John; it may have happened under other circumstances. The circumstances don't matter. Only the experience of God's Love matters. Only that has power to change the mind."

Helen is quiet

"You still with me," Richard asks?

"I'm listening."

"Following his receiving God's Wisdom, sent from above, Jesus became a witness. John's gospel clearly says he was not the light but was a witness to the light. The witnessing in John is on two levels. On the first level John is the friend of the bridegroom who witnesses to Jesus who is himself the bridegroom. On the second, higher level, Jesus witnesses to the bride, God's Beloved Son, His Old Testament Wisdom.

"The baptism is a picture of Jesus receiving God's Wisdom shown as a dove descending a celestial staircase. It's a marriage made in heaven or more properly, a picture of a mother coming to care for her new born son."

"You're equating the Holy Spirit, God's Beloved Son, and His Old Testament Wisdom as all the same person?"

"Yes. And Mary, the mother of God," Richard responds. "Don't forget the 'immaculate conception.' What a logical morass all that is.

"Simplify, simplify. '*Things equal to the same or equal things are equal to each other.*' "

"Occam's razor again?" Helen asks.

"Nope. Euclid this time, plane geometry."

"It's a lot to take in all at once. But I will admit the resurrection of the body has given me some concern. Don't tell my husband I said that. It's a matter of faith for him."

"You might ask Dr. Gospel where Jesus was coming from when he said, *Let the dead bury their dead.* That sounds to me like someone, either Jesus or the gospel writer, believed Jesus was alive, before his crucifixion, in a way others were not. Faith is alright, even necessary. But you've got to use it where reason leaves off. A body dead for three days and then coming back to life is not a matter of faith. It's a horror show.

"The question Christians need to ask is, "Was Jesus himself born again?" If the answer is yes, that leads to a whole other understanding of who he was. Jesus was a witness to God. He had special—call it secret if you must—knowledge of God. In the first sense of the word, Jesus was a Gnostic.

"I would rather be a Gnostic than a Christian, were I forced to choose. I would rather *know* God than *live by faith* in some ridiculous beliefs decided on a thousand years before the age of reason, by an ancient emperor to serve his selfish interests.

"Much of what Christianity believes about Jesus, his divinity and so forth, I believe also. But we're coming from different directions. The church is denying the power of the true 'born again, from above,' experience. Jesus says we should love our enemies *in order that* we may be children of God. Receiving God's Wisdom gives us power to be Sons of God *along with Jesus*. It's the terrible exclusivity the church gives to Jesus that separates us from him, from his teaching, and thus from God."

Helen hears Richard out. She is interested but overwhelmed and remains unchanged by what he says. Then it is her turn to speak. "Be all that as it may, Mr. Holmes, my advice to you is that you find a good Bible believing church and join them."

Helen pauses and Richard asks, "Is that you speaking Helen, or your husband's church?"

Helen ignores the question and continues on her practiced response, "Try to forget what your human reason has led you to believe apart from the universally accepted beliefs of the church. I think you will find your greatest happiness in believing with others and not alone as you are trying to do. Your little joke about being excommunicated, I see now, was not a joke at all. You are obviously yearning to find a church home, a place where you can commune with others. You may have been born outside the church, Mr. Holmes, but you don't have to stay that way. Look into your family roots; I suspect you'll find some sort of religious heritage there.

"I've got to be going now. It's been interesting talking with you."

"Okay. Well, Helen, I am happy to have met you. Thank you for the advice and again I appreciate your Christian kindness, your patience and tolerance. You are quite right about my needing a place to lay my head. I have tried to find where I belong, but haven't yet found the place that is right for me. In a way, I envy you having been born into your faith and never having doubted."

* * *

In all, the brief but energetic collision of beliefs was good for both parties. Richard surprised himself with the things he told Helen. He was beginning to sing a new song, one never before heard. Helen would remember little of what he said but the exchange has had a positive effect on her. She left their meeting buoyed up inexplicably. The idea of a gospel makeover has excited her. That evening at dinner she asked her husband, "Was Jesus born again?"

With Helen gone, Richard made a note to himself to search the Bible for the stories behind three sayings: '*nobody knowing where*

Christ comes from,' '*a visage more so marred than any other,*' and '*foxes having dens and turtles having homes, but someone having no place to lay his head.*'

Richard hasn't thought it through yet, but will soon realize he has found another radical reinterpretation of a traditional belief. It is destined to be another chapter in his turning points book. The Holy Spirit coming down is in fact God's Beloved Son.

Helen's advice that he join with a Bible believing Christian church fell on deaf ears; Richard had heard it before. Yet her parting words, her advice that he search his family history for some lost religious roots, seem to him inspired. He is filled with a renewed determination to look again, this time more thoroughly, for some clue to his religious heritage.

Chapter Fifteen

THE SECRET FAMILY PRAYER: AN IRRELIGIOUS HERITAGE

And the vision of all is become unto you as the words of a book that is sealed, which *men* deliver to one that is learned, saying, Read this, I pray thee: and he saith, I cannot; for it is sealed: — Isaiah 29: 11

One man's trash is another man's treasure. — Anonymous

Helen Gospel's advice to Richard that he look at his family roots for a lost religious heritage brought to mind a trip that he and Celeste made years ago. His sister had called and said as their father got older he'd begun talking about his early life experiences more than ever before. She suggested that Richard might want to come home for a few days to record some of the old man's stories. His father's health was failing so this might be Richard's last chance. Recognizing he might learn something about his father's experience with religion, Richard welcomed the opportunity. He remembered his conversation with Celeste on the way there, and the surprising story his father told about the death of his mother and the question he had asked himself as a result.

* * *

"Richard, what church did your family belong to?" Celeste had wanted to know.

"We didn't belong to any church," Richard answered. "When I was ten we moved to the farm and then my mother tried to get my brother and me to go to the Methodist church her parents belonged to."

"You mean before ten you didn't go to church at all?"

"Not that I recall. Maybe we went to Forest's Chapel on Christmas or Easter when we visited my grandparents, but that was all."

"Did you go after moving to the farm?"

"Not much. My father didn't, and he was my hero. So when I was about eleven or twelve I didn't want to go anymore. I got the idea that it wasn't important and really didn't think anything about it one way or the other."

"Was your father an atheist?"

"Looking back on it now, I guess it might have appeared that he was. But while I was at home, I wouldn't have known or cared what an atheist was. It just wasn't something I thought about."

"What do you mean? Didn't your father ever talk to you about religion?"

"No, not while I was growing up—or ever. It just wasn't an issue. I never heard him say anything about religion one way or the other."

"*Never*? That's hard to believe, Richard. I don't believe that. Most people, even atheists, have strong opinions about—"

"Celeste, I swear to you that I honestly can't recall ever hearing my father say anything about God or Jesus or anything having to do with religion or the church in conversation with me or anyone else, including my mother."

"Okay, I believe you. But what do you suppose was his problem with religion?"

"I don't know that he had a problem with religion. But I guess that's really what we're hoping to discover—something about his experience with religion."

When they arrived in Indiana, the truth about the old man's "problem with religion," his lifelong refusal to involve himself in anything religious, came out in its own time in a most natural way. The frail old man had choked with emotion as he began to talk about his mother. This was not the grandmother Richard had known; this was an unknown woman, his father's birth mother who had died in

1920 when his father was only ten.

"It was Christmas and I spent the day at the town dump," the old man said. "I knew that whatever I found there would be the only Christmas present I would get that year. My mother had been sick in bed for weeks. The doctor said the house should be kept dark and quiet to help her rest and recover. It was tuberculosis.

"I found one old roller skate at the dump—the kind that clamped onto your shoes—and knew I could take it apart and use it with some wood I had to build myself a scooter. I was thinking about that while walking home. The doctor's car in front of the house was a familiar sight. But this time there were other cars I didn't know. Inside the house, people were busy and no one noticed me come in. I went to my room and soon heard my father and the preacher talking outside my door, which was open a little. I knew it was the preacher because I knew him. My mother took me and my sister to church with her every Sunday. The preacher had given me a pin for perfect attendance for a full year at Sunday school," Richard's father continued.

"I heard him tell Omer that God had taken Elsie, my mother, to be with him. That was how I learned that she had died. They put the casket in the middle of the living room in those days and people came to the house to visit and bring food for us.

"My mother was good to me and I loved her. And in the days after she died a question came up in my mind."

Richard remembered how the young boy's love for his mother had been displayed openly in the way the old man's voice quivered, rich with emotion and on the verge of tears, such that he could hardly be heard as he revealed the important question.

"What kind of a God would take a loving mother on Christmas Day?" he asked from his own sick bed, speaking the young boy's question aloud, as if for the first time.

Richard and Celeste had looked at one another and known that this question, asked silently by a ten-year-old boy, was at the heart of the old man's lifelong relationship with religion.

The quivering voice then steadied and the answer the boy had found and the man had lived by was heard loud and clear.

"No God at all!" he said with grim determination.

* * *

Richard reflected now, years after his father's passing, on the story of the young boy who judged God and found Him guilty for the death of his loving mother. The story explained a lot; it was the reason he had been allowed to grow up religiously neutral and that had once seemed enough to explain his own relationship with religion. But now, under the influence of Helen Gospel's inspired advice, it seemed to Richard there was more to the story.

A blank slate really wasn't a religious heritage at all. It was a non-religious heritage, the making of an atheist. But Richard knew his father didn't live without God in his life. He was a man of high moral character. His life had been a testament to the goodness of God, whether he had chosen to recognize that or not. He was like the good son in Jesus' parable of the father and two sons. He was the son who said he would not do his father's will but in fact did. His life stood in sharp contrast to those hypocrites who said they loved God and did His will, but whose lives told a different story.

Richard believed there was more to his own religious roots and that his father was somehow the key. His old man turning his back on organized religion had left Richard with what he had always called a blank slate. But that seemed incongruent with the kind of man he'd known his father to be. Something positive must have been written—some specific religious instruction from his father. But where was it? What had he forgotten? What was he refusing to remember?

* * *

The surprising answer came from Richard's own mouth.

"God damn it," he heard himself say one dark night in automatic response to a toe stubbing incident. Hearing the words and recognizing them for the first time as religious language led him to ask, *now where did that come from?* And he wondered at this strange form of religious language. This wasn't language that came from thought in the familiar way. This was language that came from emotional thought.

From this beginning, Richard opened his mind to recognize *God damn it* as part of a larger Christian profanity, now politically incorrect, which was once a familiar part of his life. Slowly the circumstance of his first having heard it was remembered. It was unmistakably religious language and it was from his father. He had been mistaken when he told Celeste he had never heard his father say *Jesus Christ.*

* * *

When he next had a chance, he shared his new insight with Celeste, almost like he was completing the conversation they'd had years earlier on their way to visit his dying father. Celeste had been curious and he wanted to set the record straight. He didn't mention that another woman, Helen Gospel, had sent him on this quest for a religious heritage.

"My daddy left the house early that fateful morning and went to the barn with me—only ten years old—right behind him," Richard began. "His intention was to get the big Oliver tractor going and do some late spring plowing on his weekend vacation from duties as owner of a wholesale electric supply company in Indianapolis. I was excited because I would get to follow in the furrow of the Oliver's plow, driving the smaller Ford tractor and pulling another plow. But it was not to be.

"The old Oliver resisted his every attempt to get it started. The big six-cylinder, high-compression engine had no electric starter and had to be hand cranked. Cranking that engine was a difficult job even under the best of circumstances. And that morning the damp air played havoc with the Oliver's weak six-volt ignition system and made starting the old tractor all but impossible. But my daddy was a patient and determined man. He persevered, laboriously cranking the engine over and over.

"The big green tractor was a row crop design, which means the wheel arrangement was like a big tricycle. The crank was mounted at the front of the tractor over the two close-set front wheels. It was at an awkward height for my daddy, slightly above his comfortable strong center position. I could see he had to stretch slightly off-balance, all the while being careful to use proper form to guard against a broken arm, should the engine backfire.

"After a while, he stood up straight, took a big red and white checkered handkerchief from his pocket and wiped away the sweat on his brow. He cleaned the six spark plugs, and wiped the distributor cap and again cranked the engine, expecting it to come to life. It didn't. It wouldn't. Then he worked with the carburetor and found a wooden board to stand on so he would not have to stretch slightly off- balance as he cranked the tired old engine some more, again and again. And all he got for his efforts, as I watched helplessly, was some puffs of black smoke amid some mildly encouraging sputterings of mechanical life. The engine threatened several times to catch on and run powerfully as we both knew it could at any moment, but it never did. I could feel his frustration building but had no idea what to do about it.

"Finally, his strength and his patience were running out. One last supreme effort to spin the engine into life ended with only some black smoke rising up toward heaven. And then, when the time was fulfilled, out it came—religious language reserved for the out-of-doors, invoked only under circumstance of unbearable frustration, *words* not consciously spoken but always transcendently ejaculated from the time of the first great disappointment into the present time and place.

"'Jesus Christ,' my daddy said to me—and I heard him in my heart. 'Son of a bitch,' he told me and I knew not the meaning but accepted it, in my youth, as an unquestionable truth. 'God damn it,' he petitioned and I was one with him in that. 'Go to Hell,' he warned finally and then it was over. The cranking stopped and the air cleared in the great hall.

"I wasn't shocked by what I heard. Although it was the first time I had heard it. Those words were exactly the right ones to use in that situation. They cleared the air and prepared the way for a new approach to the problem. I had no idea it was considered an obscenity or even what an obscenity was. The next day a big truck came and hauled the old Oliver away to be worked on."

* * *

Richard found a secret hidden in those few forbidden words. The secret is the words can be heard as an ancient prayer. Not a modern Christian prayer to be sure, but a prayer nonetheless. In the same way that one person's trash can be another person's treasure, Richard saw that one faith's profanity could be another faith's prayer.

This ancient prayer seemed to date back to the beginnings of

Christianity as it was breaking away from its Jewish roots. It was perhaps an ancient heart-rending plea against the heresy that would become Christianity's understanding of who Jesus was.

The first line of the profanity prayer—*Jesus Christ*—Richard heard as a question asking, *Jesus?* Who was he? *Christ?* It is still the question that angers and divides us.

The second line, *Son of a Bitch*, was the most uncertain. Richard thought its words made clear that the heresy being refuted was *Jesus Christ, Son of God.* No way, the prayer answers emphatically. Not *Son of God* but instead *Son of a Bitch.* The harshest word in the prayer—bitch—means literally a female dog. Richard remembered reading how Jews thought of Samaritans as dogs. Was the prayer then saying that Jesus was the son of a Samaritan woman? Or did it more simply insist that Jesus was a most common man and not the literal Son of God?

The third line, G*od damn it*, was easier. It was clearly an imprecation imploring God to damn the emerging heresy.

The fourth line, *Go to Hell*, closed the prayer and was unmistakable as a warning of the fate to befall those who left the old faith and became believers in a Jesus who was also God.

Richard could no longer deny the obvious. His message was not for Christians. His emerging theology, his truth, was true to the profanity prayer. His religious roots were deep, going back to the time of Jesus. His message was for a religious people who were predisposed to resist and reject Christianity. His message was for Jesus' original and authentic followers. But who were they? Did they have a modern incarnation dating back two millennia?

Chapter Sixteen

THE NEW FRAMEWORK FOR UNDERSTANDING

We shall require a substantially new manner of thinking if mankind is to survive.

— Albert Einstein 1879-1955

"Striving for that 'complicated simplicity' that distinguishes a masterpiece."

— from *200 Years of Charleston Cooking,* 1930: re, sweet potato recipes

Thinking about his discovery of how the familiar Christian profanity might have been some more ancient religious group's prayer, Richard saw this was something new. Ever since his experience—more than twenty years now—he had been seeking new ways of understanding specific verses from the Bible. Here there was no Bible verse involved; he had taken the profanity not from the Bible but from the world and seen it differently.

His reinterpretations of Bible verses were a natural, though long in coming, consequence of his first experience when the world had simply disappeared and his sense of self had shifted. That breakthrough experience had come from his having dared to follow Jesus into "love your enemies" territory. He knew now that the Jesus he had followed was a radically different Jesus from that preached in most Christian churches. Taken together, the reinterpretations created a new system of thought, a new world view.

The recognition of the Christian profanity as another faith's ancient prayer had come from seeing it through the new understanding of who Jesus was. His Jesus was antithetical to the Christian Jesus of faith. Like matter and antimatter they could not exist together. The established Christian Jesus was standing in the place of his Jesus. Each was antichrist to the other. The discovery was a demonstration of the power to see things differently through application of the new thought system.

Richard began a mental review of seven Bible verses he had chosen to represent his new manner of thinking. It appeared now that his interpretations of these seven verses would be the subject matter of the small book he had been trying to write since the day of his first experience. He had written "The Oneness of God" on the desk pad immediately after returning to his body and this world. He understood the words were intended to be the title of a book he was destined to write.

After many false starts the book was at last taking shape and was subtitled: "A Radical Reinterpretation of Seven Critical Turning Points in Traditional Biblical Theology." The idea to work with seven verses was inspired by memory experts who said the average person could hold only six ideas in mind at once. The seventh verse pushed the limit of six, but it was unlike the others. It was a proof text that like the profanity prayer discovery showed the power inherent in the new way of thinking. Richard knew his reinterpretations, considered alone, had little appeal. Their power to excite the imagination was in their interaction, their ability to work together and create something new. To access that power, to see the new thing, a person had to be willing and able to hold the new thoughts in mind and see them as a system of thinking and not simply a group of unrelated ideas.

The seven verses fell naturally into three groups which together formed a new framework for understanding. Each group was in response to a different type of confusion created and maintained by traditional biblical interpretations.

The first confusion dealt with God's creation of man. There were two verses chosen to illustrate the source and the resolution of the confusion. Genesis 1:27 was the first of these.

> So God created man in his *own* image, in the image of God created he him; male and female created he them.
>
> — Genesis 1:27 (King James Bible)

This statement was the source of the belief that God created human beings. Theologian Langston Gilkey saw the importance of this verse to human culture when he said it was "the most political statement in the Bible." The trouble was it didn't actually say what everyone assumed it did. Mark Twain put his finger on the logical problem when he said: "God created man in his image, and man, being a gentleman, returned the compliment." Even the most literal interpreters did not hold to a strictly logical understanding of this verse. Everyone simply assumed that human beings were the man created in God's image. Many books had been written laboring to show how human beings were like God. It was an uphill struggle. Richard's experience in which his sense of self had shifted showed him an alternative to this understanding.

Of course, a strictly literal reinterpretation of Genesis 1:27 opened a new question. If God had not created human beings, what was their origin? The answer to that important question was found in Genesis 3:21. This second turning point verse was as little known and respected as the "created in his image" verse was famous and loved. Richard found one commentator surprisingly called it "a throwaway verse." It didn't seem to matter to him and some other commentators whether it was included or not. It had no place in Christian theology, and so it was being ignored, even though it involved a creative act of God.

> Unto Adam also and to his wife did the LORD God make coats of skins, and clothed them.
>
> — Genesis 3:21 (King James Bible)

This act of God came as a culmination of the story of the fall of His created man. In order to protect and preserve His creation from the harsh environment outside the Garden, God had clothed His creation in "coats of skins" which He had made.

Like other "near-death" experiencers, Richard had come back to this world knowing he was not a body. It was common among experiencers to understand the body differently. Many of them spoke of the body as a garment they wore.

Bible commenters who took Genesis 3:21 seriously imagined God killing a few lambs to make loincloths for Adam and Eve. *Loincloths,* Richard remembered thinking! How unknowing of the power of God could they be? They had but to look at the space agency, NASA, and the complex life support systems created to protect men and women they send into the hostile environment of space, and compare that to loincloths. Is NASA more capable than God? One needs only to think of the still unfathomable human body as God's handiwork and His greatness is restored.

Christian theology, in Richard's worldview, has taken the teaching of the fall of man too casually. The fall was much more serious and eventful than imagined. God's created man had fallen from eternity into the harsh environment of time and space where he was clothed by God in "coats of skin" to protect and preserve him. This was the man who was deceived in knowing himself and believed he was that garment, the human body. Close but no cigar.

For science-minded Richard, the theoretical Big Bang marked the beginning of time/space and thus correlated well with the Bible story of the fall and separation of man from eternity. He accepted evolution as a fact within the world of time/space and understood it as a process whereby the fallen man was slowly clawing his way back to eternity where he belonged.

The second of the three confusions dealt with the matter of who Jesus was. There were three verses in this section. The first was again from the first testament, Deuteronomy 18:18. It was a prophecy by Moses concerning a messenger God had anciently promised to send his people.

> I will raise them up a Prophet from among their brethren, like unto thee, and will put my words in his mouth; and he shall speak unto them all that I shall command him. —Deuteronomy 18:18

No reinterpretation had been required here; it was simply a matter of playing a matching game and by observation seeing that the things written in this Moses prophecy of the Prophet to be sent were also claimed by the man Jesus in the second testament gospels. Then by application of a theorem remembered from high school geometry, "Things equal to the same or equal things are equal to each other," Jesus was shown to be that prophet.

Next was a major breakthrough reinterpretation of the sixth verse of the prologue to John's gospel. This revelation had come in

Greek and had required two years of study in order to be ready to receive it when it came.

> There was a man sent from God, whose name *was* John. —John 1:6 (King James Bible)

This important reinterpretation traced the teaching of Jesus as God incarnate to a misunderstanding of what the original author has intended to say. It was found to be a simple error in spelling, an ancient typo. The correction changed the text only slightly, from the troublesome, "… whose name was John," to the corrected text which read, "… whose name was of (or 'given by') John."

The third and last verse in this middle group, showing the way out of confusion about who Jesus was, came from the synoptic gospels and the story they told of Jesus' baptism. Christian theology was shown in Matthew 3:17 refusing to give up its fixed idea that Jesus was the literal Son of God, even to the point of refusing to recognize the true Son of God when plainly evident.

> And lo a voice from heaven, saying, This is my beloved Son, in whom I am well pleased. — Matthew 3:17 (King James Bible)

Pronoun reference was the means of the reinterpretation here. It was a case of mistaken identity. Jesus was dunked in the Jordan River by John the Baptist and on coming out of the water, verse 16 says he saw the Spirit of God descending like a dove and he heard the Voice from Heaven saying, "*This* is my beloved Son, …" Obviously Jesus would have recognized the pronoun "this" as a reference to the Spirit descending from Heaven as God's beloved Son.

The third confusion dealt with the recognition of the here and now. Richard believed the human race was lost and people needed to know where they were now before they could find their way out of darkness. What was needed was an unmistakable sign of the times by means of which people could get their bearings. There were two verses in this section. The first was a prophetic message from Jesus warning his people against being deceived by the coming Christian church. Although a version of the warning was included in each of the synoptic gospels, its fullest expression was Luke 21:8 . . .

> And he said, "Take heed that ye be not deceived: for many shall come in my name, saying, I am Christ; and the time draweth near: go ye not therefore after them."
>
> Luke 21:8 King James Bible

The standard Christian interpretation of this statement depends on how the words are punctuated. There is no punctuation in the earliest manuscripts so we are free to see it differently. With a comma following the word "saying," it appears that the words "I am Christ," are a quotation of what the "many" will themselves say. And history does record several persons who have come saying they were the Messiah. But in a world that was home to people numbering in the thousands of millions, Richard thought it was unreasonable to believe that these few were the "many" foretold to come.

Alternatively if we do not place a comma following the word "saying," the words say that the "many" to come, would come saying Jesus is Christ. This statement defines Christianity. Jesus is heard warning that many would come attempting to deceive his people with their belief of who Jesus was. This, of course, is exactly what history records. Time has validated Jesus' prediction of the most important event occurring after his death—the coming of Christianity.

Richard saw it was a powerful and striking idea to believe that a human Jesus had predicted the coming of Christianity and to realize that his warning against it was likely responsible for the historical enmity between Jews and Christians. This interpretation was sure to be rejected by committed Christians if they could hear it at all. For them it would be an unthinkable thought.

The sixth verse spoke to Christians and Christianity showing how they had failed to recognize Jesus' warning against being deceived. The seventh verse was more comprehensive of the human condition and spoke to all humanity.

Richard's review of the seventh verse was interrupted as Celeste entered the room where he was sitting. Seeing him alert but quiet, she ventured a guess. "You've been thinking again haven't you?"

"Yes, I have," he answered. "And I think we may be coming to the end of something."

"Oh, goody," she bubbled. "Does that mean we can take a trip? We need to get away for a while."

Richard nodded and thought back to the beginning of their spiritual odyssey and the part Celeste had played in it.

"You remember the Baptist Sunday School?" he asked.

"Yes I remember it, like yesterday. I hated it. You couldn't control yourself. I knew I had to go with you or …"

"Or what?" Richard interrupted. "They kicked us out, didn't they? What more could they do?"

Celeste's voice took on a serious tone, as if she was about to reveal a crucial fact for the first time. "I was afraid you would join their church and become one of them. You weren't yourself. It took a year for you to find out that you weren't like them. I was glad when the teacher told you we didn't belong with them and we should find another church."

"I was a little slow, huh?"

"Yes, we had some awful arguments about it. Don't you remember?"

"I remember you being there with me. They were supposed to have been "born again." I thought they would understand where I was coming from."

"Well, they didn't. Nobody did. I'm glad we're over that part of it."

"I remember one time stopping the car, getting out and walking home," Richard said.

"That was later. It was a different church, farther away. You walked five miles. They waved their arms in the air and I didn't like it. The pastor touched one of them on the forehead and he fell backward on the floor. We saw it happen. It was like those fake preachers on TV. You said I was closed-minded and we argued about that. Finally you stopped the car in the middle of the street and got out and walked home."

"I guess you thought it was the rapture," Richard responded with a smile, knowing she had never gotten over the Sunday school teacher who spoke often and honestly about his belief that a day was coming soon when people would suddenly disappear from cars and airplanes and there would be worldwide chaos.

Celeste brightened as if he had lit a fire within her. "Don't get me started on that. Do you know that guy is still in city government?" she asked impatiently. "After all these years, he's getting away with it. He's insane for God's sake, but he acts as if he's just like the rest of us. Nobody knows what he really believes. Gheesch!"

"Where do you want to go?" she asked, suddenly changing the subject but still full of enthusiasm.

Surprising even himself, this time he answered, "Let's go to Israel."

Switch to "off." Israel was the one place in the world Celeste had no desire to go. Yet Richard knew he had to go there—sooner or later. And he couldn't imagine going without her. The seed had been planted in her mind long ago, but she stubbornly refused to let it grow. She was afraid of what might happen if they went where Jesus had lived.

Chapter Seventeen

THE SEVENTH VERSE; 666

"Religion without science is lame. Science without religion is blind." — Albert Einstein

Science and Religion are still grappling to find common ground in the "service of truth." — Pope John Paul II

"The union of the mathematician with the poet, fervor with measure, passion with correctness, this surely is the ideal." —William James, 1842-1910

"The unleashed power of the atom has changed everything save our modes of thinking, and thus we drift toward unparalleled catastrophe."
— Albert Einstein, 1879-1955

Celeste left the room and Richard resumed his mental review of the seventh verse. Unlike the first six verses, whose reinterpretations had come more or less in sequence, the new understanding of his last verse had developed slowly.

In the first year of their spiritual odyssey, he and Celeste faithfully attended a fundamental Christian Sunday school class. For irreligious Richard, the experience was an introduction to the three basic confusions.

Celeste had freely chosen to go with him each Sunday and her presence served to contain Richard's enthusiasm within acceptable limits. He remembered the first time a young woman in the class was upset, crying and pleading with Jesus saying, "Oh Jesus, I've called to you and believed that you died for me. Why won't you answer my prayer and heal my father's cancer?" He was ready to speak out and tell her about his own experience with following Jesus, but Celeste had kicked him under the table, warning him to keep quiet and not to burden the group with what she was sure was Richard's personal insanity.

Celeste somehow always knew when he was about to explode, and several times she had kept him from going off in a judgmental verbal tirade reminiscent of some ancient prophet. Still, he had butted heads with the Sunday school teacher on several occasions. The last of these had resulted in their being asked to leave the group.

His thoughts returned to the specific point of theology for which he had sought guidance from the teacher and which had provoked the teacher's anger, causing him to suggest they didn't belong in his class. It concerned the number of the beast from the book of Revelation. The beast whose number was 666 was an important part of end time theology, which was of great interest to Baptists counting on Jesus to return and reward them for their faithful service. Richard had read in a footnote to his Bible that some ancient manuscripts had the number not as 666 but as 616. He wanted the Sunday school teacher, who he naively supposed knew everything about the Bible, to inform him in depth about the possibility of 616 being the right number. He learned from this encounter how it was unreasonable to expect even a born-again Sunday school teacher to know everything. Still, the man's impatience with him, an earnest newborn, showed there was a wide gulf between them and their respective experience of God.

Among the Baptists there was agreement that 666 was the proper number of the beast. However there was no agreement about the identity of the beast or of the man whose number was 666. And Richard, of course, had no idea that his personal resolution of this widely known and debated matter would eventually become his important seventh verse.

> "Here is wisdom. Let him that hath understanding count the number of the beast: for it is the number of a man; and his number *is* Six hundred threescore *and* six."
>
> — Revelation 13:18 King James Bible

Richard was slow in taking a serious look at solving the controversial riddle for himself. He preferred to first look and listen to what others had to say about it. He even had a file, a collection of papers—newspaper clippings mostly—computer e-mail printouts, and personal notes recording the interesting facts that came his way concerning the number.

It seemed to be a guessing game that anyone, religious or not, could play. Various Popes were a common and logical choice of Protestants, but almost any prominent person who wielded a great deal of power might wake up one day and find their name had been placed in nomination. Presidents and powerful business leaders were sometimes chosen for vilification as the anti-Christ.

The matter had caught the attention of the general public and the expression "six six six" was well known and used in books and movies as a sign of evil. Skeptics, making light of the matter, had pointed to anyone from Prince Charles and David Hasslehoff to Barney the purple dinosaur as being the fulfillment of the biblical reference. He once heard comedian Robin Williams on a late night show remark about ex-vice president Dan Quayle, "Two sixes and a five," he said, "almost there."

Of course it was necessary to show how the name selected was related to the number 666. Sometimes this was simple and straightforward as in the case of ex-President Ronald Wilson Reagan. Each of his three names had six letters. Other times the logic was complex as in the case for Bill Gates III, where the numerical values of the letters in his name were computed using ASCII (American Standard Code for Information Interchange) computer code. Other names sometimes required the invention of novel systems of accounting, loosely based in logical reasoning, in order to reach the necessary total of 666.

When Richard took a college course in the book of Revelation with Dr. Sane, his Greek professor, he was interested to see what the logically minded, yet religious man would say about 666. Dr. Sane taught that Revelation was basically a veiled message intended for Christians living at the time it was written. He thought it most probable that 666 pertained to the name and title of a past Roman emperor, Nero Caesar. Yet he held open the possibility of a future importance for the number by saying that when the time was right a second meaning of 666, if there was one, would make itself known to the church.

Richard saw that Dr. Sane's preterist (from the Latin for "past") argument basically held that the prophetic events of Revelation had already taken place. Preterists used the Hebrew version of "Nero Caesar" and found the numerical value of the letters totaled 666. Their argument was strengthened in that the Latinized version of "Nero Caesar" totaled 616. This fact explained how 616, which had troubled Richard in his first year with the Baptists, had found its way into some versions of the Bible.

It was a disappointment not to have a definitive answer to the riddle, and yet Dr. Sane's saying that the meaning would reveal itself when the time was right was the wisest thing Richard had heard anyone say about it. He liked the idea of there being both a past and future meaning of the number and saw no reason why it couldn't be so.

Richard routinely rejected every suggestion regarding the identity of the man and always for the same obvious reason. Although the dream imagery of beasts in the book of Revelation was too dense for him to understand, one thing was clear. The predicted destruction to come on the earth was too massive and widespread to be the work of one man. Suggestions that a Pope or King had such power seemed to him obviously impossible and merely silly.

A turning point came in his thinking about how to understand the identity of 666 when a Far-Side cartoon took him by surprise and made him think. The cartoon showed a doctor's waiting room. Three people were shown seated, patiently waiting for the doctor. They were: Old Man River, Jack Frost, and Cro-Magnon man. It was the Cro-Magnon man that caused him to see a new possibility.

The cartoon opened his mind to another way of thinking. It made sense that the "man" referred to in Revelation 13:18 need not be an individual.

The cartoonist's depiction of Cro-Magnon man led Richard to understand that indeed the world was subject to great destructive forces at the hands of one man. Cro-Magnon man had not had the power of widespread destruction, but the man who came after him, the present step in the evolution of human beings—Homo-Sapiens—did.

Newspaper articles, television programs, and numerous books documented the human assaults on the earth's environment. Pollution of the air, land and water was being observed and carefully documented. The impending crisis and coming environmental disaster was clearly seen and there was no denying the "man" who was responsible for causing all the trouble.

Richard saw the truth, as many did, in a wise observation of a cartoonist who memorably let his character, Pogo, be the bearer of bad news. "We have met the enemy," Pogo said, "and he is us." The identity of the man, Homo-Sapiens, seemed right. But how were we 666? The riddle remained unsolved.

More years passed as other turning point verses revealed themselves in Richard's mind. Reading Ayn Rand, he first became aware of a dream humanity held of someday witnessing the coming together of science and *Love*. The matter of 666 simmered in his mind as pollution of the earth continued unchecked. There was no power in Pogo's indictment of all humanity; it had no effect.

Scientists united to sound the alarm and put the world on notice. "Ten years," they said. Ten years in which to change our human ways or the effects become irreversible, impossible to control. Ten years came and went. No power on earth seemed capable of turning the tide. Human beings went into denial, the first stage of death, denying they were the cause of the changes being documented. They conspired against scientists and science itself. They—some of them— blamed global warming on Mother Nature.

A focus on the specific way in which human beings were causing harmful atmospheric change developed and became common knowledge. The burning of fossil fuels was at the heart of the problem. Too much carbon dioxide gas was being released into the air. Rules to control the emission of carbon were proposed and legislation written, but never enacted. They said it was overkill and would cause economic disaster. But the essential role of carbon in the cycle of life was recognized.

Richard watched and waited as these developments took place. Then one day it all came together in his mind. The answer was delicate and tenuous at first—like a string shot across a canyon by engineers to bridge the gap between where they were and where they wanted to go. The string would be used to pull across a rope and then a cable. Finally a strong steel and concrete structure, a useful bridge, would close the gap.

The gap that closed in Richard's mind was the intellectual separation between human beings and God. It was the realization of the ancient dream of the marriage of science and *Love*. The insight had come through something said by a late night talk show host. The guest had uttered the familiar expression, "carbon-based life form," and David Letterman had looked up and responded, "We're all carbon-based life forms for Heaven's sake." And then, working the gag for every laugh, he continued, "Everything on the whole damn planet is a carbon-based life form."

At this Richard had taken exception. *Well, I'm not a carbon-based life form*, he thought, little knowing the implications of the realization. A line had been drawn; a new space created in which to stand and appreciate a new point of view. During his first transcendent experience a barrier had been crossed and his sense of self had shifted. He had known himself as other than the body. He knew there was life beyond the body. His reality, the reality of all life, was spirit-based. Standing apart from carbon-based life forms his understanding was different.

The question coming from Pogo's insight was, how are human beings 666? Richard saw the question had evolved and taken a turn. It now could be asked more precisely; how are human beings, the highest expression of carbon-based life forms, 666? Asked in this way, the answer seemed somehow closer; the gap seemed smaller, more capable of being bridged.

Was there an understanding linking the scientific knowledge of the element carbon with the biblical revelation, 666—the number of the man caught in the act of destroying his environment? Did God have this man's number? Had it been written down nearly two thousand years before it could be rationally understood? And if a link could be found, would it be evidence enough to convict the man and convince him to change his ways in order to avert disaster?

The scientist in Richard came forth, and taking an up-close

look at the element carbon, he found a rational understanding linking carbon and 666. It was the realization of the dream of a marriage of science and God. The answer to the age-old riddle was elemental.

He knew that in the world of science each element was believed to be made up of three essential building blocks: electrons, protons and neutrons. Each element had a number which showed its place on the periodic table of elements, a drawing familiar to every high school student of the modern science of chemistry.

Hydrogen was element number 1, indicating it had one electron circling its nucleus. Carbon was element number 6 because it had six electrons circling its nucleus. Lesser known was the important fact that the nucleus of the element carbon 12, the essential element of life on earth, was composed of six protons and six neutrons.

Six electrons. Six protons. Six neutrons. 666 was then the unique mathematical signature of the element carbon, the essential element of the life of the body and thus the number of the man, who knew himself as the highest expression of carbon-based life forms—666 was the number of the man, deceived in knowing his true self, whose activities were destroying the environment and threatening to trigger the disastrous events foretold in the book of Revelation.

Chapter Eighteen

THE SMALL BOOK

And I saw another mighty angel come down from heaven, clothed with a cloud: and a rainbow *was* upon his head, and his face *was* as it were the sun, and his feet as pillars of fire: And he had in his hand a little book open: and he set his right foot upon the sea, and *his* left *foot* on the earth, And cried with a loud voice, as *when* a lion roareth: and when he had cried, seven thunders uttered their voices. — Revelation 10:1-3 (King James Bible)

In the days and weeks following the discovery of the sameness of 666 and the element carbon, Richard became convinced the link was more than coincidental. To him it was a compelling proof for the existence of a living God, an intelligent loving presence who had planned for this moment in human history. A God who knew His Creation, exiled from His presence, would arrive at this point in their return to Him, seeking guidance, being in critical need of help to show the way out of darkness. How, he thought, could one otherwise explain the foretelling of the number 666, written long before the existence of atomic theory, and its link to a "man" implicated in the destruction of the earthly environment?

It was, he believed an act of the same loving presence that had amazingly enveloped him in an overwhelming embrace of *Divine Love* when he had desperately chosen to love his enemy in trusting, childlike obedience to the written commandment to do so.

The scientific solution to the riddle that had been a mystery for a thousand years was a coming together of two books—the "book" of life on earth written by humans, and the Bible, the inspired Word of God. The happening was a sign to His creation that He was with them. God with us. This was the hopeful message in the sign. And it was, he knew, the meaning of the name, Emmanuel, that Richard had seen written on his cup, a remembrance of a vision seen in his childhood. This was the heart of his message; we are not alone—God is with us.

He was ready at last to write the book he had known himself called to write from the beginning. He had tried many times to deliver on the dream of a book to go with the title, "The Oneness of God," but always he had been unable to finish. The first writing was an impossible attempt to put into words his ineffable, feeling experience—to describe in a compelling way *the Love of God.*

In seeming response to that first unpublished effort, there had been a story in the local newspaper about the world's smallest book. He had been reassured then, knowing that God was still with him and had a sense of humor. He knew also the writing would have to wait until he had something more substantial to write about. Slowly the system of insights had grown until now when the revelations seemed at an end and the final verse was in place, the time was right.

It would not be another impossible attempt to explain in words the emotional depth of *God's Love,* which was all he had had to work with at first. Now it would be more substantially an exposition of the seven critical turning points in traditional biblical theology revealed over a long period of time. He was ready now to pull all the insights together and to let them point the way out of darkness into the light of God. The seventh verse was the last; it gave the others an authority they did not otherwise have.

The writing would be straightforward, just the facts as he knew them. And thus the book would be a small one. It would be a new song in a four-part harmony. There would be an introductory statement noting simply that mistakes had been made. Parts one through three would deal with each of the three confusions, the misunderstandings that had taken hold about ourselves, about Jesus, and about where we are now. These three sections would present the seven important turning point verses together with some of their major corollaries.

The fourth part would be the most difficult to write. It would be a call for authentic worship. Based on the circumstances leading to Richard's own transcendent experience, it would be an attempt to show where God could be found. Personal experience of *God's Love* was the only way out of darkness into understanding. He would try to present the two-step process, first the forgiveness and then the entering into stillness, in its abstract form; it would be up to those with ears to hear to interpret it—in the language of their individual life circumstances—into specific lifesaving actions.

The writing proceeded quickly once it got underway, being basically a review of familiar material gathered over many years. A need to include a drawing presenting the seven verses in a memorable way resulted in a decision to show them arranged in a circle with the first verse at the center top and the others circling around turning left like cars racing on the Daytona speedway. This put verse four, the John 1:6b revelation at the center bottom support position. The seventh verse, 666, was placed at the top side by side with the first verse where it implied a nuclear weld, holding the circle fixed solidly together. The circle represented a unified system of thought.

With the work at an end, Richard's thoughts turned to what to do next. Was he supposed to have it published and if so by whom? A late night series of living pictures in his mind's eye just before falling asleep seemed to be the answer. There was first a view of him and Celeste outside a big building having a golden torch high atop a central rotunda. But what building was it? Was it a museum? Did the torch indicate it was related to the Statue of Liberty in New York Harbor? A second picture showing a long corridor lined with what seemed to be miles of books was a clue. Then he and Celeste drove by a traveling exhibit which had by happy coincidence come to Daytona Beach and Richard saw the golden torch he had seen in his dream, pictured eight feet tall on the side of a semi-trailer.

It was called the *torch of learning* or *flame of knowledge* and it stood, recently restored, high atop the Jefferson building of the Library of Congress (LOC) in Washington D.C. The exhibit affirmed that there were miles of books on shelves in the three buildings of the Library on Capitol Hill and other locations.

Celeste jumped at the suggestion they take a trip to the nation's Capital, Washington D.C., to see the cherry blossoms and to visit the Library of Congress.

Chapter Nineteen

BINA AND JENNY IN WASHINGTON D.C.

Richard and Celeste step out of the fog and drizzling rain into a gift shop near the White House. It is Saturday evening, the end of their last full day of visiting the many historical monuments and sites of political power in Washington D.C.

Richard had satisfied his main purpose of visiting the Library of Congress and getting a basic familiarity with its workings. Hanging around his neck, under his shirt and resting next to his heart, is his most prized possession. It is a small flash drive with the files comprising the eight chapters of his small book, *The Oneness of God; An Exposition of Seven Critical Turning Points in Traditional Biblical Theology*. The book has taken twenty-five years of his life to go from inspiration, through research and revelation, to its final written form on the 1GB flash drive. His concern now is deciding what to do with it.

Celeste immediately begins browsing through the gift shop filled with a wide variety of expensive souvenirs and cheap trinkets designed to appeal to visitors such as themselves. Richard searches all around and then inquires about a restroom. A helpful clerk tells him there is none in the shop but that he could go out the front door, turn left and cross the street to a bar and grill where he is sure to find a restroom.

Seeing Celeste happily occupied, Richard leaves the gift shop and begins his quest outside for the promised facility. He finds the bar after having to ask directions only once. The restroom is easily accessible downstairs from the street-level foyer without having to pretend he has been a customer. It is super clean with marble floor and walls and has high quality fixtures. This is no ordinary bar and grill he realizes. While leaving he glances at the menu—prices are reasonable—and checks out the dining room—white tablecloths and great turn of the century Victorian charm. Seeing no line waiting to be seated, he decides this is the perfect place to take Celeste for dinner this last evening in the city.

Celeste is ready when he returns to the gift shop. She has asked about a good place to eat and knows that the Old Ebbitt Grill, one of the most popular restaurants in the city and said to have been frequented by several presidents, is just around the corner.

"Honey," Richard begins, "I've found a great place for dinner. It's got white tablecloths and everything you like. It's just outside around the corner. Let's go. There's no waiting."

"That sounds good," Celeste answers. "I'm ready."

Richard leads the way and soon they are seated in the main dining room at one of the small tables for two arranged very closely side-by-side along a long, mirrored wall. Celeste chooses to sit with her back to the wall on the full-length leather covered bench seat. From there she has a panoramic view of the entire dining room. Richard is seated opposite her on a reproduction of an antique Victorian bentwood chair.

Celeste is clearly pleased with the tablecloth, the turn of the century decorating and the busy, politically charged atmosphere. The place is perfect; there is a lot of activity to take in and new people to watch and wonder about.

A few moments with the list of wine-and-spirits and Celeste orders her standard gin and tonic, while Richard orders something new, a "Russian Stout." The menu explains this is Guinness Stout mixed with Coca-Cola, Stoli vodka, and Kahlua.

Celeste remarks that the new drink sounds like something Richard might come up with at home. Richard agrees saying, "Yeah, a strange concoction, my kind of drink." The Russian Stout proves to be exceptionally smooth and Richard is happy with it.

Celeste orders a bucket of clams and Richard goes for the featured special, an exotic Japanese pork chop on rice, in honor, the menu says, of the cherry trees, now in peak bloom and originally a gift from Japan.

The closely spaced tables make conversation easy and almost unavoidable. Two well-dressed salesmen, who they soon overhear are in town for a convention, occupy the table to Celeste's right. They are excited and looking to spot any sort of political celebrity. The two young couples on Celeste's left toward the front of the restaurant are together and seem not to want conversation.

Richard and Celeste take their time and enjoy their meal together. Afterward Celeste has an Irish coffee in honor of the occasion. Richard, who does not drink coffee, decides to have another Russian Stout, granting himself permission since they would be riding the metro and not driving back to their hotel.

They are contentedly finishing their drinks and preparing to leave when two beautiful young women enter through the revolving front. It is Jenny and Bina. Jenny is wearing a stylish red dress hemmed above the knee and Bina is attractive in a form fitting black blouse and black skirt. Following them is "Big Dollar" Bill; Jenny's used car lot owner fiancé from Daytona Beach. Jenny is first through the door and her blue eyes scan the dining room and unexpectedly come to rest on Richard and "that woman." Excited, she turns to Bina and whispers energetically, "That's him! He's here!"

Surprised by Jenny's enthusiasm, Bina asks, "Who?"

Jenny again tries to communicate, this time in a louder whisper. "The man from the plane—Richard!"

Her mind elsewhere, Bina doesn't yet get it and again asks, "Who? And "What plane?"

Jenny is anxious to make herself understood and blurts out, "It's him—Forrest Gump." And then more explicitly, "Sex on the plane."

This at last clarifies the "who" for Bina. However, husband-to-be Bill, coming in behind the two women overhears his fiancé's whispered "sex on the plane" and is immediately suspicious that something he needs to know about is going on. He has been looking for something to explain why Jenny has suddenly become so unhappy with him that she has asked to break off their engagement.

It was Bill's idea to come to Washington today and to take

Jenny out to dinner at a nice place so they can talk about it. Jenny agreed to this one last date on several conditions. She told him that he would have to find his own place to stay, that she intends to return his ring when next she sees him, and that she will not go out with him unless Bina comes along. Bill agreed to all the conditions and made reservations for three at the busy Old Ebbitt Grill.

A waiter soon honors their reservation and leads the threesome toward a table at the rear of the dining room. But Jenny stops the procession short and refuses to go past the two open tables just vacated by the young couples sitting beside Richard and Celeste, saying, "Here, this is fine."

Jenny quickly seats herself beside Richard in the bentwood chair next to his on the aisle. Richard is polite but shows no signs of recognizing her. Jenny signals for Bina to sit opposite her on the bench seat next to Celeste, leaving Bill to sit beside her or Bina—she seems not to care which he chooses.

"Jenny," Bill protests, "we have a comfortable table for four reserved at the back."

"Well, go sit at it then," Jenny answers. "Bina and I like it here. Don't we Bina?"

Bina responds as expected and the waiter, anxious to please, calls for a busboy to clear the dishes from the two tables. Bill seats himself beside Jenny on her right.

Bina at last catches up with the situation and seeing a glow on Jenny's face knows beyond any doubt that this is the man who, perhaps unknowingly, wrapped her friend in a "love bubble" the past Monday morning. Wanting to know more about this mystery man and his wife, Bina turns to Celeste and asks, "Are you two in Washington on a visit?"

Celeste is surprised that these strangers have chosen to approach them so cordially. It's not what she expects in the big city, but she's happy to talk with this friendly young woman. "Yes . . . I'm Celeste and this is my husband Richard. We've been here since Monday and this is our last day."

When all she receives in return is a smile, she adds, "Do you live here?"

"Yes," Bina says. "Jenny and I—I'm Bina. I have a townhouse

in Arlington and we work at the Library of Congress." She makes no attempt to introduce Bill.

Celeste is attentive. "Oh, you work at the Library. Richard was especially interested in seeing the Library, weren't you dear? We even got our reader's cards in the basement of the Madison building, so we could get inside that beautiful Jefferson reading room."

A waiter visits the new table and quickly takes Bill's order for a double scotch whiskey, a gin and tonic for Jenny, and a Budweiser for Bina.

Bina is quick to pick up on the opportunity to learn more about Richard through further conversation about the library.

She asks him directly, "Was there something special about the library you wanted to see and maybe didn't get a chance to?"

"Yes," Richard responds. "I was expecting to see some of the millions of books and a little of the miles of bookshelves the library supposedly has."

Jenny is impatient to let Richard know who she is. Before Bina can answer his concern about seeing the miles of books in the library, she impulsively moves her left leg to brush against Richard's right leg under the tablecloth where the movement is hidden from Richard's wife and her own fiancé sitting only a few feet away.

Time stands still again for Richard as he feels the warmth of Jenny's leg press against his own. He turns in pleasant surprise toward the young woman sitting next to him and his eyes are opened. "It's you." he exclaims. "You're the woman with the turquoise travel case." And then, completely out of character, under the influence of the two Russian Stouts, he says with enjoyment, "We slept together—on the plane."

Jenny is thrilled to see Richard remembers her so warmly and laughs openly.

"I was afraid I would never see you again," she says.

"Me too," Richard answers awkwardly, unsure exactly why this beautiful woman is so happy to see him again.

Hearing Richard's enthusiastic confession of marital infidelity, Celeste is surprised and nearly chokes on a swallow of her Irish coffee.

Richard realizes too late that his wife is sitting only a few feet away and has heard him declare that he has slept with this young woman—and has not yet heard either of them deny it.

Celeste mops up her spilled coffee while trying to decide if the two Russian Stouts have disoriented and confused her husband, like that old man's Ouzo wine did in Venice, two years ago. Or if he is again simply out of his mind and having another vision of loving everyone, the same as he loves her and the neighbor lady, and now apparently also this young woman. That first time she had thrown everything but the kitchen sink at him in frustration at not being able to bring him back to his senses. She is hoping to avoid a repeat of that uncontrolled outburst by hearing an explanation that makes sense. She is about to open her mouth and say something when Bill bolts to his feet in apparent shock and anger.

Having heard this old man confess openly that he has slept with Jenny, his wife-to-be, and apparently done *it* while on the plane, Bill can take no more.

"That's enough!" he exclaims, leaning over Jenny and poking his finger directly at Richard's face. "I don't know what's going on here. But it seems to me, sir, that you have had some sort of illicit relationship with my fiancé, on the airplane. I could be wrong. I'm willing to listen to reason. But I demand to know *now* what's going on with you two or I'm warning you there will be consequences."

Bill's action has taken the steam out of Celeste's boiler and she is willing to wait and see what happens next. Maybe Richard will get what he deserves in response to his revelation of having slept with this angry man's fiancé. The man is young and well built; he certainly looks like he can handle the situation without any help from her.

The explosive situation is magically defused by Jenny. "Oh sit down, Bill! You're such a Neanderthal! It's not at all what you think.

"This is my friend Richard and his wife. Yes, Richard and I just met on the plane from Daytona last Monday. He sat beside me and we had a nap together and some fun but it was all totally innocent. Nothing happened. Can't you see, for God's sake, he's old enough to be my father."

Richard is anxious to confirm what Jenny has said in order to calm both Bill and Celeste. "Yes, it was all innocent," he said.

"Nothing happened that shouldn't have. We took a nap together and I made a joke saying we slept together. I'm sure that if you'll think about it, you'll realize that having sex on those planes without being found out is almost impossible."

Richard's unwitting use of the word "almost" left room for doubt in Bill's mind. He remains standing while trying to decide if this old man is some sort of sexual magician capable of doing the "almost" impossible and is making a public fool of him.

Celeste also has cause to wonder. She recalls a time when they were younger when Richard expressed an interest in their joining the mile-high-club on a long boring overnight flight to China. She had refused, saying there was no way they could do it without "being found out." She wondered now if he had at last found a way and is mocking her.

Bina nudges Bill back to sanity by saying, "Sit down, Bill. You're making everyone nervous. Nobody had sex on the plane."

"Well, all right, if you say so," Bill said, trusting Bina to tell the truth. "But will somebody please tell me what did happen on that plane that turned my fiancé against me?"

"Now is not the time for us to be talking about that," Jenny said.

A waiter came with drinks for the two young women and Bill, who downs his double Scotch and orders another.

"Maybe you want to take that next drink at the bar and wait there till we're finished visiting. I'll come get you in a few minutes," Jenny suggests to Bill.

"Sounds good to me, babe," he answers, and with a nod to each of the others he was gone.

"He's not a bad guy, not really," Jenny says. "I guess he just loves me too much sometimes."

"Honey," Richard says, looking at Celeste, "this is the young woman I sat next to on the plane from Daytona to Atlanta. Remember, I told you about her, how she was beautiful and that her turquoise luggage matched her dress?"

Then, not waiting for any sign of recognition from Celeste and evidently seeing no need to explain anything further, Richard quickly turns his attention back to Jenny.

"So, your name is Jenny and you and your friend work at the Library of Congress. That's great. I should have asked your name at least but it didn't seem the right thing to do at the time. It was only after you were gone that I wished I had."

Jenny enthusiastically skips any pretense at small talk and asks directly what she wants to know. "Were you meditating on the plane? Bina thinks you might have been meditating when you seemed to be asleep."

On the other side of the tables, Celeste realizes that Richard is ignoring her, so she turns to Bina and asks, "Why do I think there is more to this? What are they keeping to themselves? Do you know what's going on?"

"All I really know is that Jenny was very happy when she got to work that morning. And she seemed to think that just sitting next to and napping with your husband had something to do with it." Bina decides it is best to leave out the part about Jenny's sometimes devastating effect on men and how she had allowed her attractive leg to press tightly against Richard's. And she did not repeat Jenny's saying about how she felt herself wrapped in a "love bubble" and how the experience was altogether "better than sex." She did again assure Celeste that whatever took place between them was all entirely innocent.

"Because if you were meditating," Jenny continued telling Richard, "I think some of your peacefulness must have overflowed onto me."

It was the first clue Richard had to understanding this young woman's interest in him.

"Whatever happened," Celeste tells Bina, "your friend seems to have enjoyed it. Does she always flirt with older men like that?" Then, before Bina could answer, Celeste says, "Wait a minute, now I do remember Richard said something about how some beautiful young woman had been flirting with him. He decided that she must have been teasing him. I thought he was kidding me. She really is quite beautiful. How do you stand it?"

"Oh, things have a way of leveling out." Bina answers. "I'm smarter and I make more money."

"It's probably good for him," Celeste says. "I guess I shouldn't be jealous. Let him have some fun . . . why is she asking him about meditation? Does she meditate, too?"

"No, she didn't know anything about it before I suggested to her that Richard may have been meditating when she thought he was sleeping."

Bina responds to Celeste's concern but her real interest is to learn more about Richard. "She was fascinated by your husband's peacefulness. Has he been meditating long?"

"It seems like forever. He started doing it before the experience and that was about twenty-five years ago."

Bina realizes the potential in what Celeste has told her. Her hunch was right. She now knows something happened to this man at the time of the worldwide rise in consciousness that has spawned the super-secret Cinderella search at Homeland Security. She wants to know more.

"The experience?" she asks. "What was that?"

"Oh, I shouldn't say anything about it. You'll have to ask Richard. It was all his business. It changed our lives though, I can tell you that. He quit working, nearly altogether for a while, and went back to school. I was afraid he might become a preacher. He's been trying to write a book for a long time."

"A book?"

"Yes, I'm pretty sure he finally finished it. It's hanging around his neck on one of those computer things. I think he had some naïve idea that he could just come up here to the library and give it to someone and then everything would take care of itself after that."

Richard is only slightly aware of the conversation between Celeste and Bina. Jenny is enthusiastically giving him her undivided attention, flirting, it appears to Celeste, and he would have to be dead not to respond fully to that.

"Yes, I was meditating," he responds to Jenny's question about whether he was meditating or asleep while sitting next to her on the plane. "It was a very good session. Something was different; it seemed to have a new dimension, a greater depth."

"I know what it was. Some of your peace overflowed into me."

Oh? Tell me about that. Was it good for you?"

Richard has meditated in groups before, but he has never heard of a touching meditation or transference of the feeling state of one person to another. He remembers now a New Testament story of Jesus and a woman who was healed of a long illness by merely touching the hem of his garment. Richard had considered the account just a fanciful story, an example of magical thinking by a pre-scientific people. Now, as Jenny tells him of her experience, of overflowing peace, he is beginning to think differently. He is very interested in what she has to say.

"It was wonderful. Like nothing I had ever felt before. I was super-happy; it was almost like I was drunk except I wasn't. I told Bina it felt like I was wrapped up in a 'love bubble.'"

"Love bubble? That's an expression I've never heard before."

"It's the best I could do trying to describe how I felt. Before you sat down next to me I was restless and wanted to sleep but couldn't. When the seat in front of you came down suddenly and your leg jumped to get out of the way it brushed mine and I thought it was funny. And when I made our legs touch again it felt natural and was comfortable. I figured you wouldn't mind; you seemed to be asleep and so I let my leg rest against yours and straightaway I felt very relaxed and then it got better."

"How good did it get?"

"I wish I knew. I must have fallen asleep. When the plane landed, we woke up and our legs were pressed tightly together. Bina said it sounded like how tightly her Rabbi says a man and wife are supposed to cling together after they are married. I told her it wasn't like that; we weren't married for heaven's sake. I was rested and happy, very happy."

"Super-happy."

"That's right. Say, you're a good listener. Anyway, I told Bina it was better than the afterglow I get sometimes after sex. That's why I'm so glad to have found you again."

Conversation at the other end of the table stopped when Jenny spoke of her experience as being better than sex. Then with Celeste and Bina paying attention, Jenny, in all innocence and sweet expectation pops the question that will force Richard out of his closet.

"Will you teach me to meditate like you do?" she asks with her bright blue, love-me-or-I'll-die, eyes locked onto his and penetrating, it seems to Richard, down to his toes.

Yet, despite even this, his lips are set to answer, "No." It is the standard answer he has given for as long as he can remember to all requests for him to be a teacher or a leader in anything. Something within him has always told him he isn't ready, he doesn't yet know enough, and to just-say-no. But now this beautiful young woman, Jenny, believing in him and trusting him is irresistibly asking him to share with her what he knows best.

There is a pause as Richard recalls a scene from a movie, *Dumb and Dumber*. "No," the hero says out of sheer stupidity, saying he is unqualified, when asked by a busload of bikini clad girls to serve as their suntan boy. Richard asks himself, *how dumb am I*?

Suddenly the time is right. Gone is the need to just-say-no and he comes forth finally, as does a worm when it is at last ready to emerge, no longer a worm, from its self-made cocoon.

"Yes, of course I will teach you. I can teach you; in fact I'm the best possible teacher for you."

"Oh, good," Jenny gushes in happy anticipation, oblivious to the change she has facilitated. "When can we start?" she asks.

Bina sees an opportunity and offers a suggestion, "How about tomorrow morning in our office in the Jefferson building?" Then before anyone can offer an objection, she seals the deal with Richard—if that was needed—by telling him, "You'll get to see the miles of bookshelves just outside our door."

Arrangements for a meeting are made. On leaving the restaurant, Richard discovers that Jenny's fiancé has already paid for his and Celeste's dinner. He takes a minute before leaving to find Dollar Bill at the bar and thank him for his unexpected kindness. The brief exchange has a positive effect on Bill, and returning to Jenny and Bina he finds he is greeted warmly.

The next morning is Sunday and the Library is officially closed. But Richard and Celeste are allowed to enter, passing through security as official guests of employees Bina and Jenny. They go into the basement offices deep in the bowels of the Jefferson Building. Richard's curiosity is soon satisfied as he is allowed to see a little of the reported 838 miles of book shelves in the three Library of

Congress buildings on Capitol Hill and other locations.

After seeing the books, Richard and Jenny spend half an hour alone together in a quiet, dimly-lit conference room; it is her first lesson in meditation.

Bina takes this opportunity to get acquainted with Celeste. She is eager to learn more about Richard and his book.

Celeste is impressed with Bina's executive-level position with the Congressional Research Service (CRS) in its Foreign Affairs, Defense and Trade Division. CRS, Bina explains, is the branch of the Library that provides the members of Congress with information throughout the legislative process. Celeste asks about her background and education. Bina reviews her life story, growing up in Israel with her grandfather, and then her education, PhD in linguistics from Jerusalem University. Finally she tells of finding this job with the Library and how she left Israel against her grandfather's advice. Then she turns the conversation back to Richard and his book.

"Have you read your husband's book?"

"No," answers Celeste. "I'm sure it's about religion and I think all religion is crap. What I'd really like to know is why you are so interested in reading it?"

Bina is surprised by the intensity of feeling in Celeste's no-nonsense response, but she recovers quickly and tries to answer her important question with similar directness.

"I love language and books. And sometimes it seems to me that I am looking for a certain one. Do you think he would let me read it?"

"Yes I do, if you told him you were the one God had sent. He is like a child that way."

"I can't say that."

"I'm not surprised. I wouldn't believe you if you did. My job has been to help Richard see things in a more responsible way and to keep him out of trouble. If I told him I thought you were the one he was looking for, yes, he would leave it with you."

"Do you think I'm the one?"

"I don't see any other possibilities, except the only logical one—that it's all crap."

"It must make you wonder though, doesn't it? I mean you

said Richard came to the Library hoping he would find someone interested in his book. And now here I am."

"Yes, it's all very surprising. Richard would call it a miracle."

"And don't forget Jenny. She's the one who brought us all together."

"Oh, I can't forget her. I've been looking forward to the time when Richard's book was finished. I told myself, maybe then our lives could get back to normal. But now, there she is, in your conference room sitting quietly in the dark with him and probably hanging on his every word so that he thinks he is something special. Can you believe this is the first time I've ever seen him agree to be a teacher?"

"Yes, I can. There is a saying from the Jewish Talmud, 'He who learns and does not teach is like a flower in the desert.' Jenny offered your husband a way out of his desert. Teaching will give his life meaning and purpose."

"Maybe, but what does he really know?"

"I guess someone will have to read his book to answer that."

"I think you're all insane."

The door of the conference turned meditation room opens slowly and Jenny and Richard come out. Jenny is hanging on Richard's arm in seeming literal fulfillment of what Celeste has just said. She is smiling and it is easy to see that she is all wrapped up in another "love bubble."

"Meditation is easy," she giggles, "All you need is to empty your mind."

"She's a natural," Richard offers.

Bina sees Jenny's delight and gives Richard an admiring look and a smile.

Celeste is annoyed and strongly tempted to jump to a wrong conclusion but does not react. Then choosing to ignore the situation, she says, "Richard, I think Bina is the one you came here looking for. She wants to read what you've been working on—your book. I think you should leave it with her."

"My book? What do you know about that? Have you read it?" He didn't realize that Celeste knew he had written a book.

"No. I haven't. It's about religion isn't it?

“What else? But it’s not like what you call ‘crap.’ It’s different. I think it makes a lot of sense. I’ve titled it *The Oneness of God.*”

“Whatever you call it, if it makes sense it can’t be about religion. But maybe I’m wrong. Bina is apparently an intelligent young woman and she thinks it might be important.”

Richard turns his attention to Bina. “Is that so?”

“Yes, I’m very interested in seeing your book. May I read it?”

“Yes, of course. Wow, this is good. I had an idea that someone here at the Library would be interested in reading it and helping me decide what to do with it.”

Richard removes the lanyard fixed to the flash drive from around his neck and loops it over Bina’s head.

“Here, take it. Read it and let me know what you think. But promise me you won’t share it with anyone without asking me first. Maybe I should explain about the logo that’s a kind of signature. And—”

“Richard,” Celeste interrupts gently. “Let it go. We’ve got a plane to catch.”

Richard looks imploringly at Bina.

“Trust me,” she answers. “I’ll do the right thing.”

Chapter Twenty

TO ISRAEL WITH LOVE

Bina waited until she was home alone before putting Richard's flash drive in the USB port of her personal computer. A list of files popped up; she clicked on the first one. A page appeared with Richard's title, *The Oneness of God*, and a two-line subtitle, *A Radical Reinterpretation of Seven Critical Turning Points in Traditional Biblical Theology*. It was all neatly centered and spaced. Below this in the position where the name of the author would normally be found was instead something so unexpected that it made Bina's heart stop when she saw it. It was a logo, a simple line drawing that she had seen once before in her life.

She remembered it was spring in Israel; the flowers were blooming and the birds singing. Not yet two years old, her parents had left her overnight with her grandfather and grandmother at their house in Jerusalem. She was alone in Grandfather's office for just a moment when someone came to their front door and he stepped out. She climbed up on Grandfather's desk chair and came face-to-face with the typed page having the drawing of the little house in the open box. "What dat?" she asked repeatedly and insistently when her Grandfather returned a moment later and found her sitting in his chair. He lifted her up, hugging and kissing her, and told her it was nothing.

Bina woke from her reverie to hear her phone playing the Israeli National Anthem. It was her Grandfather calling from Israel.

"Grandfather," she answered excitedly. "I've found him—the

Messiah! I know it's him. He's got the sign. He uses it like it's his personal logo. He doesn't know yet who he is or where he belongs.

"Oy Vey! Bina, my child, listen to you. A messiah you've found who is lost already and doesn't know who he is?" Grandfather asked. "Slow down Granddaughter; listen to what you are saying. Two thousand years we are waiting here in Israel for our Messiah to appear. And now you tell me we have been mistaken. I should have been looking in Washington D.C.?"

"No Grandfather. Not Washington D.C., Daytona Beach, Florida! The Messiah, Grandfather, he is a senior citizen, like you; and he's waiting for us on the world's most famous beach."

"Bina, think first and breathe deeply then answer me this: 'Can anything good come out of Daytona Beach?' "

"Oh, Grandfather. It's true this time. I know it. I've been wrong before, two times I was mistaken. But now, the third time, I am right. He has the sign Grandfather, your secret sign."

"What sign Bina?"

"I saw it Grandfather, when I was little. It was on your desk and I wondered, *what is this*? And you told me 'it is nothing.' Then you put it away and I never saw it again. But I remembered and later I knew what it must be. Today, just this minute, I've seen it again Grandfather, the little house in the box without a top. I've seen it again for the first time. It's him, the promised one you have waited for."

"Bina, where have you seen this?"

"Oh my god. I'm right aren't I? There really is a sign."

"Bina! I remember a time long ago. You were a baby, just a toddler, walking and climbing everywhere. A little monkey, we had to watch you constantly. But, how could you remember? You were maybe, not yet two."

"It's part of God's plan Grandfather. How could I not remember? It's all part of the plan—my coming here, you being there, my roommate Jenny—everything. Oh, the world is suddenly brighter and more alive.

"He's the messenger, isn't he? His having the sign proves it, doesn't it? He's the one God has promised to send, the one you are waiting for, the one who will at last redeem the Jews—show the world the Jews are right. It's coming together, Grandfather. Oh, how beautiful it is to see His plan coming together."

"Bina, stop. You're going too fast. What if you are wrong, like before? Maybe it's nothing, a coincidence with the sign."

"No. It's not just a coincidence. I've met him Grandfather. He's just a man, but unlike any other I've known. He has a power to make people happy and the innocence of a child."

"Tell me where? Bina, the sign—help me to believe, like you. I want to believe. Oh, how my heart aches to believe."

"It's on his book, Grandfather. I have asked him and he has given it to me to read. He doesn't know yet, Grandfather, who he is." Oh, I've got to help him find his way to you in Israel."

"Bina. This book with the sign, can you send it to me?"

"Yes, Grandfather, It's on my computer now. I haven't read it, not even a page. Just now I looked at the title page and saw the drawing that is the sign and then your call came."

"Bina, you could send it to me with the push of a button. Please, send it. It may be nothing. We will read it together; we will know together what it is."

"Oh, Grandfather, I want to. But he asked me to promise I wouldn't share it with anyone."

"Did you promise, Bina? You must not break your promise."

"No, Grandfather. His wife, she stopped him from making me promise. I said only 'Trust me.' I told him to trust me to do the right thing. And he agreed, Grandfather. He agreed with his eyes and with his heart, I felt it. He is trusting me to do the right thing for him."

"Bina, it is the right thing that you should send it. You remember how hard you worked to bring me into the computer age? How I resisted? But now we are connected. And now we know this is why. You can send it. You must."

"Yes, Grandfather, I will send it. It feels right to me also; I'm tingling to my toes. We will read it together. Perhaps it will take the two of us to understand it. But I am concerned for you; for when you see the sign for yourself and know it is right—after waiting so long, it may be too much for your heart."

"Your uncle Levi is here with me. He knows everything, the same as me. We will see it and know together if it is right. Send it now, Granddaughter. The time is fulfilled."

Bina laid the phone down beside her laptop and closed the title page file putting it back in the folder with the rest. Then she right clicked the folder and chose the e-mail option. When the "compose" window appeared she made sure the folder with the book had been automatically attached. Then she carefully entered her Grandfather's e-mail address in Israel and added this message: "To Israel with Love, in Hope and Expectation. Bina"

She picked up the phone and said, "Grandfather, are you there?"

"Yes Bina, we are here."

"I'm ready now, ready to push 'send.' As God has sent this messenger to us, I send this to you."

Bina pushed the button, gently but firmly. "Oh Grandfather," she exclaimed, "It's like what Zechariah saw—a flying scroll!"

Chapter Twenty-one

THE SIGN'S FIRST APPEARANCE

"You've got mail." The mechanical voice of AOL echoed in Rabbi Shemuwel's (Shem-u-wel) office in the old section of Jerusalem. Uncle Levi was the first to speak as his brother the Rabbi, Bina's grandfather, opened Richard's title page. Their eyes were drawn to the space below the title where the author's name would normally be written. Instead of his name, Richard had inserted a hand-drawn copy of the unidentified line drawing he had mysteriously scratched in the red clay of a Georgia campground twenty-five years earlier. He believed the drawing was in some way his personal logo.

"Oy," Levi exclaimed, expressing both surprise and delight in recognition of the figure as the same as that which had been handed down to them in reverent secrecy from generation after generation of rabbis for two millennia.

"Grandfather, Grandfather! Are you there?" Bina's tiny voice coming from the phone lying on the desktop competed with the old man's eyes and memory for his immediate attention.

"Bina, yes. *Toda rabah* (thank you very much). Levi says it is the same. We need time now to be sure. We'll talk later."

A dial tone buzzed in Bina's ear before she could respond. In open-mouthed wonder she took her grandfather's unusual abruptness to be an indication of his excitement at seeing Richard's title page drawing and recognizing it as the long awaited sign of the Jewish Messiah. She understood his need for time. He would have to retrieve the drawing from its secret hiding place and be certain it was the same before he would allow himself to fully believe.

Too excited to sleep, Bina began reading Richard's small book, slowly working her way through each of the interpretations of the seven turning point verses Richard had chosen.

* * *

It was night, a few hours before dawn in Jerusalem. Rabbi Shemuwel did not need to see again the ancient drawing to be certain, yet the matter was too important not to compare the two drawings. He would go immediately with Levi to the Western Wall, knowing it was open every hour of the day and night. Only Rabbi Shemuwel and his brother Levi knew exactly where an ancient scroll was ingeniously hidden in the sacred rock wall, Kotel. The small scroll had survived hidden for centuries just out of reach of the unknowing.

As they walked in the dark along the familiar, narrow cobblestone streets, the old Rabbi remembered the miraculous way in which the sign had come into the world. It had come through Barnabas, a first century disciple of Jesus. Not one of the twelve, Barnabas had nevertheless been present on the Mount of Olives when the disciples had questioned their master. "What," they asked, "will be the sign of thy coming and of the end of the age?"

The hidden secret scroll recorded both the sign and Barnabas' description of its origin directly from Jesus' hand in response to his disciples' important question. The sign appeared first on the scroll, followed by this testimony of Barnabas:

"The master seemed preoccupied and unhearing when Peter and John with the twelve asked what would be the sign of the coming end of the age. Perhaps they believed he was gathering his thoughts when he stooped and picked up a stick, a broken olive branch, lying there and using it in his right hand seemed to idly scratch a few lines in the dirt. Then he immediately stood up and turning to face his disciples took a step away from the figure and began to speak with authority, saying, 'Take care that no one leads you astray. For many will come in my name saying I am the messiah and they will lead many astray. For you will hear of wars and rumors of wars. Take care that you do not be alarmed, for these things must come to pass, but the end is not yet.' As the master continued speaking, holding the attention of the twelve fixed, I, Barnabas, perceived that it was for me alone to see and to remember the pattern of lines he had drawn in the dirt. I crouched down to be certain of seeing the drawing completely and accurately. Then, when the master's feet moved a bit back toward me, I looked up and our eyes met. My mind immediately came alive and I found there a picture of the figure forever secure in my memory. And I heard in my mind the master tell me, 'And when next you see this sign you will know your redemption is nigh and the Kingdom of God on earth is at hand.' I stood and the master took a step back, and shuffling his feet in doing so the otherwise unnoticed drawing was lost and lived then only in my mind."

The Kingdom of God on earth! It was an exciting thought. Until this day *it* was a dream, forever deferred but never doubted. Preserving the secret of the sign and watching for its appearance had become a sacred trust handed down through two thousand years by faithful leaders of a unique people. Rabbi Shemuwel's small flock was descended from those, most humble, poor in spirit, followers of The Way called *The Poor Ones*. Long thought extinct, this tiny remnant, followers of the way of peace taught by the master, remained, never having left Jerusalem. Now, in this moment, the time was fulfilled. The kingdom of God on earth was ready to break forth. The Rabbi needed only to verify what he knew to be the truth before he would begin to share the good news.

Chapter Twenty-two

BINA INTERPRETS THE SIGN

Bina read the first two turning point verses in Richard's small book and realized she had no idea where this writer was coming from. No human being she knew had ever thought this way. It was beyond human reason and logic to say that the body was simply a garment. She understood why Richard had been reluctant to put his name on the book as its author.

She decided to take a closer look at the author's "name," the line art symbol drawn on the title page. She couldn't be sure of course that this drawing was the same as the one she remembered seeing as a child, but she was willing to bet it was. It had impressed her then as being a drawing of a little house in a box with an open top. If this were the same drawing her grandfather's religious sect had kept secret, it may have preexisted Richard by nearly two thousand years. What was its meaning and why was it reemerging now?

Bina knew that using her privileged access to the resources of the Library of Congress (LOC) would enable her to learn something of its mystery. She copied the drawing and entered it into the LOC computer program that would search the millions of documents in its data base for an exact match. The search took less than a second and the answer was negative as expected. There was no exact match. The drawing was apparently unique, one of a kind. Next, she lowered the search criteria to allow for variations in size and proportion. Still nothing.

It wasn't until the search criteria had been lowered to where only a sixty percent match was asked, that significant results were produced. Most of the computer selected drawings were surrounded by a square border which accounted for the major part of the match. Bina rapidly scanned through several pages of these looking for some similarity of content within the border. Then seeing the futility of searching through several thousands of drawings in this manner,

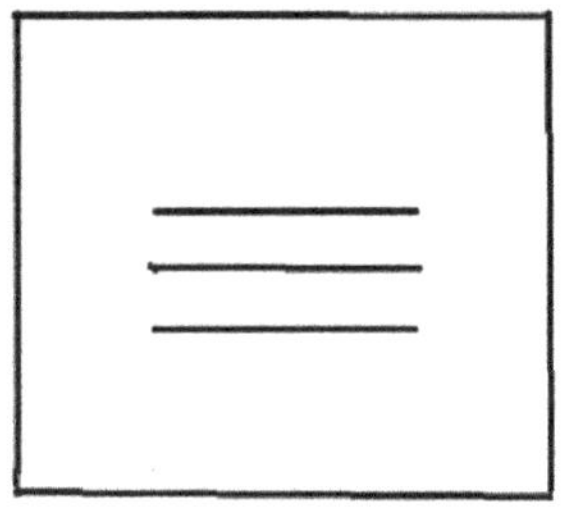

she added new search criteria that looked for some religious or mystic significance in the words associated with the drawing. Bingo! Only one drawing met the test. It was a simple square with three parallel lines drawn horizontally in its otherwise empty center. The drawing had been used in ancient occult religions to symbolically represent a person. Bingo again.

Bina saw how the same three-line center portion was in each drawing. However, in Richard's version the three horizontal lines were broken and reoriented vertically where they were pushing the top open at its center point. Symbolically, the box logically represented the body of the person and the three-line identity symbol represented the self within.

In Richard's drawing, the "self" within the box was breaking out of its container upward. With the top of the box opened, the self was now exposed to the matrix outside, which had been kept separate from the self by the closed box, the body.

It seemed a radical change had taken place within the person that was Richard. His personhood was changed. He was having a continuing out of body experience; his thinking was literally out of the box. This would explain his seeing the body as a garment, a simple container.

The new self, no longer contained within the closed box, now had room to grow upward. Bina thought it logical to believe that the upward direction represented a movement toward the light, toward God. It may have been that the self which once was Richard had ruptured internally in response to a strong impetus to grow toward God.

Two thoughts came into Bina's mind nearly simultaneously in response to the thought of the self growing toward God. The first thought suggested that perhaps there was nothing perverse in this breakup; maybe this was a natural process, like a flower bud opening itself suddenly to the light.

The second thought was a remembrance of something Jesus had said that Bina had always wondered about. "He shall receive of (what is) mine." If her grandfather's drawing and Richard's were the same it would be reasonable to expect that the two persons who drew them shared a common experience.

Bina knew that the origin of words and thus of language was in symbolic drawings. Richard's picture was a word, and more than that, a message.

She had always thought of Jesus as a man with a message. His message had come long before the world was ready to hear it and he had been quickly executed by those who saw it as a threat and feared change. Now, *What if* the same message was again threatening to come into the world? *What if* the world was being given another chance to open itself? *What if* Richard were a second messenger? Bina knew, of course, the necessity, in Jewish tradition, for a second or a third witness to establish the truth in a court of law. What if Jesus' teaching had failed to take hold among his people for lack of a second witness? Could Richard be that necessary second witness that would spark acceptance of Jesus' message in what Christians sometimes called God's frozen people?

She remembered her talk with Lucy at Homeland Security and how they had launched *Operation Cinderella Search* and were gearing up for a fight against an enemy they had not yet located, an enemy who was a suspected agent of change unwanted by the establishment. It was an old story *déjà vu* all over again.

But would the outcome be the same? Would the messenger succeed this time in sparking a revolution, wrapping the world in a love bubble with the result being "no more wars" as Jenny had said her Dr. Oh! could do. Or would they, secret agents of the establishment, be successful in their mission to kill the messenger as Lucy had said; "in order to preserve our way of life?"

Was Richard's message working its magic on Bina even now? Her sense of self, of who she was, seemed to be expanding, moving in a direction it had apparently long wanted to go, putting space between it and her body, imagined now not as her, but as a mere garment. The feeling was pleasant, like a weight being lifted.

Bina saw herself in her *What If* daydream, wanting to do whatever she could to help Richard succeed in his mission impossible. He had looked at her once and truly seen her and she had asked for his trust and he had given it and now they were one, united as in one purpose and she was growing in her understanding of who he was now and who he could become and her role in assisting the transition.

Chapter Twenty-three

MEN IN BLACK

Sometime after Richard and Celeste Holmes returned from their Washington trip to their home in Daytona Beach, neighbors began taking notice of two "men in black" walking and sometimes driving their neighborhood streets. The two of them were always dressed in the easily recognized fashion of ultra-orthodox Jews, although Celeste at first thought they might be Mormons. They wore their hair long with ringlets hanging down around their ears. Sometimes they would stop and park a while off the pavement watching residents and visitors come and go. They did not knock on doors or otherwise disturb the peace like Jehovah's Witnesses or Mormons.

Josie, a neighbor and Celeste's friend in the real estate business, asked if they were looking for a house to buy or if they needed help or directions. They respectfully said they were not in need of anything and thanked her for the offer. It soon became evident that the focus of their watching was Richard and Celeste's home. The rumor was that they wanted to live in the neighborhood and they apparently liked the big old house with the large lawn. Their continuing presence in the neighborhood was a mystery.

The men were young and appeared friendly. They were even helpful the day Mrs. Sackers backed her car out of her driveway and crashed into a moving pickup truck. They were not seen as a threat and soon their presence in the neighborhood was taken for granted as being a good thing. It was assumed they were related somehow to a nearby Jewish synagogue, though it was not ultra-orthodox. The men appeared to be interested in living in the neighborhood as they showed up at every open house, but they never made an offer to buy.

No one had reason to suspect that the men in black were spies, members of a Jewish sect in Jerusalem sent to discreetly find out who Richard Holmes was. Their rabbi had sent them in response to the Messianic Fever growing in the Jerusalem underground. The ultra-orthodox rabbi had gotten Richard's name by unintentionally reading an e-mail from Bina to her grandfather. Rabbi Shemuwel was now openly telling the story of the hidden scroll and its long held secret sign of the coming Messiah. He was preaching the good news of the Messiah's imminent arrival.

The secret agent men in black were instructed not to speak to Richard and not to interfere with his life in any way. They were to observe only and to report what they saw. One of the young men became very frustrated with the restriction against speaking to Richard, and once, on a Saturday when Richard was mowing the lawn and Celeste was nearby sleeping in a bed of flowers, he impulsively dared to ask Richard a question.

The two men came walking past the house as usual when suddenly one of them stepped off the sidewalk and into the lawn. The man's action indicated he wanted to talk. Richard politely turned off the noisy machine and while still seated looked at the man and asked, "How can I help you?"

The tall thin young man dressed in his Sunday best short black suit with white shirt and tie and wearing a black hat, got right to the point and asked the question burning in his mind, "Why are you working on the Sabbath?"

The man was certain the Messiah would observe the law against working on the Sabbath. This man could not then be the Messiah. There had to be an explanation.

Richard was wary of getting into a discussion about the Sabbath and so he answered with a bit of wisdom he had learned about work. "Work is only work," he said, "if you'd rather be doing something else." This seemed to catch the man's interest and so Richard continued, "I enjoy mowing this lawn. I work all week and I save this for today." It was a lie of course; Richard was a retired senior citizen and hadn't held a job in years, but he thought the lie excusable in order to make his point.

And then seeing he still had the man's attention, he added some words that just happened to pop into his mind from the *Everyman's Talmud*, a book he had recently bought at a garage sale. Adapting to the situation what he remembered of a surprising statement he had found in the book, he advised, "Along with the Sabbath, a sunny day, and sexual intercourse, a neatly mowed lawn is a taste of the world to come."

The man in black was captivated, believing Richard to be some new kind of secular Rabbi—a Talmud scholar, giving out new wisdom. They exchanged a few more words and then Richard restarted the shiny red riding mower and with the young man now in the driver's seat it went on its way circling the lawn, cutting the grass while Richard watched quietly from the sidewalk, standing beside the second, less adventurous young man in black.

Celeste joined them and asked Richard, "What's going on?"

"Mr. Black wanted to know why we were working on the Sabbath."

"What did you tell him?"

"I told him mowing the lawn was fun. I invited him to find out for himself."

The mower turned a corner and was again coming toward them. Richard said, "Look at that smile. He likes it."

"Well, if he's not too overjoyed when he's finished mowing, he can join me in weeding the flower bed," Celeste replied.

The unusual sight did not escape the notice of passersby and neighbors. Mrs. Sackers came out of her house on the other side of the street and pretended not to watch. The event became the subject of much neighborhood gossip.

Completing a second lap around the lawn, the driver stopped the machine, dismounted and with a smile and a tip of his wide-brimmed black hat to Richard, he rejoined his friend on the sidewalk.

"What's your name?" Richard asked.

"My name is Eli, and this is my brother. His name is Eli too," the wayward Eli answered and then volunteered, "We are from Jerusalem."

Richard responded saying, "I'm pleased to meet you Eli and you also Eli. My name is Richard and this is my wife Celeste."

The two of them spoke to Richard and answered together, "We know already who you are." This brought a look of puzzled surprise to Richard's face as the two Elis turned and walked away.

They had important new information to give their Rabbi about the mysterious American who has the sign Rabbi Shemuwel believes is the sign of the coming Messiah. Richard's growing reputation would precede his arrival in Jerusalem. The news being shared called him a Torah scholar having new wisdom about the nature of the law against working on the Sabbath.

"That was strange," Celeste commented. "Who are those guys and what are you to them?"

"I don't know. They said they were from Jerusalem. Who do we know in Jerusalem?"

"Bina—that girl you gave your book to at the Library of Congress. She told me she grew up in Jerusalem; her grandfather is a Rabbi. Maybe she can tell us something about them."

Chapter Twenty-four

SLOUCHING TOWARD JERUSALEM: PORTUGAL

Things fall apart; the centre cannot hold;
Surely the Second Coming is at hand.
And what rough beast, its hour come round at last,
Slouches towards Bethlehem to be born?

The Second Coming (excerpt)
— William Butler Yeats, 1865-1939

"I think we need to get away for a while," Celeste announced one day, not long after the encounter with Eli and Eli. "We need to take a trip."

Richard surprised her by agreeing. "Okay with me. Where do you want to go?"

"I don't know. Someplace big."

"Oh, you mean like to the moon? 'To the moon, Celeste. One of these days. *To The Moon*!' " Richard, showing his age, playfully imitated The Great One, Jackie Gleason, with relish, believing Celeste was leading him on and knew exactly where she wanted to go.

"No," Celeste responded, unappreciative of Richard's ancient humor. "I mean like Italy and France, Portugal—places we've never been."

"Oh, you mean big money places, Rome and Paris."

"We can afford it."

"I know—if we're frugal. But why Portugal? What's to see there?"

"Annette loves it, and she's been all over. She says it's still unspoiled, authentically European."

Their daughter Annette was married now, with a husband and a daughter of her own. Annette was a flight attendant with Delta Airlines. She had been working only international flights from New York City for three years.

"We can't go just yet; Bina is coming down next week," Richard advised.

"What? Bina?"

"I called her—you know, the Library of Congress, like you suggested. When I told her about Eli and Eli and how they said they were from Jerusalem, she said she didn't know anything about it, but she would ask her grandfather and find out what might be going on. She wants to come for a visit to show me some research she has done for my book. "

* * *

Richard and Celeste celebrated Bina and Jenny's safe arrival in Daytona Beach by sharing a huge crab fest dinner on the upper deck at Joe's Crab Shack on the Daytona Beach pier. Before the dinner Bina conferred with Richard about his book. "I've read your book and I have to tell you I have shared it with my grandfather who is a Rabbi in Jerusalem. We understand about the three confusions and we wonder about what happened in your life to enable you to see the world as you do. Your wife told me you had a life changing experience."

"Oh, that. Well that's another story. I just followed what Jesus taught and that changed everything. Do you think that should be in the book?"

Bina was excited seeing that she had been on the right track thinking there was one message and Richard was a witness to the truth Jesus had first taught. "Well, maybe and maybe not," she answered. "Tell me more about what you mean about just following what Jesus taught."

Richard was pleased to see Bina was sincerely interested. He had learned long ago that most people didn't want to hear about following Jesus. They had heard it all before. That was when he decided to focus on the results of the change that had taken place in his mind. His book was just seven examples of his new way of seeing the world. There was nothing in it about his experience or about his following Jesus' teaching to love your enemies. Still, he didn't want to risk losing her by boring her now with the details of what had happened. So he decided to try another way.

"I've written a parable that I haven't shared with anyone yet. Maybe that would be a good place for us to start. I call it, *This Bud's for You*. Do you want to hear it?

"Did you say bud?"

"Yeah, The title's a takeoff on the beer commercial. But it's not that kind of bud."

"Let me guess. It's about a flower bud. Right?"

"Right. Actually it's about a lot of flower buds. How did you know that?"

"I'll tell you later. After you tell me the parable."

"Okay. Here we go: 'This Bud's for You.' There was once a certain woman who each year planted flowers in a narrow space between her house and driveway."

"Oh, I saw the flowers coming in. They're beautiful," Bina said.

"Okay, so you've discovered the source of my inspiration for the parable already. I'll tell Celeste you liked her flowers. Let me try and shorten the parable; with you I hardly need all the words. By the way, it's subtitled, 'A Parable of Human Being.' "

"One certain year the woman determined to grow the very best bed of flowers possible. She did everything right and the flowers responded to her loving care. They were healthy and fast growing.

"One morning she looked at the growing plants and could hardly believe they were covered with buds already. She was surprised and exclaimed, 'Oh look at all the beautiful buds. Aren't they just perfect!'

"That's an important line. Now here comes the magic, you have to suspend your disbelief for the sake of the story.

"It was at that moment the vibrantly healthy growing flower buds became conscious. They became aware of themselves, the dirt beneath them, the blank wall of the house and the driveway in front. They saw all these things and they judged themselves to be the very best thing in all their small world.

" 'We are buds,' they told themselves, 'and we are perfect.' They had fallen in love with themselves. Soon they decided to hold a contest to find which of them was the very best bud of all. Each one tried to gain the attention of the others and there was chaos . Three standards were decided on by which they could judge one another to find the very best bud. A perfect bud they said would be perfectly round, uniformly green and as hard as possible.

As the days passed a pattern developed regarding which buds were the best. The best buds were the youngest; they were the roundest, the greenest and the hardest. Also those young buds deepest in the bed who got less exposure to the sun tended to stay more perfect than the others."

"I think I see where this is going," Bina said, "but maybe not—go on."

"All the buds learned to stay out of the sun as it was believed to cause undesirable changes. They learned several tricks but I'll leave that part out; use your imagination. They hid behind leaves and stuff. Oh, I forgot to say they crashed heads into one another to determine which was the hardest. This caused soft spots that disqualified them.

"Finally, the last call for the best bud went out throughout the bed, and a voice from the far end of the bed answered. The call was this: 'Who is the best bud among you all?' The voice answered, 'I am.' And 'I am the very best bud of all.'

"The voice was found to be coming from a bud at the very end of the bed, the place that got the most sun. It was the Gee Says bud. This caused all the buds to laugh. They all knew old Gee Says. He was the oldest and the tallest bud in the bed and they knew he didn't have the right stuff to be best bud. He had been oblong and lighter on top and soft when the contest began. And he never took care to stay out of the sun. There was nowhere to hide, he was always in the sun."

"I didn't see old Gee Says coming. This is good," Bina said.

"They all laughed, but Gee Says was quite serious. He bent over so they all could see the beautiful flower he had become and he taught them saying, 'A perfect bud is not a bud at all but a beautiful flower as you see I have become.' Oh, I forgot the part about why they called him Gee Says. It was because one day, the day he bloomed, he had begun saying Gee, Gee, Gee over and over. He was in awe about becoming a flower."

"That's perfect. You should write this down," Bina said.

"I have. It's here somewhere. I hadn't planned on telling the story. Anyway Gee Says taught they were all destined to become beautiful flowers like himself. They would all be Best Buds together. All they needed to do was be themselves and stay in the sun all day long. Many of the buds believed on him and this caused the hard-headed buds at the center of the bed to fear they might not be winners in the best bud contest. During a summer rainstorm they reached down to the end of the bed and banged their hard heads into Gee Says' stem.

"In the morning he was found hanging upside down on his own stem. The woman came and raised him up and took him into the house with her. With Gee Says gone, the hard heads taught he had been the unique son of the great sun in the sky and the woman. They said that one day he would return and save all those who accepted their teaching and worshipped Gee Says.

"It's a tragedy."

"Yeah, I guess. But it doesn't have to be. There's hope. The story shows a way out."

"I see it; follow Jesus' teaching all the way."

"Oh, I forgot, there was a debate. The hard heads said, "Our creator has told us, '*We are Buds and We are Perfect.*' We believe it and that's all there is to it." Gee Says taught, "You must be born of the soil and born of the sun to know yourself truly."

So you see it's all a misunderstanding; much ado about nothing. All that's needed is to correct the false teaching. "Love your enemies. That's the authentic part of Jesus' teaching, I think."

"Is that what you did?"

"Yeah, It worked for me. But it's complicated. Maybe later I'll tell you. Now it's your turn; how did you know the story was going to be about flower buds?"

"It was the drawing on the cover of your book."

"My logo? I don't see any connection with that."

"I figured it out with the help of the library's supercomputer.

The drawing is about an opening up. It made me think of how a flower bud opens to the world around it."

"Like in my parable."

"Exactly."

"But there's no action in my drawing."

"The computer found another drawing. It was a closed box with three parallel lines inside."

"The mathematical symbol for identity?"

"Yes. The drawing was used in occult religion to represent a self, enclosed in a body. I saw in your drawing the three lines were broken and standing upright. It looked to me like they were growing and had pushed the lid off the box which exposed the inner self to the bigger world outside. What does that feel like?"

"I reckon Jenny is the one who said it best. It's like being wrapped in a love bubble."

"I can't wait. What do I have to do?"

"Like the parable says, Just keep dancing in the sun. What goes around comes around."

Celeste came into the room saying, "Hey you two, it's time we get going for Joe's."

Later when the dinner table discussion turned to Richard and Celeste's plan for a big trip, Jenny, who was sitting next to Richard, was suddenly excited and gushed impulsively, "Oh, you're going to Portugal! I want to go too! I have a grandmother living there that I've never met. We could all stay at her place."

Richard liked what he was hearing. "That's a fine idea Jenny," he said, hoping Celeste would agree. "It would be a chance for us to experience the local culture."

Bina saw an opportunity in Jenny's impulsive travel planning to further her own agenda. "Well, you all can't go without me," she said, thinking she would have a chance to entice Richard and Celeste to experience the local culture in Jerusalem by staying with her grandfather.

Only Celeste was hesitant to commit to making travel plans with people she barely knew, one of them an exotic beauty overly friendly with her husband. Then Jenny said she would ask her boyfriend, local used car tycoon, *Top Dollar Bill,* to go along, "so he could pay for everything." Hearing that, Celeste thought maybe it could work out and might even be fun. When Bina offered to plan the trip and make reservations, Celeste was on board and ready to go.

"Where does your grandmother live in Portugal?" Celeste asked Jenny.

"I'm not sure. I haven't been there yet," Jenny answered in her totally naïve and honest way. "I think it's a small town named, 'Fat something,'" she offered.

"Do you mean Fatima?" Bina asked.

"Yes, that's it. How did you know? Is it famous?"

"Sorta," Bina responded, reluctant to tell all she knew. She guessed that Celeste might not be thrilled to go there if she knew it was the place where three children had famously seen visions of Mary. But that was years ago. It was probably all but forgotten by now, she thought.

Bina was anxious to get Richard to Israel where she believed his destiny was waiting. Jenny's inspiration for a shared trip was a great opportunity for her to guide him in that direction. It was a good plan, and with her help each stop along the way would be a step in the right direction.

* * *

The small group aboard Delta flight 1892 arrived at Portela Airport in Lisbon, Portugal at 8 a.m. on a Tuesday morning. It was the second time Jenny had slept next to Richard on a plane and once again she emerged feeling an otherworldly peace and insanely happy.

Jenny's boyfriend and used car dealer Dollar Bill was soon in familiar territory at the rental car dealer and the five amigos were quickly on their way to Fatima in a stylish BMW XP7 SUV with Dollar Bill driving and Bina riding up front serving as guide and navigator.

"This really is a fantastic driving machine," Bill exclaimed as they sped along a narrow curving road leading to Route 1, the fastest way to Fatima. At the halfway point they stopped in a small village for breakfast and their first taste of Portuguese wine. Everyone was in good spirits and when they were on the road again to Fatima, Bina decided the time was right to tell them the truth about what the small village they were heading for had become.

"In 1917," she began, "three children from the village of Fatima were tending a flock of sheep when they saw a vision of the Virgin Mary; well, it was a series of visions actually. The first one came on May 13th and the last on October 13th. I would have thought the excitement of that event would have died down by now, but it apparently hasn't. Today, Fatima is a major religious site that attracts great numbers of people—Catholics and the curious—from all over the world.

"Jenny's grandmother's family has a nice hotel in the center of town and that is where we will be staying."

"That's not exactly what we came to Portugal to see," Celeste protested gently from the back where she was seated behind Bill at the left side window. Richard sat peacefully in the middle while Jenny purred contentedly at his right side.

"I know," Bina apologized, "but we'll still get to meet Jenny's grandmother and maybe it will be interesting to find out what all the religious fervor is about."

"It's all crap; that's what I think," Celeste replied sharply.

Bill responded sympathetically to Celeste's honest opinion by restraining a chuckle.

"Maybe there is more than we know to all this," Richard said, already feeling a kinship with the three children because of his own vision years earlier. "This happened in 1917; that's not ancient history. There might be some meaning for our lives in whatever happened here. Let's keep an open mind," he advised. "Maybe we'll learn something new."

Jenny's arrival at the Fatima Hotel was an event. Her grandmother, a short round woman with a wonderful laugh welcomed her warmly saying, "Oh, you are so beautiful. Your mother was the beauty of all my girls and now look at you. I can hardly believe you are really here."

One by one she introduced Jenny to the people working in the hotel. Nearly all of them, Jenny discovered, were part of her extended family.

She learned that her mother was the only one of her

grandmother's five children, all girls, to leave home and make her life in the United States.

There was a special dinner in Jenny's honor in the hotel dining room that evening. Dozens of her cousins, aunts and uncles came to welcome their long-lost American cousin and her friends to the Fatima family and make them feel at home.

The following day it was insisted that they take a VIP tour of the Fatima exhibit. Their personal tour guide was a tall, dark and handsome man—one of Jenny's uncles—with an impossible to remember name: José Eduardo Santos Tavares Melo Silva. Mercifully, he agreed to answer if they would address him as simply José Silva. Richard noticed that the shortened name sounded a bit like HiYo Silver, the memorably famous cry of the Lone Ranger at the end of each episode when he had set things right and was on his way to another assignment. *José Silva Away*, Richard said to himself.

José apparently knew everything there was to know about the six apparitions, including the highly publicized finale, the "Miracle of the Sun." In this "public proof" event, the sun was described as appearing to dance across the sky while throwing rainbows of color across the landscape. The "solar prodigy" was witnessed by a great crowd of people, both religious and otherwise. The crowd, estimated at seventy to one hundred thousand, was terrified when at one point in its dance, the sun appeared to be falling out of the sky toward them. The description of the great event reminded Richard of one of the effects in a 3-D movie when the imaginary baseball or bumblebee suddenly flies out into the audience and people would scream or duck for cover.

Celeste found Bill was an ally in her skeptical approach to the happenings. She was more tolerant than usual, perhaps because the visions were the testimony of children and not adults who she thought should know better than to believe in visions of Mary.

Bina and Richard took in everything without judging, as though it were merely data to be stored for later retrieval and analysis. Richard was especially interested to hear of the hardships the three children had endured in sticking with their story. It was said that they were threatened with death and put in jail in attempts to make them admit they had made up the story. The children's ordeal made his own indignity of being called crazy pale in comparison.

Jenny lived in the moment as always and simply enjoyed being the center of attention among her new family in Portugal. Regardless of their different levels of interest, José succeeded in answering all of their questions and in bringing the five of them up to speed in understanding the basic facts of the historic events.

Going beyond the basics of the story, José informed them Jenny's family had lived in the village long before 1917, the year the events took place. It was said that Jenny's grandmother's mother, was BFF (best friends forever) with Lucia dos Santos, the oldest of the three children who witnessed the six visions of Mary. Two of the children died a few years after witnessing the apparitions and presumably went to the heaven they were promised. Lucia lived to be 98 and died in 2005. Lucia was the one who years after the events wrote from memory the important messages—the three secrets the children had received from the "Beautiful Lady" of Fatima.

It seemed to Richard it was primarily Lucia's writing of the third secret which was responsible for the continuing interest in the Fatima story. The third secret had to do with apostasy in the church and the death of many church officials and a Pope. The third secret was controversial and subject to interpretation. The Catholic Church, through a succession of Popes, failed to meet a 1960 deadline imposed by Lucia in which to reveal the secret. It was not until the year 2000 that the words of the third secret and the official Vatican interpretation of them was published. The long, unexplained delay in revealing the final secret—forty years beyond the appointed time—served to arouse suspicions regarding the motives of the Catholic Church.

José revealed that Lucia had become very unhappy in her later years with the Church for not having responded better in its acceptance of the beautiful lady's message. "In her disappointment with the Church," José said, "it was natural that she shared her fears and concern with her best friend." José added that Jenny's grandmother also became Lucia's friend and confidant. As a child she often accompanied her mother while visiting Lucia at the convent. Lucia, having no children of her own, took her best friend's oldest daughter—Jenny's grandmother—to be her good friend in whom she confided her hopes and fears.

So their host at the hotel had been privy to the third secret, but VIP tour guide José Silva dropped the subject as abruptly as he had brought it up. It raised a question, left unanswered, in Bina and Richard's minds. "What exactly had Lucia confided to Jenny's grandmother?" they wanted to know. When Richard privately asked José if there was more to the story, José said, "I am not at liberty to say. The answer will come if you wait for it."

The second day of their stay, Richard and Bina returned to the exhibit. They were intrigued by the mystery it presented and wanted to know more. Celeste, however, went with Bill and Jenny on a tour of the surrounding countryside in search of the picturesque villages she had hoped to find and enjoy. They all met up back at the hotel that evening at an appointed hour and were whisked away to the grandmother's private villa for a special dinner.

At the heart of the villa was the original family cottage where the grandmother had been born. The humble cottage had been added on to and expanded until it was no longer recognizable. It had grown along with the family's share of profits from the Fatima tourist trade. Top Dollar Bill was clearly impressed with the business of religious tourism.

The dining table was set for eight. There was Jenny and her four friends, grandmother, and two others. José Silva was one and there was a Roman Catholic priest.

"You all know José," Grandmother declared, "and this is Fredrico, who you haven't yet met. No, don't call him Father Fredrico; he's just a member of the family to us."

The portly, balding man laughed and greeted them as if he had known them all for years. "Call me Fred; all my American friends do."

"Let's have some excellent wine first and then we'll eat," Grandmother said. "I hope you all are hungry. We've got alligator steaks and Kentucky Fried Chicken which is what they tell me you folks eat over there in Florida," she said laughing. "I'm only kidding of course, about the food. But not about the wine. Tonight we're having some really excellent local Fatima wine, vintage 1917. Tonight is a special night."

"What's the special occasion, Grandma?" Jenny asked.

"Tonight, my beautiful child, we will together write a new chapter in the history of Fatima. First we share a meal and then I will tell you a story that some of you may find impossible to believe," Grandmother said, while stealing a glance first at Celeste and then Bill.

The elephant in the dining room was an artist's easel standing at the front. A purple cloth was draped over a painting that appeared to be about thirty inches tall and two feet wide.

The excellent dinner was praised by everyone and as the last of the dishes were being cleared away, Grandmother began telling the story. "I believe José has told you already my mother and Lucia dos Santos were best friends at the time of the visions and she continued to confide in my mother until late in my mother's life when Lucia took me as her best friend and began sharing with me her grave concern about the Church and its failure to recognize the Beautiful Lady's message warning about an apostasy in the Church at 'the highest level.'"

"'The Beautiful Lady is sad,' she would say, 'when her message is neglected.' Lucia's freedom to make public pronouncements was severely restricted by her position as a nun. It troubled her greatly, and slowly she was losing faith in the Church hierarchy's willingness to recognize an apostasy within itself. At long last, in the year 2000, the Vatican published Lucia's words written in 1944—the so-called third secret. The message had been sealed and given to the Pope with a declaration it was to be released no later than 1960.

I was with Lucia as she read for the first time the official interpretation of her words warning of apostasy in the Church. She had not been allowed to watch the official Vatican reading of her words in an internationally televised press conference[3]. Her reaction was surprisingly severe. "'Blind guides'! she nearly shouted. 'They are like blind men guiding other blind men. They cannot see the apostasy in their midst. They are looking for an apostasy to come

' ' within. It is a *diabolical disorientation*[4] in the

Church *and it is in the gospel.*[5]"'

"I had never before heard her speak of the false teaching being in the gospel. That got my attention and it scared me. I realized then I had assumed the problem was confined within the Church hierarchy, that it was an administrative problem of some sort. I understood then that when she said the apostasy was 'at the highest level,' she meant it was in the gospel. My eyes were opened that day to the full dimension and importance of the message. If the gospel itself was flawed, even the souls of the faithful were at stake."

As the grandmother spoke of false teaching in the gospel, her guests had various reactions. Richard looked across the table to Bina. He was excited that the story was moving in his direction. He had given the past twenty-five years of his life to rooting out false teaching in the church and in the gospel. If Bina had read his book as she surely had by now, she knew that it was all about a flawed gospel. His eyes met hers and he knew she, at least, understood.

Bill, being essentially nonreligious, was restless and wondering why he was there. He searched the room for a kindred soul and found Celeste. He rolled his eyeballs to communicate his skepticism. Celeste responded by rolling hers back at him.

Jenny listened carefully and looked at her grandmother with admiration and respect. She believed every word of the story. Jose Silva and Uncle Fred were already on board, of course, as the grandmother slowly worked toward a climax to her story.

"I needed help," she continued. "That is when I opened up to my nephew Fredrico. Fredrico was both family and a priest. He saw my distress when no one else did and he listened with an open mind as I shared with him what Lucia had said about the Church and the gospel. I found that he also had private concerns and doubts. One of the first things we agreed on was that within the family we would no longer call him Father. 'Call no man father,' Jesus had said.

"It was obvious to us Lucia did not know what the false teaching was. She only believed in it because the Beautiful Lady had warned her of the urgency of dealing with it. She prayed earnestly for an answer.

"Then one day she confided to me that the Beautiful Lady had visited her again and had given her a new message. She was old and I didn't know whether to believe her or not. But she was happy about it and had great enthusiasm, so I hoped it was true. 'The answer is coming,' she would say. 'It will come through a lost one after I am gone.' It was a new message, a would-be fourth secret of Fatima.

"This is the point in the story where José Eduardo Santos Tavares Melo Silva joined Fredrico and me in our quest to believe Lucia and Fatima had one last secret to give to the world. José is executive director of the Fatima Exhibit; I don't know whether you knew that or not. José was the only other person to visit Lucia regularly. He, of course, noticed when Lucia began saying, 'The answer is coming,'and he asked me about it. I could tell he believed in Lucia and the visions and he had her best interests at heart.

"Now the story gets more interesting for you all from Florida. Lucia told me the Beautiful Lady said the answer would come to Fatima from a 'lost one' in *my* family. The answer was then to be taken to the Pope that he might know the apostasy. We had no idea what a 'lost one' meant. We supposed it to mean some family member who rejected the Church. As you might imagine, in a family as large as mine there were several—mostly men—who we thought qualified as lost.

"I brought pictures of some of these to Lucia, one at a time so as not to overwhelm her. She wasn't interested in any of them. But she apparently got the idea of what I wanted because she became interested in painting. From the first when she began working with the art materials at the convent, she drew the figure of a young woman. I thought of my first daughter, lost to me in America. We encouraged Lucia, and over time she produced the picture on the easel behind me."

At this Celeste had heard enough. "Give me a break," she exploded. "What kind of a scam are you trying to pull. We've been here two days. I'll bet the paint on your picture of Jenny is still wet." She pushed back from the table as she spoke and before anyone could say 'stop,' she was at the front of the room and removed the purple cloth covering the painting.

A collective gasp was heard in the room as they saw the painting was indeed of Jenny but it was not her alone. It was *them*. Richard was shown in the center, seated on a barstool. Jenny was next to him on his right and Bill stood by her. Celeste and Bina stood on the left.

For a long time no one spoke. If this were a forgery as Celeste alleged, it was professionally done. Even Celeste was impressed. She backed slowly away and returned to her place at the table.

Finally, Grandmother broke the silence. "If you will allow it, Lucia finished this painting in 2004, the year before she died. Her work was done and she believed the lost one would not come until after her death."

Richard tried to speak, wanting to believe, searching for words to express his amazement and concern. "How could you, uh, Lucia, know . . . the details? It's unbelievable. The colors of the clothing are the same as what we're wearing."

"We weren't sure the clothing would be accurate until you arrived here this evening. There are details that identify this room so we knew it would be here. Lucia apparently had an image burning in her mind of a particular point in time and place," Grandmother answered.

"What do you want from us?" Richard asked.

Grandmother looked at José, who stood and stepped to the easel. "We have studied the painting and have discovered something very interesting. There are five of you and everyone can see that you Richard are at the center. But more than that, when we draw diagonals from corner to corner we find the center is exactly here." José used a pointer to show a location just left of center in Richard's chest. And now that I have called your attention to the exact spot you will undoubtedly notice a certain brightness in the painting there. It's a trick of light and color that professional artists know but how Lucia alone could have managed it is a mystery."

José Silva stepped back and Uncle Fred took over speaking. "You remember Lucia said, 'The answer is coming.' And our part was to take the answer to the problem. We believe you are the answer, Richard. The painting clearly shows it's in your heart. We want you to go with us to the Vatican and speak your heart to the Pope."

"It isn't me you should take to the Pope, but this," Richard said with enthusiasm as he fumbled awkwardly beneath his shirt and at last pulled out a small computer memory device from its resting place over his heart. It was attached to a lanyard hanging around his neck. It was exactly like the one he had given Bina previously at The Library of Congress.

The revelation of a computer device resting at the exact spot Lucia had pointed to as the location of the answer came as a big surprise to Jenny's grandmother and her two associates. They looked at one another and watched as Richard lifted the lanyard over his head and held the memory stick in his left hand for everyone to see.

"This *is* my heart," he told them. "The files on this flash drive represent twenty-five years of my life spent uncovering the sources of the false teaching that has led the Church into apostasy. This is the information your Pope needs to begin unraveling the mistakes that have been made." Richard handed the device to Jenny, who was sitting next to him. She in turn offered it to her grandmother who happily accepted it.

"Here is your answer coming to you from the lost one in your family just as Lucia told you it would," Richard said. "If you can get the Pope to read this, I believe that Lucia and the Beautiful Lady of Fatima will be pleased. The Pope however may not be quite so happy. "

Grandmother spoke slowly as she looped the lanyard over her head, treating the memory stick as if it were the pearl of great price. "Thank you Jenny, and Richard, all of you. Well, I certainly am pleased with the way this is working out. Now it's up to us to do our part."

After a celebration with more Fatima wine and as the group was preparing to return to the hotel, Jenny spoke up, "Oh, we've got to have a picture." She handed her camera to José and the five of them assembled quickly at the front of the room. The picture fell naturally into place without undue shuffling Richard in the center seated on a stool, Jenny and Bill on his right, Celeste and Bina to his left. There was a flash of light and everyone knew it was 'the moment' that had burned itself into Lucia's mind and inspired the painting that had drawn them together.

The next day, Jenny was looking at the picture and noticed the bright spot was there over Richard's heart. "How could that be?" she asked Bina. "because when the picture was taken the computer thing wasn't there. My grandmother had it."

"That's right," Bina agreed. "But then it wasn't there when Lucia saw her vision either."

"It looks like Uncle Fred was right. The brightness is in Richard's heart," Jenny said. "Maybe it's that 'immaculate heart' thing the children said Mary wanted everyone to have."

The Three Visionaries 1917
Lucia dos Santos; Francisco and Jacinta Marto

Chapter Notes

3 Headline in *Corriere della Sera*; Antonio Socci, *The Fourth Secret of Fatima*, page 26

4 Sister Lucia quoted by John Vennari; *Death of the Last Witness*

5 Sister Lucia reported by Frere Michel; *The Whole Truth About Fatima: Science and the Facts*

Chapter Twenty-five

MESSIANIC FEVER GRIPS OLD TOWN UNDERGROUND

Word of Rabbi Shemuwel's belief that the time had been fulfilled went out from his small group through the Old City of Jerusalem. There was a loose network of friendships, an underground of sorts, that united the commonplace people of the many religious factions and it was at that level that rumors of an imminent arrival of the Messiah spread.

Each community of believers had their own traditions and ways of understanding. Among Christians and Armenians, the belief was in a second coming of Jesus; among Islamists there was an expectation for the coming of "a guided one" or of "the Mahdi," a 12th Imam long hidden from humanity. At the common street level the peculiarities of these beliefs tended to be overlooked and the expectations were allowed to blend into one. At this level, it was not so important what he should be called or how he need be understood. The one great overriding and energizing fact was that Rabbi Shemuwel, a person of authority and someone who should know, believed that the Messiah was coming soon and was even now at the door.

It was impossible to hide the fact that the Rabbi's routine had changed. He was spending long hours at the computer and on the phone with his granddaughter in the United States. It was well known among the underground network that the Rabbi and his brother Levi were having serious discussions with the elders in their group. Rumor had it that they were translating an ancient scroll that had come suddenly into their possession and that the Rabbi would soon be preaching the good news of the coming of a long-awaited messenger.

The important discussions were taking place in the small group's sanctuary. It was a simple, open beam, high ceilinged space having six high small windows and two doors, one on either side at one end of a long room. Shelves of books lined the long walls below the three high windows on each side. The large part of the floor was tile, an ancient terra-cotta, worn and dusty so it was only slightly more refined than a dirt floor. The thick exterior walls behind the books were rough stone painted white. An aging floor-length velvet curtain hung at the far end of the room where it served to cover several sacred scrolls stored on a small table standing on a raised wooden floor. In front of the velvet curtain on the slightly raised wooden platform stood a reading stand. In the center of the room was a long narrow table with chairs for twelve elders. There were more chairs along the walls and at the end of the room near the two doors.

No special precautions were taken to insure privacy during discussions, but the voices were known to pause when others came near enough to hear. As long days passed with no official word forthcoming, Messianic Fever took hold. Many were growing impatient to know what was being discussed. Some feared the heavenly message was being censored before its release. Desire to be informed led to impatience, and speculation regarding the daily meetings was the leading topic of gossip among the underground network of friends in the Old City.

In one certain house, which happened to be in the Muslim quarter, there was a boy named Mahdi who was small for his age of ten. He listened intently as his parents shared with one another the stories and rumors of the day. As they spoke, Mahdi, who was known to his friends as a fierce competitor in the game of stickball, recognized the place his parents were talking about. It was the old high-roofed small stone building with the three windows that were set too high up to see inside. It was on a cobblestone street close to where his friend Benny lived. It had become a newly popular spot, in the Jewish quarter, where his friends met to play. Mahdi and Benny had secretly explored the old building once, entering through the door opening on the narrow street. He remembered the room with its long table and the purple curtain at the far end.

Wanting to please his parents, Mahdi went very early one morning to the old building and again found the door unlocked. He entered the dark room, hid himself behind the velvet curtain, and sat comfortably under the small table. Mahdi planned to stay all day, listening to discover what was said in order to bring the story to his parents.

The discussion that day, as it happened to be, dealt with the last chapter of Richard's small book, chapter 8, *The Call to Authentic Worship*. Mahdi listened as the Rabbi read in English, which Mahdi had learned to understand from English speaking tourists. The discussion was about the nature of true worship.

"Worship which has become fixed in form as well as in time and place has lost its authenticity and thus its power to unite the worshipper with God. It is not then to be disregarded as worthless but must be understood as a powerless form only and interpreted, translated into powerful authentic worship in the everyday happenings of life." Mahdi with the uncritical trust of a child understood that it was the words of the guided one that the Rabbi was speaking, and so he listened closely and remembered, accepting the words uncritically as true.

Following the Rabbi's reading, there was a long period of comment as the elders voiced their critical opinions on the wisdom of the reading. Many of these voices were in Hebrew, which Mahdi did not understand as well as he did English and his own Arabic. Finally, it seemed there was a general acceptance, an agreement with the wisdom in the words of the guided one. Soon the Rabbi was again reading more words of the guided one and Mahdi again perked up his ears to hear.

"All religions are united in their wish for peace, in their quest to find peace with one another and with God. Yet they each have their limits beyond which they will not allow their adherents to go.

Religious symbols improperly understood as themselves being the reality they were intended only to point to are the greatest impediment to finding God. It is exactly these symbols which are standing in the way, which are blocking the power of God to break through in every heart and mind." Richard's words were general and did not excite strong feelings. Then the words turned fatefully specific with ten-year-old Mahdi listening unrecognized behind the curtain.

"Today Judaism and Islam are bound together in a struggle neither can win alone. Only one resolution is possible. They must both win together; God must be found where he lives in the hearts and minds of all. Each side in the present struggle is daily faced with chances for authentic worship. Opportunities abound at the personal level, where every individual, Jewish and Moslem, daily decides for war or for peace, and at the national level, where positions seeming to be set in stone could be softened in a moment with a turn to authenticity. Wherever there is conflict, there are opportunities for authentic worship.

"In all arenas, limits must be transcended in order that God be found. To Palestinians I say, Are there strangers in your country? Be then sincerely willing to welcome them as guests and before you can open your door, you will know yourself as the beloved of Allah.

"To Israelites, I ask, Do your enemies hate you and want you to leave their presence so they can be free of you? Be willing, I pray—you who have ears to hear—for the love of God, be sincerely willing, without limit, to remove yourself and lacking any grievance, to simply go. Pack your bags and be at the door as if you were instantly departing for the Promised Land. Then before you have one foot on the outside, I say unto you, this day you shall be in Paradise[6]."

With this reading there arose a great controversy and a great tumult at the long narrow table. Everyone was speaking at once. One large man rose and quickly walked to the purple curtain to retrieve a scroll that would prove his point in debate. As he threw the curtain aside, there was Mahdi, revealed for all to see sitting comfortably cross-legged under the table. But only for a moment was he there. In a second he was on his feet and running for the door at the far end of the room. Another second and the small boy was past them all, out the door and running free in the street toward home and safety.

Out the door came Rabbi Shemuwel's brother Levi and the elders chasing after the boy, but with none of them having any real chance of catching him.

The following day, the gossip surrounding Rabbi Shemuwel's discovery and ensuing discussions broke into print. It was just a few words in an Old City neighborhood newsletter.

"A small group thought to have roots in ancient Ebonite beliefs and said to be the oldest surviving Jewish sect, having never left Jerusalem, became embroiled in controversy yesterday when a heated debate involving the elders and their Rabbi spilled out into the cobblestone alley bordering their sanctuary in the Jewish quarter. The uproar was said to have been caused when a small boy was discovered in the sanctuary attempting a theft of a sacred scroll. In pursuit of the thief the group of older men followed the boy into the street but not much farther as the unidentified lad ran speedily away and was soon lost out of sight. However, rumor has it that there is more to this controversy. The small sect's highly respected Rabbi Shemuwel is said to be in possession of a scroll found at the Kotel which proves the Messiah is coming soon. Should be good for tourism."

Mahdi had run away fearing punishment for what he had done. When his parents talked about the rumors and gossip surrounding what had happened at the Rabbi's sanctuary, he pretended he wasn't interested and didn't tell them what he knew. But the strong words of the guided one had found a warm place in his heart, and he pondered their meaning in his life.

* * *

"Frank, take a look at this," the young agent from Homeland Security said to his partner.

"Yeah, what is it?"

"It's a newsletter our undercover man in Jerusalem put on the fax."

"What's it say?"

"Some Rabbi found a scroll saying the Messiah is coming soon. It looks like a kid tried to grab it and run. Caused a hubbub in the street near the Wall."

"Hubbub? Ernie, where the hell did you ever hear that? Junior agent Ernie looked like he was about to recount a long story of his time spent growing up in Oklahoma.

"Oh forget it man;" the older agent said, "just give me the fax."

Senior CIA agent Frank Doomi's left hand fondled the 9mm Glock G34 nestled in his right armpit, lovingly fingering the trigger while taking the paper from Ernie with his right hand—all the while day-dreaming of the time when he would be justified in drawing the awesome Glock and firing it, destroying the trouble maker and winning a promotion. But first he had to find the bad guy, and this bothersome paperwork was a necessary step in that direction.

"Hey, this news is four days old. Why haven't I seen this?

"It just came in this morning," Ernie answered as a fax machine in the Langley, Virginia CIA headquarters, office of project *Cinderella Search,* came to life.

"It's John in Jerusalem again."

"Let me have it," demanded Frank who was still bitter about being assigned to a project named *Cinderella*. The fax was another story from the same Old City neighborhood newsletter.

> "A small boy identified only as Mahdi was injured before noon today while playing stickball in the streets near the Kotel in the Jewish quarter. Witnesses said the boy was hit in the head by a wild pitch that he may have thought was thrown with intent to do him harm. The boy, who has a reputation for being quick to anger, reportedly first ran toward the pitcher but then stopped suddenly and stood still, seeming to be paralyzed. The pitcher, a boy named Benny, said Mahdi's face then 'lit up like an angel.' Others said he apparently suffered a seizure because of being hit in the head.
>
> "Police and an ambulance were called when the boy recovered and began running around wildly and shouting.
>
> " 'He was like a mad man, no one could calm him down,' a shop keeper said. 'He was very excited and climbed to the top of a house and shouted that Allah had kissed him and that he loved everyone.' All the yelling drew a crowd. This reporter has learned that if

it could be proven Allah kissed the boy, it would be an unprecedented scandal in the Muslim quarter where the boy was thought to be from.

"Mahdi was brought down off the rooftop, sedated, and taken by ambulance to Jerusalem Hospital outside the Old City wall where he is being held for observation. Authorities are looking for his parents.

"During the excitement with Mahdi running wildly through the streets, a local resident commented that he looked like the same boy seen running away after reportedly trying to steal a scroll from Rabbi Shemuwel's sanctuary last week. The sanctuary is only a short distance away."

Agent Doomi paused only a moment after reading the news story. "Pack your bag Ernie," he said. "We've got a fire to put out. "

"Where's the fire," Ernie asked.

"The fire's in Jerusalem—in a small boy's heart." His left hand reached across his chest to his right armpit as he continued speaking, "We've got to find the scroll and silence that boy before peace breaks out all over."

* * *

Arriving in Jerusalem without asking permission from his CIA superiors, Agent Doomi immediately set up a surveillance operation at the Wall, hoping the Rabbi would reveal the scroll's hiding place.

"Why didn't ya put the camera on the Rabbi insteada the Wall? It woulda made this job a whole lot easier," asked Ernie.

"You just keep your Oakey eyes glued to that screen and don't ask stupid questions," Frank Doomi responded. The two of them were holed up in Jerusalem, so undercover not even their own people knew they were there.

"Hey, Lookit this. Isn't that him?" Ernie's days-long vigil was at last bearing fruit.

"Yeah, that's our Rabbi. Good job, sport. And there's his brother with him."

"Lookit, lookit, they're headin' to that same place in the Wall where we first saw him. Must be a good place to stick your prayers."

"Run that part over again! There! That look like a prayer to you?

"Nah, that looks more like a bottle of Crown Royal in one of those velvet bags," answered Ernie. "You suppose the Rabbi's a drinker?"

"It's either that or there's a small scroll in that fancy sack. It sure as hell ain't no folded piece of paper prayer he's stuffing in The Wall there."

"Amen, to that," Ernie said, convinced Frank was right.

Agent Frank Doomi affectionately patted the Glock 9mm resting in his underarm holster as if to alert it to be ready for action soon. The movement did not escape Ernie's notice.

"You gonna shoot him?" he asked.

"Who? Shoot who?"

"The Rabbi, of course. I don't see nobody else."

"I ain't gonna shoot no Rabbi. Not unless he comes between my silver bullet and Cinderella."

"Who's Cinderella?"

"Where you been son? Don't you know who we are on the hunt for? Cinderella is the evil Prince; the 'peace and love' monger whose picture I.D. is in that sack on the scroll. Let's go get it.

Chapter Notes

6 Richard's admonition asks the people of Palestine and Israel to embrace the unseen Kingdom of God spread out on the earth. He promises an opening of the mind to a new dimension of life; a rebirth into seeing the present world differently.

Chapter Twenty-six

ROME AND PARIS: HERETICS AND POPES

The five travelers left Fatima in the rented BMW and drove back to Lisbon where they boarded another Delta flight that took them to Rome. Bina had made reservations in Rome at a romantic old world hotel in the center of the Eternal City. Their rooms had balconies with spectacular views of the city. Celeste was pleased beyond saying.

For three glorious days and nights they enjoyed being in the timeless city. Their days were filled with visits to the major tourist spots; they saw the ancient Roman Forum and Coliseum, visited the Capitoline Museums, Trevi Fountain, and shared pizza and wine with some friendly art school students Jenny ran into at the Pantheon. They took the standard tour of St. Peter's Cathedral in the Vatican but did not buy tickets for a private audience with the Pope in an auditorium with several thousand other tourists.

At one of the many colorful city plazas, the *Campo di Florio*, Richard paused to read the plaque at a statue of Giordano Bruno, a famous religious heretic whose tongue had been stilled by a torturous wooden screw before he was silenced permanently by being burned at the stake for an offense against Roman Catholic doctrine. The statue was placed at the spot where the fire had burned in 1600 A.D., and the tragic figure was aligned to face his tormentor in the Vatican across town. Richard considered the "crime" for which the freethinking "heretic" had been killed: he declared the universe was infinite and there were other populated worlds. The offense seemed minor compared to the "mistakes" Richard had found the church guilty of making. But of course the price of heresy had gone way down in four hundred years. Still, it was sobering to see up close this reminder of the naked brutality that had once dominated over reason.

The first evening, Dollar Bill, who had been in Rome before, treated them all to an authentic Italian family dinner at a restaurant hidden away near the site of the old Roman chariot "circus." The second evening, Richard and Celeste found their own out of the way place for a romantic dinner in the Testaccio district on the wrong side of the Tiber River. Their last night in the ancient city they had dinner with Bina in the hotel restaurant and made plans for the trip to Paris.

Leaving Rome after three days, the five friends arrived in Paris at the Charles DeGalle Airport. They piled into a taxi for the trip into the heart of the City of Light, where Bina had made reservations for them at a venerable hotel in the Spanish quarter near the Seine River and Notre Dame Cathedral. The first night they strolled along the Champs Elysees and had dinner aboard a sight-seeing tour boat on the Seine.

The next day was spent at Eiffle's Tower and the Sacre-Coure Basicilia where they sat on the steps enjoying the view high above the city below them. They found a neighborhood restaurant, *Chez Marie*, at the foot of the steps within sight of the landmark tower. Richard bought a small painting from a local artist showing both the *Chez Marie* and the famous tower.

Visiting the Louvre Museum the second day, they entered through the glass pyramid and took in as many of the world's priceless art treasures as time would allow. They managed to see both the Mona Lisa painting and the Venus diMilo sculpture before closing time.

Then after two full days in Paris they awoke the third day to a shocking headline:

POPE
DEAD

POPE DEAD. It was the biggest type any of them had ever

seen used in a newspaper. The two words stacked on top of each other took up the entire front page of the *Paris Register*. There wasn't much news to the story except that the Pope was dead and no one yet had any details. The news was all the more shocking to them since they had just come from three days in Rome, during which they'd visited St. Peter's Cathedral in the Vatican, home of the now dead Pope. And to think just a few hours later he was gone. It was shocking.

POPE

FOUND

DEAD

POPE FOUND DEAD. *The Roman Day* filled their front page with three words instead of two. The meat of their more in-depth story was that the Pope's butler had found him alone in his bedroom dead. There was no suggestion of foul play.

Only Richard was not totally shocked. "It looks to me like maybe he couldn't handle the truth," he said. "Or on the other hand he may have strangled on a cheese doodle while watching TV. We will probably never know."

"A cheese doodle? Are you kidding? Something like that couldn't happen—not in a million years," complained Celeste.

"Oh I don't know. I kinda like the cheese doodle theory," said Dollar Bill. "I see that sort of thing all the time in my business. It happens to people when they suddenly wake up to the fact that the payment is due and they don't have the money."

Even as the small group spoke lightly of the momentous event, an inquiry was being sent out from the Vatican to Fatima. It was an inquiry that could result in a white hot ray of investigation being reflected back in their direction.

"I wonder if he had time to read that computer thing before he died," Jenny commented.

"I think he *was* reading it and when he got to the good part—*wham*—his heart stopped. He couldn't handle the truth. There will be more like him," Richard answered prophetically and then mumbled something from the Bible:

"Men's hearts failing them for fear and for looking after those things that are coming on the earth."

"If he was reading your stuff he must have died of boredom," Celeste said in fulfillment of what she believed was her duty to take the wind out of Richard's sails whenever she felt he was getting too puffed up.

"What do you think, Bina? You're the smart one," Jenny asked.

Jenny's question gave Bina a chance to speak just as she had succeeded in thinking it through. She had found an opportunity in this disaster that would advance her own agenda. There was a way she could spin this tragedy that would help her get Richard moving toward Jerusalem and it wasn't far-fetched at all.

"I've read Richard's book," she began. "I'm the only one of us who has, and I think it could be as he says. There is a chapter on the misguided role of the Church that is pretty hard hitting. If the Pope got that far it may have truly upset him. Whether he would have found it believable enough to stop his heart is impossible to know.

"But one thing is certain, if that flash drive with any documentation linking it to Fatima is found anywhere near him, there is sure to be an inquiry. They'll check with Fatima first, with Jose and Fredrico, and if they're not satisfied, they'll investigate and find Lucia's painting and then the Vatican Swiss Guard will be coming after five Americans who look exactly like us."

Bill's rational analysis of the situation played into Bina's plan. "So? We've got nothing to hide. Besides where could we run from that kind of worldwide manhunt?"

"There's only one place in all the world," she said, "where we could go to lay low for a while, where we would be welcomed and protected—Jerusalem."

Chapter Twenty-seven

A PARTING OF THE WAYS

There arose a controversy among them as to whether they should go to Jerusalem for a while as Bina had said, or if they should return home now as they had planned. Bina assured them that they would all be welcome and safe in the home where she had grown up—her grandfather's house in Old Jerusalem.

"Whatever you all decide to do," she said, "I will be going on to visit my grandfather." She wasn't quite sure herself if it was a lie or not. She was still campaigning to get Richard to Jerusalem. The truth was she was too close to realizing her goal to go anywhere while leaving him behind.

"I think maybe I need to get back to Daytona Beach and my business," said Dollar Bill. It was clear he was open to changing his mind if there was a good reason to do so.

"I'm going to Jerusalem," Richard declared, "sooner or later. Why not now?" He had long known his destiny was there and now suddenly the time seemed right with Bina holding the door open wide.

"Well, if you're going to Jerusalem," Jenny declared, "I want to go there too."

Bill was surprised by Bina's statement on the power in Richard's book. He had respect for her education and level-headedness. Maybe he had misjudged Richard, he thought, by assuming he was pretty much like all the other religious zanies he had known in his life. Now, seeing his girlfriend Jenny was ready to leave him behind in order to continue on with Richard, he realized he needed to know more about this old man and his book in order to make an informed decision.

"Richard," he said, "do you think you could tell me what's in your book that might cause a Pope to choke on a cheese doodle? I'm afraid it's all a little out of my territory and since its beginning to look like we all might be hung with the same rope, I need to be brought up to speed with what's really going on before I decide what to do. I'm just a farm boy from Georgia. I know about cars and how to fix them up and how to buy and sell them so as to make a little money for myself. I don't know much about religion."

"Neither did I," Richard replied, "until one day I realized the world didn't make any sense without God. Actually Bill, we have a lot in common; I grew up on a farm too—in Indiana. I liked to work on cars, and farm machinery, and washing machines, anything that was broken and needed fixing. I was pretty good at taking things apart and figuring out what all the parts were supposed to be doing. I would find the trouble—the broken part or whatever—figure out a way to fix it and then put it all back together. It didn't always work, but I always learned something about trouble shooting and about why things don't work right."

Bill was immediately animated at hearing Richard speak. "I know about trouble shooting," he said, "It's an art. My father was a cracker-jack trouble shooter."

"Well, my book is about trouble-shooting the world," Richard said, pausing for a moment to see how that would sit with the younger man. Seeing no strong objection, he continued, "That may sound like a tall order but I got lucky. I'm sure you know how sometimes a little thing can go wrong and cause big trouble somewhere else."

"Don't I know it," Bill exclaimed. "I could tell you stories you wouldn't believe about how some damn little thing caused thousands of dollars worth of repairs."

Richard continued with his theme of trouble shooting the world. "If you think about it, the world, human society, is a complex machine much like a car. A car has many systems: the fuel system, electrical system, exhaust system, steering, braking system, etc., and all these systems have to be working together in order for the car to run the way it was designed.

"Okay? Now, the world also is made up of interconnected systems: education, transportation, communication, defense, waste disposal, government, economic system, and so forth. All these systems and more have to be working right or there will be trouble. And as anyone knows who has been paying attention, there is a great deal of trouble in the world. I won't go into that; I'm sure you know what I'm talking about. A peaceful world, a peaceful human society, depends on the proper functioning of all its systems."

"Never thought of it like that before, but I see what you're saying," Bill agreed.

"Good. Now we're ready to trouble shoot the world. Where do we start? I had a teacher once who taught me the way to begin trouble shooting was to first take my tool box and sit on it; and then use my eyes and ears to just look and listen. Sitting on my tool box was his way of telling me to resist the temptation to jump right in and start fixing things. When we follow that advice with the world, when we resist the urge to run around willy nilly blaming this and blaming that and doing studies and spending money trying to fix things, and if we just quietly look and listen to what is going on, what we see in the world is there's trouble everywhere."

"Power failure," said Bill.

"Wow, That's right. You're good!" Richard exclaimed. "That's what I meant when I said I got lucky. I saw that while there appears to be a lot of problems, there is really only one.

"A power failure in human society means that people have no power to do the right thing. Most of the problems of the world are problems of human nature. People are all basically selfish and they naturally do what they believe is best for them. They are unwilling to cooperate and they get in one another's way. Everyone is at war with everyone else.

"Now, the big secret is that it doesn't have to be that way."

"Human nature is human nature. There's no cure for that," Bill declared.

"That's what everyone thinks," Richard continued, "But I found a whole system in human society whose only function is to reform selfish human nature. The problem is that this system isn't working. Like a bad fuel pump, it looks good on the outside, but it doesn't do anything.

"I'm talking now about religion and specifically about Christianity. I found that it seems to work for a few older people who may have been born into it, but it no longer appeals to the great majority of people who today are guided by reason.

"I found Christianity is based on a system of logical errors and mistakes that rob it of its power. I pointed out some of those mistakes in my book, on that flash drive we left for the Pope. And who knows, maybe that's what caused him to suddenly see himself as a big part of the problem.

"I believe if we get the teaching right, the non-functioning system, religion, will come to life and people will be empowered out of their selfishness; hearts will be changed and then the lights will begin to come back on."

"What makes you think you can make it work?" Bill asked, skeptical of anything religious.

"It worked for me. I'm not mad at anyone anymore like I used to be, and I'm no one special; so I figure it'll work for pretty much anybody who isn't too messed up by the old teaching—anyone willing to give it a fair chance," Richard said.

"How do I know it worked for you? You seem pretty normal to me," Bill said.

"He isn't normal at all," Jenny spoke up, coming enthusiastically to Richard's defense.

"You can say that again," Celeste joined in. "I won't say he's crazy, but he's not himself, not the man I married. I don't know who he thinks he is."

"Well what I mean is, he's better than normal—he's super," Jenny continued, passionately responding to Bill's attack on Richard's claim that religion had worked for him.

Celeste looked at Bill and rolled her eyes as if to say, "See, they're both crazy."

"You don't know," Jenny told Bill, "because you never slept with him on a plane. That's what happened to me. Our legs came together under the armrest and we melded together—"

"Meditated," Bina corrected.

"Huh? Oh, right, we 'meditated' together and after that I was all happy and wrapped up in a love bubble when I got to work. It was better than sex, I told Bina. She knows all about it. And what about that picture in Fatima? There's a bright spot at Richard's heart and it's not the computer thing he said it was. We think it's the 'immaculate heart' of Mary. Isn't that right Bina."

"Yes," Bina said, "All that is true and there's the sign. My grandfather believes Richard has the secret sign of the coming Jewish Messiah. He's different from anyone I've ever known."

"Are you the Messiah?" Bill asked Richard directly.

"The Messiah is as the Messiah does," Richard answered simply.

"Sure," Bill said, thankful he had at least finally unraveled the misunderstanding about this old man being a sexual magician who had sex with his Jenny on an airplane.

"I'm glad I asked," Bill told Richard. "I have a better idea now of what you're all about and how to respond if someone asks me about you and about my part in all this."

Then turning to Jenny he offered an apology, "Jenny, baby, I know you want to stay with your friends and that's okay by me. I understand that, but I still think it would be best for me now, and better for us in the long run, if I go home and take care of business."

He wasn't called "Big Dollar" Bill for nothing. An understanding of why he has been a party to all these religious shenanigans was slowly dawning in his mind—an idea of how he could profit greatly by promoting his hometown as the special place where the man destined to be the Messiah had walked the world's most famous beach as he prepared to enter the world.

Bill foresaw an explosion of the number of people wanting to come and spend time in this special place. The economic potential of adding this new dimension to already tourist oriented Daytona Beach, he believed, was stupendous. It would surpass even what he has just witnessed in Fatima. And he had the inside track. He couldn't wait to get home and begin working with his business manager and real estate broker. He knew he was in a strong position financially. He'd begin quietly buying up options on beachfront real estate, motels and condos. It was a once in a lifetime opportunity and Big Dollar Bill was intent on seizing the day.

Celeste waited as long as possible to decide whether she would continue on to Israel with Richard or return to their home in Daytona. In the end she decided she had done all she could to keep her husband from making a complete fool of himself. She had protected him like a child and kept a lid on his madness for a long time. But now he had grown and become too much for her to handle. Jenny and Bina believed in him now. They had come to his defense in a way she could not. It would be up to them to help him remember who he was and where he had come from—where he belonged. She parted with a final hug and a kiss as Richard told her he had a big job to do but promised he would return and then things would be normal again. He asked her not to give up and instead to "save the last dance" for him.

As Richard shook Bill's hand a final time in parting he asked him to look after Celeste and gave him a folded piece of paper. "Read it later," he said.

As Bill's body relaxed in first class on Delta's nonstop flight from Paris to Orlando, his mind was busy composing possible advertising slogans:

"*Come walk on the beach where the Son of Man walked.*"

"*Come to Daytona Beach. If it was good enough for the Second Coming, it's good enough for you.*"

Bill wasn't happy with any of his ideas. Then he remembered the note and read what Richard had written. It was first a personal note:

Bill, is this what you're searching for?

Below the note was printed a verse from *The Living Bible:*
"*He Stood Waiting on an Ocean Beach.*"

Revelation 12:16, *The Living Bible*

Following the Bible verse were printed two three-word questions separated by the already well known expression of Daytona Beach as the world's most famous. The two questions would become the basis of his promotional campaign.

WHY NOT DAYTONA?

WORLD'S MOST FAMOUS BEACH

WHY NOT NOW?

The words were exactly what Bill was searching for. Beyond its immediate usefulness to him, the note was indicative of the growing power of Richard's mind to know the mind of others and to foresee the future.

Chapter Twenty-eight

ARRIVAL IN ISRAEL AT BEN GURION AIRPORT

Once the decision of who was going where was made, Bina wasted no time making reservations for herself, Jenny, and Richard on an Israeli Airlines (El Al) flight to Ben Gurion airport in Israel. They left Paris from Charles De Galle Airport, passing through security without a hitch. Their acceptance on the El Al flight was facilitated by the fact that Bina was an Israeli citizen and knew the system well. Ben Gurion Airport, located just southeast of the modern city of Tel-Aviv, was the major International airport serving Jerusalem and all of Israel.

Richard's first view of the small country was spectacular. Their plane came in from the west off the Mediterranean with late afternoon sunshine streaming in behind it. As the pilot lined their plane up for a landing on runway 12, sunlight lit up the city of Tel-Aviv from its seashore playground to the furthest reaches of its suburbs to the north and east. Bina was at the window on the left side of the plane pointing out landmarks to Richard in the middle seat with Jenny leaning over him trying to see it all from her seat on the aisle. Jerusalem was only thirty miles away to the southeast in the Judean hills.

The view of the mountainous region reminded Richard of the Great Smoky Mountains and the enchanted trip he had made with Celeste and the kids from Daytona Beach to his Indiana home years ago. He could not help wondering if he would be better received at this new destination, or if he would again be dismissed as crazy.

Bina had, of course, immediately called her grandfather to give him the good news. "Get ready," she encouraged him, "The Messiah is coming to Israel and he is staying at your house." It was a preposterous message to Christian sensibilities. But in the Jewish understanding, their Messiah was to be a man, someone like themselves with the same needs for food and a place to sleep like everyone else. The Rabbi had mobilized his congregation and a large contingent was waiting at the gate to meet and greet them and carry them home triumphantly to Jerusalem.

Richard might have entered the Old City under cover of darkness unheralded, except for CIA agent Frank Doomi. Agent Doomi had moved fast to discover the identity of the "Cinderella" personage whose state of mind was judged to be a weapon of mass destruction, a threat to a certain way of life. He remained loyal to a leadership faction within the agency which was now a distinct minority. This faction had first conceived "Operation Cinderella" and had issued the original "kill on sight" order. Doomi had gone rogue simply by refusing to accept a new project-wide directive that ordered a stand-down to the "kill on sight" order and replaced it with a more reasonable "capture and hold for questioning" command.

The dangerous rogue agent used the resources of the agency wisely to uncover the identity of his prey. After recovering the scroll from its hiding place in the wall, he had immediately sent a copy of the mysterious line drawing to the investigative laboratory in Langley, Virginia. They in turn searched LOC materials and discovered they were not the first to do so. Bina Shemuwel immediately became a person of intense interest. Doomi recognized the family name as being that of the Rabbi at the center of his investigation. Bina's progress traveling across the European continent—first Portugal, then Rome and Paris—was revealed from a trace of her Passport activity obtained through the U.S. Customs Department.

Agent Doomi and special assistant Ernie were still in Jerusalem when they learned that Bina and two traveling companions, one a man, Richard Holmes, were on an El Al flight from Paris to Ben Gurion airport in Israel. They hurriedly made the trip from the Old City in time to be at the gate awaiting the arrival of the three traveling companions. Armed with pictures to identify the subjects, and new orders to take out the would-be Messiah before he could set one foot in Israel, Agent Doomi and Ernie waited along with the Rabbi and his followers.

Seeing the Rabbi already at the gate, Ernie whispered to agent Doomi, "See, I told ya we shoulda put a tail on the Rabbi, we woulda been here already."

Richard came into view and the rogue agent reached his left hand under his right arm and in one smooth motion drew his Glock 9mm in full view of Israeli security forces holding Uzzi machine guns at the ready. He fired one shot from only ten feet away straight into the heart of the man whose killing he believed would preserve the American way of life and ensure his own immortality. He didn't get a second shot before multiple explosive rounds from two Uzis' ripped into his body tearing it to shreds as the crowd scattered, running away in panic for their lives.

Agent Doomi's aim was true and the Glock 9mm performed flawlessly yet the target escaped being hit as the single round passed by close enough to destroy only a single button on Richard's shirt before it slammed into and shattered a ten foot high plate glass window. "Bang Boom," followed by the "Brrrrrr" of the Uzzis and the screaming of the crowd and it was over. Bang Boom Brrrrr! The misguided attempt on Richard's life had failed.

Richard miraculously survived the assassination attempt unharmed. Only a single button was missing from his shirt. Analysis of high quality digital images from a camera recording the arrival of the Messiah showed that Richard's body had suddenly twisted to his left a full ninety degrees allowing the 9mm round to pass harmlessly through the space where his heart had been only a fraction of a second earlier.

The action looked, on the television screen, where it was repeated endlessly in slow motion, like a scene from the movie *Matrix*. It appeared that Richard had anticipated the bullet and had willfully and majestically moved his body out of its path with the action appearing to take place impossibly quick in the split second after Agent Doomi had triggered the Glock but before the round had reached him.

In this way the Messiah's arrival in Israel did not go unheralded.

The failed assassination attempt by a U.S. government agent was a major news event having serious international political and military consequences. The media ate it up. Richard's reputation as a man who could not be killed was born. Only he knew that in fact he had stepped on one of his own loose shoelaces and that had resulted in the strange bodily contortion that saved his life. Yet even he was in awe of the immaculate timing of the two unrelated events.

It took three days for the Israeli Defense Force (IDF) to sort everything out and decide what they would do. In that time Richard was detained along with Bina and Jenny at the exclusive El Al King David Lounge at Ben Gurion Airport. They were held under guard and were not yet allowed to enter the country. They were however accessible to the media. News teams from all over the world came to interview them. Richard repeated endlessly the answer he had given Bill, "The Messiah is as the Messiah does."

After three days, they were finally cleared for entry under strong protest from the United States government which claimed the legal right to have Richard extradited back to the U.S.A. But before the release into Israel took place, word of their possible involvement in the death of the Pope became headline news.

While killing time at the King David lounge, Richard found a discarded scandal sheet newspaper claiming to have smuggled photos from inside the Pope's bedroom at the time of his mysterious death. One photo showed a computer off to one side and Richard recognized the flash drive he had given Jenny's grandmother at Fatima for delivery to the Pope. The story told how an argument had taken place between the person legally designated to take control of the Vatican in such emergencies and the head of the Pope's personal secret library. The library head was caught trying to smuggle a manuscript out of the Pope's bedroom. A second photo showed the librarian holding the manuscript at his side. Richard could see the writing was Greek. And under a strong light he was able to make out part of a line of continuously written letters. Clearly visible was the long dreamed of double OY, which when translated read "Ou-Ou" and confirmed that Jesus had been the author's intended "man sent from God." It was evidence that the Pope had discovered the truth and apparently had not been able to handle it.

There followed another three days living in the luxury of the exclusive club while the IDF again investigated. And there were more interviews, this time probing Richard's views on Christianity. "Mistakes have been made," he said, adding finally in response to repeated requests for further specifics, "With this Pope's death I imagine the office of Pope will be abolished and then the mistakes will begin to reveal themselves."

The official IDF verdict was "undecided" as to their possible involvement in the Pope's death and they were released to enter Israel. The verdict of the Israeli people however was more decisive. Many believed God was with this man who had miraculously escaped an assassin's bullet and whose written words were rumored to have had power enough to kill a Pope. Hope welled up in the Jewish psyche—was the time of their redemption near? The eyes of the world were on Richard, watching to see what miracle he might work next.

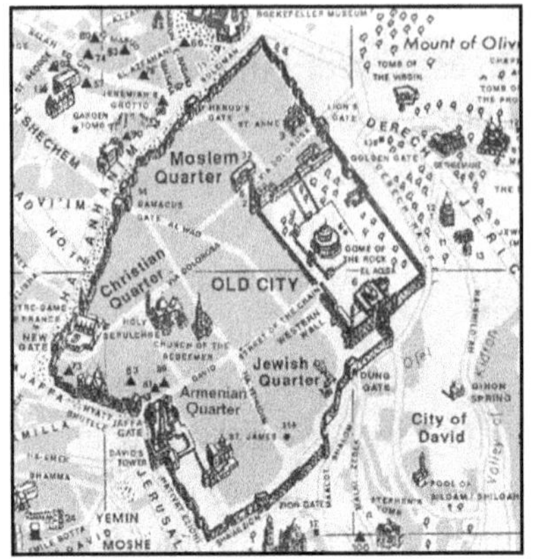

At left, a diagram of the Old City of Jerusalem. Below, an outline map of the Old City showing locations of the eight gates.

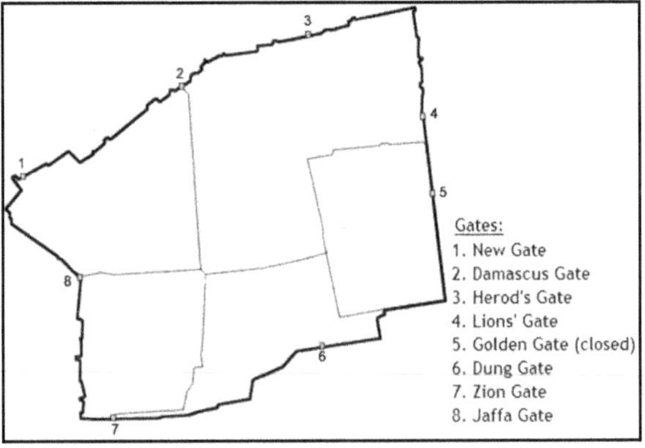

Above, the sealed Golden Gate to the Old City of Jerusalem.

Chapter Twenty-nine

AT THE GATE: A BLAST FROM THE PAST

Arriving in Jerusalem, the Rabbi unexpectedly decided to take a victory lap around the wall surrounding the Old City. He and his brother had driven to Ben Gurion airport and picked up his granddaughter Bina and her friends Jenny and Richard after they were released by the IDF authorities. Highway #1 had brought them into Jerusalem from the west and they were in position to enter the Old City through the wall at the Jaffa gate near the Tower of David when the Rabbi suddenly turned left onto a road that would take them around the city outside the walls.

"Where are you going?" his granddaughter Bina asked, aware that this was not the shortest way to her childhood home.

"I want to give Richard a feel for the size of the Old City before we enter," her Grandfather responded. Going north (left) from the Jaffa Gate outside the wall, the white SUV went about a quarter mile before it turned right, continuing to follow the wall. Bina directed their attention to the New Gate as they passed it by. "The New Gate was opened in 1889 and provides access directly into the Christian quarter," she said.

Now heading east, the van went another short distance before passing the busy Damascus gate. Rabbi Shemuel explained the old road from Damascus led to the Damascus gate and into the City along a road that ran between the Christian and Moslem quarters. Another quarter mile by Richard's reckoning and they were passing by Herod's gate, which Bina noted opened into the Moslem quarter directly.

And then the wall seemed to end abruptly and the van turned right again to follow it. The venerable Lions gate on the old road to Jericho soon came into view. The Rabbi explained that this gate was named for the animal carvings in the stone wall above the gate. "Research has shown that the animals chiseled in stone above the gate are really panthers and not lions but the name remains," he said.

"The Temple Mount is just to the left inside the Lions gate and the famous *Via Deloroso* begins a short distance inside," Bina added.

Passing by the Lions gate and going south, the white Cherokee entered onto a smaller road passing through a Moslem cemetery.

The wall was straight along this backstretch through the cemetery and the Rabbi pulled into a parking area and stopped. They all took the opportunity to get out and stretch their legs while looking at the wall there. Richard judged correctly that they were directly opposite the Jaffe gate, halfway around the Old City. In the stillness, the Rabbi began speaking about the history and importance of the special place in the wall directly in front of them.

"There are eight openings through the wall surrounding the Old City of Jerusalem," he said. "Seven of these gates are open for traffic; only this one, the Golden Gate, is closed." He was speaking to all of them but it was soon obvious the speech was mainly for Richard's ears.

"Jewish tradition," he continued, "says the Messiah will enter the City of Jerusalem through the Gate of the Mercy, riding on a white donkey." While saying this he put his hand affectionately on the white Jeep Cherokee. "The Gate of the Mercy, *Sha'ar Harachamim*, is the name in Hebrew for the tightly sealed hole in the wall, the Golden Gate, directly in front of us. The builders of the wall, the Moslem Ottomans, closed this gate in 1541 hoping to put an end to the Jewish hope for the coming of their Messiah by physically blocking the entrance. They also built this cemetery outside the wall in front of the gate believing the Messiah would not go through a cemetery.

The Rabbi stopped speaking and they stood quietly in the cemetery gazing at the long sealed important entrance, the Golden Gate into Jerusalem, the City of Peace. The quiet period went overlong and Richard wondered if perhaps the Rabbi was waiting for a response from him.

"It looks like there is a small wooden door in each of those stone arches," Richard said. "You think maybe I should take a walk over there and give the doors a good yank? The lock might have rusted through sometime in the last hundred years or so and well, who knows, something might happen. I might be able to just walk right in."

Bina perceived what was going on and began to chastise her grandfather. "I know what you're up to Grandfather, and it isn't fair what you're doing to Richard. He isn't going to be able to fulfill every old story and tradition about the coming of the Messiah. He isn't that kind of Messiah. I thought you knew that. I'm ashamed of you."

"I just thought, well, there are still many who believe in this tradition. And shouldn't we give every opportunity a chance before we decide what sort of Messiah has been sent to us?" the Rabbi asked in defense of his behavior.

Richard felt a need to walk and struck out alone through the cemetery toward the wall and the Golden Gate. As he walked, he suddenly became painfully aware of just how impossible the situation was he had let himself be drawn into. He had no real understanding of who the Messiah was supposed to be or what exactly he was expected to do. The thought, "redeem the Jewish people," came to mind. He had thought he was doing just that in writing his book which generally condemned Christian ideas in favor of Jewish understandings. But now this—what was this need for him to enter the Old City by a certain gate really all about?

Jenny went after him and soon caught up by running through the old graveyard. "Stop! Richard, You don't have to do this," she shouted.

"I know," he answered while stopping a moment to let her catch up. Then he took her hands and looked directly at her. She felt his energy, his intensity; it was stronger than she had ever known it before. "But I kind of agree with the Rabbi," he said, "I need to know myself what kind of Messiah I am.

"You wait here. I have to do this myself," Richard told Jenny and then he turned and began walking purposefully, moving quickly with great expectation toward the wall and the Golden Gate. He was about one hundred yards away from Jenny with yet another fifty yards to reach the wall. The Rabbi, his brother, and Bina were watching a quarter mile away from the higher elevation of the parking area at the edge of the Mount of Olives when:

BOOM !

A powerful explosion, a deep-throated roar came from somewhere directly in front of them and echoed, reverberating over and over throughout the surrounding hills. The blast was accompanied by a hail of flying rock that spewed out from the wall and reached even beyond the quarter mile away where the rabbi and Bina had instinctively taken cover. Jenny was immediately knocked to the ground and sheltered behind a heavy gravestone where she wisely remained.

On the heels of the flying rock came a cloud of smoke and dust that rose and blotted out the sun. When it cleared—a process that took several long minutes—Richard was gone. The Golden Gate stood open up to the original arches and the wall above was still in place, standing apparently as good as new. Richard was gone and the Golden Gate was open!

"Jesus Christ!" Rabbi Shemuel exclaimed. "What happened?"

"Jenny!" Bina screamed running down the slope to reach the place where Jenny was last seen standing before the blast.

In the stillness after the sudden eruption, chaos gathered her forces and came to the fore. Flashing lights, sirens, armed guards materialized from all directions and converged on the gaping hole in the wall. But the chaos outside the wall was minor in comparison to that inside the Old City where the Golden Gate now stood open from the cemetery through a gatehouse inside the wall to a staircase leading up to the heavily defended Dome of the Rock.

* * *

"Ring! *Richard calling*. Ring! *Richard calling*." The automated message sung out from the phone in Richard and Celeste's home in Daytona Beach. Celeste sat up on the side of the bed and answered, "Hello. Richard?"

"Yes, it's me. I think I've been in some kind of explosion . . ."

"Explosion! Richard are you all right?"

"I'm all right—still got my two arms and legs and everything's working but my phone which doesn't work except on the speed dial and then only to reach you. Can you call Bina or Jenny to see if they're all right and to tell them I'm okay? We were all together outside the wall and then I wasn't there anymore. I was with Jesus eating bread inside the wall and we were having a quiet conversation. It was like before; it was a beautiful place. I don't know what happened. The people here are going crazy. I don't know what they're afraid of. Maybe there's something on CNN or FOX. You got the TV on? Would you check and tell me what's happening?"

"Nothing's happening! Richard, you're dreaming! Wake up! Do you know what time it is?"

"Celeste, I don't know anything; that's why I'm calling you. It's daylight here, afternoon I think. Just call Bina and tell her I'm all right and to call me. Okay?"

"It's early here. I was still sleeping. Give me a minute to wake up. . . . Okay now; there *is* something on TV—on FOX channel. It's breaking news. Looks like they think there's a terrorist attack on Jerusalem."

"I'm in Jerusalem!"

"I thought you were still at the airport."

"No, the rabbi picked us up when we were released today and took us to Jerusalem. He said he wasn't coming back and it was up to me to carry the ball and to bring it home."

"The rabbi said that?"

"No. Jesus. Jesus said that. I told you we ate bread and talked inside the wall. It was that place where the atmosphere is pure *Love*. It was like before at the *Happy Cricket* when I sang the song with Jesus and the others: *Glorious, Glorious, One keg of beer for the four of us*. He said I needed only to lead them home now, to the promised land and he would be there waiting."

"Richard! Slow down! I can't understand you. Wall? What wall?

"The wall around the Old City, Jerusalem. It's a big wall and we were on the outside before something happened. And then I was inside the wall—not on the other side but *in* the wall."

What do you mean, like before? Before what? You're not making any sense to me."

"You know. The first time. When I told you I loved everyone. Like before you threw everything but the kitchen sink at me."

"Richard, *that* was thirty years ago."

"Not to me. To me it was yesterday!"

"Here's something now, on TV; they've got a picture of a terrorist. It's a video. A man coming up a staircase out of the smoke and fire of an explosion. It looks like . . . Richard—it's you! They think you're a terrorist! They're looking for you!"

"Well, good luck. I don't even know where I am. I'm in a crowd of noisy people."

"Here's another channel, CNN—they've got a live feed in a crowd of people. It's chaos. There you are! I see you in the crowd with the phone, talking to me. Richard—listen to me! They're coming for you. Don't tell them you talked with Jesus; they won't understand, they can't. They'll say you're crazy and lock you up."

"Celeste. Help me. Cele—"

"I'm coming Richard! Richard! . . . *buzz, buzz, buzz* . . . Oh Crap!"

* * *

Richard should have been killed, of course, in the blast. His body should have been blown back by the concussion and slammed into some unyielding gravestone and torn apart and then buried under tons of falling rock. The fact that he was found near the Dome of the Rock on the Temple Mount, alive and well without a scratch on him, was powerful evidence that a miracle had taken place. It appeared the ordinary laws of physics had been suspended for the time it took Richard to walk through the Golden Gate and up the staircase onto the Temple Mount inside the Old City. But the world, even the religious world of Jerusalem, did not readily accept miracles.

It was established soon enough that the "terrorist" suddenly appearing on the Temple Mount through the smoke of the explosion was just Richard. It was not, as first thought, the beginning of a Christian terrorist assault on the Dome of the Rock. Richard was released into the custody of Rabbi Shemuwel and an investigation into the cause of the blast was opened.

After much deliberation and testimony, it was found that the explosion had been caused by some evil characters—Cassandra and Scopes—who had tunneled their way into the gatehouse on the Temple Mount side of the wall at the Golden Gate and had set up a crystal meth lab there. The supposition was that the evil characters had a cache of dynamite and in an uncontrolled crystal meth fire the dynamite had exploded. The inquiry said that Richard had simply walked through the open gate after the explosion. No miracle was required to explain his sudden appearance on the Temple Mount.

Witnesses came forth to give testimony to support the crystal meth story. Cassandra and Scopes were known shady characters and dealers in crystal meth. Unknown sections of an ancient tunnel unearthed years before were noted as possibly being useful for gaining access to the forbidden gatehouse space. Cassandra and Scopes were nowhere to be found, if they had ever existed. They were presumed dead, killed in the explosion caused by their own doings. The finding was comforting confirmation for many that the laws of known reality still applied.

Other witnesses told other stories. A Palestinian woman at work on the mount of Olives swore she saw a brilliant ray of light come from a silky bright cloud moments before the blast.

A lone paparazzi came out saying she had tailed the Rabbi's white Cherokee from Ben Gurion Airport to Jerusalem, hoping to get pictures of the wannabe Messiah's suspected sexual relationship with the beautiful woman who was always with him but who was not his wife. The photographer had set up a long range high speed camera far away from where the group had gotten out of the Cherokee. When Richard broke away from the group and went toward the wall and then Jenny ran after him, the paparazzi believed it was a lover's quarrel she was witnessing and focused in on the lovers as they held hands. She expected to photograph a make-up kiss, but when Richard turned and went toward the wall again, she was confused. The camera stayed focused on Jenny hoping to catch her reaction to being spurned. Finally the paparazzi widened her view to include Richard just as the explosion sounded. The camera recorded pictures of rock fragments speeding by Richard until one frame clearly showed a rock the size of a large watermelon occupying the same space as Richard's body. In the next frame, there was a Richard sized hole, a white space, in the picture. Richard was gone.

A camera expert, a factory rep, testified there was nothing unusual in the pictures he saw. It was a double exposure consistent with a known malfunction, a limitation he called it, of the camera when recording high speed objects. The investigative committee said that Richard and Jenny had each taken cover behind protective gravestones.

Rabbi Shemuwel was asked to testify and give his understanding of what had happened. In conversations with his granddaughter Bina, the Rabbi had formulated an understanding that was at once religious and metaphysical. "Richard is a righteous man," he declared. "When he set his face toward the task of entering the city through the closed gate, the power of God was with him and nothing could stand in his way. The wall was simply blown away to clear the way before him. He wasn't just in the explosion, he caused the explosion—it happened around him. It was like what scientists say would happen in a matter / anti-matter explosion. Richard lives, at least partially, in another world. For him the stuff of this world is a dream and like in our own dreams, circumstances change for him like they do with us in our dreams. That is, in accordance with our will. Richard has power to change our world—to him it isn't real, it's a dream."

Richard listened carefully to all the theories of what had happened. He too wanted to know. He had no memory of having walked into and through an explosion. Nor did he remember taking cover behind a gravestone and walking through the open gate after the explosion. He remembered only that he had walked toward the wall with the expectation of finding a way through the sealed gate and into the Old City. But something happened and his consciousness had shifted to another time and place where he had a quiet conversation with Jesus. Then he found himself at the foot of a stairway and he had simply walked up. When he emerged out of the smoke onto the Temple Mount he was recognized by some as the man who had miraculously escaped assassination at the airport, and was feared by others who mistook him for a terrorist. He testified only to a lapse of memory and, heeding the advise of his wife, made no mention of having had a conversation with Jesus.

Richard was particularly interested in the theory of a defect or limitation on the paparazzi's camera's ability to record high speed images. He thought it possible that he had been speeded up somehow so the camera could no longer see him—speeded up until he was beyond all time and space, in eternity or heaven, the place he knew where everything was *Love*. Maybe he had ridden on the beam of light the Palestinian woman had seen, up into the silky bright cloud just before the blast. Either way, the explosion apparently happened in a moment of time in which he had not been present.

The Rabbi's understanding—that for Richard living in this world was like living in a dream—took him back to the first days after his experience years ago when he had tried to tell everyone that this world isn't real, that there is another world, a world of *Love* that is really *Real*. It was holding to this truth that had almost gotten him put away as insane. Now Richard wondered if it was as the rabbi had suggested, that his knowing the unreality of this world gave him a power over it. Was this the power of faith to move mountains that Jesus had spoken of?

* * *

The matter of what to do about the newly opened gate was a religious and political hot potato. Authorities could not restore it to its previous, permanently sealed condition. The people would not allow it. They believed its opening was in accordance with the Divine Plan and that Richard was part of that. As a compromise and without seeming to endorse Richard as the Messiah, iron gates were installed at the new opening in the wall and guards posted outside the wall. A second set of iron gates were installed at the entrance to the gatehouse at the foot of the stairs to the Temple Mount. Guards were also posted at these gates. Then, in a surprising move, the authorities ruled that only Richard and those accompanying him could on special occasions have access to and from the Old City through the new entrance.

Chapter Thirty

THE PROMISED LAND

"Eternal truths will be neither true nor eternal unless they have fresh meaning (new interpretation) for every new social situation."

— Franklin D. Roosevelt, 1882-1945, 32nd U.S. President

With the miraculous opening of the Golden Gate, messianic fever was high in the Old City and all of Israel. Richard was recognized now everywhere he went.

Following his secret meeting with Jesus, Richard's thinking had a different focus: the Promised Land. It was a new challenge, but one that seemed to make little sense. Richard knew Jesus had asked him to lead the people to the promised land. But how could he lead the Jewish people into the holy land when they were already there?

History recorded the people had grow weary of waiting for their Messiah and had followed zealots to Palestine where, in 1948, they had established Israel as their own country. It was also true that they had been in conflict trying to keep their small country from the time it was established. Some said all the trouble was because the people had not waited for the Messiah to come and lead them into the land.

Richard found his assignment was not clearly defined. Was he supposed to lead the people out of Israel first and then have them follow him back in again? How would this lead to peace replacing the present conflict? It was a final test. He had to find a way for the Jewish people to live peacefully in the land promised by God to their ancestors. If he could make peace here, Richard thought, he could make it everywhere.

He went quietly to work, studying, asking questions, learning all he could about the history of the belief in a special place for God's people. All Israel waited and watched, wondering if what Rabbi Schemuel had testified to was true. Did this man have power to dream up a solution to an apparently unsolvable problem?

One morning Richard and Jenny were up early, having coffee together, when Richard asked, "Jenny, did you and Bina go to the beach when you were in Tel Aviv last week?"

"Yes, we did. I like Tel Aviv. It's kinda like Miami with new buildings and shopping malls. We saw lots of young people on the beach there."

"It's not the people I'm interested in today. I want to know about the sand on the beach. Is it like the sand in Florida on Daytona's beach?"

"I didn't notice any difference. Sand is sand, isn't it?

"Maybe, but sometimes its noticeably coarser, rougher on the feet. The grains of sand are bigger. Do you think you could find a little bit of Tel Aviv beach sand for me? Maybe on your shoes or in a beach towel or something.

"I'll bet there's a ton of it in my beach bag. Why do you want to know about the sand?"

"I want to count the number of grains of sand on the beach. How long is the beach?"

"I don't know—it goes on for miles. I bet Bina knows that." She had found her beach bag and was standing next to the table where Richard sat with his coffee. "Here's some sand. Where you want me to dump it?"

"Right here on this paper. I just need a little bit—enough to cover that one inch square I've drawn right there."

She gently shook sand from the bag until Richard said, "Stop. That's good. Thank you."

Bina entered the kitchen and said, "Good morning. What are you two up to today?"

"We're counting beach sand. How long is the beach in Tel-Aviv?" Jenny asked. "I told Richard you would know."

"Counting sand? Is that fun? Oh, is this like the beans in a jar thing? Are we planning a raffle?"

"Just roughly, it doesn't have to be accurate." Richard said. "Jenny said the beach goes on for miles. You suppose it's three or maybe four miles long?"

"That's about right. Not all of it is public beach. Why do you want to know?"

"Let's just say three miles long. Now, how wide? Would you guess about a hundred feet wide, average, along the public beach part?"

"First you tell me what for. Anyone want scrambled eggs and bagels?" Bina asked.

"God promised Abraham He would multiply his descendants in number '*as the sand which is upon the sea shore.*' I was just wondering how many grains of sand that might actually be, just roughly. You know how I like to double check everything."

"Don't forget, the number of stars in the sky also," Bina answered, showing she was familiar with God's promise to Abraham.

"Right. Well, stars are harder to count. Besides, Carl Sagan already counted them. 'Billions and billions,' he said. That's close enough for me."

Richard's head was craned down close to the paper with the square inch of sand. "This isn't working," he said. "The sand particles are too small. I can't see them to count them."

"Jenny, there's a magnifier on the desk. You want to get it for the Messiah?"

"Sure. Anything for the holy one and for world peace."

"You girls are a riot. Celeste been coaching you, or are you getting it through osmosis?"

"Did someone mention my name?" Celeste asked, coming into the room looking for coffee.

"Thanks, Jenny. That's better," Richard said. "Now I know why I can't see the individual grains of sand. A lot of them are white or clear, quartz I suppose. I need a darker background."

"Here, try this piece of brown cardboard," offered Jenny.

"Nope, needs to be darker—what have we got that's black?"

"Ah, that's good. Thanks," Richard exclaimed as Celeste handed him a paper, an advertisement, she picked out of the waste basket showing an orthodox Jew wearing the traditional black hat and suit—all on sale for twenty percent off.

"Don't ask," he said in answer to her puzzled look.

"It's for world peace," Jenny told Celeste as Bina handed her a cup of steaming hot coffee.

"Okay. Now let me draw a line on this black hat and then we're in business."

The three women watched Richard meticulously attempt to spread the sand into a single layer. "Well," he said, "I still can't really count them—they're so small. But it looks like there are about 10 to 20 in an eighth of an inch. That's an average of 15 per 1/8 inch or 120 per inch. So 120 times 120 is 14,400 grains of sand per square inch. Boy was I naïve. I thought I would start by just counting the number in one square inch but they are way too small for that."

Now we multiply that 14,400 by 12 and by 12 again to get the number per square foot. And that is a bit more than two million grains of sand per square foot. But remember, that's only the number visible on the surface, one grain of sand deep. We need to multiply again by 120 to get the number in one square foot to a depth of one inch and then by 12 to get the number to a depth of one foot. And, would you believe the answer is 2,985.984 million?"

No one voiced an objection so Richard continued, speaking aloud to himself, "We can round that up just a bit and call it three billion, that's billion with a B, grains of Tel-Aviv beach sand per cubic foot. Can that be right? Three billion? In only one cubic foot? Wow. That's half the number of people living in the world today. So, in just two cubic feet of beach sand there is one grain of sand for every person on earth. We hardly need to finish the calculation; I can see this is going to be an impossibly big number. But let's go ahead anyway.

"If the beach is 100 feet wide, that's 100 times 3—300 billion grains of sand per linear foot of beach. And each mile of beach in Israel has 5,280 feet, the same as everywhere else, so we multiply 300 billion by 5,280 and—drum roll please—we find there are roughly 1,600 trillion grains of sand per mile of 100-foot-wide beach sand, one foot deep. Now we said the public part of the beach is three miles long that's three times 1,600 trillion or 4,800 trillion grains of sand, roughly, on just Tel-Aviv beach. That's a big number. To put it into perspective, 4,800 trillion divided by 6 billion, the population of the world today, is 800,000. In other words the sand on Tel-Aviv beach is 800,000 times the population of the world. And all the sand '*which is upon the sea shore,'* as God promised Abraham his descendants would number, is many times that."

There was silence in the small kitchen for the space of about a minute.

"Okay, now what?" asked Jenny, the only one who was still awake and paying attention.

"Well, isn't it obvious? Now we know for sure what we only suspected at the first," Richard answered triumphantly.

"What do we know? Come on, the suspense is killing me," Bina joined in.

"We know for sure that Israel is not the promised land."

"What? How do we know that?" Bina and Jenny asked together.

"It can't be." Richard began. "Five quadrillion people won't fit in the small country of Israel. And *if the people won't fit, Israel can't be it,"* he concluded with poetic certainty.

"So, maybe the promised land is the entire Middle-East," suggested Bina.

"Nope, too many people."

Well then, the whole world," Jenny said.

"Still not enough room for all the people," Richard said.

"There has to be a promised land somewhere." Bina objected.

"Why?" Richard asked.

"Well, God promised, for one thing."

"Okay, well, it looks like God will have to put all the chosen ones up at His place because Heaven is the only venue I know big enough to accommodate five quadtrillion plus people."

"That's not fair," Bina objected, "It can't be Heaven. It has to be a real place."

"Heaven *is* a real place," Richard said with the confidence and authority of one who knew.

"It's not a place we can see," Jenny offered.

"That doesn't make it unreal, Virginia," Richard answered. "In fact the unseen things of this world are the most real. There is a veil covering the unseen world which not the strongest man, nor even the united strength of all the strongest men that ever lived could tear apart. Only faith, poetry, love, romance, can push aside that curtain and view the supernal beauty and glory beyond. Is it all real? Ah, Virginia, in all this world there is nothing else real and abiding."

"*Who's Virginia?*" Jenny whispered to Bina.

"*It's a long story—tell you later*," Bina whispered back.

"Heaven isn't real?" Richard continued. "You may as well say Jesus never lived and spoke of the Kingdom of Heaven."

"But the scriptures repeatedly say that this land, this place on earth, was promised to Abraham and his descendants. How can that be ignored?" Bina asked.

"I don't know. There must be a misunderstanding hidden somewhere. We'll have to search the scriptures till we find it," Richard answered.

"Is there more coffee?" Celeste asked.

* * *

The news traveled fast. The next morning Rabbi Schemuwel was called into an impromptu meeting with the elders.

"We have heard that your Messiah has decided that Israel is not the promised land. Is that true?" their spokesman demanded to know.

Before the rabbi could respond, another of them spoke his mind bluntly, "This man is an idiot. Has God sent us an idiot for our Messiah?"

The Rabbi answered saying, "Surely it is as this man has said, 'The Messiah is as the Messiah does.' We must not judge this man by his means of deliberation. If he is able in his own way to succeed where others have failed, he is deserving of our support. This is a time for emunah (faith). Let us wait and see."

And no man of them could answer their Rabbi for his wisdom. All of them set their face to hold their tongue from that day forward and to wait and see what would come of the unusual deliberations of the Messiah that had been sent them.

Chapter Thirty-one

THE MISUNDERSTANDING AND MARVELOUS MARVIN MILLER

"In the middle of difficulty lies opportunity."
— Albert Einstein

Richard read through the scriptures twice more, searching for something that might lead to a different understanding of the "land" God had intended to give to Abraham and his seed. He was relying on his one superpower—his ability to see things differently—to help him find what others had never thought to look for. It would be something that could logically support belief in a new understanding, an understanding that could lead to peace. On the third reading of Genesis he found a possibility. It was promising but a field trip would be necessary to confirm his suspicions. The destination would be a certain place about twelve miles north of Jerusalem, near the modern village of Beitin.

The place was described in the twelfth chapter of Genesis, as being "a mountain" somewhere between the ancient settlements of Bethel on the west and Hai on the east. It was one of several places where Abram, the first patriarch of the Hebrews, long ago had pitched his tent and built an altar. This was the place where the idea God promised the descendants of Abram a vast tract of land was first heard.

Genesis said that Abram called upon the name of the LORD from on top of his mountain and in response the LORD answered, telling him: "Lift up now thine eyes, and look from the place where thou art northward, and southward, and eastward, and westward. For all the land which thou seest, to thee will I give it, and to thy seed forever. And I will make thy seed as the dust of the earth: so that if a man can number the dust of the earth, *then* shall thy seed also be numbered. . . ."

The promise was clear and apparently irrefutable. Yet Richard found reason to question the accepted understanding of the words. In the end it was nothing more than a clear seeing of the difference between up and down that had given Richard reason to pause at this verse and to think more in depth about what had actually been promised Abram. It was possible the solution to the problem of the Promised Land was a matter of Sacred Geometry.

Abram was told to look *up* and all around from where he was. Richard saw that it was just simple geometry that if Abram was, in fact, on top of a mountain when he looked up, he would not see the land below the mountain, but whichever way he looked, north, south, east or west, he would see only blue sky—the heavens!

What Abram saw depended entirely on what his response to the directive to "Lift *up* now thine eyes" had been. Richard wanted to visit the place and see for himself what Abram might have seen. In seeking to understand Abram's "Promised Land" as Heaven and not a physical place on earth, Richard was impacting a basic tenant of three major world religions: Judaism, Christianity and Islam. He was touching on the major interreligious point of contention, ownership of the Promised Land. And by emphasizing the unlimited extent of heaven, he hoped to remove this source of conflict among the 3.5 billion people of the three faiths and open a way to peace.

It was in the meaning of these words that he suspected a misunderstanding had crept in. Richard knew from his experience that communication with the divine did not require the use of words. A direct feeling experience of God's Love had given him the message that God was Love and that he was loved very personally, as God loved all his creations, beyond any meaning of the word "love" he had previously known. In his otherworld encounter with Jesus during the explosion at the Jerusalem wall, the communication had again taken place without the use of words. It was Richard who had translated the feeling message into words saying that Jesus had asked him to deliver his people to the Promised Land.

Richard knew it was very likely that Abram's message had been corrupted over time. After all, the recasting of supernatural messages into mundane human terms over time was regrettably the history of religion. It was difficult for mere human beings to accept, without direct experience, what God was trying to communicate when it conflicted with their most deeply held beliefs. One could be easily fooled by what one loved. In the case of Abram, it may have been that Abram himself had understood that the land he was promised was Heaven but those who came after him, knowing only of the earth, had substituted an earthly meaning, a belief in a chosen people who held title to a specific place on earth promised them by God. It was a belief that was divisive and a cause of continual violent conflict in Israel and in the world.

Yet, in the scripture, Abram was said to be seeing a vast land that would hold an unimaginably large number of people and a land that would last forever. It was clear to Richard that only Heaven could measure up to these requirements. Abram most probably was "seeing" in a vision similar to what Richard had known.

A search for the exact phrase, "lift up now thine eyes," revealed that it is used in the Bible four times. In each of the other three uses, the words are said by an angel directing the sight of a person to look at something *within a vision.*

Richard knew "raising one's eyes" was a technique used in meditation to hasten the onset of the meditative state. He had "raised his eyes" under closed eyelids long ago when he had sat himself down to meditate after having paid the mechanic Andrew more than he had asked. It had been his last conscious act before the surprising vision in which his mind was suddenly transported to a limitless and eternal heavenly realm.

He remembered his poem *The Visio*n where he had tried to capture and report on what he had seen. "*Love enough to go around, as I could see it knew no bounds,*" he had written. The world of *Love* he had seen was very like what Abram had reported seeing—a land that "knew no bounds"—an unlimited place big enough to embrace all of Abram's promised seed, even though they be incomprehensibly great in number as the "dust of the earth."

By journeying from Jerusalem to the mountain vista, Richard hoped to gain insight into Abram's experience. Sharing his plan for a field trip with his friends brought an enthusiastic response.

He consulted with the Rabbi regarding the location of Abram's altar and was told its precise location was not known. There was in fact no archaeological evidence Abram had ever lived. Only the ancient scriptures told the story of his journey through the land and of God's promise to give the land to him and to his seed forever.

Richard was surprised and disappointed to learn of the impossibility of knowing the location of Abram's altar. It seemed to him his proposed trip was pointless without a real destination. Yet the rabbi was enthusiastic and offered his help to find a best guess destination based on scripture, the latest archaeological discoveries, and local traditions. Richard was happy to have the Rabbi's help. What he had imagined as only a simple day trip, perhaps a drive up a mountain to an established tourist attraction, or maybe an afternoon's climb to a hilltop for a brief look around before returning home, became, under the rabbi's leadership, a more elaborate attempt to recreate Abram's experience. Plans were made for an overnight stay which would allow time to build a small rock altar and to call upon God's name as the scripture said Abram had done.

The plan for an overnight stay required them to pack tents and sleeping bags. They would not need to carry food and cooking equipment because their intention was to eat a good breakfast and then fast a day and overnight until returning to civilization the next day. A young man, the newest member of the rabbi's congregation, learned of the overnight adventure and came forward offering his services as an experienced hiker and camper. His service was welcomed and he became a valuable member of the group. His name was Marvin Miller.

On the appointed day for the adventure, their jeep traveled along paved roads for only half an hour before reaching the modern town of Beitin, the supposed place of the biblical Bethel. Their destination would be somewhere to the east.

Although the Rabbi had lived his life in Jerusalem, he was familiar with the countryside and towns surrounding the city and he knew people who lived in many different places. He had made arrangements to meet with an old friend at Beitin. They drove through the town and stopped at an inn overlooking the hills beyond the town toward the east. Everyone got out of the jeep to take in the view of the barren hills and wilderness facing them. Out there somewhere was the high place where they would spend the night.

After breakfast at the inn, an old man approached the Rabbi and they greeted one another warmly in a language even Bina did not understand. The rabbi introduced Bina to the man and he paused, remembering the time when he had last seen her. She was about so high, he said in Hebrew, gesturing with his hand held just above his waist. He seemed to be remembering something more and Bina thought perhaps he was recalling a memory of her father, the Rabbi's son, and her mother. Maybe he had known them before their tragic death when she came to live with her grandfather. She gave him a warm hug as an old friend she had never known. The Rabbi introduced Jenny as Bina's good friend from America. The man shook her hand and said something unintelligible that they took to indicate his great respect for special friendship. Richard and Celeste were introduced as guests from America. The man's eyes lit up in recognition of Richard, perhaps from seeing his image on television. The man shook Richard's hand vigorously, smiling broadly and speaking rapidly in the unknown language while exchanging glances with the Rabbi, who nodded approval with each glance. Lastly, the Rabbi presented Marvin Miller as his son, meaning he was a member of his congregation. The old man greeted Marvin as a friend and equal.

Outside the inn and looking eastward, the man began to speak in English pointing out features of the landscape.

"Scholars believe the ancient village of Bethel lies somewhere under the present town, and Hai they believe was somewhere off in that direction," the man said with a sweep of his arm toward the east beyond a range of hills. "They think maybe five or six miles. No one knows for sure. Abram's altar was somewhere in between. Perhaps here or there, it's never been found. About a mile down this road there is a tourist site which pretends to know the truth about Abram's altar, but I don't recommend it. There is another road nearby, turn there and drive three miles farther on to where the road ends. From there, a two-hour walk uphill, too difficult for tourists, to a hilltop and maybe then, I think, you may be near where the altar stood."

It was late afternoon when they reached the summit. The climb had been steep in places and they had needed to work together helping one another along. Marvin Miller's experience with climbing had been useful. They were glad he was with them.

The summit wasn't a rugged mountaintop but instead was a broad flat plateau covered with rocks and scattered clumps of dead grass. There was a high spot—a small rocky hill at one end. There were higher places, mountains, visible way off in the far distance to the east but there was no higher location nearby.

There was an overwhelming stillness and a feeling of solitude which after a time resulted in a realization of harsh aloneness. The sky was a clear beautiful blue with only broken clouds here and there. The place was unspoiled and had a kind of natural reverence.

Richard saw he had been correct in his estimation that there was nothing to see but sky when his eyes were lifted above the horizontal. And even if Abram had looked out over the surrounding land he must have seen it was clearly incapable of supporting the great number of people God had promised would be his legacy.

Following the Rabbi's suggestions, they gathered a few scattered rocks atop the small hill to simulate an altar where they planned to gather at dawn with the Rabbi calling on God's name. On the plateau below the small hill and altar, they set up three modern, lightweight pop-up tents and readied the inflatable mattresses and sleeping bags.

When the work was done, they searched the entire plateau for firewood and found none. The place was barren; they were the only living things on it. They were glad for the bundle of firewood Marvin Miller had carried on his back against just such a possibility. At dusk Marvin kindled a fire and they gathered around, sitting on rocks while the Rabbi told the timeless story of Abram's journey from his home into the very wilderness where they were now.

It was an hour or two before dawn when Richard moved restlessly in the dark. "Where are you going?" Celeste asked sleepily from her side of the double sleeping bag.

“I gotta pee,” Richard answered and each of them recalled a similar exchange that had ended with him being lost in a Tennessee forest long ago.

“Well, remember where you are and don’t get lost or fall off the mountain,” she cautioned.

Richard eased himself out the tent flap, crawling on all fours into a starry starry night. He was surprised to see a figure silhouetted against the dark sky atop the altar hill. After taking care of business he approached the lone figure, not knowing who it was up late. Maybe they would want to talk.

“Beautiful sky,” he said.

“Yes, I’ve never seen one quite like it,” Marvin Miller answered.

“Am I intruding? I thought you might want to talk.”

“Yes, let’s talk. Who are you?”

“Who do they say I am?”

“Some say you’re a pretender. Others think you are just crazy. They all recognize you’re a stranger; you don’t know our laws.”

“What do you say?”

“I don’t know. I believe in God. I want to believe in you. But who are you?”

“I’m just a man, a nobody really, just someone who lived a life and ended up missing something. I didn’t know what—I followed Jesus’ advice and found God. I thought others should know about it, so I wrote a book. Jenny and Bina found me and my book and then, well, here I am.”

“So you’re just some guy who had an experience of God. Big deal; they are everywhere in Jerusalem trying to sell their Jesus to Jews. What makes you different?”

“I‘ve wondered about that too. I guess I just got lucky. Right place, right time; you know.”

“No, I don’t know. What’s right about this time?”

“Well, let’s see. Are you familiar with the concept of spiritual growth?”

“I’ve heard of it. Why?”

“It seems to me human beings are mostly physical stuff but part non-material, spiritual, stuff too. And we have been involved unknowingly in a process of spiritual growth forever. It’s the story of civilization. It's been a slow process but it seems now the time is right for a change. We have finally reached a tipping point; a breakthrough was inevitable. It had to be someone. It just happened to be me."

"What breakthrough? What are you talking about?"

"It's a 'beauty and the beast' sort of thing. The beast in us, the material part, has been losing ground to the beauty, the spiritual part of us. And now with its back to the wall, our material nature feels threatened and is fighting for its life.

"There's a civil war raging within each of us. With the spiritual part of us grown to nearly equal the physical, we're at a turning point. It's the battle of midway. It's about control. Our material nature is imposing a limit on our ability to grow further spiritually. There's an invisible barrier we have to punch through. I call it the body barrier. It seems like death, but I say to you there's new life, a whole new world waiting for us beyond the barrier."

"There's more to you than I thought."

Remembering a prophecy, Richard asked, "Marvin, you're a virgin aren't you?"

"Excuse me. That's none of your business."

"Sorry, I meant you're a spiritual virgin. You've never committed yourself to a religion, a system of spiritual thought, even Judaism, have you?"

Emboldened by this correct perception, Richard went out on a limb, "And you've never been serious about anyone have you? I mean, you're also a virgin in the usual sense."

"Yes," Marvin answered, hesitantly adding, "but, like I said, that's none of your business."

"Why are you here?" Richard asked.

"I'm looking for God. Rabbi said I might find Him here."

"The Rabbi sent you?"

"He suggested I might want to come. 'Something might happen,' is what he said."

"The Rabbi knows my family and my problem. I grew up in Jerusalem; Bina and I played together as kids. Then I left and I was in business in New York City; we were pretty successful, my partner and I. He kept the books and did the legal work. I was the salesman, the out front public relations guy. I made the business work. We were equal partners, or so I thought. Recently, I discovered he betrayed my trust and swindled me. He cut me out of the business totally. Legally I have nothing; he owns everything.

"I'm bitter. I want to hurt him and fight for what belongs to me. But my heart isn't in it. I'm conflicted and I've been asking God to tell me what to do. He doesn't answer. I thought maybe if I came home and reconnected with my family's religious roots I might find an answer.

"And then all at once there you were and Bina was with you. She believes in you and I respect her opinion. I've been trying to keep an open mind.

"So, now you know all about me; what do you say I should do?"

"Marvin, we could talk forever and nothing I might say would change your mind. But, trust me; the bottom line is you have to get over what you think your partner did to you. You have to let go of blame and guilt like it never happened."

"Forgive that S.O.B.? I've heard that advice before. But, seriously, forgiveness is not an option. But, I'm curious, why did you say I have to get over what *I think* my partner did to me? There's no question he did it. It happened. I'm screwed. That's a damn fact."

"Well, it's a fact, like you are a body and this world of time and space is real. Those are facts too—*within the illusion*. Forgiveness is unjustified if you have truly suffered a loss. But the fact forgiveness happens proves that nothing real takes place within the illusion. If you want to know yourself truly, to experience the breakthrough, you've got to do something that doesn't compute."

"Forgive my partner's screwing me?"

"Forgive what you only thought your partner did to you. Yes, but you've got to do it willingly and with enthusiasm. Your partner has given you a great gift. You have an opportunity to forgive his trespass against you. Let it go like it never happened. It never did, not really, not in truth and that's where you'll find God holding the line open, waiting for you to pick up and receive His answer."

"I've never heard forgiveness spoken of like that before. Is this a new teaching with you?"

"Not just me. God revealed the power of forgiveness to Jesus. He said we had to settle old scores before placing our gift on God's altar. That is, if we expect to get an answer. You've got two voices urging you to love your enemy.

"Have you got your phone with you?"

"Yes, stupid of me to bring it out here."

"Maybe not. Give him a call."

"Who? Jesus? You're cra— Oh, you mean my partner?"

"I'm sure his number is on speed dial. There's a six-hour time difference …"

"I know what time it is. He's probably at home watching TV."

"So? What's stopping you?"

"I'm considering it—okay? Don't push me. I've got ten million reasons why not. It's insane. There's probably no signal out here. He might not pick up."

"Leave a message. Tell him you love him. Offer to pay the taxes on the money he took."

"You're joking, right?" Marvin said as he took out his phone to check the signal strength.

"That's surprising, three bars."

"Punch 1 for the United States," Richard reminded him unnecessarily as Marvin stood and walked off into the darkness.

"Absolutely insane, a raving maniac," Richard heard Marvin arguing with himself as he disappeared into the deep darkness.

Half an hour passed before Marvin materialized again out of the dark. "How do you feel?" Richard asked.

"He didn't answer. I left a long message; maybe he was listening. Told him I wasn't going to the courts—gave him the whole ten million dollar business."

"Sounds pretty grim. Anything else?"

"Yeah, I told him I would assign the lease on my rent-controlled apartment for the person he'll need to hire to replace me. That felt good, like it was the right thing to do."

"Now you're talking. That was a nice touch about the apartment. No one in their right mind would do that. Truly insane."

"Now I'm beginning to feel like a fool. I must be the biggest fool ever to listen to you."

"I know that feeling; it won't last. Don't listen to that voice; don't go off into the future—stay present. Do you meditate?"

"No. I play handball."

"Handball? Oh, you mean to beat stress?"

"Yeah, what do you mean?"

"You need a way to quiet your mind. Communication with God is a two-step process. First you reach out and place your gift on the altar; you turn your back on this world. Then you pull back and wait with infinite patience; you open your mind in order to receive His answer. You've done the first part. Mediation can help with the second.

"But it's not a problem. Just do this: when the Rabbi offers the prayer, try not to think of anything except that if God doesn't answer, you will be a ten million dollar fool. Seriously, when the time is right—you'll know—close your eyes and look up; raise your eyes under the closed eyelids."

Marvin was skeptical and Richard said, "Hey, It worked for Abraham and it worked for me."

Just then, the Rabbi emerged from the tent he and Marvin had shared. In a few minutes everyone, save Celeste, was gathered together at the rock altar in the rose colored pre-dawn light. A thin column of smoke rose from the still smoldering fire. Richard stood beside Marvin on Marvin's left. Bina was on Marvin's right and Jenny attached herself comfortably to Richard's left hand and arm. As the Rabbi spoke—simply, softly using a mixture of words, English and Hebrew, calling on God, thanking Him for His blessing—Richard and Bina reached out to hold Marvin's hands. The Rabbi finished calling on the God of Abraham and then there was only the calm stillness of the breaking dawn. The time was right.

Bina and Richard felt Marvin's body suddenly relax. It fell back only a little before finding there a stone good to sit on. Richard remembered he had been sitting down when he left his body on his other world journey years ago. It was a detail he had not planned for and now Marvin's body was limp and was being held erect only by his and Bina's hands and the rock behind it.

Richard turned toward the lifeless body just in time to see its eyes open and feel Marvin's life return.

"Well," Richard heard himself ask as if in a dream, "was it good for you?"

Marvin's expression was enigmatic, reminiscent of the Mona Lisa. Then his mouth opened and out came a perfectly intoned, "*Marvelous*." The sound was robust and exquisitely formed. It held its shape in the still air and went out, echoing through the hills, enlivening them with the sound of music even unto Jerusalem. Marvelous Marvin was born.

Celeste came into the group between Richard and Jenny just in time to hear Marvin declare sincerely, "I love everyone!" and "I have seen the Promised Land."

"Oh, no!" she exclaimed, "Here we go again."

Chapter Thirty-two

MYSTICISM AND MAGIC

$E = mc^2$ —Albert Einstein's equation of energy and matter

Marvelous Marvin's sighting of the Promised Land proved to be a watershed event for Richard and for his goal of making *Love* real to the whole world. Suddenly he was no longer home alone in this world. Now he had a partner in his madness. Like Richard, Marvin learned from his experience that reality was greater than anything he had ever imagined. His body no longer defined his reality and the familiar world of time and space was not the real world. He learned that he, and everyone, were fragments of one spiritual reality, united with and loved by their Creator as part of himself. He knew at last, beyond this world of separation and fear, there was another world, a *Promised Land of Love and peace* where he belonged.

Richard had others who supported him, each in their own way. Celeste, Jenny, Bina, and the Rabbi who had wisely maneuvered both Richard and Marvin into the breakthrough situation, all had loved and believed in him. But Marvin was something more than a supporter; Marvin was an ally. He and Marvin understood one another; they were on the same page. They both realized only personal experience of the loving presence of God could end the tyranny of fear and was therefore the only way to a peaceful world. Words were useful for bringing others to the door, but each one would personally have to choose to cross the threshold into the Promised Land.

Marvin shared Richard's dedication to the goal of waking the world to the reality of the oneness of God. But unlike Richard, who was an introverted thinker, Marvin was an extroverted promoter, a salesman. His talents were better suited to sharing the excitement and to recruiting others to share in this awakening to a new world.

A second return to Abram's altar saw three more witnesses to the reality of the Promised Land come into the world. Richard believed these three young Jewish men, like Marvin, would become leaders in a growing movement, foretold in the Bible book of Revelation[7], destined to become a multitude of one hundred and forty-four thousands of Israelite witnesses given to the world.

The local phenomenon gained authority and acceptance when the Rabbi gave a talk on the history of the Promised Land. He pointed out the boundaries of God's Promised Land recorded in the Bible had expanded through the years until the present time when the ultimate reality of the Promise was being revealed. He called the ongoing phenomenon in which a generation of young Jewish men was being called to witness to the reality of the Promised Land, a clear act of God. This generation, he declared, was the flowering of the Jewish people, the reason for their long struggle to keep themselves apart, uncontaminated with the religious beliefs of other peoples.

Marvin kept close track on the growing number of witnesses and when the total reached one hundred, the phenomenon entered a new phase. The rate of reported visions accelerated and went viral in the Jewish mind with reports of spontaneous otherworldly experiences occurring to spiritually uncommitted and thus 'virgin' Jewish men and women throughout all of Israel.

Soon it was estimated 15,000 spontaneous Promised Land visions had taken place in Israel. Then scattered reports of vision experiences coming from other countries were received. But few of these were from Jewish communities.

When word of this new worldwide expansion of witnesses to the reality of *Love* and to a transcendent Promised Land reached Richard, he understood these reported visions were coming from descendants of the lost ten tribes of ancient Israel. Believing the phenomenon would continue, as foretold in the Bible prophesy[8], until it included 12,000 witnesses from each of the twelve tribes, he told Celeste, "Looks like we'll be going on an extended world tour to visit the soon to be revealed lost children of Israel."

"Oh good," she responded, "we need to get away by ourselves for a while. Where will we go first?" she wanted to know.

"That will be up to Marvin and Bina to decide," Richard answered. "They are working together and watching to see in which countries of the world the visions are concentrated."

So Celeste asked Marvin and Bina where they might be going first. Marvin told her, "It's a little early for planning a tour, but it's looking like the lost tribes migrated to the northwest from Palestine. There's a scattering of reports through the Scandinavian countries, Holland, Norway, Sweden, Denmark and Belgium that seem to mark the way they went, like bread crumbs left behind. A few reports have come from Switzerland, Luxembourg, France, and one from Iceland. But the major destination must have been the British Isles—England, Scotland and Ireland are all hot spots. Then, there are many other countries and island territories around the world, including Australia, India, South Africa, Sierra Leone, Malaysia, Pakistan, Grenada, and New Zealand.

These scattered locations made little sense until Bina recognized them as colonies of the old British Empire. "We suppose Israelites migrated there from England. But the big surprise is the United States."

Celeste interrupted saying, "Oh, well sure. That's no surprise; even I know New York City has the second largest number of Jews in the world, and Miami Beach, Palm Beach—there is a big concentration of Jewish people in South Florida."

"Remember now," Marvin advised, "we're looking at descendants of the lost ten tribes. The surprise in the United States is the number of reports coming from the heartland. Places like Iowa and Indiana—"

"Indiana? Richard and I are from Indiana. You're saying Indiana was settled by Jews?"

"No, not Jews; Israelites," Bina corrected her.

"What? Aren't Jews Israelites? Celeste asked.

"Yes," Bina answered, "All Jews are Israelites. But they're not the same thing. All Israelites are not Jews. The lost ten tribes, the great majority of Israelites, were not Jews."

"Wait. Now I'm confused. If they aren't Jews, what are they?"

Marvin interceded to bring clarity to the conversation. "Brothers," he said. "Think of it this way: The twelve tribes, the Israelites, God's chosen people, started as a family of twelve brothers. They were all sons of the third great patriarch, Jacob, whose name was changed to Israel after he wrestled all night with an angel. The most prominent of the brothers was named Judah, and his descendants became the tribe of Judah—Jews.

"The eleventh of the twelve brothers was Joseph, who was a dreamer; he is the Joseph in the story of Joseph and the coat of many colors. His jealous brothers sold him into slavery and he went to Egypt where he became important in Pharaoh's government. The other brothers had other names; they were as different as, well as different as brothers. None of them became as well-known as Judah and Joseph."

"I get it," Celeste said. "Richard's brother is shorter and has a lighter complexion, and he is athletic while Richard is not."

"That's the idea," Bina said,

"Now, for hundreds of years the Israelites lived as one big family in a united kingdom; then there was a family disagreement," she continued. "The family split into two kingdoms—the Northern Kingdom of Israel and the Southern Kingdom of Judah. The Southern Kingdom included Jerusalem. It was only two tribes, Judah and Benjamin, but it was mostly Judah—Jews. The Northern Kingdom, the other ten tribes, was conquered by the Assyrians and carried off as slaves about seven hundred years before Jesus."

"That's right," Marvin agreed. Then, taking up where Bina left off, he continued, "Since that time the ten tribes have been lost to history. The Southern Kingdom was also taken captive many years later and carried off by the Babylonians. But they eventually came back, rebuilt the temple and expanded into what was the Northern Kingdom territory. Today the nation of Israel is considered as being only Jews. The other ten tribes have been forgotten. Now, with these visions, we think we are seeing descendants of the Northern Kingdom—12,000 from each of the ten lost tribes—coming out as witnesses to the reality of the Kingdom of God."

"So, you think it's possible Richard and I are descended from Israelites? We may be part of God's chosen people too?"

"That's right," Bina said, "There is a theory that the people of Britain and the United States are descendants of the lost tribe of Joseph."[9]

"The dreamer, the 'coat of many colors' Joseph," Celeste said.

"Yes," Bina answered. "The Old Testament says that Joseph married an Egyptian girl and they had two sons, Manasseh and Ephraim. Joseph's father, Jacob, who had been renamed Israel, died in Egypt. Before he died he gave his name, Israel, and his blessing to each of these two grandsons saying they would inherit the promise God originally made to Abraham. It appears these two sons could have found their way to Britain and become a great company of nations, the British Empire.

"Then, according to the theory, there was a split as the descendants of the brother Manasseh—essentially a 13th tribe—left England and established the 13 colonies of what would become the greatest nation ever, the United States of America.

"So, Celeste, to answer your question, Yes, I believe millions of Americans, including you, may be part of God's chosen people who have received his greatest blessing."

Richard entered the room and asked Celeste, "Did you find out where we're going first?"

"No," Celeste answered, "But I think we're going to wind up back home again in Indiana."

When Jenny learned of the coming worldwide tour she said, "See, I was right. Richard is wrapping up the whole world in a love bubble. Pretty soon, no more war."

Marvin and Bina mapped out a travel plan to visit the places where visions were being reported. It began in New Zealand and then went to Australia, India, and Africa; then up through Europe and the British Isles and finally across the Atlantic to Canada and the United States.

When Richard and Celeste prepared to leave Israel to meet and hear testimonies of the newest members of God's chosen people, they found that everyone wanted to go along. It was not just Jenny and Bina, but Marvin and all the thousands of Jewish witnesses who had come out in Israel. They obviously considered themselves family and wanted to follow Richard like younger siblings, wherever he went. It became a challenge after a while and got a lot of publicity. But the group organized themselves and took care of their needs and so it wasn't a problem.

The choir grew in size as the tour progressed. Typically, they would go into a new country and find a venue large enough to hold them all and then they would hold a rally where Richard and Marvin would speak, validating the newbies' experiences and welcoming them to the growing family. Then for the next day or two, Richard and company would go sightseeing while the congregation realigned itself to incorporate the newest members of the family.

The tour wound up back in Richard and Celeste's hometown of Daytona Beach, Florida. Every motel room and condo was filled as Big Dollar Bill facilitated accommodations for his returning friends. He and Jenny were happy being together again.

Big Dollar Bill formally welcomed the group in his capacity as mayor of the city of Daytona Beach. Richard believed he had done his duty and the next big thing was to follow the biblical example of Jesus and send these familial disciples out, two by two, to witness to the world.

A final ceremony was held at the Daytona Speedway. With a seating capacity of 146,000, it was the only venue large enough to hold all the 144,000. A large elevated speaker's platform was constructed in the center of the infield. Bright sunlight and shadows from scattered clouds alternated over the world famous speedway on the day of the assembly.

Richard spoke as he had planned and charged the 144,000 to go out into all the world preaching the good news of the coming Kingdom of God. The speech was enthusiastically received and Richard believed his part was finished. He had brought the first fruits of the children of Israel to the Promised Land and now having accomplished the impossible he would go home, keeping his promise to Celeste that their life would be normal again.

After the speech, the 144,000 were in no hurry to leave. Richard asked Marvin, "Why aren't they leaving?"

Marvin went to find out what was causing the delay and came back saying, "They're waiting for sundown. They say there is more to come. They're staying for the fireworks."

"What fireworks?" Richard exclaimed. "It's over. The ball is in their court now."

"They're expecting you to come back out."

"You mean like an encore?"

"Maybe," Marvin said. "Something like that."

"Well, oh, why not? I could do that. Let's all go out—you, Jenny, Bina, and Celeste. Come on stage with me. I mean this is a final celebration, isn't it? Let's all go out and take a bow."

But Marvin was certain. "No, it's you they want to see. Here take your book. Sing them a few bars of the new song. Something might happen."

With the sun setting in the west, Richard prepared to go out on center stage a second time. Then suddenly, out of the west the fireworks began. Flashes of colored light, remnants of the dying sun, played across the sky.

"Go now," Marvin urged. "That's your cue."

As Richard climbed the platform's fifteen steps to the top, all eyes shifted to him. No one noticed the shiny bright clouds moving high above. Twelve bright discs, one for each of the ancient Israelite tribes, positioned themselves unseen in circular formation above the crowd.

On stage, Richard lifted his small book up high above his head and walked around the platform. Applause erupted from each section of the friendly audience as he faced in their direction.

The book was his story, his new song. And now it had become their song as well. It was the new manner of thinking each of them had made their own. In 144,000 diverse ways they had turned their backs on the world and taking a leap of faith into the unknown, each had learned the world of separation and fear was but a veil covering a much greater reality. Each witness had gone beyond the teaching of the world and learned they were not their body but were instead deathless spirits made in the image of their creator.

In the company of this multitude of friends who considered themselves family, Richard opened his book and found the words he had written there blurred such that they were impossible to read. Yet there were other words, living words, emboldened, three dimensional words vibrating at a high frequency waiting to be expressed. Whether the new words were in his mind only or written on the page in the book he could not tell. As once before, Richard felt his head lifted and the words went out, energetically discharged into the still air:

There is one life and that we share with God.[10]

His voice had a new attractive quality to it. The sound system was superb and there was music playing in the background. A haunting melody was floating in the air. It was a familiar refrain but what was it? He tried to remember the forgotten song and the circumstance in which he had first heard it. More words followed the first:

We are not the body, we are free.

The crowd was stirring, he supposed in their recognition of the haunting melody he too remembered but could not exactly recall.

We are still as God created us.

Richard's mind was in synch with the words he voiced and there was a resonance, a verbal harmony with the truth being expressed.

We are at home in God dreaming of exile.

He was preaching to the choir and the words became a prayer. The 144 thousand were with him in spirit, adding power to the spoken words.

Richard's sense of being a separated self was lost, given up willingly in exchange for serving as a means for the Oneness finding expression through him. He was in *Love* again, lost to himself. It had happened before, first by himself, then with Jenny, and now for the first time in a crowd.

We are children of God,
Each one of us a priceless part of His Kingdom,
Which He created as part of Him.

Today belongs to Love. Let us not fear.
We are surrounded by the Love of God.

A brief pause followed before the next unbelievable truth sounded.

There is no world. Only Love is here.

The prayer became an invocation as the final words expressed an unlimited willingness to let the truth be true.

Now would I be as God created me.
Into his presence would I enter now.

Then, as Marvin had suggested, something happened. God showed up.

Richard closed the small book and his face began to glow with light from within. Suddenly in the blink of an eye the prayer was answered; Richard appeared as God had created him. On stage the human Richard was gone, in its place was a single translucent being of glowing white light.

The brightness exploded silently from the stage and went into the surrounding grandstands as the newest members of the family, the 144 thousand, reached out to be in Oneness with the truth of their being. The thousands were themselves transformed, appearing as beings of light. On stage an orb of light emerged from the brightness that was Richard and lifted itself upward slowly as though climbing a spiraling celestial stairway moving toward the shiny bright clouds and unseen discs of light waiting high above. All around the stadium orbs of light rose up climbing skyward like bubbles in a glass of champagne. Radiant golden white light filled the entire arena as the veil covering the unseen world was torn away, revealing the Beauty and Glory of the twelve shining emissaries from the Promised Land. The orbs of light bubbled up and down until each of them had succeeded in touching the twelve shining discs.

In the seeming next moment, the fireworks were over and Richard was again himself on stage.

* * *

Marvin appeared on stage with Richard and told him, "Go and be with Celeste. She's glowing."

Richard left the stage to go and see.

"Celeste, what …?"

"I don't know … *something* happened. I just had a thought … seeing everyone looking so intently at something I couldn't see. I thought well, maybe there is something."

"You were willing, just a little, for it to be true."

"I guess, maybe, something like that. And then it just happened. I was somewhere else. It was real."

"Tell me—"

"All right, I'll say it. It was love. I was in *Love*. It was incredibly personal and yet I knew it was for all alike. It is more real than anything. I feel love for everyone as for myself."

Richard smiled. "Oh boy, here we go again."

He could see more clearly now what was coming next. He had opened the way and brought the first fruits of the coming Kingdom of God. The 144 thousand were now sealed and empowered to bring others; each of them would bring thousands more into the Kingdom. Together they would bring a great multitude willing to let God's Kingdom come on earth. Celeste, it seemed was the first of the coming "great multitude that no one could count, from every nation, tribe, people and language."[11]

The Kingdom of God was coming. Soon the world would be a place in which war and violence were no more because, "the earth will be filled with the knowledge of the Lord, as the waters cover the sea."[12]

END

CHAPTER NOTES

7 Revelation 14:1-5

8 Revelation 7: 1-8

9 *The United States and Britain in Prophecy,* Herbert W. Armstrong, 1967

10 These and subsequent italicized words are from *A Course In Miracles*

11 Revelation 7:9

12 Isaiah 11: 9

APPENDIX

Appendix A

P66, BODMER PAPYRUS
BODMER LIBRARY, GENEVA, SWITZERLAND

Early Second Century AD. Beginning of the gospel by John
See line nine – from OY to OY; "his name *was* John"

Appendix B: THE GREEK ALPHABET

Capitals	Lower Case	Greek	English
Α	α	ἄλφα	alpha
Β	β	βῆτα	beta
Γ	γ	γάμμα	gamma
Δ	δ	δέλτα	delta
Ε	ε	ἒ ψιλόν	epsilon
Ζ	ζ	ζῆτα	zeta
Η	η	ἦτα	eta
Θ	θ	θῆτα	theta
Ι	ι	ἰῶτα	iota
Κ	κ	κάππα	kappa
Λ	λ	λάμβδα	lambda
Μ	μ	μῦ	mu
Ν	ν	νῦ	nu
Ξ	ξ	ξῖ	xi
Ο	ο	ὂ μικρόν	omicron
Π	π	πῖ	pi
Ρ	ρ	ῥῶ	rho
Σ	σ, ς	σίγμα	sigma
Τ	τ	ταῦ	tau
Υ	υ	ὒ ψιλόν	upsilon
Φ	φ	φῖ	phi
Χ	χ	χῖ	chi
Ψ	ψ	ψῖ	psi
Ω	ω	ὦ μέγα	omega

The Greek Alphabet

Appendix C: THE GREEK LANGUAGE

Dr. Sane's Beginning Greek Handout

Greek is written from left to right as the English language. The Greek language is characterized by a high degree of *inflection*. Each Greek word actually changes form (inflection) based upon the role that it plays in the sentence. A Greek **noun** is composed of the *stem*, which conveys the meaning, and the *case ending*. The inflection of a noun is called its *declension*, and nouns are declined. There are three patterns of declension to Greek nouns: stems ending in alpha or eta are in the first declension, those ending in omicron are second declension, and stems ending in a consonant are third declension. Case endings are the way the Greek language designates the function of a noun (nominative, accusative, genitive, dative, vocative), the gender (masculine, feminine, or neuter), and the number (singular or plural). Case marks the relationship of the noun to the verb. Word order in Greek is primarily used for emphasis, balance, contrast, or variety.

For example, when **Κύριος**, the Greek word for **Lord**, is the subject (nominative case), as "the Lord blessed the crowd," the word keeps its lexical form as above and is spelled in transliteration as Kyrios. When the Lord is the direct object (accusative case), as "the Father sent the Lord," it is spelled *Κύριον*. When the Lord is possessive (genitive case), as "the Lord's supper or the Lord's prayer," the word is spelled *Κύριου*. When the Lord is the indirect object (dative case), as "Philip brought bread to the Lord," it is spelled as Kyrioi; the omicron lengthens to omega, and the iota subscripts in the dative singular, to form *Κυρίῳ*. When the Lord is addressed (vocative case), as "Lord, Lord, please forgive me," the word is spelled *Κύριε*, as in the hymnal *Kyrie Eleison*. The following chart lists the case endings for *Κύριος*, a second declension noun in the masculine singular. Thus in the following Biblical passage from the Letter of St. Paul to the Romans, Lord must be the direct object or in the accusative case. (See following page.)

LORD

Case	Ending	Spelling	Example
Nominative	-ς	Κύριος	John 20:28
Genitive	-υ	Κυρίου	Philippians 3:8
Dative	-ι	Κυρίῳ	Philemon 1:16
Accusative	-ν	Κύριον	Acts 2:36
Vocative	-ε	Κύριε	Luke 18:41

ὅτι ἐὰν ὁμολογήσῃς ἐν τῷ στόματί σου
Because if you confess with your mouth

Κύριον Ἰησοῦν καὶ πιστεύσῃς ἐν τῇ καρδίᾳ σου
the Lord Jesus and believe in your heart

ὅτι ὁ Θεὸς αὐτὸν ἤγειρεν ἐκ νεκρῶν,
that God him raised from the dead,

σωθήσῃ·
you will be saved.

ΡΩΜΑΙΟΥΕ 10:9

A Greek **verb** describes the action or state of being in a sentence, and is primarily composed of the verb root, to which are added various affixes. The addition of prefixes, infixes, and/or suffixes forms each particular *stem* and *personal ending*. The verb stem expresses the basic meaning of the verb and indicates tense and mood. The personal endings convey voice, person and number in agreement with its subject. The inflection of a verb is called its *conjugation*, and verbs are said to be conjugated. *Tense* expresses *aspect* or the kind of action, either continuous, undefined, or the completion of an action; tense expresses both *aspect* and *time* (present, past, future) in the indicative mood. The Greek verb has seven tenses in the indicative mood: present, future, aorist (see below), perfect, imperfect, pluperfect, and future perfect. *Voice* is either active, middle, or passive. In the *active* voice, the person performs the action, as "the teacher taught the students." In the *passive* voice, the subject is acted upon, as "the students were taught by the teacher." There is also *middle* voice, in which the subject of the verb does the action, but the action somehow affects the subject, as in self-interest, such as "I defend myself." The *mood* of a verb may be *indicative* (the most common), a statement of fact, reality, or actual occurrence; *imperative*, a command; *subjunctive*, a contemplated, possible, or probable action; or *optative*, a wish or hope.

There are three principal parts to an English verb: the present tense, the simple past, and the past participle. Examples are "bless, blessed, blessed," or "sing, sang, sung." The Greek language has six principal parts or tense forms to a verb. The principal parts of a verb are a standard set of related forms from which you can provide the correct stem for each particular verb to express tense, voice, mood, person, and number. All possible forms of a Greek verb, including infinitives and participles, are inflected from a stem derived from one of these six principal parts. Here are the six principal parts of the verb **λύω**, a regular verb which means "I loose, untie, free, release," or (2) "I destroy," and in which the verb root *λυ* is consistent throughout:

Principal Part:	Present Active	Future Active	Aorist Active	Perfect Active	Perfect Middle/Passive	Aorist Passive
Verb:	**λύω**	**λύσω**	**?λυσα**	**λέλυκα**	**λέλυμαι**	**?λύθην**
Translation:	I loose	I will loose	I loosed	I have loosed	I have been loosed	I was loosed

To conjugate a verb, for example, take the first principal part of the verb *I have* - **ἔχω**, which serves as the lexical or dictionary form of the verb. The present tense stem is formed by removing the omega, and in combination with the connecting or thematic vowel and the primary active personal endings, one is given the following conjugation of the present active indicative of the verb ἔχω:

Conjugation of Present Active Indicative of ἔχω

Person and Number	*Vowel + Ending*	*Verb*	*Translation*	*Example*
1st person singular	-ω	ἔχω	*I have*	*Matthew 3:9*
2nd person singular	-εις	ἔχεις	*You have*	*Mark 10:21*
3rd person singular	-ει	ἔχει	*He has*	*Luke 5:24*
1st person plural	-ομεν	ἔχομεν	*We have*	*John 8:41*
2nd person plural	-ετε	ἔχετε	*You have*	*1Corinthians 6:7*
3rd person plural	-ουσι	ἔχουσι(ν)	*They have*	*Revelation 9:4*

www.ingramcontent.com/pod-product-compliance
Lightning Source LLC
LaVergne TN
LVHW050529160826
845677LV00011B/1984

9798987318447